BALTHAZAR JONES AND THE TOWER OF LONDON ZOO

This book should be returned to any branch of the Lancashire County Library on or before the date shown

Lancashire County Library
Bowran Street
Preston PR1 2UX

Lancashire
County Council

www.lancashire.gov.uk/libraries

BALTHAZAR JONES AND THE TOWER OF LONDON ZOO

Julia Stuart

WINDSOR
PARAGON

First published 2010
by HarperPress
This Large Print edition published 2010
by AudioGO Ltd
by arrangement with
HarperCollins*Publishers*

Hardcover ISBN: 978 1 408 48774 7
Softcover   ISBN: 978 1 408 48775 4

British Library Cataloguing in Publication Data available

11706218

Printed and bound in Great Britain by
CPI Antony Rowe, Chippenham and Eastbourne

We can judge the heart of a man by his treatment of animals.

Immanuel Kant

For Digby

Acknowledgements

I am indebted to the authors of numerous guidebooks for sale at the Tower of London. *The Funeral Effigies of Westminster Abbey*, edited by Anthony Harvey and Richard Mortimer, provided insight into the Abbey's curious exhibits, though the story told here of the Duchess of Richmond and Lennox's very real stuffed parrot is a flight of fantasy. Daniel Hahn's wonderful *The Tower Menagerie: The Amazing True Story of the Royal Collection of Wild Beasts* was a fascinating source of reference. My thanks also go to Dr Elijah R. Behr, my super agent Gráinne Fox, and all at HarperCollins. No animal was harmed in the writing of this novel.

1

Standing on the battlements in his pyjamas, Balthazar Jones looked out across the Thames where Henry III's polar bear had once fished for salmon while tied to a rope. The Beefeater failed to notice the cold that pierced his dressing gown with deadly precision, or the wretched damp that crept round his ankles. Placing his frozen hands on the ancient parapet, he tilted back his head, and inhaled the night. There it was again.

The undeniable aroma had fluttered past his capacious nostrils several hours earlier as he lay sleeping in the Tower of London, his home for the last eight years. Assuming such wonderment had been an oasis in his usual gruesome dreams, he scratched at the hairs that covered his chest like freshly fallen ash, and descended back into ragged slumber. It wasn't until he rolled on to his side, away from his wife and her souk of competing odours, that he smelt it again. Recognising instantly the exquisite scent of the world's rarest rainfall, the Beefeater sat bolt upright in the darkness, his eyes open wide like a baby bird.

The sudden movement of the mattress caused his wife to undulate for several seconds like a body drifting at sea, and she muttered something incomprehensible. As she turned away from the disturbance, her pillow fell into the gap between the head of the bed and the wall, one of the many irritations of living within circular walls. Balthazar Jones reached down into the dusty no-man's land and groped around. After carefully retrieving the pillow, he placed it gently next to his wife so as not to disturb her. As he did so, he wondered, as he often had throughout their marriage, how a woman of such beauty, the embers of which still glowed fiercely in her fifty-fifth year, could look just like her father as she slept. For once, he didn't feel the urge to poke her awake in order to rid himself of the harrowing illusion of sharing his bed with his Greek father-in-law, a man whose ferocious looks had led his relatives to refer to him as a good cheese in a dog's skin. Instead, he quickly got out of bed, his heart tight with anticipation. Forgetting his usual gazelle's step at such times, he crossed the room, his bare heels, cracked as a dry riverbed, thudding on the emaciated carpet. Nose and white beard against the pane, which bore the smudges of numerous previous occasions, he peered out. The ground was still dry. With mounting desperation, he scanned the night sky for the approaching rain clouds responsible for the undeniable aroma. In his panic not to miss the moment for which he had been waiting for more than two years, he hurried past the vast stone fireplace to the other side of the bedroom. His stomach, still bilious from the previous evening's hogget, arrived first.

Grabbing his dressing gown, its pockets bearing the guilty crumbs of clandestine biscuits, the Beefeater pulled it across his pyjamas, and, forgetting his tartan slippers, opened the bedroom door. He failed to notice the noise the latch made and the subsequent incomprehensible babble it produced from his wife, a slither of hair skimming her cheek. Fingers sliding down the filthy rope handrail, he descended the corpse-cold spiral printed with matching envelopes, and set up the St Heribert of Cologne Club, named after the patron saint of rain, hoping to compare notes with fellow wet weather enthusiasts. He placed adverts in various newspapers around the world, but the only correspondence he ever received was a heavily watermarked letter from an anonymous resident of Mawsynram, in north-eastern India, which suffered from one of the world's heaviest rainfalls. 'Mr Balthazar, You must desist from this utter madness at the most soonest. The only thing worse than a lunatic is a wet one,' was all that it said.

But the lack of interest only fuelled his obsession. The Beefeater spent all his spare time writing to meteorologists around the world about his discoveries. He received replies from them all, his fingers, as lithe as a watchmaker's, quivering as he opened them. However, the experts' politeness was matched by their disinterest. He changed tack and buried himself in dusty parchments and books as fragile as his sanity at the British Library. And with eyes magnified by the strength of his reading glasses, he scoured everything ever written about rain.

Eventually, Balthazar Jones became convinced that he had discovered a variant that, from what he could make out, hadn't fallen since 1892 in Colombo, making it the world's rarest. He read and reread the descriptions of the sudden shower, which, through a catalogue of misfortunes had resulted in the untimely death of a cow. He became adamant that he would recognise it from its scent even before seeing it. Every day he waited, hoping for it to fall. Obsession eventually loosened his tongue, and one afternoon he heard himself telling his wife of his desperate desire to include it in his collection. With a mixture of incredulity and pity, she gazed up at the man who had never shed a tear over the death of their son, Milo. And when she looked back down at the daffodil bulbs she was planting in a tub on the Salt Tower roof, she wondered yet again what had happened to her husband.

*   *   *

Standing with his back against the Salt Tower's oak door, the Beefeater glanced around in the darkness to make sure that he wouldn't be spotted by any of the other inhabitants of the fortress. The only movement was a gentleman's voluminous white vest and a pair of flesh-coloured tights swinging on a washing line strung up on the roof of the Casemates. These ancient terraced cottages built against the fortress walls housed many of the thirty-five Beefeaters who lived with their families at the Tower. The rest, like Balthazar Jones, had had the misfortune of being allocated one of the monument's twenty-one towers as their home or, worse still, a house on Tower Green, the site of seven beheadings, five of them women.

Balthazar Jones listened carefully. The only sound emerging through the darkness was a sentry marking his territory, his footfall as precise as a Swiss clock. He sniffed the night again and for a moment he doubted himself. He hesitated, cursing himself for being so foolish as to believe that the moment had finally come. He imagined his wife emitting an aviary of sounds as she dreamt, and decided to return to the warm familiarity of the bed. But just as he was about to retrace his steps, he smelt it again.

Heading for the battlements, he noticed to his relief that the lights were off at the Rack & Ruin, the Tower's tavern that had been serving the tiny community for two hundred and twenty-seven uninterrupted years, despite a direct hit during the Second World War. He did well to check, for there were occasions when the more vociferous arguments between the Beefeaters took until the early hours to be buried. Not, of course, that they remained that way. For they would often be gleefully dug up again in front of the warring parties by those seeking further entertainment.

He started down Water Lane, the cobbles slimy underneath his bare feet from the fallen leaves. As he approached Wakefield Tower, his thoughts turned to the odious ravens, which had been put to bed in their pens in the tower's shadow. Their luxurious accommodation, with its running water, under-floor heating, and supply of fresh squirrel meat at the taxpayer's expense, had been a constant source of irritation ever since he had discovered the true depth of their villainy.

His wife had taken an instant dislike to the famous birds when the family first arrived at the Tower. 'They taste of shrouds,' announced Hebe Jones, who, with the exception of peacock, which she deemed inauspicious, claimed to have eaten most species of animals.

However, the ravens had been an instant source of curiosity to Balthazar Jones. During his first week, he wandered over to one perched on the wooden staircase leading to the entrance of the White Tower, begun by William the Conqueror to

7

keep out the vile and furious English. As the bird eyed him, he stood admiring the thousands of colours that swam in the oily blackness of its feathers in the sunlight. He was equally impressed when the Ravenmaster, the Beefeater responsible for looking after the birds, called the creature's name, and it arrived at the man's feet following a shambolic flight due to the fact that its wings had been clipped to prevent it absconding. And when Balthazar Jones discovered that they had a weakness for blood-soaked biscuits, he went out of his way to provide them with a splendid breakfast comprised of the delicacy.

Several days later, Milo, who was six at the time, shrieked 'Daddy!' and pointed to a raven standing on top of Mrs Cook, the family's historic tortoise. All affection instantly vanished. It wasn't just that it was extraordinary bad manners to hitch a ride— albeit at the most sedate of paces—aloft another creature that infuriated Balthazar Jones. Neither was it the fact that the bird had just left a copious runny deposit on top of his pet. What drove the Beefeater into a state of fury was the raven pecking at Mrs Cook's fleshy bits with its satanic beak. And given the tortoise's age of one hundred and eighty-one, there was a noticeable delay before she was able to draw her head and limbs into her worn shell away from the vicious assault.

It was by no means an isolated incident. Several days later, Balthazar Jones noticed that the ravens had assembled into what was indisputably an attack formation outside the Salt Tower, once used to store saltpetre. One of the birds squatted on top of the red phone box, three stood on a cannon, another perched on the remains of a

8

Roman wall, and a pair sat on the roof of the New Armouries. The situation continued for several days as it took considerable time for Mrs Cook to explore her new lodgings. Eventually, she was ready for a change of scenery. But as soon as she set a wizened leg out of the front door, there was a uniform advance of one hop from the massed ravens. The birds displayed remarkable patience, for it took several hours for Mrs Cook to make sufficient ground out of the door to warrant a second hop. The Ravenmaster blamed the fact that it was well past their lunchtimes for what happened next. Balthazar Jones, however, vehemently insisted that their scandalous behaviour was not only a result of their allegiance to Beelzebub, but how they had been raised, an insult that pierced so deeply it was never forgotten. Whatever the reason, one thing was for certain: by late afternoon Mrs Cook, the oldest tortoise in the world, no longer had a tail, and one of the Tower ravens was too full for supper.

*   *   *

As Balthazar Jones passed Wakefield Tower, the sound of the Thames lapping through Traitors' Gate seemed louder than usual in the darkness. He looked to his left and saw the vast wooden watergates that had once opened to let in the boats carrying trembling prisoners accused of treason. But he spared not a thought for such matters, the details of which he had to relate countless times during his working day to the tourists who were only interested in methods of torture, executions and the whereabouts of the lavatories. Instead, he pressed on, past the Bloody Tower with its red rambling rose, said to have produced snow-white blossoms before the murder of the two little princes. Neither did he notice the dancing candlelight at one of its windows, where the ghost of Sir Walter Raleigh nibbled the end of his quill as he sat at his desk in what had been his prison for thirteen years.

Climbing up the stone steps, the Beefeater quickly reached the battlements. In front of him stretched the Thames where Henry III's white bear had once swum for its dinner. But Balthazar Jones kept his pale blue eyes raised as he tried to work out from which direction the precious rain would come. Touching his white beard with his fingertips as he made his calculations, he scoured the sky through which the dawn was starting to leak.

*   *   *

Unable to sleep since her husband woke her as he left, Hebe Jones sneezed twice, irritated by the dust on her pillow. Rolling on to her back, she dragged a clump of damp hair from the corner of her mouth. Instead of coursing down her back as it had done during the lusty days of youth, it meandered slowly to her shoulders. Despite her age, apart from the odd strand that flashed like a silver fish in certain lights, it was the same luminous black it had been when Balthazar Jones first met her, a defiance of nature that he put down to his wife's obstinacy.

As she lay in the darkness, she imagined her husband walking through the Tower's grounds in

10

his pyjamas, clutching an Egyptian perfume bottle in a hand that no longer caressed her. She had tried her best to rid him of his compulsion. During his first few attempts, she had caught him before he reached the bedroom door. But he soon improved his technique, and before long he was able to make it halfway down the stairs before he heard the seven words which he had grown to dread, uttered with the same red breath as his mother's: *And where do you think you're going?* However, dedication to the high art of vanishing resulted in a number of spectacular successes.

Hebe Jones began to monitor the escape manuals he borrowed from the public library, and locked the bedroom door before they turned out their reading lights, hiding the key while her husband was in the bathroom battling with the loneliness of constipation. But the trick backfired one morning when she could not remember where she had put it. Through a mouthful of humiliation which threatened to choke her, she asked him to help her in her search. He removed the loose stone next to one of the lattice windows, but all he found were the more aromatic love letters he had sent her during their courtship. He then strode to the fireplace, put his hand up the vast stone hood, and retrieved an old sweet tin from a ledge. Upon opening it he discovered a pair of silver cufflinks bearing his initials in the most alluring of scripts. His wife revealed that it was a gift she had bought for him four Christmases ago, which she had never been able to put her hands on. Her joy at seeing them again, and Balthazar Jones's delight at suddenly receiving an unexpected present, distracted them both from their predicament. But

11

before long, the hunt resumed until Balthazar Jones found what was indisputably a sex aid in the drawer of his wife's bedside table. 'What on earth is this for?' he asked, pushing a button. Their dilemma was forgotten again for the next thirty-four minutes, during which many questions were asked. The answers that were forthcoming led to further questions, which in turn produced a series of accusations from both sides.

It was over an hour before they returned to their search. By then the cufflinks were back in the tin up the chimney with the announcement that he would have to wait until Christmas for them. Eventually, the pair admitted defeat, and Balthazar Jones reached for the phone and called the Chief Yeoman Warder to release them. The man made four attempts before the spare key sailed through one of the open windows. It was then that Hebe Jones spotted the original still in the keyhole, and she secretly removed it.

From then on the bedroom door remained unlocked, and no amount of protests would keep the Beefeater from his nocturnal wandering. It was with relief that Hebe Jones took the news one morning that her husband had been caught by the Chief Yeoman Warder. However, her relief turned to indignation when the rumours quickly followed that Balthazar Jones was carrying out a secret liaison with Evangeline Moore, the Tower's young resident doctor, who quickened the heart rate of many of her patients. The claim was not without credibility as most affairs conducted by the Tower's inhabitants took place within its walls, as they were locked in from midnight. While Hebe Jones knew instantly that there was no truth in the rumour—since Milo's death her husband hadn't allowed himself the pleasure of love-making—she nevertheless banished him from the matrimonial bed for a fortnight. Feet either side of the taps, Balthazar Jones slept in the bath. He endured the cramped, damp conditions dreaming amongst the spiders of being lost at sea in a sinking boat. Each morning Hebe Jones would get up early to run a bath, being careful not to remove her husband beforehand, and always ensuring that she ran the cold water first.

*   *   *

Now, as she looked at the bedside clock, fury coursed through her veins at yet another night of disturbed sleep. Her usual revenge, performed each time her husband returned to bed reeking of the night, was an anatomical masterstroke. Once she heard the muddy breath of a man descended deep into his dreams, she would suddenly leap from the bed and make the short journey to the bathroom with the gait of a demented sentry. Once installed on the lavatory, she would proceed to empty her bladder with the door wide open. The clamour of the catastrophic downpour was such that her husband would immediately wake in terror, convinced that he was lying in a nest of snakes. When the infernal hissing eventually came to an end, the Beefeater would instantly sink back to his dreams. But several seconds later, in a feat of immaculate timing, his wife would release a second, much shorter but equally deafening cascade, which would finish with a tone-perfect rising pitch, and wake her husband as brutally as the first.

Pulling the shabby blanket up to her chin, Hebe Jones thought of the cabinets of Egyptian perfume bottles filled with rain in the top room of the Salt Tower, and then of the cruelty of grief. Compassion suddenly chilled her rage. Ignoring the glass of water on her bedside table that she usually drank in its entirety on such occasions, she turned back on to her side. When her husband eventually returned home with his empty vessel after the clouds had fled, Hebe Jones pretended to be asleep. And when the torment of a full bladder woke her an hour later, she rolled on to her back to alleviate the suffering that eventually reached her ears.

2

It was the sight of her husband's dressing gown hanging on the back of the bedroom door, an Egyptian perfume bottle still in its pocket, that reignited Hebe Jones's anger the following morning. She pressed down on the latch with irritation, having lost all compassion for her husband because of a headache brought on by her broken night's sleep. She descended the stairs in her pink leather slippers and nightclothes, recalling the previous occasions that her dreams had been disturbed by her husband's obsession. When he joined her for breakfast at the kitchen table, she placed in front of him a plate of eggs that had been scrambled more vigorously than usual, then released the full fury inside her.

14

Several minutes later, the Beefeater's stomach shrank again as she suddenly veered away from his compulsion, and launched into the many injustices of living within the fortress. She started with the Salt Tower roof that was such a poor exchange for her beloved garden at their house in Catford, which the wretched lodgers had let go to seed. Then there was the gossip that spread through the monument like fire. And finally there were the mournful sounds that permeated their home, once the prison of numerous Catholic priests during the reign of Elizabeth I, which both had pretended to Milo that they couldn't hear.

For a moment Balthazar Jones closed his ears, having heard the complaints on countless previous occasions, and picked up his knife and fork. But suddenly his wife came up with a wholly new deprivation that caught his attention. Despite her unrepentant aversion to Italian food, which her husband put down to her nation's historic distrust of Italy, she suddenly declared: 'All I want in life is to be able to get a takeaway pizza!' He remained silent as there was no escaping the fact that they lived at an address that cab drivers, washing machine repairmen, newspaper boys, and every official who had ever given them a form to fill in, assumed to be fictitious.

He put down his cutlery, and looked up at her again with eyes the colour of pale opals, something people who met him never forgot. 'Where else could you live surrounded by nine hundred years of history?' he asked.

She folded her arms across her chest. 'Virtually anywhere in Greece,' she replied. 'And it would be a lot older.'

'I don't think you realise how lucky I was to get this job.'

'A lucky person is someone who plants pebbles and harvests potatoes,' she said, evoking the Greek mysticism of her grandparents. She then hunted around, searching amongst the rubble of their relationship for past hurts that she held up again in front of him. Balthazar Jones responded in kind, taking her examiner's torch and shining it on ancient grievances. No shadow was left unlit and by the time they left the table, every fissure of their teetering love had been exposed to the damp morning air.

With furious, quick steps, Hebe Jones scuffed back up the stone spiral staircase to the bedroom. Dressing for work, she thought with regret at the part she had played in helping her husband secure a job at the Tower after his second career failed. As he had been a master stitch in the army, responsible for altering the magnificent Foot Guard uniforms, tailoring had seemed an obvious choice when he finally hung up his bearskin. When he suggested renting some premises, his wife thought of the mortgage they were still paying off, and warned: 'Don't extend your feet beyond your blanket.' So he commandeered the front room of their terrace house in Catford, and built a counter behind which he presided, his measuring tape hanging around his neck with the sanctity of a priest's stole.

A year later, Milo arrived after two fruitless decades of conjugal contortion. Balthazar Jones took care of him while his wife was at the office. In between customers, he would set the infant's basket on the counter, pull up a chair, and proceed

16

to tell his son all he knew about life. There were warnings to work hard at school 'otherwise you'll end up an ignoramus, like your father'. The child was informed that he happened to have been born into a family whose members included the oldest tortoise in the world. 'You'll have to look after Mrs Cook when old age turns your mother and I cuckoo, for which your maternal grandparents have always shown a natural disposition,' he said as he tucked in Milo's blanket. And it was pointed out that of all the blessings that would come to him in life, none would be greater than having Hebe Jones as a mother. 'I've pitied every man I've ever met for not being married to her,' Balthazar Jones admitted. And Milo would listen, his dark eyes not leaving his father for a moment as he chewed his own toes.

For a while it appeared that he had made the right decision in opening a tailor's. But gradually fewer and fewer customers knocked at the house with the tiny Greek flag flying from the roof of the birdhouse in the front garden. Some stayed away, unsettled by having to wait while a nappy was being changed. Later, others blamed the brevity of their trouser legs on the attention the bewitched tailor gave to the boy, who ran round the shop as his father refused to send him to nursery. And when Milo was finally at school, some of the new trade that Balthazar Jones managed to pick up never returned after being measured, unsettled by the brutal honesty of a former soldier.

When he realised how precarious the family's finances were, Balthazar Jones thought about the ways in which other soldiers earned a living after leaving the army. He remembered the time he had spent on sentry duty at the Tower of London, and the Beefeaters in their splendid uniforms, who went by the exalted title of Yeoman Warders of Her Majesty's Royal Palace and Fortress the Tower of London, and Members of the Sovereign's Body Guard of the Yeomen Guard Extraordinary. Not only were they all former warrant officers from Her Majesty's Forces, but each had an honourable service record of at least twenty-two years. Fulfilling both requirements, he posted off an application form. Four months later, a letter arrived informing him of a vacancy for the historic position, which had once entailed guarding prisoners, as well as torturing them, but since Victorian times involved acting as an official tour guide.

Hebe Jones, whose own earnings were modest, knew that their savings would never stretch to the university education they both wanted for their son. Ignoring the dread that set like cement in her guts, she dismissed her husband's warning that they would have to live at the Tower if he were successful. 'It's every woman's dream to live in a castle,' she lied, not turning round from the stove.

When Balthazar Jones discovered that she had never visited the famous monument, he asked how it was possible since she had spent most of her childhood in London. She explained that her parents had only ever taken their four daughters to the British Museum to see the Elgin Marbles. The sound of Mr and Mrs Grammatikos weeping as they stood in front of the Greek exhibits pilfered by the English was so catastrophic that the family was eventually banned from the museum for life. The couple consequently refused to visit any

British landmarks, a protest Hebe Jones had kept up in adulthood out of familial solidarity.

In case his wife wasn't aware, Balthazar Jones pointed out that not only was the Tower of London a royal palace and fortress, but it had once been England's state prison, had witnessed numerous executions, and was also widely believed to be haunted. But Hebe Jones simply disappeared into the garden shed, and emerged with a blue-and-white striped deck chair. She sat down and pulled out from a carrier bag a guide to the Tower that she had purchased to prepare her husband for his interview. With the ruthlessness of a gunner, she started to fire questions at the man who had failed his history O-Level to such a spectacular degree that the astonished marker kept a copy of his paper to cheer herself up during her most debilitating bouts of depression. Hebe Jones maintained the battery as her husband paced up and down the lawn, scratching the back of his neck as he searched for the answers in the empty birdcage of his head.

His wife's determination was absolute. Balthazar Jones would receive a call at lunchtime asking not what he fancied for supper, but the name of the woman who was sent to the Tower in the thirteenth century for repulsing the advances of King John, who subsequently poisoned her with an egg. She would return home from work and enquire, not how her husband's day had been, but in which tower the Duke of Clarence had been drowned in a butt of his favourite Malmsey wine. Bathed in sweat after love-making, she would lift her head from his chest and demand not that he reveal the depth of his devotion for her, but the name of the seventeenth-century thief who made it as far as the Tower wharf with the Crown Jewels. By the time the job offer arrived in the post, Balthazar Jones's brain had been unsettled by so much English history, that it provoked in him a mania for the subject that afflicted him for the rest of his life.

*   *   *

Rev. Septimus Drew woke in his three-storey home overlooking Tower Green, and glanced at his alarm clock. There was still some time before the gates of the Middle Tower would open to let in the loathsome tourists, the worst of whom still thought that the Queen Mother was alive. At times the chaplain rose even earlier to capture more of this exquisite period. The place was never the same when the infernal hoards eventually left, the gates shut swiftly behind them, as the air in the chapel remained as putrid as a stable's until nightfall.

His mind immediately turned to the new mousetrap he had painstakingly laid the previous evening. With the mounting excitement of a child about to inspect the contents of his Christmas stocking, the clergyman wondered what he would find. Unable to wait any longer, he swung his legs out of bed, and opened the windows to clear the room of the mists of unrequited love that had clouded them overnight. The movement sent tears of condensation running down the panes. He dressed quickly, his long, holy fingers still stiff from his endeavours in his workshop the night before. Pulling on his red cassock over his trousers and shirt, he screwed his sockless feet into his shoes, not bothering to unlace them. As he rushed down the two staircases, he clutched the front of his cassock so as not to trip, the back pouring down the battered wooden steps behind him like crimson paint. Despite his purchase of a jar of thick-cut Seville orange marmalade from Fortnum & Mason, he didn't stop for breakfast in the tiny kitchen with its window overlooking Tower Green, screened with a net curtain to prevent the tourists seeing inside. Not, of course, that it stopped them from trying. The chaplain was forever coming out of his light blue door to find them with their hands cupped against the glass, jostling for position.

His beetle-black hair still in turmoil, he walked the short distance across the cobbles to the Chapel Royal of St Peter ad Vincula. He had never got used to it being included in the Beefeaters' tours. Many of the sightseers ignored the instruction to take off their hats before entering, only to receive a retired soldier's reprimand once inside. Some even attended the Sunday service, and the chaplain would watch them from the altar, his fury mounting as they sat amongst the Beefeaters and their families, gazing at the walls around them. And he knew that their wonderment had nothing to do with being in the House of God, but everything to do with the thrill of sitting in a chapel which housed the broken remains of three Queens of England who had been beheaded just outside.

He naturally blamed the tourists for the rat infestation, assuming they showered the place with tantalising crumbs as they snacked, listening to the Beefeaters' talks. However, the sightseers were

21

entirely blameless, for any food they made the grave mistake of purchasing from the Tower Café, which made a rude profit from dismaying the tourists, went straight into the bin after the first mouthful. The truth was that the current rat population were descendants of the rodents that moved in not long after St Peter's was first built as an ordinary city parish church outside the Tower walls, before being incorporated into the castle following Henry III's extensions. The rats had decamped briefly on the two occasions when the chapel was rebuilt, and for a third time during the nineteenth-century renovations when more than a thousand human corpses were discovered under the floor. But the vermin soon returned, lured by the succulence of the new tapestry kneelers. They had harassed a succession of chaplains to such a degree that each was obliged to wear his cassock several inches above the dusty chapel floor to prevent the ends from being ravished whenever he stood in contemplation. But it did nothing to stop the nibbling while they knelt in prayer. Rev. Septimus Drew found such radical tailoring one humiliation too far, and had devoted his eleven years in the post to the extermination of the creature not worthy of a mention in the Bible.

His time had been spent studiously converting the humble mousetrap into a contraption of suitable robustness to annihilate a rat. First he turned one of the empty bedrooms, which he had hoped would be used by the family he had longed for, into a workshop. It was there that he laboured on his inventions late into the night, the shelves lined with books on basic scientific laws and theories. Numerous plans with perfectly to-scale drawings lay unfurled on a desk, weighed down by anaemic spider plants. A series of models, made out of pieces of cardboard, off-cuts of wood and garden twine, were laid out on a table. The arsenal of weapons included a tiny sling and marble, a razor blade which had once formed part of a doomed guillotine, a tiny trebuchet, and a pair of minuscule gates complete with murder holes in the top, through which deadly substances could be poured.

Arriving at the chapel door, he pressed down on the cold door handle. His hopes mounting for a formidable body count, he pushed open the door and made his way across the worn tiles to the door that led to the crypt. As he approached the tomb of Sir Thomas More where he had set up his latest apparatus (which had taken two months of planning and execution, as well as a call to a weapons expert at the Imperial War Museum), he heard a sound in the main body of the church. Irritated at being disturbed at such a delicious moment, he retraced his steps to determine the source of the noise.

His resentment at being interrupted immediately evaporated the moment he recognised the figure sitting in the front row of chairs next to the altar. Caught off guard by the sight of the woman who had chased away his dreams, he quickly hid behind a pillar and stood with his palms flat against the cold, smooth stone. It was the moment he had been imagining for months: a chance to speak to her alone, take her hand in his and ask whether there was any hope that she might feel for him the way he did about her. While still uncertain of the merits of such an antiquated approach, he

considered it the best out of all those he had
thought of since his heart had taken flight. But in
all the wistful fantasies he had concocted as he
stood at his window overlooking Tower Green
hoping for a glimpse of her, his hair had always
been perfectly combed into the style first inflicted
at the age of eight, and his teeth had been brushed.
Cursing himself for having left the house with
hangman's breath, he looked down at his skinny,
bare ankles and deeply regretted not having taken
the time to put on his socks.

As he berated himself for his unsavoury state, a
burst of sobbing echoed round the ancient walls.
Unable to ignore a soul in anguish, he decided to
offer her comfort, despite his wretchedness. But at
that very moment came a thud and a high-pitched
squeak from the crypt. The woman jumped to her
feet and fled, no doubt in fear of one of the many
spectral apparitions said to haunt the Tower. Rev.
Septimus Drew remained where he was, playing
the scene over in his mind with a spectacularly
different ending as the incense, which he burnt in
copious amounts to mask the stench of rat
droppings, curled around his skinny, bare ankles.
When, eventually, he returned to the crypt, not
even the sight of a slaughtered rat improved his
mood.

*   *   *

When Balthazar Jones had recovered the will to
report for duty after his disastrous breakfast, he
clambered into his dark blue trousers and pulled
on the matching tunic with the initials ER
emblazoned in red across the front, surmounted by

a red crown. He reached up to the top of the wardrobe for his hat, and pulled it on with both hands. Like all the Beefeaters before him, he had initially worn the Victorian uniform with pride. But it hadn't been long before it became a source of utmost irritation. The outfits were unbearably hot in the summer and insufferably cold in the winter. Not only that, but they itched from the clouds of moth repellent sprayed on them twice a year while the Beefeaters were still wearing them lest they shrank.

Descending the Salt Tower's stairs, he locked the door behind him, and turned right past the Tower Café. Assigned the post outside Waterloo Barracks, which housed the Crown Jewels, he chose a spot at sufficient distance from the sentry who had won a fistfight with a Beefeater the week before. His pale blue eyes instinctively searched the sky, and his thoughts drifted with the clouds on their way to drench the washing of the residents of Croydon. When his concentration briefly returned, he braced himself for the battery of ludicrous questions from the tourists who had started to seep in.

An hour later, Balthazar Jones had failed to realise that it had started to rain. Such was his expertise, his subconscious had instantly dismissed the downpour as a particularly common variety for January. He remained in exactly the same position, staring intently but seeing nothing, while the visitors had long since run for cover. When the man from the Palace eventually found him, he was still standing in the same spot, completely sodden and smelling fiercely of moth repellent. On hearing his name, Balthazar Jones turned his head, causing a raindrop to fall from the end of his nose on to the red crown embroidered on the front of his tunic. The man in the dry coat immediately covered the Beefeater with his silver-handled umbrella. Introducing himself as Oswin Fielding, an equerry to Her Majesty, he enquired as to whether he might have a word. Balthazar Jones hurriedly wiped his beard to rid it of water, but then found that his hand was too wet to offer. The man from the palace suggested that they had a cup of tea at the Tower Café. But as they approached, he sniffed twice, flinched at the affront to his nostrils, and headed straight for the Rack & Ruin.

The tavern, from which members of the public had always been barred, was empty apart from the landlady, who was cleaning out her canary's cage. Oswin Fielding walked past the empty tables, and chose one against the back wall. He hung up his coat, and approached the bar. Balthazar Jones, who had forgotten to remove his hat, sat down and tried to distract himself from his anxiety about what the man wanted by studying the framed signature of Rudolf Hess hanging on the wall. It had been given to a Beefeater during the Deputy Führer's four-day imprisonment at the Tower. But Balthazar Jones had studied it so many times before, it failed to hold his attention.

The Beefeater's hope that Oswin Fielding would be seduced by the real ales evaporated when he returned with two teas and the last Kit Kat. He watched in silence as the man from the Palace removed the red wrapper, and offered him half, which he refused on account of his fluttering insides. The equerry proceeded to dunk each finger before eating it, a process that doubled the length of consumption, while at the same time enquiring about the pub's history. Balthazar Jones answered as briefly as possible, and failed to mention the fact that the man had chocolate on his chin lest it deterred him further from getting to the point. When the courtier spotted the framed signature of Rudolf Hess, the Beefeater instantly dismissed it as a fake as he could no longer bear waiting for the executioner's axe to fall.

But much to his annoyance, Oswin Fielding started to talk about a golden monkey called Guoliang, which had belonged to the Queen. 'It was a gift from the President of China following his state visit in 2005,' he explained.

Balthazar Jones was not the least bit interested in golden monkeys, royal or not. He glanced out of the window and wondered whether the equerry had come about his lamentable record for catching pickpockets, which was the worst amongst the Beefeaters. By the time he opened his ears again, he realised that Oswin Fielding was still discussing the late Guoliang.

'The creature's death has caused Her Majesty immense personal sorrow,' the equerry was saying, shaking his head, which barely possessed sufficient hair to warrant such a meticulous parting. 'Someone at the Palace looked up its name, and discovered it means "May the Country Be Kind", which makes its demise even more unfortunate. It caused the most stupendous diplomatic row. Golden monkeys are indigenous to China and there aren't many of them left. We explained that we even got in a feng shui expert to redesign the enclosure as soon as it appeared off-colour, but the Chinese didn't seem that impressed. For some reason they had got it into their heads that it would be kept at Buckingham Palace. But with the exception of horses, the Queen keeps all animals given to her by heads of state at London Zoo. Which is just as well, as the Palace is enough of a monkey house as it is.' The courtier paused. 'Don't repeat that,' he added hastily.

Just as Balthazar Jones could take no more, Oswin Fielding adjusted his rimless spectacles and announced that he had something of the utmost importance to tell him. The Beefeater stopped breathing.

'As you will know, relations between Britain and China are in a rather delicate state, and as an emerging super power we need to keep them on side,' the courtier said firmly. 'No one has forgotten those unfortunate comments made by the Duke of Edinburgh, either. As a gesture of goodwill, China has sent Her Majesty a second golden monkey. Shame, really, as they haven't got the most attractive combination of features—a snub nose, blue cheeks and hair the same colour as Sarah Ferguson's. Anyway, the Queen is stuck with it. To make matters worse, the Chinese also noticed the similarity in hair colour, and have named it the Duchess of York. The Queen is understandably rather unsettled by that.'

The Beefeater was about to ask why exactly he had wanted to see him, but the equerry continued.

'While the Queen has the utmost respect for London Zoo, she has decided to move the new monkey, as well as all her other gifts of animals that are kept there, to a more intimate location. The problem is that foreign rulers always take it as a personal slight if their creature dies.'

The courtier then leant forward conspiratorially. 'I'm sure you've guessed where the animals are to be newly lodged,' he said.

'I can't imagine,' replied Balthazar Jones, who was contemplating fetching himself a pint.

Oswin Fielding then lowered his voice and announced: 'They are going to be transferred to the Tower to form a new royal menagerie.'

The Beefeater wondered whether the rain had rusted his eardrums.

'It's not as daft an idea as it sounds,' the man from the Palace insisted. 'Exotic beasts were kept at the Tower from the thirteenth century. Foreign powers continued to send the monarchy animals over the years, and the menagerie became an immensely popular tourist attraction. It didn't close until the 1830s.'

Like all the Beefeaters, Balthazar Jones was well aware that the Tower had housed a menagerie, and often pointed out the remains of the Lion Tower to the tourists. He could even have told the equerry that the elephants were given red wine by their keepers to banish the cold, and that the lions were rumoured to have been able to determine whether or not a woman was a virgin, tales he used to stun the more irritating visitors into silence. But he didn't utter a word.

Oswin Fielding continued: 'Her Majesty very much hopes that the new menagerie will increase the number of visitors to the Tower, which has been declining.' He paused before adding: 'Hirsute gentlemen in antiquated uniforms are not much of an attraction these days. No disrespect to you, your trousers, or your beard.'

He paused yet again, but the only movement that

came from the Beefeater was a raindrop plunging from the brim of his hat. Slowly, the courtier raised his eyes from the spot where it had landed.

'It's a little-known fact that Her Majesty is rather partial to tortoises,' he said. 'She is aware that you are in possession of the world's oldest specimen, which, of course, is a source of great national pride. Such an animal undoubtedly requires the most tender care.' And with a triumphant smile the man from the Palace added: 'The Queen can think of no one better than you to oversee the project.'

Oswin Fielding patted Balthazar Jones on the shoulder, and then reached underneath the table to dry his hand on his trouser leg. As he stood up, he warned the Beefeater not to tell anyone of the plan, particularly the Chief Yeoman Warder, as details had yet to be ironed out. 'We're hoping to transfer the Queen's animals in about three weeks' time, and give them a few days to settle in before opening the menagerie to the public,' he said.

Announcing that he would be in touch shortly, he put on his coat, and walked out with his splendid umbrella. Balthazar Jones remained on the red leather stool unable to move. He didn't manage the monumental task of getting to his feet until he was asked to leave by the infuriated landlady who complained that the stench of mothballs had caused her canary to faint, and it had landed in the slops tray.

*   *   *

It had stopped raining by the time Hebe Jones returned to the Tower, having left work early on account of her headache. The sky remained an obstinate shade of used bathwater, ready to disgorge a second filthy load at any moment. She nodded at the Yeoman Gaoler, the Chief Yeoman Warder's deputy, who was sitting in a black hut at the entrance to the Tower, a three-bar electric fire preventing the damp from decomposing his toes. When he enquired about the visit from the man from the Palace, Hebe Jones replied that there had been no such thing, or her husband would have called to inform her. But the Beefeater backed up the sighting with a further nine eyewitness accounts, each of whom he named while unfurling a plump finger.

'Don't sprout where you haven't been planted,' Hebe Jones snapped, and continued through the gates. Her passage was soon thwarted by a suffocation of tourists staring at the Beefeaters' terrace houses along Mint Street. Feeling more than ever the weight of her supermarket shopping in each hand, she squeezed her way sideways up Water Lane, wishing that the visitors would indulge their lunatic weakness for British history elsewhere. As she passed Cradle Tower, she was struck sharply in the chest by a rucksack whose owner had turned to see the window from where two prisoners had escaped on a rope stretched across the moat in the sixteenth century. Once she had caught her breath, she continued on her journey, seeing nothing but the Greek cottage of her fantasies.

Arriving at the Salt Tower, she searched for the key that failed to fit into a pocket, and discovered that it had already torn the lining of her new handbag. After turning it in the lock, a feat that

31

required both of her doll-sized hands, she made her way up the steps with half her bags, the narrowness of the spiral stairs preventing her from carrying them all up in one go. As she started her descent for the second load, gripping the filthy rope handrail that still bore the sweat of the condemned, she wondered, as she often did, how many of them had kept their heads.

She put away the shopping, and started to wash the breakfast dishes, remembering the argument with her husband that morning. After losing Milo, instead of clinging to each other cheek-to-cheek as they had throughout their marriage, the couple had found themselves swimming in opposite directions as they battled to survive. When one needed to talk about the tragedy, the other wanted to experience the fleeting seconds of tranquillity they had found. They eventually ended up collapsed on distant shores, marooned by their grief, and aiming their anger over losing him at each other.

As she scrubbed, she looked up at the picture on the wall in front of her depicting the Salt Tower in wobbly pencil strokes, coloured in with felt tip. Great care had been taken, but not always achieved, to keep within the lines. Next to the Tower stood three smiling figures, two tall, one short. Only the artist's parents had recognised the small object next to them, which was also smiling, as that of the oldest tortoise in the world. And she peered, with mounting distress, at the colours that had started to fade.

Suddenly she heard the thud of the Salt Tower door. Not long afterwards, her husband appeared in the kitchen and silently presented her with a warm, flat cardboard box. Hebe Jones, unable to admit that she still detested pizza, set the table, and forced down the white flag in small mouthfuls that threatened to choke her. And for the rest of the evening the air in the Salt Tower was so fragile that they spoke to each other as if the place were filled with a million fluttering butterflies that neither dared disturb.

3

Hebe Jones unbuttoned her coat next to the drawer containing one hundred and fifty-seven pairs of false teeth. It was a ritual she performed every morning upon arrival at London Underground's Lost Property Office, even during the summer, a season she vehemently distrusted in England. She hung it on the stand next to the life-size inflatable doll, a deep red hole for a mouth, which no one had yet dared to claim. Turning the corner, she stood at the original Victorian counter, its shutter still closed, and studied one of the ledgers to remind her what had been brought in the previous day. As well as the usual several dozen umbrellas and best-selling novels, some with a bookmark tragically near the end, the yield included one lawnmower, a Russian typewriter and sixteen jars of preserved ginger. The last item brought in was yet another abandoned wheelchair, increasing the office's hoard to the spectacular figure of thirty-nine. It was proof, if only to the staff, that London Underground could perform miracles.

She switched on the kettle on top of the safe that no one had been able to open since its discovery on the Circle Line five years ago. Opening the fridge, currently the subject of a standoff about whose turn it was to clean, she took out a carton of milk and raised it to her nose. Satisfied that the boisterous odour came from something no longer recognisable on the lower shelf, she poured some into a teacup. As she waited for the water to boil, the woman who felt the weight of loss more acutely than most gazed with regret at the graveyard of forgotten belongings on metal shelves stretching far into the distance, covered in a shroud of dust.

Passing the long, black magician's box used to imprison glamorous assistants while sawing them in half, she took her tea to her desk. It was scattered with a number of recent items whose owners she was still trying to trace: a stuffed humming bird in a little glass dome; a false eye; a pair of tiny pointed Chinese slippers with lotus leaf embroidery; a gigolo's diary which she hoped wouldn't be claimed before she had finished reading it; and a small box purporting to contain a testicle belonging to an A. Hitler found in the Albert Hall. Standing on a shelf above the desk was a line of faded thank-you cards kept as proof of the more considerate side of human nature, one that was easily forgotten when dealing with the general public.

Opening a drawer, she pulled out her notebook, hoping that the deeply satisfying task of reuniting a possession with its absent-minded owner would take her mind off her troubles. She read the notes she had made during her search for the manufacturer of the false eye, but her thoughts kept finding their way back to her husband.

She smelt the arrival of her colleague before seeing her. The still-warm bacon sandwich in greaseproof paper tossed on to the neighbouring desk knocked over an Oscar statuette, which had been waiting for collection for two years, eight months and twenty-seven days. Despite the fact that Hebe Jones had repeatedly told her that it was a fake, borne out by all the letters sent to the actor's agent remaining unanswered, Valerie Jennings was of the utter conviction that one day Dustin Hoffman would arrive in person to reclaim it.

Years of frustration, made bearable by the odd spectacular triumph, had bonded the two women like prisoners sharing the same cell. While they rejoiced in one another's successes as keenly as their own, they were equally susceptible to feeling the dead weight of the other's failures. It was a job of highs and lows. As a result, neither woman could bear the shafts of boredom that would eventually shine their way into the working day, often with the handing in of the morning's thirty-ninth set of door keys. It was then that they would long for the arrival of something either exotic, edible, or, if luck would have it, both. And while during particularly intense periods of stress Hebe Jones was able to escape to the sanctuary of the magician's box, where she would remain entombed with her eyes closed, Valerie Jennings, whose marvellous girth thwarted such pleasure, resorted to trying on the contents of an abandoned box-set of theatrical beards and moustaches, and admiring the many splendid permutations in the mirror.

The two women, who irritated each other as much as siblings, but who loved each other just as fiercely, ruled London Underground's Lost Property Office with a queenly air that only slipped to that of the filthiest of brothels during moments of intense frustration. Their honesty was utmost. Everything that was handed in by Underground staff, or kindly members of the public, was written down with the penmanship of a monk in perfectly ordered ledgers. The only items the women claimed as their own were perishables, which they were forbidden from storing for more than twenty-four hours, though they made a secret extension for inscribed birthday cakes, which unsettled their hearts more than their taste buds.

The women greeted each other with the casual indifference earned from having spent over a decade at each other's side. As Hebe Jones raised the counter's metal shutter, which emitted a gruesome wail, Valerie Jennings inspected the Oscar statuette for damage, then stood it back on its feet. Just as she was about to pick up her sandwich, instinct told her that something was not as it should be, and she peeled back the top slice of white bread. Her suspicions confirmed, she cursed the owner of the greasy spoon for omitting the tomato ketchup. And, with the commendable hope she always bore when faced with adversity, she enquired whether any ketchup had been handed in.

The Swiss cowbell rang before Hebe Jones had a chance to reply. She got up from her seat to allow Valerie Jennings the dignity of an uninterrupted breakfast. On her way to the counter she tried to open the safe, as was the office custom. But

36

despite yet another combination of numbers, the grey steel door remained tightly shut.

Samuel Crapper, the Lost Property Office's most frequent customer, was standing at the counter dressed in a brown corduroy suit and striped blue shirt, concern threaded across his forehead. A distant descendant of the famous plumber with a glut of Royal Warrants, his family had given him the best private education money could buy. But they paid an even higher price than they had thought. The cruel words in the playground made his cheeks flare, which invariably led to the loud declaration by his tormentors that he was 'flushed with pride'. Despite his protestations that it was an urban myth that Thomas Crapper invented the flush lavatory, and it was in fact Queen Elizabeth I's godson, Sir John Harington, they would lie in wait, striking at any opportunity to force his head down the pan. The trauma of the bullying affected his memory, and he tried to compensate for it by purchasing two of everything. However, he failed to realise that if something went missing it didn't prevent its double from going the same way.

On seeing Hebe Jones approach, his agitation mounted as he realised he couldn't remember what he had lost. Staring at the floor, he ran his fingers through his ochre-coloured hair, which had never regained its ability to lie flat since the brutal years of being constantly flushed. A smile suddenly appeared as he recalled the object, but it swiftly slid away again when he remembered that it was no longer in his possession.

'Has a tomato plant been handed in, by any chance?' he enquired. It was no ordinary specimen, he went on to explain, as it was descended from one of the first such plants ever to have been grown in England, courtesy of the barber-surgeon John Gerard in the 1590s. After several years of infiltration, he had managed to procure the seed from a contact in the tomato world. Such was the magnificence of its fruit, he had decided to enter it into a show. 'Unfortunately, I left it on the Piccadilly Line yesterday on my way there,' he confessed. 'I'd forgotten that the show actually takes place this afternoon.'

'Just a minute,' replied Hebe Jones, disappearing from view. She returned within minutes, carrying the plant in front of her, and slid it silently on to the counter with the words 'Don't worry about the retrieval fee.' Skipping her usual chat, she said goodbye and disappeared again with unusual determination. And Samuel Crapper walked joyfully away, clutching the plant to his corduroy jacket, having completely failed to notice the four missing tomatoes that Hebe Jones and Valerie Jennings had enjoyed in toasted cheese sandwiches the previous day.

When Hebe Jones returned to her desk, her colleague was looking inside the fridge in readiness for elevenses, despite the fact that there was some time to go before the sacred hour. During those magical fifteen minutes, the shutter was closed, phones remained unanswered, and the two women would serve themselves Lady Grey tea in bone china cups, yet to be claimed, along with whatever cake, tarts or biscuits Valerie Jennings had brought in.

Her appreciation of the fine work of Messrs Kipling and McVitie developed after she returned home from the office one day intending to suggest to her husband that it was time that they start a family. But instead of the night of reckless passion she had been hoping for, her husband turned from his newspaper and told her with the frigidity of a lawyer that he was leaving her. He explained that the marriage had been a mistake, and insisted that no one else was involved. Valerie Jennings was so distraught at the revelation of his lack of affection, she let him handle the divorce. Several months after the decree absolute came through, she heard he had got married barefoot on a Caribbean island, and she threw out the travel brochure she discovered in the drawer of his bedside table. Only then did she take down their wedding photograph from the mantelpiece, and put it in the attic along with the album, both almost too painful to touch.

When, several minutes later, the Swiss cowbell rang again, Hebe Jones got to her feet. Standing at the counter was Arthur Catnip, a London Underground ticket inspector of limited height, whose waistline had been softened by a weakness for fried breakfasts. Over the years he had learnt to detect a fare dodger at a hundred paces. He put his talent down to the same intuition that had warned him he was going to have a massive heart attack fifteen days before the colossal misadventure took place. After taking annual leave, he attempted to check himself into the nearest hospital in readiness for the disaster. But the tattooed ticket inspector was detained against his wishes in the psychiatric wing. His prophetic warnings were noted down by a squeakily bald doctor thrilled at the thought that he had discovered a whole new subset of insanity. When the medical emergency eventually took place, the only reason Arthur Catnip survived the massive onslaught was because during the height of his suffering a flood of boiling vindication coursed up his body from his toes, pushing through his blocked artery with the thrust of a stallion. As the scent of self-righteousness filled the wing, two patients more sane than their keepers decided that this was their moment, and escaped with their suitcases after a combined stay of forty-nine years.

Over the years, Arthur Catnip had received numerous cups of tea from the ladies for his willingness to hand in everything he found. A number of his colleagues, exhausted by the amount of forgotten belongings choking the network, left the least suspicious items where they were in the hope that they would be stolen. Arthur Catnip, however, took everything that he found immediately to the Lost Property Office. Not only were the two ladies the only people in the entire workforce who ever thanked him for his efforts to make London Underground a bastion of British glory, but the thought of visiting the antiquated department in Baker Street made the former seaman's innards roll as if he were back on one of his ships. Several months ago, he had caught Valerie Jennings in one of her theatrical beards, a sight which had thrilled him beyond measure. The vision instantly reminded him of the wondrous bearded ladies he had seen on his voyages around the Pacific, who had once been guarded by spear-waving elders against circus owners with voluminous nets. The women's undoubted charms had earned them the highest regard in their village, where they were worshipped as deities and presented with the biggest turtle eggs. They used the golden yolks to gloss their beards, and the whites to oil the succulent flesh that covered their bodies in tantalising handfuls.

Arthur Catnip had vowed not to trust women again when his eleven-year marriage collapsed on the chance discovery that his wife was having an affair with his Rear Admiral. He left the Navy before he could be discharged for breaking the man's jaw, and, not wanting to see the light of day, applied for a job with London Underground. But the spectacular vision of Valerie Jennings produced in him such yearning that from then on he always arrived at work doused in eau de toilette. Having never seen her crowned with such lustrous facial hair again, he eventually convinced himself that the wondrousness had been an illusion, and he was left with a ghost of the vision that haunted him during his working day as he rattled through the Victorian tunnels seeking out fare-evaders.

The ticket inspector, whose hands had never recovered their smoothness after years of rope-pulling, placed on the counter a camellia, a pair of handcuffs, sixteen umbrellas, thirteen mobile phones and five odd socks. He waited in silence, one elbow on the counter, as Hebe Jones noted down the items in a number of ledgers with inscrutable coded cross references. Just as she closed the final volume, and returned it to its place, Arthur Catnip picked up a modest blue holdall from the floor next to his feet and placed it on the counter with the words: 'Almost forgot this.'

Hebe Jones, her curiosity as potent as the first day she started the job, unzipped the bag and

41

stood on her toes to peer inside. Still uncertain of its contents, she reached in a hand and retrieved a plastic lunch box containing the crusts of a fish paste sandwich. Feeling something else inside, she drew out a wooden box with a brass plaque inscribed with the words 'Clementine Perkins, 1939 to 2008, RIP'. And neither of them spoke as they stared in horror at the urn of ashes before them.

After Arthur Catnip had left, wondering out loud how someone could mislay human remains, Hebe Jones noted it down in the ledgers. But her hand shook to such an extent that her penmanship no longer resembled that of a monk. She carried the item back to her desk, and put it on top of the gigolo's diary without a word. But her mind was no longer on the wooden box in front of her with the brass nameplate. Instead, with the twist of a knife, it had turned to the small urn that stood in the back of the Salt Tower's wardrobe.

*   *   *

When Hebe Jones had received the call from the undertakers to say that Milo's remains were ready for collection, she instantly dropped the vase of flowers that had just arrived from Rev. Septimus Drew. Once Balthazar Jones had swept up the glass from the living-room carpet, he fetched the car keys from the hook on the wall, and they made the journey in brittle silence. Balthazar Jones didn't put on Phil Collins' 'In the Air Tonight' so he could play the air drums to the music while they waited in traffic, and nor was there anyone on the back seat joining in with his father at the best bit.

The couple only spoke when they arrived, but neither of them could say the purpose of their visit, and all they offered were their names. The receptionist continued to look at them expectantly, and it wasn't until the funeral director came out that the awkwardness ended. But it started again as soon as he presented them with the urn, as neither of them could bear to take it.

On their return to the Salt Tower, the heady fumes of white lilies flooding the spiral staircase hit them. Hebe Jones, who had clutched the urn while sitting in the passenger seat in a private state of agony, placed it on the coffee table next to Milo's kazoo on her way to the kitchen to make three cups of tea. The couple sat on the sofa in suffocating silence, the third cup abandoned on the tray, neither of them able to look at the thing on the table that induced in them both a secret wish to die. Several days later, Hebe Jones noticed that her husband had placed it on top of the ancient mantelpiece. The following week, unable to bear seeing it any longer, she put it in the wardrobe until they had decided upon Milo's final resting place. But each time one of them brought up the subject, the other, suddenly caught off guard, had felt too bruised to reply. So it remained at the back of the shelf behind Hebe Jones's jumpers. And every night, before turning off her bedside light, the mother would find an excuse to open the wardrobe doors and silently wish her child goodnight, unable to abandon the ritual she had performed for eleven years.

4

For what he considered to be very good reasons, Balthazar Jones decided not to tell his wife about the visit from the equerry with the splendid umbrella. When, several days later, at the demonic hour of 3.13 a.m., Hebe Jones sat bolt upright in bed and asked: 'So what did the man from the Palace want?', the Beefeater muttered with the colourful breath of a man still embedded in his dreams that it was something to do with the drains. He instantly regretted his reply. Hebe Jones remained in the same erect position for the following eleven minutes as she pointed out that while their lavatory may very well be connected to an historic garderobe, the monstrous smell of petrified effluent left by centuries of prisoners that hung like a fog in their home whenever the drains blocked was not protected by any royal decree.

The Beefeater had considered Oswin Fielding's proposal to be utter lunacy. Once the tourists had been locked out of the fortress for the day, he spent the rest of his afternoons collapsed on his blue-and-white striped deckchair on the battlements engulfed in the creeping darkness, hoping that royal enthusiasm for the menagerie would wane. While he didn't suffer from his wife's natural horror of them, animals offered little in the way of interest for him. The one exception was Mrs Cook, whom generations of Joneses had completely forgotten was a tortoise. She was regarded more as a loose-bowelled geriatric relative with a propensity for absconding: such a

44

protracted habit that nobody realised she had vanished until weeks later as her sedate trajectory across the room was forever burnt on their memories.

It was only after being summoned to the office in the Byward Tower that the Beefeater realised that being in charge of the Queen's beasts might in fact be to his benefit. He pushed open the office's studded door to see the Chief Yeoman Warder sitting behind his desk within the cold, circular walls, his fingers, as pale as an embalmer's, laced over his stomach. He looked at his watch with irritation, and then gestured to a seat. Balthazar Jones sat down, placed his dark blue hat on his lap, and held on to its brim with both hands.

'I'll get straight to the point, Yeoman Warder Jones,' the man said, his grey beard clipped with the precision of topiary. 'Guarding the Tower and capturing the professional pickpockets are very much part of the job for which thousands of retired British servicemen would give their back teeth, if they still had any, to be selected.'

He leant forward and rested his elbows on the desk. 'You were one of our best when you first arrived,' he continued. 'I remember the time you rugby-tackled that chap on Tower Green. He had five wallets on him at the time, if I recall correctly. I know things haven't been easy, what with that dreadful business with the little chap. But time has moved on. We can't afford to have a weak link. Let's not forget the Peasants' Revolt when all those hoodlums stormed the place.'

'That was back in 1381, sir.'

'I'm well aware of that, Yeoman Warder Jones. But the point is that the Tower is not infallible. We

45

must be alert at all times, not gazing around the place enjoying the view.'

The Beefeater looked through the arrow slit behind the Chief Yeoman Warder's head as he remembered the last time he had been called into the office. On that occasion, the man had bothered to get to his feet when he came in, and immediately offered him his condolences. 'I know exactly how you feel,' he had insisted. 'When we lost Sally we were just devastated. She had such an extraordinary character. One of the most intelligent dogs we've ever had. She'd been with us for nine years. How old was the little chap again?'

'Eleven,' Balthazar Jones had replied. He then looked at his hands, while the Chief Yeoman Warder's gaze fell to his desk. The silence was eventually broken with an offer of more time off work, which Balthazar Jones refused, insisting that the three days had been sufficient. He left to walk the battlements, hoping to find a reason to live.

*　　*　　*

'Are you listening, Yeoman Warder Jones?' the Chief Yeoman Warder asked from behind the desk.

The Beefeater, his cloud-white hair flattened from his hat, turned his gaze to him and asked: 'How's the new dog?'

'She's fine, thank you for asking. Top of the obedience class.'

Balthazar Jones's gaze returned to the view through the arrow slit.

The Chief Yeoman Warder studied him with a frown. 'I don't think you realise that your future

46

here hangs in the balance. I suggest you sit there for a while and think things over,' he said, getting up. 'This can't go on.'

The Beefeater jumped as the door slammed. He looked down at his hat, and slowly wiped away the raindrops that shone like diamonds on its crown. Too defeated to get to his feet, he stared ahead of him. His mind turned once more to the night Milo died and his terrible, terrible secret. When his stomach eventually settled, his eyes dropped again to his hat, and he wiped it with the tips of his fingers, though nothing was there. Standing up, he put it back on, tugged open the door, and returned to duty.

By the time the letter arrived from Oswin Fielding asking him to come to the Palace to discuss the new menagerie, Balthazar Jones had convinced himself that his new duty would protect him from losing his job, which had given him a reason to get up in the morning when the weight of remorse pinned him to the sheets. He slipped the letter into his tunic pocket, where it remained hidden from his wife, along with the crumbs from the biscuits she forbade him to eat to safeguard his heart.

*　　　*　　　*

On the morning he was due to meet the Queen, the Beefeater sat on the bed in his dressing gown waiting for the final echo of his wife's footsteps as she descended the spiral staircase. He scurried to one of the lattice windows to check that she was on her way to work. Through the ancient glass he recognised instantly the gait of a woman determined to reunite a lost possession with its absent-minded owner. He fetched from the wardrobe his red and gold state dress uniform, which Oswin Fielding had insisted he wore for the occasion. And, with the thrill of a woman about to put on her most alluring underwear, he retrieved his white linen ruff from the trouser press.

He started to dress in front of the mirror, which for the last eight years had stood on the floor as he had been unable to mount it on the circular walls. It was a miserable room, as miserable as the living room downstairs, despite the efforts he and Hebe Jones had made to disguise the Salt Tower's repugnant past as a prison. The cheerful curtains he had made for the windows not only failed to keep out the draughts, but threw into sharp relief the wretchedness of the place.

The couple had pushed the wardrobe in front of the worst of the pitiful carvings by the prisoners who had scratched on to the walls their hopes of keeping their heads. But the others could still be seen. At night, when the couple were unable to sleep, fearing the catastrophic dreams inspired by their lodgings, they were convinced they could hear the mournful sound of chiselling.

When the family first arrived at the fortress, Hebe Jones had insisted that all the Salt Tower's decrepit furniture be taken away and replaced with their own. But it was a decision both of them regretted. While a bed, a chest of drawers, and a desk had been easily carried into Milo's bedroom on the ground floor, there was little they could manoeuvre up the spiral staircase to the floors above. As a result, the furniture had to be dismantled outside and brought up piece by piece.

Not only did it refuse to fit back together correctly, but it failed to stand flush against the curved walls, a problem neither of them had foreseen. Despite the folds of cardboard that Balthazar Jones had wedged underneath, the furniture stood at precarious angles, made worse by the pitch of the floor, until the next thunderous collapse that invariably happened in the middle of the night.

Savouring the opportunity to put on the famous uniform reserved for royal visits to the Tower and special ceremonies, Balthazar Jones clambered into his crimson tights. Pulling in his stomach, he managed to do up the matching breeches, which he concluded must have shrunk while they were hanging in the wardrobe. After putting on the tunic with the initials ER embroidered in gold thread across the chest, he tucked in the ruff's hem, and saw in the mirror the remains of a man who had dedicated his life to serving his country. Gone were the waves of hair that his wife, an amateur artist driven by hope rather than talent, had once declared was the precise shade of mummy brown, a paint whose pigment came from the dusty remains of ancient Egyptians. Over the years, the rich, earthy crests had been replaced by a low, grey undulation that had suddenly turned white. And his once clean-shaven cheeks were hidden by a beard of identical colour, grown as insulation against the wretched damp.

Sitting down on the edge of the bed, he attached red, white and blue rosettes to the sides of his knees, and then to the front of his black patent shoes. Stepping over Mrs Cook, he headed for the bathroom where the cold penetrated with such intensity a woollen hat was required during the solitude of constipation. And, as he brushed his teeth with the vigour required for a royal appointment, he prayed that the button on his breeches wouldn't burst when he bowed.

As he walked down Water Lane towards Middle Tower, a sight that sent the tourists into raptures, he refused to tell his colleagues he met on the way the reason for his attire. Once outside the fortress, he hailed a black cab, his ability to drive thwarted by his Irish linen ruff. After shutting the door, he settled himself on the back seat, and leant towards the glass. 'Buckingham Palace, please,' he said, straightening his tunic over his garnished knees.

*   *   *

Rev. Septimus Drew returned from his morning walk around the grassy moat, which had been drained of its pestilent waters by 1845. He had spent the time contemplating his next Sunday school lesson for the Tower children, during which he would explain how animals such as unicorns appeared in the Bible, whereas rats, for example, didn't. Just as he was about to enter the fortress, he spotted Balthazar Jones getting into a cab wearing state dress, and he was once again filled with regret over the collapse of their friendship.

There was a time when the Beefeater had been a regular guest at his dinner table, and they would enjoy together the delights of a plump game bird and a bottle of Château Musar. Other evenings had been spent in the Rack & Ruin inventing stories about the mystery bullet hole in the bar as they sampled the real ales. When weather permitted they used to be found on the Tower's bowling green, where they upheld their unspoken gentlemen's agreement to overlook one another's cheating. The chaplain was able to ignore the fact that, as a former soldier, the Beefeater had been prepared to kill for his country, just as Balthazar Jones had been able to ignore his friend's unfathomable attachment to religion.

Such had been the two men's mutual appreciation that even Milo had got over his initial terror of the chaplain, said to have been driven mad by the eleven-fingered drumming from Anne Boleyn's tomb. The boy would seek him out in the chapel, and the pair would sit on a bench outside as the clergyman told him tales of the Tower that had never appeared in the guidebooks. And when, one afternoon, Milo was eventually discovered hiding in Little Ease, the tiny prison cell in which no grown man could stand, he never admitted who had told him its secret location.

But since the boy's death, the Beefeater had only once accepted an invitation to supper with the chaplain, and his bowling shoes had remained in the bottom of the wardrobe. Despite the clergyman's best efforts to lure him into having a drink with him in the Rack & Ruin, Balthazar Jones had always gone alone, preferring the company of solitude.

Arriving back at his home that overlooked Tower Green, the chaplain ran himself a bath in which he was unable to linger on account of the desperate temperature of the room. He searched for a pair of underpants that would afford him the appropriate dignity for what he was about to do. After putting on his favourite mustard corduroys, that revealed a breathtaking expanse of skinny

51

ankle on account of his excessively long legs, he scrabbled inside his sock drawer and selected a pair that hadn't been worn since its arrival in the Christmas post. Shrouded in his red cassock, he padded off to the bathroom lost in the silent ecstasy of wearing new socks. Looking into the mirror dappled with age spots, he carefully combed his dark hair into the style first inflicted at the age of eight, and took particular care in brushing his teeth. But despite his efforts, when he looked at his reflection, all he saw was a man who had reached his thirty-ninth year without having experienced one of God's greatest gifts: the love of a wife.

He made the short journey to the chapel, glad that there was still time before the tourists would be let into the Tower. Pressing down the cold handle, he descended the three steps, and made his way to the crypt where he sat out of sight, hoping that the woman who had stirred the very sediment of his soul would return. After the first hour had passed, he reached into his briefcase for his copy of *Private Eye*, and searched for the unholy adventures of his fellow clergymen. For a while it managed to keep his mind off his predicament as he contemplated a particularly tantalising revelation, the details of which included a female lighthouse-keeper, a sou'wester, a bottle of absinthe, and a cauliflower. But once he had finished the magazine, and the joy of its scandal had faded, his mind turned yet again to the woman he was waiting for. As another hour creaked past, he wondered again why he was still single.

His married friends had done their best to lift him out of the quagmire of bachelorhood. To each of their dinner parties they had invited a good Christian woman whom they insisted would be a perfect match. Forever hopeful, the chaplain would arrive freshly shaven and armed with one of his more treasured bottles of Château Musar. At first, it would seem that his hosts had been right. The woman would be instantly captivated by the engaging clergyman whose job obliged him to live at the Tower of London. Despite his hairstyle, he was perfectly agreeable to the eye. Not only did the man admit to a passion for cooking, music to a modern woman's ears, but he recounted the most riveting tales about escapes from the fortress, which had everyone either wide-eyed or roaring before they had finished their cocktails. By the time the guests took their seats at the table, the woman would be flushed with desire. But despite the encouraging start, the evening always followed the same fault line whenever someone inevitably asked: 'So how many people died in the Tower?'

The chaplain, who had grown wary of the question, knew from experience to keep his reply brief. Crossing his excessively long legs underneath the table he would state: 'Despite popular belief, only seven people were beheaded at the Tower.' But either the exceptional Lebanese vintage, or the interjection of a fellow guest with surprising historical insight would get the better of him, and Rev. Septimus Drew would find himself disgorging the whole wretched truth:

'But there weren't only the beheadings, of course. Henry VI was said to have been stabbed to death in Wakefield Tower. Many people believe that the two little princes were murdered in the Bloody Tower by Richard III. In the reign of

Edward I a senior official called Henry de Bray tried to drown himself on the boat ride to the Tower by throwing himself bound into the Thames. Once he was inside, he committed suicide in his cell. In 1585 the Eighth Earl of Northumberland shot himself in the Bloody Tower. Incidentally, Sir Walter Raleigh also tried to commit suicide while imprisoned in the Tower. Who else? Oh, yes, nine Royalists were executed during the Civil War. Then there were the three men from the Scottish Black Watch who were shot for mutiny in full view of their regiment next to the chapel. They had been ordered to wear their shrouds underneath their uniforms. Who have I forgotten? Oh, yes. Poor old Sir Thomas Overbury. While he was imprisoned in the Bloody Tower he was given poisoned tarts and jellies. He suffered a slow and agonising death over several months and was finally finished off with a mercury enema. Most painful.'

Assuming he had finished, there would be a momentary pause of condolence. But as soon as the guests reached again for their cutlery, the chaplain would continue:

'Then there was the Duke of Clarence who was drowned in a butt of his favourite Malmsey wine in the Bowyer Tower. Simon Sudbury, the Archbishop of Canterbury, was dragged from the Tower during the Peasants' Revolt and, after several attempts, beheaded outside. You can see his mummified head in the church of St Gregory at Sudbury in Suffolk . . .

'Where was I? Oh yes. Arbella Stuart, James I's cousin, was imprisoned and possibly murdered in the Queen's House. Her ghost is in the habit of strangling people as they sleep. There were eleven men of various nationalities shot by firing squads for espionage during the First World War. A German spy was shot during the Second World War in 1941. He was the last person to be executed at the Tower, by the way. We've still got the chair he was sitting on at the time somewhere. And I suppose I should mention the one hundred and twenty-five-odd Tower prisoners who died, mostly by beheading, on Tower Hill, just outside the fortress, watched by thousands of unruly spectators. Well, that's some of them, anyway.'

By the time Rev. Septimus Drew had finished answering the query, the dinner was inevitably cold, and the woman's cheeks had drained to the colour of the white linen napkins. When she would leave at the end of the evening, guarding her telephone number closely, the apologetic hosts would insist that his home was to blame. 'What sort of woman would want to live in the Tower of London anyway?' they would ask. And each time the chaplain would agree with the explanation. But whenever he returned to his empty home on Tower Green, and sat in the dark in his carpetless study, he always came to the bitter conclusion that the fault was solely his.

*　　　*　　　*

Once he had finally accepted that the woman who invaded his dreams wasn't coming, Rev. Septimus Drew got up, and headed through the chapel to the door. As he stepped out, the wind instantly rearranged his hair, and he headed home, the snowmen on his socks visible in the gap between the bottom of his cassock and the cobbles. He searched in his pocket for the key to his blue front door, which he kept locked ever since the day he returned home to find two Spanish tourists in his sitting room, eating their sandwiches on the sofa. After locking the door behind him, he went into the kitchen that still smelt of the treacle cake he had baked using his mother's faded recipe, and took down his solitary teapot for one.

*   *   *

Balthazar Jones arrived at the gates of Buckingham Palace having spent the journey trying not to crush his ruff against the back of the seat each time the taxi driver hit the brakes. A police officer escorted him into the palace via a side door, then handed him into the care of a mute footman, whose polished buckled shoes were equally silent as they passed along a corridor of dense blue carpet. It was flanked with marble-topped gilt tables bearing billowing pink arrangements made that morning by a weeping Royal Household florist, whose husband had just asked her for a divorce. However, her tears were not those of sadness, but of relief, for she had never got used to the idea that her husband left for work each morning wearing what was irrefutably a skirt, tartan knee socks and no underpants. Married to the Queen's Piper for three disappointing years, she had found his talent for the bagpipes as insufferable as the Monarch did. His historic duty, dreamed up by Queen Victoria at the height of her Scottish mania, was to play every weekday under the Sovereign's window. The commotion started at the absurd hour of nine o'clock in the morning and lasted for a full fifteen minutes, much to Elizabeth II's infuriation. There was no escaping the man as he would follow her to her other residences at Windsor, Holyrood and Balmoral, where he continued the loathsome ritual with undiminished devotion.

The mute footman opened the door to Oswin Fielding's office, and indicated a green seat upon which Balthazar Jones was to wait. Once the door was shut silently behind him, the Beefeater sat down, and removed from his left crimson knee a piece of fluff that upon inspection he failed to recognise. Looking up, he surveyed the room. On the pale blue walls were hung several engravings of Buckingham Palace mounted in thin gold frames, which were part of the courtier's private collection. As he leant forward to inspect the photographs on the formidable desk, a drop of sweat started its descent inside his thick crimson tunic, tickling the valley of his chest as it fell. He picked up the nearest silver frame and staring back at him was Oswin Fielding, almost unrecognisable with a profusion of hair, in hiking gear with his arm around a blonde woman in a baseball cap. He surveyed the man's legs, which he immediately concluded were not as good as his own, despite his advanced years.

Suddenly the door opened and in strode the equerry accompanied by a waft of gentleman's scent. 'I must say you're looking splendid,' announced the courtier, undoing the button on his discreet suit jacket. 'Her Majesty has been delayed unfortunately, so I'm afraid it's just the two of us after all. Still, always fun to put on the old crimson

57

breeches, I'm sure!'

The Beefeater slowly took off his black Tudor bonnet and rested it on his lap in silence.

'What we both need is a cup of tea,' the courtier announced as he sat down behind his desk. After making the call, he sat back. 'It must be fun living in the Tower,' he said. 'When my children were younger they were always asking whether we could move there. Have you got any children? All I seem to know about your personal circumstances is your tortoise.'

There was a pause.

The Beefeater's gaze fell to the desk. 'A son,' he replied.

'Is he still with you or has he gone off to join the Army like his father?'

'He's no longer with us, no,' replied Balthazar Jones, looking at the carpet.

The silence was broken by the arrival of a footman with a silver tray. After setting it down on the courtier's desk, he poured two cups through a silver strainer, and left again without a sound. Oswin Fielding offered the Beefeater a plate of shortbread. Balthazar Jones declined, unsettled by the unruly shape.

'Pity, they're one of Her Majesty's specialities. Almost as good as her scones. Admittedly, they do appear a little strange. Apparently she couldn't find her glasses,' said the courtier, helping himself.

The Beefeater looked with regret at the shortbread made by royal fingers, and then at the equerry who had just taken a bite and seemed to float in a momentary state of ecstasy. Once Oswin Fielding came to, he took a file from a locked drawer and opened it. He then went through the planned building works for the menagerie, pointing out that not only would enclosures be constructed in the moat, but a number of the disused towers within the monument would be converted for the keeping of the beasts.

'I've no idea where any of them should go. I know nothing about exotic animals—I'm more of a labrador man, to tell you the truth—so I'm leaving all that up to you,' said the courtier with a smile.

Balthazar Jones pulled at the band of his ruff to ease the constriction around his neck.

'Now I expect you're wanting to know which animals are to be transferred along with the Duchess of York,' the equerry continued, turning to another page. 'Some toucans. If I remember correctly, they came from the President of Peru. There's a zorilla, which isn't, as one might imagine, a cross between a zebra and a gorilla, but a highly revered yet uniquely odorous black-and-white skunk-like animal from Africa. In the Sudan they call it "father of stinks". We were hoping to send that back before the Queen saw it, but she spotted it and said it was rude to return a gift, no matter how foul smelling. There are a number of Geoffroy's marmosets from the President of Brazil, and a sugar glider from the Governor of Tasmania. Sugar gliders, by the way, are small flying possums that get depressed if you don't give them enough attention. There's also a glutton, sent by the Russians, which looks like a small bear and has an enormous appetite. It costs the Queen a fortune in food. What else? A Komodo dragon from the President of Indonesia. Komodo dragons are the world's largest lizards, and can bring down a horse. They're carnivorous and have a ferocious bite, injecting venom into their victims. So I'd watch that one, if I were you.'

The Beefeater gripped his armrests as the equerry turned a page.

'What else?' Oswin Fielding asked. 'Ah yes, some crested water dragons, otherwise known as Jesus Christ lizards. The President of Costa Rica sent that lot, God knows why. And there's also an Etruscan shrew from the President of Portugal. It's the smallest land mammal in the world, and can sit in a teaspoon when fully grown. It's also very highly strung—some die from anxiety just being handled. They say moving is one of life's greatest stressors, so best of luck. Let me remind you that the Anglo-Portuguese Alliance, signed in 1373, is the oldest alliance in the world still in force. We wouldn't want anyone to come along and mess that up. Well, here's the list. You can read about the others at your leisure. There will, of course, be a vet at your disposal, should you need one, but it should all be pretty straightforward. Just make sure they're fed and watered. And jolly them along, I expect.'

The Beefeater reached out a white-gloved hand and silently took the file. Just as he was about to stand up, the man from the Palace leant forward. 'A word of warning,' he said, lowering his voice. 'Remember to keep the lovebirds separated. They hate each other . . .'

5

Hebe Jones ignored the urn sitting on her desk as she had done every day since its arrival, and picked up the false eye. As she held it up to her own, the two pupils looked at one another for several seconds. Eventually stared out, she admired the artistry of the tiny brushstrokes on the hazel iris. Her curiosity sated, she picked up the phone, hoping to reunite the item with its Danish owner.

It hadn't taken her as long as she had feared to find a number for him. The breakthrough had come when she spotted the manufacturer's name and a serial number on the back of the prosthesis. The print's mouse-like dimensions had meant that she had needed to borrow Valerie Jennings's glasses in order to decipher it, a habit that had become a particular source of irritation. The request evoked a sigh of despair that stirred the worms in the earth below, but which Hebe Jones never heard. Valerie Jennings disappeared into a labyrinth of petrifying smears as she waited for their return, and suggested once again that Hebe Jones had her eyes tested. 'Everyone's sight gets worse as they get older,' she said.

'The old hen is worth forty chickens,' Hebe Jones replied, when she finally handed over the spectacles.

After dialling the owner's number in Århus, given to her by the receptionist at the eye manufacturer's, Hebe Jones doodled on her pad as she waited.

'Hallo,' came the eventual reply.

'Hallo,' Hebe Jones repeated cautiously. 'Frederik Kjeldsen?'

'Ja!'

'This is Mrs Jones from London Underground Lost Property Office. I believe we may have something that belongs to you.'

There was a moment of pure silence, after which Frederik Kjeldsen began to weep with his good eye. When the damp sound eventually came to an end, the man apologised, and began to explain what had happened.

'Two years ago I lost my eye in a road accident, and spent seven weeks in hospital,' he said. 'I was too scared to drive again and had to give up my job as a teacher. I was so depressed, I didn't bother getting a . . . what do you call them?'

'A prosthesis?'

'Ja, a prosthesis. It wasn't until my sister announced her wedding that I decided to get one to save her the humiliation of my solitary eye in the wedding photographs. I made the decision that, once the celebrations were over, I would take my own life.'

There was a pause during which the two strangers held on to each other through the silence.

'I had to take two buses to reach the manufacturer's,' he continued. 'But the moment the eye-maker lifted her head from her instruments, and spoke to me with the voice of an angel, I fell for her. After eight months, and what I have to admit were many unnecessary appointments, I proposed to her under the same fir tree that my father had proposed to my mother. Our wedding emptied the florists for miles. I was so happy I cannot tell you.'

After swallowing loudly, Frederik Kjeldsen continued: 'Ten days ago, I was travelling back to the airport after a weekend in London to see my niece when the Tube suddenly stopped. I banged my head against the glass and my eye flew out. There were so many feet and suitcases in the carriage I wasn't able to find it before arriving at Heathrow. If I had stayed looking for it any longer, the train would have taken me back to London, and I would have missed my flight. I needed to get back in time for work the next day, and I had such a headache you wouldn't believe, so I put on my sunglasses and got off. Of course my wife has made me another eye, but I so wanted the one that had brought us together. And now it seems that you have found it. It is truly a miracle.'

After Frederik Kjeldsen apologised again for his salty state, Hebe Jones assured him that she would get it into the post immediately. As she put down the phone, Valerie Jennings approached and peered at the eye over her colleague's shoulder, scratching her nest of dark curls, clipped to the back of her head. She then walked to one of the shelves and returned with a box containing a hand-blown glass eye purporting to have belonged to Nelson, and another made of porcelain, which, according to its accompanying label, was used by a fourteenth-century Chinese emperor whenever he slept with his favourite mistress. After showing them to her colleague, Valerie Jennings, who had started to smell the rank breath of boredom, asked: 'Fancy a game of marbles?'

Hebe Jones was certain of winning, particularly as she was prepared to suffer the indignity of lying flat on the office floor to execute a shot. She had honed her skills as a young child on the cool, tiled floors of the house in Athens, and her talent flourished when the Grammatikos family moved to London when she was five, despite the challenge of carpeting. Her ability to win even blindfolded led to the widespread belief that her expertise was due to exceptional hearing, rather than the more obvious explanation that she was peeking. She subsequently claimed to be able to hear the talk of infants still in the womb, and mothers from the Greek community, who were more ready to believe such ability in one of their own, presented their swollen abdomens to the girl to learn the first utterances of their child. After demanding absolute silence, she would sit, one ear pressed against the protruding umbilicus, translating the squeaks, whistles and centenarian groans with the fluency of a polyglot.

'No, thanks,' Hebe Jones nevertheless replied, turning over the prosthesis in her hand. 'Look. It's concave. And anyway, that poor man's eye has rolled around enough of London as it is.'

After sealing up the box with brown tape, kept on the inflatable doll's wrist by mutual agreement following one too many disappearances, Hebe Jones added Mr Kjeldsen's address, and dropped the package into the mailbag with the warm glow of victory. As she looked around her desk for the next task, her eyes stopped at the urn. Feeling a stab of guilt for having ignored it since its arrival, she turned the wooden box round in her hands and ran a finger over the brass nameplate bearing the words 'Clementine Perkins, 1939 to 2008. RIP' in an elegant script. She tried to imagine the woman

64

whose remains had been travelling around the Underground, but felt even greater pity for the person who had mislaid them. Hoping to find something to help her trace Clementine Perkins's relatives, she decided to look up her entry in the national register of deaths.

'I'm just popping out to the library,' she announced, standing up. And within minutes, Hebe Jones and her turquoise coat were gone.

Valerie Jennings watched her turn the corner and immediately regretted not having asked her to bring back a Chelsea bun from the high street bakery. Despite her patronage, she had long lamented their offerings, and had once even boycotted the establishment when she noticed two French tourists looking into its windows discussing whether its wares were for the purpose of plugging holes. But eventually she relented, defeated by patriotism and necessity.

After labelling a yellow canoe, she took hold of one end, and dragged it through the office shuffling backwards in her flat black shoes, uttering a string of profanities. Eventually, she managed to slide it on to the bottom shelf of the nautical section. Standing up, she arched her back, then made her way to the original Victorian counter, and noted down the shelf number in an inscrutable code in one of the ledgers.

It was the only office in the whole of London without a computer, the introduction of which the two women had refused with a steadfast obstinacy. When, five years earlier, they were informed that the unfathomable machines were to be installed, both immediately offered their resignation with the freaky concurrency of twins. Then, like two circus curiosities, they demonstrated their encyclopaedic knowledge of every item stored on the meticulously numbered shelves, including on which Tube line they had been abandoned.

Their invincible memories were not, however, enough to dissuade the authorities from accepting their resignations until an attempt was made to follow the logic of the cross-referencing in the ledgers. The antique code, invented by clerks to make themselves indispensable, had been handed down from Victorian times when the office was established to handle the onslaught of muffs and canes left behind on the breathtaking new transport.

As soon as management realised what they were up against, one of them filled his pockets with barley sugar, and visited the only staff still alive who had worked in the antiquated office. He found the pair propping each other up in the sitting room of an old people's home, covered in a coat of dust. But despite the joy of an unexpected visitor, and one with such treasures in his pockets, nothing could persuade them when their mists of senility temporarily parted to give up the key to the code that had ensured them a job for life. All attempts at modernisation were therefore abandoned until the next change of management, which, despite renewed tactics, always failed as emphatically as its predecessor.

Arriving back at her desk, Valerie Jennings reached into her black handbag, and returned a novel to its place on one of the bookshelves. Each volume she borrowed was brought back to the office the next day lest its owner arrived to claim it. There it would remain until she slipped it back into her bag again on leaving. And, once installed in her armchair with the pop-up leg rest, she would rampage through the pages, intoxicated by the heady fumes of fantasy.

On hearing the Swiss cowbell, she brushed away a kink of hair that had escaped from its mooring, pushed her glasses up her nose, and headed back to the counter. On the way she tried to open the safe, as was the office custom. But it remained as closed as the day it had been discovered on the Circle Line five years ago.

Turning the corner, she found Arthur Catnip partially obscured by a bunch of yellow roses. It was the second bouquet he had bought her. When he found the shutter closed the first time, his courage instantly abandoned him, and he fled to the street. He offered the flowers to the first woman he encountered, but she, along with the eleven after her, rejected the gift in the common belief that all fellow Londoners had the potential to be psychotic lunatics.

Flowers were not the only gift the ticket inspector of limited height had bought for Valerie Jennings. Recognising her weakness for literature on account of her habit of reading the back of each novel he handed in, he scoured the capital's second-hand bookshops for something to give her pleasure. Ignoring the bestselling paperbacks, he eventually came across the work of the obscure nineteenth-century novelist Miss E. Clutterbuck. Skimming the pages, he found that the female protagonist who featured in all of her work was graced with stoutness, a fearsome intellect, and a long line of suitors of varying heights. Never once did a tale end without the heroine having discovered a new country, invented a scientific theory, or solved the most fiendish of crimes. It was only then that she would retire to her parlour with a bowl of rhubarb and custard to consider her numerous marriage proposals, surrounded by love tokens of yellow roses. Arthur Catnip bought all the novelist's work that he could find, and would arrive at the original Victorian counter with his latest cloth-backed musty purchase, claiming he had found it in a carriage. Valerie Jennings's face would immediately light up at the prospect of another instalment. And she would gaze with unfettered anticipation at the colour plates of the fleshy heroine throttling a serpent in a newly discovered land, introducing her latest invention to awed gentlemen in Parliament, and stepping out with one of her elegantly moustached admirers, a number of whom were of inferior height.

Suddenly finding himself in the presence of Valerie Jennings while holding the flowers of choice of Miss E. Clutterbuck's suitors, Arthur Catnip was unable to speak.

'How lovely!' she said, peering at the bouquet. 'They must have been for someone special. Where were they left?'

Panic rattled him, and Arthur Catnip found himself uttering the three wretched words that he spent the following week regretting.

'The Victoria Line.'

*   *   *

Rev. Septimus Drew crossed the cobbles on his way back from the chapel, where he had waited yet again in vain for the woman who had unsettled his

68

heart. As he approached his front door, he looked around hoping to spot her, but all he saw were the first of the loathsome tourists who had started to seep into the Tower. As he reached into his cassock pocket for the key, he noticed that the visitors were not in fact the first, as there was someone already sitting on the bench next to the White Tower staring straight at him. Knees clamped together, and her short gunmetal hair lifting in the breeze, he recognised instantly the chairwoman of the Richard III Appreciation Society. For months she had been trying to persuade him to become a member, her passion for the maligned monarch inflamed by the gasoline of unrequited love for the clergyman. Fearing that she was going to try and convince him yet again of the injustice of the King's reputation as a hunchbacked child slayer, Rev. Septimus Drew quickly unlocked his door and closed it behind him.

He made his way down the hall to his bachelor's sitting room where he spent more time than he cared to. Avoiding the unruly spring, he sat down on the sofa, a relic from the former chaplain, along with the rest of the mismatched furniture. Picking up a biography of Jack Black, rat-catcher and mole destroyer by appointment to Queen Victoria, he started to read. But he soon found his mind wandering after the woman who had failed to return to the chapel. His gaze settled on the family portrait on the mantelpiece taken on Christmas Day when his six sisters had come to his home for lunch with their husbands and numerous children. As his eyes ran along the familiar faces, he tasted the bitterness of failure for being the only one who still wasn't married.

His nose still invaded by the smell of rat droppings from the chapel, he picked up a bottle of Rescue Remedy from the side table, and released two drops on to his tongue. His belief in the mystical powers of the blend of five flowers, and the other more lunatic offerings distilled by the druids of alternative medicine, was as strong as his belief in the Holy Spirit. As the chaplain advanced towards middle age, he had begun to grab all the defences against ill health he could find, filling his bathroom cabinet with the latest tinctures and potions brewed for the worried well. For he was firmly of the conviction that the body was more susceptible to disease without the presence of love to warm the organs.

The belief was not without its foundations, however unstable. He had watched his elderly mother, the colour of porridge, lying in a hospital bed for months, while the entire family was convinced that she would meet her maker at any moment. It was such a foregone conclusion that the music for the funeral had been chosen, and the florist put on standby for the approaching calamity. With her sheet pulled up to her whiskered chin, Florence Drew spoke of nothing other than joining her husband in heaven. Her only fear was that he would fail to recognise her on account of the disease that had infiltrated her body.

One night the man in the opposite cubicle, who had never received a visitor, got out of bed and came to sit on the grey plastic chair next to her. Switching on the night light, George Proudfoot reached into the pocket of the new dressing gown that would be his last, pulled out a paperback, and started reading to her simply to hear his own voice before he died. He returned each night, but never once did the widow acknowledge his presence.

When, one evening, he failed to arrive, she called out to him, unable to bear the thought of dying without knowing the ending. George Proudfoot, by now so close to death he was barely able to speak, eventually made his way to the grey plastic chair. With the hermit's voice that was all that was left to him, he proceeded to make up the dénouement, no longer able to read. The twist was so ingenious that Florence Drew immediately asked for another tale, and every night he arrived with his dose of storytelling. The widow would lie hypnotised, her head turned towards him, unable to take her eyes off his lips for a minute. Depending on the nature of the tale, her fingers, twisted like hazel by age, would grip the top of the sheet with dread, or reach for it to dry the tears that cascaded on to her pillow.

Suddenly, she no longer looked forward to death as George Proudfoot always left the ending to the following night, too weak to complete a whole story in one sitting. He also stopped praying that he would be taken as swiftly as possible as he wanted time to think up the ending which he was as eager to know as she was.

One night, after several weeks, he straightened the top of Florence Drew's clutched sheet, and planted a kiss on her forehead before returning to bed. The footnote to their ritual continued after every visit. The widow's colour returned with such force that the florist was stood down, and blood tests were repeated three times to check their accuracy. It wasn't long before her heartbeat started to stampede out of range again, this time in the opposite direction, sending her monitors shrieking. Eager medical students formed a queue at the end of her bed to witness the patient who was seized by the mania of love.

Eventually, the staff decided it was such a hopeless case nothing could be done, and the chaplain's mother was discharged, along with George Proudfoot who was just as badly afflicted. The pair moved into opposite rooms in a nursing home, their doors left open to continue their nocturnal courtship, and never once did the man's imagination fail him. They lived in such a state of bliss they became the envy of the young nurses whose romances were always in tatters.

When, eventually, Florence Drew died, George Proudfoot followed within minutes. Both had left instructions to be buried in the same coffin, as neither could bear to be parted even in death. Her six daughters opposed the request, but Rev. Septimus Drew insisted that the couple's instructions be carried out, as the holy state of love wasn't to be meddled with. And the couple were lowered into the ground together, the first time they had lain in each other's arms.

*   *   *

Balthazar Jones sat in the small black hut next to the Bloody Tower, no longer able to feel his toes. He had been unable to use the three-bar electric fire that usually acted as defence against the cold from the open hatch door. For, several moments after turning it on, he had been engulfed with the putrefying smell of bacon fat, a result of the Yeoman Gaoler's second breakfast the week before.

It had been a busy morning for the Beefeaters as an unfathomable dry spell had encouraged the tourists to wander round the monument instead of sheltering in the towers, and few could resist the urge to pose them a question of infinite idiocy. Balthazar Jones had already been asked in which tower Princess Diana had been kept following her divorce, whether he was an actor, and if the Crown Jewels, which had been on public display at the Tower since the seventeenth century, were real. These had come on top of the usual enquiries that came every few minutes regarding executions, methods of torture, and the location of the lavatories.

Over the centuries the Beefeaters, or Yeoman Warders as they were officially called, had kept a written record of the worst of the visitors' queries, as well as their more questionable behaviour. The leather-bound volumes included the tale of the nobleman, who, in 1587, read Everard Digby's *De Arte Natandi*, the first book published in England on swimming. Having rigorously studied the woodcut illustrations, the nobleman ignored the author's avocation of the breaststroke, and decided to attempt his first ever aquatic manoeuvres on his back. He chose as his initiation not the overcrowded Thames, but the more tranquil waters of the Tower moat. The moment the Beefeater accompanying him turned his back, the gentleman whipped off his breeches and shirt, passed his wig to his wife and scurried round to the steps next to the Byward Tower leading down to the moat. It was never clear whether it was the man's lamentable rendition of the backstroke or the pestilent waters that were to blame. Either way, his bloated body floated around the fortress until the following spring, and became the latest landmark people jostled to see, fuelled by dire warnings in the newspapers by doctors who insisted that his unsavoury ending was proof of the hazards of getting wet.

Through the hatch door Balthazar Jones explained with utmost patience to a couple from the Midlands that Mint Street, which they had spotted upon entering the Tower, had nothing to do with the manufacture of humbugs as they suspected. Rather, it had everything to do with the fact that the Royal Mint, which produced most of the country's coinage, had been located at the Tower from the thirteenth to the nineteenth centuries. Overcome by generosity, he decided to toss them another historical nugget, adding that the great physicist and mathematician Sir Isaac Newton had been Master of the Royal Mint for twenty-eight years. But the couple looked at him blankly and then asked the location of the lavatories.

As he smiled for the inevitable photograph, an evil wind sent the brittle leaves rattling noisily along the cobbles beside them. Dark spots appeared on the stones like the weeping sores of the Black Plague, and the stench of dust nine centuries old filled the air. When the tourists ran for shelter from the downpour, Balthazar Jones unbolted the lower half of the door, stepped outside and squinted at the sky with the scrutiny of a veteran horse-trader. Cheered by the sudden arrival of a new variety, he reached into his pocket for a slender pink Egyptian perfume bottle. After propping it up against the remains of a wall erected on the orders of Henry III, he returned to the black hut, shut the top and bottom doors, and sat down. The rain hitting the roof with the frenzy of a cannibal's drumbeat, he put on his reading glasses and unfolded the list of animals given to him by Oswin Fielding.

He was scratching his beard, trying to remember what a zorilla was, when there was a sharp knock on the window. The Beefeater looked up, took off his spectacles, and saw the Chief Yeoman Warder standing hunched against the rain. Balthazar Jones hurriedly opened the top half of the door.

'There are two men sitting in a lorry outside the gates insisting they've come to erect a penguin enclosure in the moat,' shouted the Chief Yeoman Warder over the downpour. 'Apparently you know all about it.'

Balthazar Jones frowned. 'Hasn't the Palace told you?' he asked.

'That lot never have the decency to tell me anything.'

It took him several attempts to persuade the Chief Yeoman Warder that there was to be a second royal menagerie at the Tower. And it took even more for him to believe that Balthazar Jones had been put in charge of it. The Beefeater had never seen such fire raging in a man whilst caught in the devastation of a rainstorm.

'What the hell do you know about looking after exotic animals, apart from that knackered tortoise? Good God, they couldn't have picked anyone worse,' said the Chief Yeoman Warder, wiping rain out of his eyes with his embalmer's fingers.

Suddenly the monument flashed silver.

'This is a fortress, not some ruddy theme park,' hurled the Chief Yeoman Warder before running for cover as the thunder rolled.

Balthazar Jones closed the door. Despite his dislike of the man, there was no denying that he was right about his lack of experience. Putting his glasses back on, he looked down at his now sodden list with magnified eyes, and struggled to remember what all the creatures were. He had expected to be entrusted with the sorts of animals that had inhabited the Tower over the centuries, some of which had been the first of their kind in England, and which by modern standards would be deemed decidedly pedestrian.

The original menagerie was a subject the Beefeater was intimately familiar with, having studied its history when he first arrived at the fortress in an effort to dispel Milo's dread of his new home. The boy's horror was a result of the tour on which some of the other Tower children had taken him while his parents were still unpacking, the tourists long since locked out for the day. When they called at the Salt Tower to meet the newest and youngest resident, the six-year-old was attempting to lure Mrs Cook out of her travelling case with a fuchsia filched from one of the tubs his mother had insisted on bringing with her. But with the obstinacy of the ancient, the creature refused to move. After each child had lain on the floor and been formally introduced to the record-holder, whose antique features resembled a tribal shrunken head, they offered to show Milo around the fortress. Hebe Jones, who had no idea what lay in store for her son, immediately agreed, assuming they were going to show him where he could ride his bike.

As the children ran to nearby Broad Arrow Tower, one of them asked Milo whether he knew what Bonfire Night was.

'It's when Daddy lets off fireworks from milk bottles in the garden, while Mummy watches from the kitchen with Mrs Cook as the noise makes their ears go funny,' he replied. The son of the Chief Yeoman Warder then informed Milo that it was, in fact, the anniversary of the day when Guy Fawkes and his gang tried to blow up Parliament. He then pointed out where Sir Everard Digby, one of the Gunpowder Plot conspirators, had chiselled his name on the wall while imprisoned, before being hanged, drawn and quartered. Milo, who had no idea what that meant, ran his tiny white finger along the carving, wondering where his father would nail the Catherine wheel now that they no longer had a garden shed. When there was no response, one of the older children elaborated: 'All the plotters were hanged, then taken down before they died. After their private parts were cut off, and their hearts ripped out, they were beheaded and cut into quarters. Finally, their severed heads were displayed on London Bridge as a warning to others.'

Feeling light-headed, Milo followed the children as they ran out of the tower. As they passed Waterloo Barracks one of them called out: 'That's where they keep the Crown Jewels, but we can't show them to you as the alarms will go off and all the Beefeaters will shout at us, and then we'll be sent to prison.'

Another child then shouted: 'It's also where the East End gangsters the Kray twins were imprisoned in 1952 after going AWOL during National Service.'

When they reached the scaffold site on Tower Green, they all sat cross-legged on the grass. One of the boys lowered his voice and said: 'This is the spot where seven prisoners had their heads chopped off, six with an axe and one with a sword.' Milo, his stomach in turmoil, immediately wanted to return to the sanctuary of the Salt Tower, but was too scared to find the way back on his own.

He followed them as closely as he could as they ran across the lawn, still pierced by the tobacco grown by Sir Walter Raleigh during his thirteen-year imprisonment. As they pushed down the cold door handle of the Chapel Royal of St Peter ad Vincula, three rats feasting on a tapestry kneeler darted underneath the organ. Once the children had gathered at the altar, Charlotte Broughton, the Ravenmaster's daughter, pointed to the spot at her feet and whispered: 'Underneath here is the arrow chest containing the remains of Anne Boleyn. Her husband, Henry VIII, got the most fashionable executioner from France to come and behead her with a sword. She had an extra finger and the sound of them drumming on the box's lid has sent the chaplain mad.'

When they left, sending footsteps echoing round the walls, Milo ran as fast as he could to ensure that he wouldn't be the last to leave.

As the evening slipped over the battlements, bringing with it the stench of the Thames, the children decided to take the boy on a ghost tour of the fortress. First they visited Wakefield Tower, which they pointed out was haunted by Henry VI who was stabbed to death within its walls. Then they stood outside the Bloody Tower and one whispered that two small ghosts in white nightgowns had frequently been spotted standing in the doorway. Next they ran along the stretch of the ramparts where the spirit of Sir Walter Raleigh strode in the most elegant of Elizabethan fashions. And, after they had visited the other dozen sites, they finally crept into Martin Tower where the apparition of a bear had startled a soldier, who later dropped dead in shock.

Despite his new stegosaurus duvet cover, and the tyrannosaurus poster that Balthazar Jones had eventually managed to fix to the cold wall, that night Milo refused to sleep in his circular room that had initially filled him with wonder. When it was time to go to bed, he clambered up the spiral staircase in his tiny slippers, and crept between his parents' sheets. He lay on his back, arms against his sides, and refused to close his eyes 'in case they come and get me'. When he finally descended into his dreams, he kicked his father in the shins as he tried to escape his tormentors. Balthazar Jones woke up shrieking, followed within seconds by his wife and son who instantly joined in the uproar.

The Beefeater tried all manner of reassurance to lighten the shadow that the Tower's abhorrent past had cast over his son. But despite pointing out that the death penalty had been abolished, the scientific world denied the existence of ghosts, and Rev. Septimus Drew was as sane as could be expected from a member of the clergy, it did nothing to calm the boy.

Holding Milo's hand, Balthazar Jones took him on a walk along the battlements. As they looked over the ramparts at Tower Bridge, the Beefeater explained that some of the prisoners had had a much more comfortable existence than the poor living in freedom outside the fortress.

'Remember John Balliol, the Scottish king I was telling you about who was imprisoned in the Salt Tower? He had a splendid time,' the father insisted, leaning against the parapet. 'He brought loads of staff with him. He had two squires, a huntsman, a barber, a chaplain, a chapel clerk, two grooms, two chamberlains, a tailor, a laundress, and three pages. And he was allowed to leave the Tower to go hunting. He had it better than we do. Your mother's already sent me out twice to the laundrette because the washing machine isn't working. Mind you, he was banished to France after serving his sentence, which was particularly cruel in my opinion.'

But Milo, who was standing on his toes to see over the parapet, wasn't convinced.

'What about Sir Walter Raleigh, then?' Balthazar Jones continued. 'Remember that man I was telling you about who discovered potatoes and was imprisoned in the Tower three times?'

'Was he put into prison for discovering potatoes?' asked Milo, looking up at his father.

'Not exactly. First it was for marrying one of Elizabeth I's ladies-in-waiting without asking the Queen's permission, then for treason, and finally for inciting war between Spain and England while searching for gold. But you're absolutely right, potatoes are a very questionable vegetable. Personally, I would have locked up the person who discovered brussel sprouts. What was I saying? Oh yes, during his thirteen-year imprisonment in the Bloody Tower, Walter Raleigh was allowed three servants. Imagine that! You'd like someone to pick up your socks, wouldn't you?'

But Milo didn't reply.

The Beefeater then told him that the explorer's wife and son sometimes stayed with him in the Bloody Tower, and that his second son had been born there and was baptised in the chapel.

'Raleigh was even allowed to grow the exotic plants he brought back from the countries he discovered in the Tower garden,' he continued. 'They let him set up a still in an old hen house there, where he experimented with medicinal cordials that he sold to the public. And he built a small furnace for smelting metals. We could get you a chemistry set, if you liked, and you could try out some experiments of your own. We could make a few explosions, and see if we can get your mother to jump higher than she does on Bonfire Night.'

But that evening Milo returned to his parents' sheets, where he juddered in his sleep as if possessed by demons. Balthazar Jones finally managed to reclaim the marital bed after a flash of inspiration during lunch in the Salt Tower's shabby kitchen.

'When can we go home to Catford?' Milo had asked, his mouth covered in bolognese sauce.

'Every time the ewe goes "baa", she loses the same number of mouthfuls,' Hebe Jones said.

The Beefeater looked at his wife, and then at his son. 'I think what your mother is trying to tell you is not to talk with your mouth full,' he said. He continued to wind spaghetti around his fork, then added without raising his eyes: 'Milo, you really do live in a very special place, you know. For six hundred years the Tower had its own little zoo as there was a tradition of giving the monarchy live animals as presents.'

Milo's eyes shot to his father. 'What sort of animals did they have?' he asked.

The Beefeater kept his head lowered. 'I'll tell you before you go to sleep tonight, but only if you're in your own bed,' he replied. 'They may or may not have been descended from dinosaurs.'

Balthazar Jones spent the rest of the day studying documents and records he prised from the covetous fingers of the Keeper of Tower History. When night fell, he closed each set of curtains he had made for his son's bedroom. He then drew the duvet up to the boy's chin, and sat down on the side of his bed.

The menagerie was started in the reign of King John, he explained, possibly with three crates of wild beasts he ordered to be brought from Normandy in 1204, when he finally lost the province. Then, in 1235, his son, King Henry III, was prodded awake while sleeping off a disappointing lunch in the Tower. The bony finger belonged to an anxious courtier who informed him that a surprise gift making the most villainous of noises had just arrived by boat courtesy of the Holy Roman Emperor, Frederick II. The King, thrilled at the thought of an unexpected present, quickly pulled on his boots and scurried down to the banks of the Thames. The crates were prised opened to reveal three malodorous leopards. But no amount of persuasion could convince the monarch that their spots were an integral part of their beauty rather than an indication of disease. And some of the rarest beasts in England were left alone to pace their cages in the Tower.

Milo, who had listened transfixed, asked: 'But if spots are beautiful, why does Mummy always get cross when she gets one?'

'Because spots are beautiful on leopards, but not on ladies,' Balthazar Jones explained.

The following night, Milo returned to his own bed, lured by the promise of the next instalment. The Beefeater sat down, saw in his son his wife's dark good looks, and continued his tale.

In 1251 another present arrived at the Tower, this time from Norway. The polar bear and its keeper turned up unannounced outside the fortress in a small, salty boat. By then the pair, who had been travelling for months after being blown off course, could no longer abide one another's company. Their journey up the Thames only increased their foul moods. Both had a rabid dislike of being stared at, and the hysteria caused by the sight of the white bear, the first to be seen in England, to say nothing of the comments made about the keeper's dress sense, brought about a monumental double sulk that grew worse as soon as they saw their ruinous lodgings within the fortress. Assuming the creature to be aged well over three hundred on account of its white fur, Henry was content to simply look at it, much like a rare antique.

'What's an antique?' Milo asked.

'Something that's very old.'

There was a pause.

'Like Granddad?'

'Exactly.'

Harald, the bear's keeper, who would take the creature to fish for salmon in the Thames while it was attached to a rope, soon realised that no one understood him, the Beefeater continued. Nor he them. He gave up trying to communicate, and spent all his time in the company of his white charge, sleeping in the animal's pen, their quarrels long forgotten. Eventually they knew what the other was thinking, though neither of them ever spoke. At night the pen would fill with dreams of their homeland with glinting snowy expanses and air purer than tears. When scurvy eventually claimed Harald's life, the white bear was dead within the hour, felled by a broken heart.

When Balthazar Jones had finished, he noticed a line of tears running down each of Milo's cheeks. But the boy insisted that his father carry on. In 1255 Henry was sent yet another animal, courtesy of Louis IX, which was also the first of its kind in England, the Beefeater continued. A number of ladies who had stopped on the banks of the Thames to witness its arrival fainted when they saw that it drank not with its mouth, but an excessively long nose.

The King ordered that a wooden house be constructed for it within the Tower. But despite the creature's docile disposition and wrinkly knees, the monarch was too terrified to enter, and he would gaze at the beast through the bars, much to the hilarity of the Tower's prisoners. It came as some relief to the King when, two years later, the animal took one final breath with its mysterious trunk and keeled over, trapping its keeper for several days before help eventually arrived.

'But why did the elephant have to die as well?' Milo asked, clutching the top of his stegosaurus duvet.

'Animals die too, son,' Balthazar Jones replied. 'Otherwise there would be no animals in heaven for Grandma, would there?'

Milo looked at his father. 'Will Mrs Cook go to heaven?' he asked.

'Eventually,' said the Beefeater.

There was a pause.

'Daddy?'

'Yes, Milo.'

'Will I go to heaven?'

'Yes, son, but not for a long time.'

'Will you and Mummy be there?'

'Yes,' he replied, stroking the boy's head. 'We'll be there waiting for you.'

'I won't be alone, will I?' the boy asked.

'No, son. You won't.'

6

After making himself some ginger tea in his sorrowful teapot for one, Rev. Septimus Drew carried it up the two flights of battered wooden stairs to his study, lifting the ends of his nibbled skirts so as not to trip. The only gesture of comfort in the room was a forlorn leather armchair, bearing a patchwork cushion made by one of his sisters. Next to it stood a mail-order reading lamp that had taken months to arrive as the address was assumed to be a joke. Above the mantelpiece hung a portrait of the Virgin Mary, resolutely Catholic in origin, the brushwork of which had seduced his father into buying it for his bride on their honeymoon. Feeling the draught from the sash windows, the clergyman looked with regret at the fireplace that he was forbidden from using since a coal escaped and set ablaze the ancient rag rug in front of it. It was assumed that the chaplain had been deep in prayer for him not to have noticed the foul-smelling smoke that reeked of thousands of pairs of unwashed feet. However, the truth was that he had been in his workshop trying to fashion a miniature replica of the Spanish Armada on wheels, fitted with fully functioning cannons.

He took off his cassock and dog collar, which he deemed inappropriate attire on such occasions, and hung them on the hook on the back of the door. His heart afloat with relish for the task ahead of him, he sat on the dining chair at the simple desk, and took out his writing pad from the drawer. As he unscrewed the lid of the fountain pen that had remained like a trusty sword at his side ever since school, he read the last sentence he had written, and continued with his description of the rosebud nipple.

While the clergyman's imagination was one of his many assets, it had never occurred to him that he would become one of Britain's most successful writers of erotic fiction. When he started creative writing, inspired by the effect George Proudfoot's storytelling had had on his mother, he had assumed that if his work were to encounter success, it would be in the mainstream market. When he finished his first novel, *A Short but Staggering Tale of Infinite Interest*, he sent it off to the country's leading publishers with a silent prayer of hope. It was only after waiting eleven months for a reply that never came that he assumed there was no interest. He then penned another work entitled *A Long and Lengthy Saga of Unfettered Intrigue*. Convinced that his address at the Tower was preventing him from being taken seriously, he rented a post office box, and sent out his new manuscript, his heart aflutter with the thrill of expectation. But the unequivocal rejection slips that eventually arrived only served to encourage him, and when each new novel was finished it was swiftly sent off with the same benediction uttered with closed eyes.

Just as he was about to put copies of his eighteenth work into the post, he received a number of envelopes that his fingers detected did not contain the standard printed card of rejection. Such was his excitement he was unable to open them for a week, and the letters remained on the mantelpiece glowing more brightly than the halo of the Virgin Mary above. But when he finally worked his ivory letter-opener into their spines, instead of the offers he was expecting, he discovered letters requesting him to refrain from ever submitting a manuscript again.

For a week Rev. Septimus Drew laid down his pen. But he soon found his holy fingers reaching once more for its slender barrel, and, having exhausted every other genre, he submerged himself in the musky vapours of erotica. His chastity was his virtue as there were no experiences to limit his imagination: everything was possible. Assuming the pseudonym Vivienne Ventress in an attempt to slip under the barbed wire erected in front of him, he sent his first effort, *The Grocer's*

Forbidden Fruit, to the prohibited addresses, minus a benediction. By the time he checked his post office box, several of the publishers had sent their third letter imploring Miss Ventress to sign a six-book deal. All of them had seen a uniqueness in her work: the glinting chinks left open for the reader's imagination; the strong moralistic tone that gave her work a distinctive voice never previously heard in the genre; and her absolute conviction in the existence of true love, a theme no other writer had explored. Rev. Septimus Drew assumed a position of infinite coyness, drizzling his replies with the lustiest of fragrances as he wrote to each one turning them down. The tactic worked as the offers were immediately raised. The chaplain accepted the highest, insisting on a clause in the contract allowing good to triumph over evil in every plot. He kept the huge advance cheque hidden underneath the brass crucifix on his study mantelpiece. And when the royalties started arriving, there were sufficient funds for him to set up a shelter for retired ladies of the night who had been ruined by love in its many guises.

The chaplain continued writing until lunchtime when he rose to the surface again, distracted from his forbidden romances by a sudden gust of loneliness. As he thought of the woman who had reduced him to a cursed victim of insomnia, he gazed down out of the window hoping to see her. But all he saw was the first of the day's tourists, one of whom had just made the instantly regrettable error of trying to pet an odious raven. His mind filled with the chaste thoughts that permeated his own romantic fantasies, and he wondered whether she could ever think of him as a husband. Lost in the devastation of love, the ambulance had already collected the sightseer by the time he came round from his reverie. He slid open the desk drawer, put away his pad, and got up to prepare himself for an afternoon of ministry with the retired pedlars of love whose shattered souls he sheltered. He left the house holding an umbrella in one hand, and a treacle cake in the other, having long ago recognised its pagan ability to comfort.

*   *   *

The rain had been driving against the door of the Rack & Ruin with such ferocity that it started to seep underneath it, spreading like a pool of blood across the worn flagstones. Not that Ruby Dore noticed. The landlady, who had been alone since the lunchtime drinkers finally left, was looking into the cage at the end of the bar trying to coax her canary to sing. The bird was suffering from a chronic bout of agoraphobia brought on by its dramatic fainting fit into the slops tray. Despite her previous attempts, which had started with cajoles, progressed to bribes, and ended in threats, nothing could induce from it even the most humble of melodies. Much to Ruby Dore's consternation, the bird was also suffering from what gut professors euphemistically called 'the trots'. They had been brought on by the feast of dainties fed to it by a succession of Beefeaters to encourage it to sing, in the hope of securing a free pint. Paper napkins had been unwrapped on the bar containing crust from a steak and ale pie, leftover Christmas pudding discovered at the back of the fridge, as well as the remains of a Cornish pasty. But the only sound that came from its cage was an intermittent quiver of yellow tail feathers followed by an unladylike splat.

Plump lips close to the bars, and a cinnamon-coloured ponytail running down her back, Ruby Dore whistled a final salvo of random notes in an order that no one of musical persuasion would ever assemble. But the bird remained mute. In an effort to distract herself from her failure, she set about dusting the cabinets of Beefeater souvenirs mounted on the tavern's walls. The collection had been started by her father, the previous landlord, who had retired with his second wife to Spain, suffering from a surfeit of bearded conversation. The cabinets contained hundreds of Beefeater figurines, ashtrays, glasses, mugs, thimbles and bells—anything on which could be stamped the famous image of a hirsute gentleman in crimson state dress, complete with rosettes on his shoes and the sides of his knees.

The Rack & Ruin had been her only home since the day she emerged from her mother, slipped through her father's tremulous fingers, and slithered headfirst on to the kitchen linoleum in the family's quarters upstairs. The night Ruby Dore was due to make her entrance into the world, the Tower doctor was in the bar below having long given in to the addiction that was to be his life's torment. When he was politely informed that the landlord's wife's contractions had started, he waved away the messenger. 'She's got plenty of time,' he insisted. He then turned back to the game of Monopoly he was playing with a Beefeater that had already lasted more than two hours. The man was the only Tower resident whom the doctor hadn't beaten, simply because the pair had never previously played together.

The doctor's reign was absolute. While Beefeater after Beefeater would languish in jail, the general practitioner would rampage across the board, buying up property in a monstrous display of avarice. Once he had acquired all the title deeds of a colour-group, he would double the rent, and, without so much as a blush, hold out his palm for payment when his opponent landed on them. It was a strategy that many claimed to be illegal. The rules were searched for but declared lost, and a number accused the doctor of having hidden them. Tempers flared in the fortress to such an extent that arbitration had to be sought from the board game's manufacturer. It sent back a closely typed letter stating that the doctor's methods did not contravene the holy regulations.

The general practitioner, who would secure the Strand, Fleet Street and Trafalgar Square as the epicentre of his colossal hotel empire, put his supremacy down to the fact that he always played with the boot. He was offered all manner of bribes to swap it for the hat with its alluring brim, the motorcar with its tiny wheels, or even the Scottie dog with its cute shaggy coat. But nothing could persuade him to surrender the boot.

When a much more urgent whisper sounded in his ear that the contractions were coming with alarming frequency, the doctor turned to the messenger and snapped: 'I'll be up in a minute.' But when he looked back at the board, the boot had vanished. He immediately blamed the Beefeater, who vehemently denied the accusation of theft. The game was stopped for thirty-nine minutes while the corpulent doctor stuffed his stash of pink £500 notes into his breast pocket, and hunted between the chair legs for the sacred object. When he returned to his seat, red-faced and empty-handed, he insisted that his opponent turn out his pockets. The Beefeater obliged, and then offered the doctor the iron with a limp smile. Just as the medic was about to declare a suspension of play, the Beefeater started to choke. Instantly suspecting what he had done, the doctor stood him up, turned him around, and proceeded to perform the Heimlich manoeuvre. And, as Ruby Dore skidded on to the kitchen floor, the disputed boot sailed from the Beefeater's mouth and landed on the board, scattering a row of tiny red hotels.

Once she had finished the dusting, the landlady returned to her stool behind the beer taps. She rested her feet on an empty bottle crate, and reached for her knitting, a diversion started to relieve the desire for a cigarette, which had since become an even more compulsive habit. But before long, her mind drifted to the test she had done in the bathroom that morning, and she thought again how the result didn't make sense. Unable to stand the uncertainty any longer, she stood up. Sidestepping the creeping pool of water on the worn flagstones, she grabbed her coat, opened the door, and pulled it shut behind her.

Lowering her chin to her chest to keep the rain out of her eyes, she ran past the Tower Café where some of the tourists had taken shelter, much to their regret after sampling its fare. Turning the corner at the White Tower, she continued past Waterloo Barracks, and when she reached the row of houses with blue doors overlooking Tower Green, a now sodden ponytail swung heavily behind her.

After a vigorous knock, Dr Evangeline Moore eventually appeared, and stepped back to let the landlady in out of the rain. Apologising for her wet feet, Ruby Dore walked down the hall to the surgery. She sat in the chair with a cracked leather seat in front of the desk, and waited until the Tower doctor had taken her place opposite her. It was only then that she announced: 'Sorry to barge in, but I think I might be pregnant.'

*   *   *

Several hours later, when darkness had crept over the parapet, Balthazar Jones hesitated outside the Rack & Ruin waiting for the courage to enter. He hadn't bothered changing out of his uniform since coming off duty, as he had been too preoccupied about the meeting he had called to inform the Tower residents of the new menagerie. Numerous rumours had swept round the fortress, the most alarming of which involved tigers being able to roam freely once the visitors had been locked out for the day. Suddenly the sign above the door depicting a Beefeater operating the rack let out a screech in the wind. He went in, and saw that the other Beefeaters, who hadn't changed either, were already sitting at the tables, each armed with a pint and a wife.

Knowing there would be considerable opposition to the project, as nothing unsettled Beefeaters more than a change to their routine, Balthazar Jones headed straight for the bar. Ruby Dore, who

93

still hadn't forgiven him for provoking her canary's fainting fit, eventually served him a pint of Scavenger's Daughter, ordered not out of admiration but as a gesture of atonement. The only ale brewed on the premises, it was, according to some of the Tower residents, even more gruesome than the method of torture after which it had been named. Balthazar Jones had only managed three reluctant sips when the Chief Yeoman Warder stood up, called for silence and invited him to explain to everyone the catastrophe that he was about to inflict on the Tower.

Placing his pint on the bar, he turned towards his colleagues, whose hair, still bearing the imprint of their hats, spanned a dozen hues of grey. He felt for the security of his beard as he suddenly forgot the words he had carefully rehearsed. He then caught sight of the chaplain, sitting at the back next to Dr Evangeline Moore. The clergyman smiled and raised both his thumbs in a gesture of encouragement.

'As most people here already know, there was a royal menagerie at the Tower of London from the thirteenth to the nineteenth centuries,' he began. 'At first the animals were just for the amusement of the monarch, but they became a public attraction during the reign of Elizabeth I. A lion was actually named after her. The health of the monarch and its lion was said to be interlinked, and the creature did in fact die several days before her.'

'Get on with it, man,' called the Chief Yeoman Warder.

'The tradition of giving the monarchy live animals continues to this day, and they are kept at

London Zoo,' Balthazar Jones continued. He paused before adding: 'The Queen has decided to transfer them to the Tower and reinstate the menagerie. She very much hopes that their presence will attract more visitors. The animals are due to arrive next week, and the menagerie will open to the public once they have settled in.'

There was an instant chorus of protests.

'But we don't need any more tourists. We're overrun by the buggers as it is,' called the Ravenmaster.

'One knocked on my door the other day and had the cheek to ask whether he could have a look around,' said one of the Beefeaters' wives. 'I told him to get lost, but he didn't seem to understand. Then he asked whether I would take some photographs of the inside for him. So I took a picture of the loo, gave him his camera back, and shut the door.'

'Where precisely are these animals going to be kept?' demanded one of the Beefeaters. 'There's no room at my place.'

Balthazar Jones cleared his throat. 'The construction of a penguin enclosure has already started in the moat, and it will be joined by a number of other pens. There will also be one on the grass outside the White Tower. Some of the disused towers will be used as well. The birds, for example, will be located in the Brick Tower.'

'What type of penguins are they?' asked the Yeoman Gaoler, whose sprawling beard covered his mountainous chins like grey heather. 'They're not the type that live on the Falkland Islands, are they? They're more vicious than the Argies. Nip your arse as soon as look at you.'

Balthazar Jones took a sip of his pint. 'All I remember is that they're short-sighted when out of the water and are partial to squid,' he replied.

'Ex-servicemen looking after animals . . . I've never felt so humiliated in all my life,' raged the Chief Yeoman Warder, his embalmer's fingers even paler than usual as he gripped the handle of his glass. 'I hope you prove better at looking after animals than you do at catching pickpockets, Yeoman Warder Jones. Otherwise we're all doomed.'

A number of Beefeaters got up to go to the bar, while the others continued to protest about the four-legged invasion. Balthazar Jones picked up his glass and walked over to inspect the canary, hoping that he would be forgotten. Bending down, he looked at the thinning bird. He reached into his pocket, and pulled out a Fig Roll filched from a packet in the office bearing the words 'Yeoman Gaoler' in black marker. He broke some off, and offered the biscuit crumbs to the mute creature through the bars. Refusing to look him in the eye, it slowly sidestepped along its perch, then took a morsel in its beak with the speed of a pickpocket. The assembled Beefeaters turned in amazement to look at the crazed creature suddenly disgorging a surfeit of notes that had built up in its chest during its protracted period of silence. But while everyone gazed at the noisy bird, Rev. Septimus Drew turned his dark eyes once more to the heavenly Ruby Dore.

As the Beefeaters struggled to hear themselves above the yellow racket, the Ravenmaster finished his tomato juice. Despite the lure of the well-stocked bar, he avoided the soothing temptation of alcohol as he needed his wits about him when handling his charges to avoid losing an eye.

'I'm just going to check on the birds,' he said to his wife, patting her on the knee. After blowing her a kiss from the door, which confused the Yeoman Gaoler who happened to be in his eye-line, he put on his hat and stepped outside. One of the few Beefeaters who had resisted growing a beard, he was immediately hit by the bitterness of the evening. Just as he was about to cross Water Lane, he saw Hebe Jones approaching on her way home from work, clouds of breath visible in the darkness as she hurried to escape the sadistic cold.

He paused in the doorway, taking his time to put on his black leather gloves. The pair had barely spoken since one of the odious ravens had relieved Mrs Cook of her tail. In keeping with the duties of a mother, Hebe Jones had helped Milo in his fruitless search for the severed appendage. The boy was adamant that it could be sewn back on like the finger Thanos Grammatikos, his mother's cousin, had lost during a misguided return to the dark art of carpentry. The six-year-old spent several hours scouring the Tower grounds, Hebe Jones on all fours next to him. Every now and again he would joyfully hold aloft a bit of twig, only to cast it aside upon closer inspection. Eventually, he came to the reluctant conclusion that it had been swallowed, one that his parents had reached much earlier, and the hunt was finally called off.

During the ensuing years, Balthazar and Hebe Jones had been obliged to remain civil with the Ravenmaster on account of the friendship that had developed between their two children. It started when Charlotte Broughton, who was eight months older than Milo, appeared at the Salt Tower one morning with what she insisted was a new tail for Mrs Cook. Hebe Jones immediately invited her inside, and followed her up the spiral staircase. The family sat on the sofa and held their breath as the girl slowly unfurled her tiny clenched fist. While his parents instantly recognised what was undeniably the end of a parsnip, Milo was thrilled with the new appendage. The two children immediately went in search of Mrs Cook, whom they eventually found in the bathroom, and lay down on the floor next to her trying to fathom how to attach it. And, with the help of a piece of green wool, for a whole morning the oldest tortoise in the world dragged behind her the browning tip of a root vegetable, until Balthazar Jones spotted the creature and put a stop to the indignity.

*   *   *

The Ravenmaster touched the brim of his hat as Hebe Jones walked past, and she nodded stiffly at him in return, her nose reddened by the cold. Once she was out of sight, he waited a few more minutes until he was certain that she had reached the Salt Tower. He then headed towards the wooden bird pens next to Wakefield Tower, barely visible for the clouds masking the moon. But when he reached them, he simply glanced at the closed doors and carried on walking, smoothing down his pigeon-grey moustache in anticipation. Arriving at the Brick Tower, he checked behind him, then felt for the enormous key he had slipped into his pocket while in the office.

He cursed under his breath at the noise the lock made when it eventually turned, and looked behind him once more. He then pushed open the door, and shut it behind him. Flicking on his lighter for a moment to get his bearings, he made his way up the steps of the tower that had once imprisoned William Wallace. Reaching the first floor, he groped in the darkness for the door latch, and entered the empty room. He looked at his watch, a present from his wife, which glowed in the gloom. Still a few minutes early, he sat down on the wooden floorboards, took off his gloves, and waited, his heart clenched with anticipation.

Eventually, the Ravenmaster heard the bottom door open and gently close again. He rubbed his moist palms on his trouser legs as the sound of heels climbing the steps echoed up the stone staircase. It hadn't taken him long to discover the delights of the Tower Café when it re-opened. However, his appreciation had nothing to do with the menu, which horrified the Beefeaters as much as the tourists, but everything to do with the delicious new chef. He immediately forgot Ambrosine Clarke's lack of talent, which some believed bordered on cruelty, the moment he saw the glow of her formidable cleavage as she leant over to stir what was allegedly turnip soup. Her mind enfeebled by poor nutrition, she agreed to meet him at the Pig in a Poke pub, a short walk from the fortress. Sitting on the bar stool, she forgave him his lack of imagination regarding the choice of venue when he whispered into her ear his insurmountable appreciation of her eel pie. She forgave his repeated assertions that ravens were more intelligent than dogs when he placed a hand on her sturdy thigh, and muttered exaltations about her tripe and mash. And she even forgave the fact that he had a wife when he ran the back of his fingers over her cheek, still flushed from the heat of the kitchen, and assured her that her suet pudding was better than his mother's.

The Ravenmaster watched as the glow from a match crept its way up the wall towards him. Suddenly it was blown out, and the tower was plunged back into darkness. He listened as the footsteps approached the door, and passed slowly through the threshold. Recognising the smell of cooking fat, he got to his feet and reached for her. And when the Ravenmaster got to taste the succulent Ambrosine Clarke, he finally forgave her catastrophic cuisine.

*　　　　*　　　　*

Once she had let herself into the Salt Tower, Hebe Jones climbed to the roof to take down the sodden washing. It was stubbornness, rather than optimism, that had made her peg it out that morning before going to work. Lit up by a bone-coloured moon that had momentarily broken free of the clouds, she worked her way along the line, dropping into the plastic basket the heavy clothes that reeked of damp from the Thames. As she struggled to take down the bed sheets without trailing them in the puddles, she glanced over to Tower Bridge, and she remembered having to convince Milo, when he was still terrified of the place, that it had been old London Bridge, down the river, that had been mounted with severed heads.

100

When she walked into the kitchen with the basket, she found her husband sitting at the table with his head in his hands, his moustache still damp from a final swig of Scavenger's Daughter to complete his reparation.

'Feeling all right?' she asked, squeezing behind his chair to get to the tumble drier.

'Fine,' he replied, moving in his chair. 'How was work? Anything interesting brought in?'

Hebe Jones's mind immediately turned to the urn still sitting on top of the gigolo's diary. 'Not really,' she replied, feeding the sheets into the machine.

Once she had finished cooking supper, she reached for the two trays propped up against the bread bin. The couple no longer ate at the kitchen table in the evening, as neither could stand the silence that sat like an unwanted guest between them. After serving out the moussaka, a recipe passed down generations of Grammatikoses which she had hoped to teach Milo, she carried the trays to the living room and placed them on the coffee table in front of the settee. It was there that she found her husband again, dressed in a pair of ancient trousers with a hole at each pocket from the weight of his hands. They ate with their eyes on the television, rather than on each other. As soon as they had finished, Balthazar Jones got up to wash the dishes, which he no longer left until the end of the evening as it gave him an excuse to leave the room. Once he had finished, he stepped over Mrs Cook, and headed for the door to the staircase.

'What do you think Milo would have looked like now?' Hebe Jones suddenly asked as he raised his

101

hand to the latch.

He froze. 'I don't know,' he replied, not turning round. After closing the door behind him, Balthazar Jones made his way up the spiral staircase, the scuff of his tartan slippers amplified by the ancient stone that surrounded him. Arriving at the top floor, he felt in the darkness for the handle and pushed open the door to the room that his wife never entered, as the chalk graffiti left on the walls by the German U-boat men imprisoned during the war gave her the creeps. He switched on the light, revealing the night at the lattice windows, surrounding him on all sides and sat down on the hardback chair at the table, the only pieces of furniture in the circular room. Picking up his pen, he started to compose his next batch of letters that he hoped would secure him a fellow member of the St Heribert of Cologne Club. And two floors below him Hebe Jones sat alone on the sofa trying to answer her own question as the cracks of her heart opened.

7

The day exotic beasts returned to the Tower of London, Mrs Cook's ancient bowels defeated her. Balthazar Jones discovered the disgrace as he made his way to the bathroom in the early hours of the morning. He hadn't slept, still seeking the courage to tell his wife about the animals' imminent arrival. He had hoped that the news would have reached her, sparing him the onerous task, but she remained completely oblivious. Her ignorance was due, he concluded, from having given up all social activities within the fortress, which included folding herself up into mysterious positions, having been indoctrinated into the cult of yoga by one of the Beefeaters' wives.

He sat in the darkness on the side of the bath, his pyjama leg pulled up to his knee as he washed Mrs Cook's indiscretion off his foot. He gazed out of the lattice window towards the Thames, glowing with the sparks of a new day. And, as he looked at the Tower wharf, his thoughts turned to the tale he had told Milo of when the ship bearing England's first ostriches arrived, courtesy of the Dey of Tunis, the North African ruler, in the eighteenth century. He and his son had been collapsed on deck chairs on the lawn in front of the White Tower, the loathsome tourists long since locked out for the day. After handing him a glass of lemonade, the Beefeater told the boy how the curious crowd that had gathered when the vessel docked at the fortress recoiled with dread as two giant birds stalked down the gangplank, shook their dusty behinds, and released a volley of evil-smelling droppings.

The Londoners quivered at the sight of their hideous two-toed feet, he continued, and gasped when a beaming crew member held above his orange turban a white egg almost the size of his head. The onlookers' horror was complete when the birds fluttered their long, lustrous eyelashes at the crowd, and lunged their pitifully small heads at the nearest bystanders to snatch a pearl button and a clay pipe, which were immediately swallowed. The pair were swiftly housed in a roofed pen to prevent them flying away. But it wasn't long before

103

one of them was dead, having swallowed too many nails fed to it by an eager public convinced of the rumour that the creatures could digest iron.

Milo had listened to the rest of the tale in silence, gripping the sides of his seat as the story unfolded. Afterwards he kissed his father on the cheek and ran off to ride his bike around the moat with the other Tower children. Balthazar Jones didn't give the ostrich tale another thought until two days later when they rushed Milo to hospital white with pain, and the doctor tapped his pen on the X-ray of the boy's twisted gut, indicating the edges of what was unmistakably a fifty-pence piece.

*   *   *

Balthazar Jones rolled down his pyjama leg and returned to bed. Convinced his wife was safely settled on the seabed of slumber, he turned his head towards her and muttered that not only was the Tower about to have a new menagerie, but that he had been put in charge of it. Satisfied that he had finally done his duty, he turned away and closed his eyes. But Hebe Jones sat up with the thrust of a sea serpent.

'But you know how much I hate animals,' she protested. 'Putting up with that geriatric tortoise has been bad enough, and I only did that because you insisted that she was part of the family.'

The argument only came to an end when Balthazar Jones got up to go to the lavatory again, where he remained for so long battling against the obstinacy of constipation that Hebe Jones fell asleep, her beauty immediately eclipsed by her resemblance to her father.

When the shriek of the alarm woke them several hours later, they got dressed on either side of the bedroom in silence. Neither had breakfast so as to avoid having to sit at the kitchen table together. And when they eventually bumped into each other the only thing they exchanged was the word 'goodbye'.

After his wife had left for work, Balthazar Jones ran a clothes brush over the shoulders of his tunic, and grabbed his hat from the top of the wardrobe. He drove out of the Tower headed for London Zoo, his hands clamped tightly on the wheel as he tried to concentrate after so little sleep. Sliding around next to him was his partisan, an eight-foot pike-like weapon that could gut a man in an instant. Usually reserved for ceremonial occasions, Oswin Fielding had insisted that he brought it along as he wanted him to look as 'Beefeatery' as possible for the press.

When he eventually found a parking space between the television satellite vans, he remained behind the wheel for a few moments trying to summon enough courage for the task ahead of him. But it never came, so he got out anyway, forgetting his partisan. He walked through the wrought-iron gates and stood watching as a single file of penguins waddled up a gangplank into a van following a trail of glistening fish. Once they were inside, a solitary bird stood at the door looking back towards the enclosure. The driver, the sleeves of his checked shirt rolled up to his elbows, shooed it inside, swiftly removed the gangplank and closed the door. Suddenly the Beefeater heard the sound of slapping. He turned to see a solitary penguin following the wet footprints, rocking from side to side as it attempted to run.

'You've forgotten one!' he yelled.

'For Christ's sake!' said the driver, who had already reached for the cigarettes he had vowed to give up that morning. 'I knew this job would be a nightmare. It'll have to come in the front with me. I'm not opening that door again. The whole ruddy lot will come out. It's taken me over two hours and a trip to the fishmongers to get them in there. They're worse than bloody kids. And I should know, I've got four of 'em. What's that you're wearing, anyway? Fancy dress or something?'

Things began to deviate wildly from what Oswin Fielding had referred to as *The Plan* when he approached Balthazar Jones and informed him that the press wanted to take a picture of him with some of the Queen's animals. After berating the Beefeater for leaving his partisan in the car, the equerry then herded the journalists towards the monkey house. He stopped outside the Geoffroy's marmosets' enclosure, seduced by the innocence of their white faces and their fluffy, black ears. What he didn't know, however, was that the creatures' keeper had been trying all morning to entice them out of their cages in readiness for their journey to the Tower. But the longer she tried to lure them with pieces of chopped fruit, the more desperately they clung on to the bars, until she gave up and went to weep in the lavatory. When the man from the Palace introduced Balthazar Jones to the press as Keeper of the Royal Menagerie, and stood him in front of them, the marmosets displayed their most defensive behaviour yet. And the monkeys continued to flash their privates long after the most sexually depraved of the journalists had blushed to the roots of their hair.

The Beefeater escaped the cameras at last, and went to the aviaries to make sure that the two lovebirds were being loaded into separate vans. On his way, he stopped to admire the herd of bearded pigs, in a state of ecstasy as they rubbed their behinds against their itching post, and he regretted that they belonged to the zoo rather than the Queen. Much later, when he had to face the consequences of his actions, he put his gross lack of judgement down to having been seduced by their stupendously hirsute cheeks, which were even more lustrous than his colleagues'. In his defence, it seemed that the animal had been entirely complicit. For when Balthazar Jones succumbed to the temptation of an open van door, and pointed in its direction, the pig quite happily trotted inside. And it only took the Beefeater seconds to shut the door behind it, in the wholly deluded belief that no one would notice its absence.

Just as he was about to fetch the Etruscan shrew, he saw the Komodo dragon lumbering away from its terrified keeper, who was attempting to shoo it into a lorry with flaps of his handkerchief. The giant lizard came to a stop next to the gift shop, and stood perfectly still, flicking its forked tongue. Balthazar Jones followed its gaze and saw Oswin Fielding tapping a box of animal feed with his umbrella, the wind lifting the remains of his hair like a palm branch. As the animal headed towards the equerry with surprising speed, the Beefeater recalled the creature's ability to swallow a small deer whole, after which it would lie in the sun for a week to digest. It was then that he started to run.

Within seconds, the ugly reptile had thundered past the equerry towards its target of a discarded hamburger. But by then Balthazar Jones, who hadn't run so fast since rugby-tackling a pickpocket on Tower Green with five wallets down his trousers, had built up such a speed he was unable to stop. He collided with Oswin Fielding with a force that brought both men to the ground in an instant, and resulted in the equerry's silver umbrella no longer being splendid. It was only when both men confirmed that they were still conscious, and struggled back to their feet, that the man from the Palace conceded that it was a good job Balthazar Jones hadn't been carrying his partisan after all.

The Beefeater was still mournfully inspecting the hole in the knee of his uniform when the cavalcade of vehicles was ready to leave for the Tower. He watched as the first van passed, a solitary penguin standing on the passenger seat looking at him through the window. He winced at the smell emanating from the second, carrying the zorilla, and then shouted as he saw the open-topped lorry bearing the giraffes approach the exit, the top of which threatened to decapitate all four of the beasts. Six members of staff then stood around the vehicle holding out tantalising branches to encourage the creatures to lower their heads long enough to pass underneath the wrought-iron arch. As soon as they were safely through, the animals raised their necks again and closed their eyes in the breeze as the lorry picked up speed. Balthazar Jones waited until the final truck pulled out, then headed to his car carrying a cage bearing the

Etruscan shrew. He placed it on the back seat, and lashed his partisan to the headrest to prevent disaster. Searching among his CDs, he selected Phil Collins' *Love Songs* in the hope of calming his highly strung passenger. The Beefeater then started his journey back to the Tower, attracting all manner of honks and two-fingered gestures on account of his pitiful speed.

*   *   *

Ruby Dore knocked at the blue door facing Tower Green, and stamped her feet to banish the cold as she waited for it to open. It had taken a week for the doctor to call, informing her that the test result was ready. She had spent the time feeling more and more distressed, knowing that as each bloodless day passed, the future she had dreamed of—a husband first and children later—was increasingly unlikely. When Dr Evangeline Moore finally appeared, the landlady searched her face, but was greeted by the inscrutability of a poker player. Ruby Dore walked swiftly along the hall to the surgery and sat down. Taking her place opposite her patient, the doctor picked up a pen from her desk, and held it with both hands in front of her. 'I'm sorry it's taken so long,' she said. 'It's just as you thought, you are pregnant.'

Ruby Dore remained silent.

'Is it good or bad news?' the doctor asked.

'Not the greatest, considering the circumstances,' the landlady replied, fiddling with the end of her scarf.

Once the consultation was over, she ran back to the Rack & Ruin, and bolted the door behind her.

She climbed the narrow wooden staircase that led to her cramped home, with its low ceilings, worn furniture she couldn't afford to replace, and smell of beer, which she never noticed. Moving aside several books, she sat down on the only sofa she had known, and closed her eyes. She immediately saw the man she had met in the village bar while visiting her father in Spain, the white Rioja they had enjoyed, and the tumultuous hour they had spent together on the beach before she crept back to the villa, accompanied by the dawn. She thought of the woman and child whose hands he had been holding when she bumped into him the following day, and his refusal to acknowledge her. And she wondered whether he lied as much to his family as he had to her in the brief time that she had known him.

Her thoughts turned to the humiliation of having to tell her parents she was pregnant. Her mother would naturally blame her father, as she continued to do for most things, despite having divorced him more than two decades ago. Her father would blame himself for not having raised his daughter well enough after her mother left, unable to bear life in the Tower any longer. It had taken him weeks to admit to his daughter that she was gone for good. When the nine-year-old asked yet again where her mother was, Harry Dore finally gave her the answer: 'Your mother is in India trying to find herself. God help her when she does.'

Opening her eyes, the landlady looked at the display cabinets containing her collection of Tower artefacts, amassed by generations of Dores while running the tavern. She remembered telling the man about it in the bar when he asked where she

110

lived, and he had even feigned interest. There was the Tower report written in 1598 complaining that the Beefeaters were 'given to drunkenness, disorders and quarrels'. On the shelf below was the mallet used in 1671 by Colonel Blood to flatten the state crown before hiding it in his coat during the only attempt to steal the Crown Jewels. Next to it was a piece of the cloak worn by Lord Nithsdale during his escape from the Tower in 1716 disguised as a woman.

Every piece had been researched and labelled, a project she and her father had shared. Harry Dore would recount the objects' history with the mesmerising delivery of an oral bard, after which his daughter would print the labels in her best schoolgirl's handwriting. But their time together had not been enough to heal the damage wrought by the years Ruby Dore had spent watching her parents serve each other their curdled devotion. Her mother had advised her to remain single. 'There's nothing lonelier than marriage,' she warned. However, Ruby Dore refused to believe her. But during her search for affection, she had found herself seeking it from the shadiest of hearts. And no matter how often she opened her bedroom window, never once had she been touched by the moonlight of love.

*   *   *

Hebe Jones had had no luck with the register of deaths. Despite searching it thoroughly, all those listed under the name of Clementine Perkins had died several decades ago. She had since put it out of her mind, and got on with easier items that guaranteed the warm glow of victory, such as handbags containing their owners' phone numbers. But the sight of the urn still sitting on her desk unsettled her.

'Valerie,' she said, looking at the brass plaque.

'Yes,' came the muffled reply. Hebe Jones turned to see that her colleague had squeezed herself into the front end of a pantomime horse, found on a bench at Piccadilly Circus station.

'It smells in here,' said Valerie Jennings, positioning herself so that she could see through the small mesh window in the neck.

'What of?'

'Carrots.'

'I need to ask your opinion about something,' Hebe Jones continued, ignoring the reply.

Valerie Jennings sat down at her desk, and crossed her matted fur legs.

'If someone died, but their death wasn't officially recorded, what would that mean?' Hebe Jones asked.

Valerie Jennings scratched the back of her leg with a brown leather hoof. 'Well, it could mean a number of things. Maybe the person hasn't died after all, and someone is pretending that they have,' she said, tugging on a cord, which sent the horse's eyes shooting left. 'Or maybe the person really did die, but someone wants to keep it a secret and they bribed the crematorium staff not to inform the authorities,' she continued, tugging another cord, which sent the horse's eyes shooting to the right.

'I think you read too many books,' suggested Hebe Jones.

'Then, of course, there's human error,' she

added, pressing a switch that sent both sets of lustrous eyelashes fluttering. Standing up, she then headed towards the fridge. But just as she secured the horse's long, yellow teeth around the door handle, the Swiss cowbell sounded. After a brief bout of wriggling and blaspheming, she found that she was firmly wedged inside. Hebe Jones got up and tried tugging on the creature's enormous felt ears. But eventually she gave up as they started to work loose.

The bell started up again, and continued with such urgency Hebe Jones quickly went to answer it, not even stopping to try and open the safe that had been left on the Circle Line five years ago.

As she turned the corner she found a man at the original Victorian counter wearing a navy uniform. Middle age had run its fingers through his neat, dark hair.

'Is this London Underground Lost Property Office?' he asked.

Hebe Jones raised her eyes to the sign above the counter.

He followed her gaze. 'Has anyone handed in a small, green case in the last fifteen minutes? It's an emergency,' he asked.

'What does it look like?' she asked.

'A bit bigger than a child's lunch box.'

'Was there anything identifiable inside?' she asked.

'A kidney,' he replied.

'As in steak and kidney pie?'

'As in organ donation.'

Hebe Jones turned the corner and called: 'Valerie! Has anyone brought in a green case in the last fifteen minutes?'

'No!' came the muffled reply.

Hebe Jones came swiftly back to the counter. 'Where did you leave it?' she asked.

'Nowhere,' the man said. 'It was by my feet as I was standing by the carriage doors. The next moment I looked down it was gone.'

Suddenly the phone started ringing in the office. When it failed to stop Hebe Jones called: 'Valerie, can you get that?'

But there was no reply. When she looked round the corner, she was confronted by the sight of Valerie Jennings bending over her desk, trying to knock the receiver off its cradle with threadbare nostrils. Hebe Jones picked up the phone. After a while she replied: 'I've got the owner with me now. We'll come for it immediately.'

Grabbing her turquoise coat from the stand, she called: 'Valerie, I've got to go out. There's a man at the counter who's lost a kidney and it's just been handed in at Edgware Road. I'm going with him to make sure he finds it.'

There was an equine nod.

Once Hebe Jones had left, Valerie Jennings sat down and looked around the office through the gauze. She peered up at the cuckoo clock and wondered how long it would be before her colleague returned to release her. Just as she was about to attempt opening the fridge door again, the cowbell sounded. She ignored it at first, but it continued clanking. Unable to bear it any longer, she got to her hoofed feet, and headed to the counter with the reluctance of a beast on its way to the knacker's yard.

When she turned the corner, Arthur Catnip returned the bell to the counter without a word,

114

and looked into the horse's eyes. 'Is that Valerie Jennings?' he asked.

'It is indeed,' came the buried reply.

'I was just wondering whether you'd like to go out for lunch some time,' he said.

'That would be fine.'

Arthur Catnip hesitated. 'Today?' he ventured.

'I'm a bit tied up.'

'What about Thursday?'

'That would be lovely.'

'One o'clock?'

'I'll see you then.'

Arthur Catnip watched as the horse seemed to momentarily lose sense of direction, went cross-eyed, and then disappeared from view.

*   *   *

Hebe Jones moved aside a discarded newspaper, and sat down in the carriage, relieved that the organ courier had finally been reunited with his case. As the train began to rattle its way out of the station, she looked up, and inspected the passengers opposite. It was the boy who immediately drew her attention. 'He must be around eleven or twelve,' she calculated. Though he looked nothing like Milo, the sight of him wounded her just the same. She studied his mother sitting next to him absorbed in a magazine, and doubted she would ignore him if she knew how easy it was to lose a child. She closed her eyes, regretting yet again all the occasions she could have spent with Milo: the times when she had told him to go and play with the other children when she was trying to find a talent for painting on the

Salt Tower roof; the times when she and her husband had left him with Rev. Septimus Drew so that they could go out to dinner; and the times when she had sent him out of the kitchen after finding plastic soldiers bobbing in the casserole.

The boy got up and offered his seat to an elderly lady who had been looking at him hopefully since the journey began. 'Milo would have done that,' Hebe Jones thought. She looked at the boy's hand holding the rail next to her. Suddenly she remembered the last time she had seen her son's hand: cold, white and perfect as he lay on the hospital bed. And she thought what a neglectful mother she had been for not knowing there had been something so terribly wrong with him.

It had taken far longer than Hebe Jones had wished to become a mother. A year into the marriage, when there was still no grandchild, her mother had presented her with a small wooden statue of Demeter with the solemnity of a holy relic. Hebe Jones put it into her handbag, and carried it with her wherever she went. But it seemed that not even the Greek goddess of fertility could make anything grow inside her. Medical tests failed to find a reason for the couple's inability to conceive. By then her three sisters had produced so many offspring, the oldest was obliged to lock her husband out of the bedroom at night out of fear of yet another nine months of craving ice.

The blood eventually stopped after twenty years of monthly disappointment. During that time, Hebe and Balthazar Jones had refused to let the thorns of infertility shred their marriage, and the roots of their love had wound round each other

116

even more tightly. Convinced she had entered the black hole of menopause, Hebe Jones wept with joy when she discovered she was pregnant. And that night in bed Balthazar Jones laid his head on his wife's soft stomach, and started a conversation with Milo that continued for nearly twelve years.

While Hebe Jones escaped the horror of morning sickness, she found herself gripped by an even more pernicious compulsion than her sister's. Balthazar Jones would return home to find his wife sitting on the floor by the fire, her swollen belly resting on her thighs, helping herself to the coals. 'I'm not doing anything,' she would reply, her teeth blackened with soot. Her husband, convinced that she was lacking a vital mineral, searched through the dusty shelves of the local grocer's for something to satisfy the yearning. He brought back one hundred and fourteen tins of squid in black ink, and presented them to his wife with the pride of a hunter. And, for a while, the Spanish delicacy seemed to work. But one evening he caught her walking out of the living room with a telltale smut on her cheek. It was then that he took irrevocable action. And Hebe Jones greeted the man who came to replace the coal fire for gas with silent tears in her eyes.

She spent her pregnancy in a state of bliss interspersed with bouts of terror that she would not be able to love anyone else as much as her husband. But her fears were unfounded. When the baby was born, she soaked him with an outpouring of affection that rained just as heavily on his father.

Balthazar Jones, who was equally lost in the madness of newborn love, thought his son so

117

beautiful he suggested calling him Adonis. Still flushed with the effort of expelling the child, Hebe Jones, who had always wanted a Greek name, welcomed her husband's capitulation. But while her baby's allure was beyond doubt, she feared taunts in the playground, and reminded her husband of the misery he had suffered being named after one of the Three Wise Men, particularly one who had turned up with such a lousy gift as frankincense.

When Hebe Jones's mother arrived at the ward to meet her eleventh grandchild, Idola Grammatikos looked at the baby and announced: 'The old chicken makes good broth.' Unable to take her eyes off her grandson for a moment, she declared him so delicious she could eat him. Milo, the Greek word for apple was then suggested, and the boy left the hospital named after a fruit. But when Balthazar Jones eventually came round from his delirium, he denied any botanical influence, and insisted that his son had been named in honour of Milo of Croton, the Ancient Greek six-time Olympic wrestling champion.

8

Opening the Salt Tower door, Balthazar Jones peered out at the silent fortress, glistening with a stubble of frost. He stood for several minutes listening for the Ravenmaster, who always rose early to feed his odious birds. But nothing could be heard. He closed the door swiftly behind him, and headed to the Develin Tower clutching a

118

grapefruit.

The Beefeater slipped a hand into his trouser pocket, and withdrew the key. After a quick glance behind him to make sure that he wouldn't be seen, he put it into the lock and turned it. Once he had closed the front door behind him, he pressed down on the latch to his right. The bearded pig immediately turned its head at the noise. The moment Balthazar Jones saw its marvellous hirsute cheeks, his guilt at having made off with the animal instantly vanished. Bending down, he held out the grapefruit, the only thing he had been able to find in the kitchen in his haste to check on the animals after their first night at the Tower. The pig, which had been in the middle of an orgy of scratching, instantly gave up pleasuring itself against the fireplace, and scampered across the straw to inspect the yellow gift with its hairy snout. Instead of sinking its teeth into the fruit, the creature promptly knocked it to the floor, flicked it across the room with its nose, and charged after it. After another butt, the pig continued the pursuit with undiminished enthusiasm, its tasselled tail flying like a flag over its fulsome buttocks. The Beefeater watched entranced, and after more than ten minutes, neither man nor beast had shown any sign of tiring from either performing or watching the grapefruit spectacle.

Vowing to return with an alternative breakfast, Balthazar Jones locked the door behind him, and headed down Water Lane to see whether the delivery of fish for the rockhopper penguins had arrived. Suddenly it dawned on him that he hadn't seen the creatures since the van passed him on its way out of the zoo, a solitary bird standing on the passenger seat looking at him.

Balthazar Jones stopped running when he reached the bridge overlooking the moat. As he stood with both hands on the wall, firing hot clouds of desperate breath into the cold morning air, he saw that the penguin enclosure was empty. He opened the gate, and clattered along the boardwalk erected to prevent the tourists' feet from turning the grass into mud. Standing at the window of the next enclosure, he looked for a huddle of short-sighted birds with magnificent yellow eyebrows. But all he saw was the reclined glutton, feeding itself another fresh egg with the self-indulgence of a Roman emperor. Moving to the next pen, he hunted between the knobbly knees of the giraffes, but there wasn't a hint of a beak.

He ran back inside the fortress, climbed the steps of the Devereux Tower, and opened the door to the monkey house. But his sudden appearance set off the howler monkeys, and he was forced to retreat after a quick glance through the bars of the cage. Standing in front of the zorilla, he encouraged it to get to its feet, but his frantic arm movements produced from the animal a particularly pungent aroma, and he backed out as soon as he saw that the creature was alone. As he stood staring at the Komodo dragon that refused to move, he realised that the birds would have stood no chance in its company anyway, and he rushed off to the enclosure next to the White Tower, hoping they had been herded inside. He then hunted between the sleeping reclusive ringtail possums, hiding behind the leaves, their tails coiled neatly below them. But never once did he glimpse a pair of beady black eyes.

Having searched the rest of the fortress, the Beefeater finally arrived at the Brick Tower. Telling himself that the removal man must have shooed the penguins in with the other birds, he climbed the stone steps two at a time. Once he had reached the first floor, he flung open the oak door and rushed to the aviary. As he peered through the wire fencing, his eyes didn't linger over the charming King of Saxony bird of paradise, its two prized brow feathers stretching twice the length of its body, a sight so extraordinary that early ornithologists dismissed the first stuffed specimen as taxidermic trickery. Nor did he gaze at the green and peach female lovebird that had been separated from its mate lest it savaged it. He didn't even admire the toucans given to the Queen by the President of Peru, with their alluring beaks believed by the Aztecs to be made from rainbows. Instead he kept his eyes on a pair of ugly feet sticking out of a small bush. Suddenly there was a rustle of leaves, and the Beefeater held his breath. But from out of the undergrowth stalked the wandering albatross, a species with such voluminous feet sailors once used them as tobacco pouches. The Beefeater sank to the floor, wondering how he was going to explain the penguins' disappearance to the man from the Palace. As he leant back against the circular wall, he let out a sigh of such momentous despair it woke the emerald hanging parrot from its upside-down slumber.

*   *   *

Rev. Septimus Drew hitched up his cassock, and knelt down by the organ. It took a moment for him to summon the courage to pick up the creature by its tail. Once he had overcome his aversion, he held it aloft and inspected it with an eye that had seen into the dusty depths of countless tormented souls. Despite a disappointing week of mechanical failures, and more pestilent droppings than usual, the sight of its tiny front paws suddenly filled the chaplain with unexpected regret. He lowered his eyes to the rat's gruesome yellow teeth that had been sunk with unfettered ecstasy into the succulent tapestry kneelers, and all pity vanished. He noted that the creature had been cleanly slain with a single blow to the back of the neck by his latest innovation, a masterpiece of engineering that had been hidden inside a miniature Trojan horse. The whiskered enemy had been lured to its minutely plotted death by the most unholy of temptations: peanut butter.

While part of him opposed a Christian burial for the vermin, rats were, nevertheless, one of God's creatures despite their non-appearance in the Bible. He dropped the stiffened body inside one of the old turquoise Fortnum & Mason paper bags that he kept for such occasions, and picked up his trowel. Pulling open the chapel's ancient door, he made his way to the Byward Tower, where he descended the steps to the moat, used for growing vegetables during the Second World War. After a quick prayer for the creature's villainous soul, he buried it in the flowerbed that ran alongside the bowling green. While in life the rodents had little meaningful purpose, in death they played the exalted role of fertiliser to the chaplain's favourite rose bushes. He then turned his back on the carefully tended patch of lawn, which had witnessed so many accusations of cheating the previous season that all bowling matches had been suspended.

As he headed home, the Yeoman Gaoler, who was looking even more exhausted than usual, caught up with him and placed a plump hand on his arm. 'No offence, but you haven't been pinching my Fig Rolls, have you?' he asked.

Rev. Septimus Drew considered the question. 'While I'd hold my hand up to the odd bit of gluttony, theft isn't my thing, I'm afraid,' he replied.

The Yeoman Gaoler nodded in the direction of the chapel. 'Nobody's happened to confess to it, have they?' he asked.

'Unfortunately we don't do confessions. Try the Catholics down the road. The priest gets to hear all manner of scandal, though from my experience he's a bit reluctant to pass it on.'

As he crossed Tower Green, the clergyman spotted Balthazar Jones in the distance weighed down by what appeared to be a bag of fruit and vegetables. He watched his journey, troubled as usual by his old friend's perpetual air of despair. The chaplain had tried his utmost to encourage him to take up his interests again. He had even offered him the custodianship of the bowling green, a duty that had fallen to him that year, knowing that there was little that gave an Englishman more pleasure than the torment of tending a lawn. But the Beefeater had declined the offer with a shake of his white head.

Rev. Septimus Drew then tried to smoke him out

of his grief by stoking his mania for English history. After service one Sunday, he cornered the Keeper of Tower History and asked him whether there was any new research that had been kept out of the latest edition of the Tower guide. Caught disarmed in the House of God, the man confessed to a revelation of such tantalising intrigue that the chaplain immediately went in search of Balthazar Jones to tell him.

He found him collapsed in his blue-and-white striped deckchair on the battlements, gazing at the sky. The chaplain strode up to him, an undignified breeze lifting the ends of his crimson nibbled skirts, convinced that he had the key to set his friend free from the prison of his depression.

Sitting down on the ground next to him, the clergyman then recounted the astonishing tale of the ravens' dubious historical pedigree. It was widely believed that the birds had been at the Tower for centuries. According to the legend peddled to the tourists, Charles II's astronomer complained that they were getting in the way of his telescope. The King was said to have called for them to be destroyed, only to be warned that the White Tower would fall and a great disaster would befall England if the birds ever left the Tower. He then decreed that there must always be at least six birds present.

'But it's all rubbish,' exclaimed the triumphant clergyman. 'A researcher just scoured the records going back a thousand years and found out that the earliest reference to the ravens being at the Tower was in fact 1895, and so the legend must have been a Victorian invention.'

But instead of the delight he expected the

Beefeater to display at the news, Balthazar Jones turned to him and asked: 'Do you think it's going to rain?'

However the chaplain refused to give up. Sweeping into the British Library, he asked to see the most obscure titles he could find in the hallowed catalogue, much to the irritation of the staff, who were obliged to push aside curtains of cobwebs in the basement in order to reach them. After several months, he finally fell upon a tale of historical fascination that had at its helm a number of doctors. Not only did it show the medical profession to be staffed by baboons, as the Beefeater insisted it was, but it was of such hilarity that the chaplain's membership was terminated on account of his explosion of mirth when he read it.

With no hint as to the delight that lay in store for the Beefeater, Rev. Septimus Drew invited him round for supper, having selected his best bottle of Château Musar from his cellar. Once he had served the watercress soup, the clergyman proceeded to tell the story of Mary Toft, the eighteenth-century maidservant who one day began to give birth to rabbits. The local surgeon was called and he helped deliver nine of them, all stillborn and in pieces. The doctor wrote to numerous learned gentleman about the phenomenon. George I sent his surgeon-anatomist and the secretary to the Prince of Wales to investigate, both of whom witnessed her deliver yet more of the dead creatures. The woman was subsequently brought to London, and the medical profession was so convinced of her affliction, rabbit stew and jugged hare disappeared off dinner tables across the kingdom. But she was eventually unmasked as a hoaxer when a porter was caught trying to sneak a rabbit into her room, and she confessed to having inserted the pieces inside her.

The tale, which the chaplain related over three courses, included a number of ambitious theatrical demonstrations. After they had finished the roast capon, the chaplain pulled back his chair and rubbed his back with both hands as if easing the pains of a rabbit gestation. After he refilled their glasses for a fourth time, he raised a finger to either side of his head, bared his front teeth and twitched his nose. And just before bringing in the summer pudding, the six foot three clergyman proceeded to execute what were undeniably bunny hops around the dining room. The Beefeater's eyes did not leave the chaplain for a minute as he related the uproarious tale. But when Rev. Septimus Drew finally wiped his tears of merriment on his white cotton handkerchief, and asked his guest what he thought of the story of Mary Toft, Balthazar Jones blinked and asked: 'Who?'

*   *   *

Arriving back at his house, the chaplain put the trowel in the cupboard under the kitchen sink, washed his hands carefully and took down his sorrowful teapot for one. As he sat alone at the table sipping his cranberry infusion, his mind turned once more to the heavenly Ruby Dore. Unable to bear the stab of solitude any longer, he stood up, fetched his pile of recipes from the drawer next to the sink, and set about selecting his weapon of seduction.

126

Once his choice was made, the clergyman picked up the mail he had collected from his post office box earlier that morning, and made his way up to his study to compose his next sermon. Sitting at his desk, he worked his ivory letter-opener across the first spine, and reached inside. When he had finished reading, he read it again to make sure that he had understood it correctly. He then folded the letter up, returned it to its envelope, and slid it into the desk drawer. And, as he sat back in his chair in astonishment, he wondered whether there was any real hope that he would win the Erotic Fiction Award, for which he had just been shortlisted.

*　　　*　　　*

Balthazar Jones stood at number seven Tower Green and knocked on the door. When, after several long minutes, there was still no reply, he put down the cage, capped his hands against the windowpane, and attempted to see through a gap in the curtain. Eventually, the Yeoman Gaoler appeared at the door, his dressing gown tied across the crest of his stomach, one hand raised against the glare of the marble clouds.

'Are you all right?' Balthazar Jones asked.

The Yeoman Gaoler scratched at his chest. 'I didn't get much sleep last night.'

'May I come in for a minute?'

The Yeoman Gaoler stepped back to allow the man to pass. 'It might be warmer in the kitchen,' he said.

Balthazar Jones walked down the hall, and placed the cage on the table. The Yeoman Gaoler sat down, and ran a hand through his tumultuous hair.

'What's that?' he asked, nodding at the cage.

'The Queen's Etruscan shrew. I was hoping you'd look after it. It's of a particularly nervous disposition.'

The Yeoman Gaoler looked at him. 'How will the public be able to see it if it's in my house?' he asked.

'They can make an appointment, but to be honest I'm not too bothered if they don't. I just want to make sure that it stays alive.'

'Let's see it then.'

Balthazar Jones stretched his arm into the cage and took the lid off the tiny plastic house.

The Yeoman Gaoler stood up and peered inside. 'I can't see anything,' he said.

'It's there in the corner.'

The man reached for his glasses and took another look. 'That thing there? Are you sure it's alive?' he asked.

'Of course I'm sure. I saw it move this morning.'

The Yeoman Gaoler continued to gaze at the creature, then scratched the back of his head and declared: 'To be honest, I don't think shrews are my thing.'

The Beefeater studied him for a moment. 'The other thing I had you pencilled in for was helping to look after the penguins,' he said. 'They were a gift from the President of Argentina. Apparently they're from the Falkland Islands after all.'

After showing Balthazar Jones out, the Yeoman Gaoler returned to the kitchen, sat down, and looked at the cage with the unfocused gaze of the exhausted. He had gone to bed at a respectable hour the previous night, dressed in a celebratory new pair of pyjamas, convinced that the horror was finally over. Before taking his evening bath, he had opened all the windows in the house and, according to the ancient remedy to drive out ghosts, stood in the corners of each room brandishing a smouldering bunch of dried sage. The vapours had curled up against the walls towards the ceiling and drifted off into the night. But shortly before dawn, he was woken by the sound of boots striding across the wooden dining-room floor below him, and the most heinous profanities deriding the Spanish uttered in a Devonshire accent. After mustering the courage to descend the stairs, which were flooded with the stench of tobacco, he found that the potatoes he had left out to fry for his breakfast were missing. Returning swiftly to bed, he locked the door, drew up his covers and listened in a state of terror to the unearthly sounds that continued until well after dawn.

*   *   *

Hebe Jones arrived at London Underground Lost Property Office earlier than usual, having been woken by the uproar of the red howler monkeys. Her irritation had been complete when she discovered not only that her husband was missing, but so too was the grapefruit she had bought herself for breakfast. As she waited for the water to boil for her cup of tea, she looked through the fridge for something to eat, and discovered a solitary Bakewell tartlet belonging to Valerie Jennings behind a carton of carrot soup. Seduced

129

by the lurid red cherry, she convinced herself that her colleague would not miss it, carried it back to her desk, and took a bite. But it was to be her only memory of the succulent almond filling. For her fingers immediately reached for the gigolo's diary, and she became so engrossed by an entry that involved the ruination of a boardroom table by one of his lover's heels, that she ate the rest without realising.

Just as she was wiping the evidence off her mouth, the phone rang.

'We do indeed,' she replied, turning her eyes towards the inflatable doll with the red hole for a mouth. 'She's blonde . . . I see . . . They're white . . . Her shoes are definitely white, I can see them from here . . . She doesn't appear to be yours then . . . We'll be in touch if she shows up . . . We always take great care of anything that's handed in . . . I quite understand . . . Not at all . . . Each to their own . . . Will do . . . Goodbye.'

Sitting back in her chair, her eyes fell to the urn, and she dusted the wooden lid with her tiny fingers. She reached for one of the London telephone directories on the shelf above her desk, and leafed her way to the residents called Perkins. Hebe Jones was not beyond looking for a needle in a haystack, a method both she and Valerie Jennings had been forced to adopt on numerous occasions. Its rare successes had meant that they both returned to it when desperate, with the dogged hope of a gambler. She looked at the first entry, and dialled the number.

'Hello, is that Mr Perkins?' she asked.

'Yes,' a voice replied.

'This is Mrs Jones from London Underground

Lost Property Office. I'm calling to enquire whether you might have left something on the Tube network recently.'

'I wish I had, dearie, but I haven't left my house in over twenty years.'

'I'm sorry to have disturbed you.'

'That's quite all right, dearie. Goodbye.'

She peered at the phone book and dialled again.

'Hello, is that Dr Perkins?'

'Who's speaking?'

'Mrs Jones from London Underground Lost Property Office.'

'She's at work. I'm the cleaner. Can I take a message?'

'Do you know whether she happened to have left a wooden box on the Tube recently? It has a brass plaque bearing the name Clementine Perkins.'

'I doubt it,' the woman replied. 'There are no Clementines in Dr Perkins' family.'

As Hebe Jones put down the phone, Valerie Jennings arrived in her usual flat black shoes. But as she hung her navy coat on the stand next to the inflatable doll, there were none of her usual complaints about delays on the Northern Line during which she had to suffer the indignity of being tightly pressed against her fellow passengers. Nor was there a word about the bitterness of the morning and a prediction of snow on account of the twitching of her bunions. And when she opened the fridge, there wasn't even a look of reproach when she searched in vain for the Bakewell tartlet that she had hidden behind a carton of carrot soup.

'You're not still worried about those ears, are you?' enquired Hebe Jones, thinking of Valerie

131

Jennings's eventual release from the front end of the pantomime horse, which had resulted in the detachment of both appendages and her lurching backwards. 'I took the horse home last night and Balthazar said he'd sew them back on and you'd never notice.'

'It's much worse than that,' she said.

'What?' asked Hebe Jones.

'Arthur Catnip asked me out to lunch while you were gone yesterday afternoon.'

'What did you say?'

'Yes . . . He caught me off guard.'

There was a pause.

'It gets worse,' Valerie Jennings continued.

'Why?'

'I don't want to go.'

*   *   *

Following a day of defeat at the office, Hebe Jones made her way up Water Lane, hunching her shoulders in the darkness. While she welcomed the fact that the tourists had been shut out of the Tower by the time she returned each evening, she dreaded the solitary walk in winter when the only light came from the fleeting appearance of the moon. As she passed Traitors' Gate, she remembered the time when Milo dived for coins dropped by tourists into the stretch of the Thames that seeped through its wooden bars. With no regard for the visitors still touring the monument, he and Charlotte Broughton had shed their clothes, and descended the forbidden steps to the water's edge in their pants and vests. They had retrieved several handfuls of coins by the time the alarm was raised. Running back up the steps, their underwear heavy with water, they dodged the Beefeater who had spotted them, and took off down the cobbles. As they headed up Mint Lane, they were seen by several off-duty Beefeaters from their living rooms who joined the chase. The pair were eventually cornered against the Flint Tower where they stood heads bowed, dripping with water. Not only did they endure the wrath of their parents and every Beefeater in the Tower, but they were summoned to explain themselves to the Chief Yeoman Warder. The coins were duly thrown back into the murky water, apart from a single gold sovereign that Milo slipped into the leg of his underpants, which he kept with his other treasures in a Harrogate toffee tin until he presented it to Charlotte Broughton two years later in exchange for a kiss.

The Salt Tower was in darkness as Hebe Jones approached, save for a light on the top floor. Passing Milo's door at the foot of the spiral staircase, she wondered whether her husband would remember that their son would have been fourteen the following day. As she changed into something warmer in the bedroom, she thought of the time when she used to be greeted on her return home. She went down to the kitchen, and while searching in a cupboard for a pan, she recalled the evenings when there had been so much noise, she had had to shut the door. If it wasn't her husband playing Phil Collins hits on Milo's kazoo, a uniquely irritating habit that had led her to hide the instrument, it was his attempts to help the boy with his homework. Unless the subject was English history, Balthazar Jones would walk around the living room suggesting answers that were wholly arbitrary. When asked a question he was unable to even guess at, he would go to extraordinary lengths to conceal the fact that he was as mystified as his young son. Leaving the room under the pretext of needing the lavatory, he would riffle through the sacred text he kept hidden by his bed that held the key to the world's most troubling enigma: how to do fractions. And he would emerge victorious through the living-room door, trying to hold the formula in his head, and the pair would wrestle with mathematics until the monster was eventually slain.

When supper was ready, she walked through the empty living room, and called up the spiral staircase to the room at the top of the tower that she never entered. When they had finished their chops in front of the television, Balthazar Jones immediately got up to do the dishes, then disappeared once more to his celestial shed. And when they met each other again, several hours later in bed, Hebe Jones looked at the outline of her husband in the darkness and thought: 'Please don't forget what day it is tomorrow.'

9

Balthazar Jones woke early, and turned on to his back away from his wife muttering in her dreams next to him. As he waited for sleep to reclaim him, the question Hebe Jones asked him the previous week about what Milo would have looked like had he lived floated back to him, and he tried to imagine how tall he would have grown, and the shape of his face that had always appeared to him to be that of an angel. He had never had the pleasure of teaching him how to shave, and the razor that had belonged to the boy's grandfather, which had travelled around India in its battered silver tin, remained in the Beefeater's sock drawer with no one to pass it on to.

Unable to bear his thoughts any longer, he got up, and dressed in the bathroom so as not to disturb his wife. He left the Salt Tower without stopping for breakfast, barely noticing the snow pirouetting down from the sky like feathers. He drifted from enclosure to enclosure, as he wondered how his son's voice would have sounded today on his fourteenth birthday. When he led the eleven o'clock tour of the fortress, he didn't have the stomach to show the tourists the scaffold site, and only mentioned its location while standing at the chapel door as they were about to file out at the end. It caused such annoyance that even the Americans, whose mystification over English history the Beefeaters always forgave on account of their famous generosity, failed to press a tip into his hand. He crossed Tower Green, and started to patrol Water Lane for pickpockets, but kept seeing his son amongst the visitors. He left to check that the Komodo dragon's enclosure was completely secure in readiness for the opening of the menagerie to the public, scheduled for a couple of days' time. But all he could think about as he tested the locks was how much Milo would have liked to have seen the mighty lizard that was strong enough to bring down a horse.

He only remembered his meeting with the man

from the Palace when he spotted him striding across the fortress wrapped up against the cold. He hurried to the Rack & Ruin, cursing himself for not having come up with a credible explanation for the missing birds with yellow eyebrows, and pushed open the door.

*   *   *

'What do you mean, the penguins are missing?' Oswin Fielding asked, leaning across the table next to the framed signature of Rudolf Hess.

'They just never turned up,' Balthazar Jones replied, lowering his voice lest someone heard.

'So where are they?'

The Beefeater scratched at his white beard. 'I'm not quite certain at the moment,' he replied. 'The removal man says he stopped for petrol and when he came back from paying, both the back and the passenger doors were open and they'd vanished.'

'Who was in the passenger seat?'

The Beefeater looked away. 'One of the penguins,' he muttered.

'Damn,' said the equerry, running a hand through the remains of his hair. 'The Argentineans are going to think we lost them on purpose. We don't want to get on the wrong side of that lot again. Listen, if anyone asks where they are, tell them that they got travel sickness or something and they're at the vets. I'll make a few discreet enquiries.'

Oswin Fielding took a sip of his orange juice while studying the Beefeater carefully. 'Is there anything else I should know?' he asked. 'I don't want any cock-ups when the menagerie opens.'

'Everything else has gone according to plan,' he insisted. 'Apart from the wandering albatross, all the animals have settled in well,' he said. 'The giraffes are loving the moat.'

The courtier frowned. 'What giraffes?' he asked.

'The ones with the long necks.'

'Her Majesty doesn't possess any giraffes.'

Balthazar Jones looked confused. 'But there are four in the moat,' he said.

'But I gave you a list,' Oswin Fielding hissed. 'There were no giraffes on it.'

'Well, someone thought they belonged to the Queen. They'd been loaded into a lorry by the time I arrived. I just assumed you'd forgotten to write them down.'

There was a pause as both men glared at each other.

'So, to sum things up then, Yeoman Warder Jones,' the equerry said, 'the Queen's penguins are missing, and the Tower of London has kidnapped four giraffes that belong to London Zoo.'

The Beefeater shifted in his seat. 'We can just send the giraffes back, and say there was a misunderstanding,' he suggested.

Oswin Fielding leant forward. 'I very much doubt that we will be able to sneak four giraffes back across London without being spotted. It'll be all over the papers and we'll both look like complete idiots. I'll call the zoo and explain that we've borrowed them. Hopefully they won't kick up too much of a fuss, and we'll send them back in a couple of months when things have quietened down. If they start being difficult, I'll remind them what they did to Jumbo the elephant.'

'What did they do to Jumbo the elephant?' the

Beefeater asked.

'They sold him to Barnum, the American circus man, for two thousand pounds. It caused an absolute stink: there were letters to *The Times*, the nation's children were in tears, and Queen Victoria was furious.'

Oswin Fielding sat back in his chair with a sigh that would have woken the dead. 'Is that shrew still alive?' he asked.

'I saw it move this morning.'

'That's something at least.'

*   *   *

Once the equerry and Beefeater had left, Ruby Dore collected their glasses and looked to see if it was still snowing. But as she peered through the window, on which was scratched an eighteenth-century insult concerning the landlord's personal hygiene, she saw that there were no traces of it left. Filled with disappointment, she remembered the winters of her childhood when her father pulled her around the moat on her sledge, and the Beefeaters engaged in snowball fights more furious than their historic battle to defend the Tower against the Peasants' Revolt in 1381.

As the canary hopped from perch to perch in its cage, she returned to her stool behind the bar and finished writing an announcement that the thirty-five-year ban on Monopoly had been lifted. It had been introduced by her father, incensed that the Tower doctor had continued playing while his wife gave birth on the kitchen floor above. The board game's prohibition had forced it underground, and a number of Beefeaters descended to their basements to brew their own ales with which to drown the torment of defeat as they played the Tower doctor in their sitting rooms. The practice, which had continued over the years, had resulted in a drop in the tavern's profits, and now that her life was about to change forever, Ruby Dore was determined to claw back some turnover.

After pinning the notice on the board next to the door, she reread the rules she had listed underneath the announcement. In order to avoid resurrecting historic grievances, playing with the boot would be prohibited. Anyone caught cheating would be obliged to pay a fixed levy on their pints for the next six months. And the Tower doctor was only permitted to play in the absence of a medical emergency.

Not long afterwards, when Rev. Septimus Drew pushed open the heavy door carrying his weapon of seduction, he was relieved to find that he was the only customer. But Ruby Dore was nowhere to be seen. He stood for several minutes on the worn flagstones, wondering where she was, then placed the treacle cake on the bar, sat down on one of the stools, and took off his scarf. Picking up the nearest beer mat, he read the joke on the back of it. He then gazed around the bar, wondering whether it was unseemly for a man of the cloth to be looking for love armed with the fruits of his oven.

Fearing that one of the Beefeaters would come in at any moment and catch him in flagrante with his Tupperware box, he quickly got to his feet, and strode out. As he stood in the cold tying his scarf, he heard a sound coming from the disused Well Tower. Unable to resist the lure of an open door, he stepped in. There, with her back to him, was Ruby Dore, instantly recognisable in the gloom by her ponytail. Just as he was about to reveal that he had left her a little something on the bar made according to his mother's recipe, the landlady turned and greeted the chaplain with the words: 'Come and have a look at the Queen's fancy rats.'

The chaplain saw behind her a flash of villainous yellow teeth.

'The Keeper of the Royal Menagerie said I could look after them,' she continued, turning back towards them. 'Aren't they sweet? I used to have one when I was little, but it escaped. One of the Beefeaters said he spotted him by the organ in the chapel once, but we never found him. It was such a shame. We'd taught him all kinds of tricks. My dad made him a tiny barrel, and he used to push it across the bar. The Beefeaters would give him a penny each time he got to the end. He was loaded by the time he escaped. Did you know that Queen Victoria used to have one?'

But when Ruby Dore turned round, all that was left of Rev. Septimus Drew was a hint of frankincense.

*   *   *

By the time Valerie Jennings arrived at work, Hebe Jones was already entombed in the magician's box used to saw glamorous assistants in two. Recognising instantly the horizontal position of defeat, Valerie Jennings unbuttoned her navy coat, hung it next to the inflatable doll, and sat at her desk waiting for the restoration of her colleague's faculties. After a few moments, she

140

glanced at her again, but her eyes were still closed and both her shoes had dropped to the floor. Eventually, she heard the telltale creak of the lid, and Hebe Jones emerged, and muttered a greeting to her colleague. She watched as she returned to her desk, peered at the phone book and picked up the receiver with renewed determination.

Valerie Jennings looked at her notebook, but found herself unable to concentrate on reuniting the yellow canoe with its owner. She glanced at the cuckoo clock, dreading lunchtime. Despite the fact that Arthur Catnip was their favourite ticket inspector, she bitterly regretted having agreed to go out with him. She had never intended to enter the maze of romance again, with its hopeless dead ends. The last time she ventured inside, she had been encouraged by a neighbour unable to bear the sight of her mowing her lawn, a job she believed to be decreed at birth to be that of a husband. She waited until Valerie Jennings was trimming the edge next to the fence, and seized the opportunity to rear her head. First she congratulated her on her crosscutting technique that her own husband also swore by. She then added in a breathless non sequitur that she had a single colleague who also liked books. But despite Valerie Jennings's insistence that single men were almost as dangerous as married ones, the woman persisted until she reluctantly agreed to meet him.

For a week she convinced herself that the man would be entirely unsuitable. But as she got ready for their evening together, a spark of hope suddenly flickered inside her, and when she closed the front door behind her a gust of loneliness fanned it into an inferno of longing. She sat in the corner of the pub with her double vodka and orange, inspecting the pattern on her new dress, looking up each time someone came in. Eventually, a man opened the door and glanced around. They held each other's gaze long enough for her to realise that it was him. She offered a timorous smile, but he turned on his heels and left with as much determination as he had entered. It was a considerable time before Valerie Jennings was able to stand. She then pulled down her dress over her splendid thighs and walked out, leaving the embers of her dreams scattered behind her.

When the door of the cuckoo clock burst open and the tiny wooden bird shot out to deliver a single demented cry, Hebe Jones wished her good luck. 'I've got some lipstick you can borrow, if you like,' she added.

'It's OK, thanks. I wouldn't want to encourage him,' she replied. She put on her navy coat over the skirt she had worn the previous day, and reluctantly turned the corner. Arthur Catnip was already waiting at the original Victorian counter, fingering a savage new haircut. The assault had taken place that morning during his tea break. As soon as the barber heard that his customer was taking a woman out for lunch, he insisted that something more dramatic was required. But instead of the transformation he had been hoping for, when Arthur Catnip raised his eyes to the mirror after the man had finally laid down his scissors, he found that a massacre had taken place. Not even the peace dove of a waived bill could appease him. And he wandered back to the staff room in defeat, hoping that Valerie Jennings would see past the carnage.

They headed out together into the cold, discussing the early morning snow that had failed to settle. As they passed the Hotel Splendid, Valerie Jennings glanced with regret at the marvellous columns and the uniformed doorman waiting on the top step, wondering where the ticket inspector was taking her.

It wasn't long before the couple arrived at the entrance to Regent's Park, and Valerie Jennings wished she was back in the warm, familiar office. As they passed the fountain, Arthur Catnip pointed to something in the distance and announced that they were almost there. Valerie Jennings peered through her smeared spectacles and saw what was undeniably a tea hut. 'I think it's going to rain,' she said.

As they passed several men prodding the undergrowth with sticks, Arthur Catnip wondered what they were searching for. But Valerie Jennings didn't even look up, as she was thinking about what she would find in the comforting foxed pages of Miss E. Clutterbuck that evening, while in the sanctuary of her armchair with the pop-up leg rest.

When they approached the tea hut, she pointed with relief to a notice on the door saying 'Closed'. But Arthur Catnip pushed it open, and invited her to step inside. Instead of the rows of battered tables and chairs filled with dog walkers and bird watchers, she looked around to see a table set for two in the centre, covered in a white linen cloth. A single yellow rose stood in a silver vase in the middle. Behind the counter was a man wearing a white chef's hat, and a young waitress dressed in black. 'Don't worry, I asked for a French chef,' said Arthur Catnip as the waitress approached to take her coat.

When the onion soup arrived, Valerie Jennings recalled the French onion seller of her childhood standing on the corner with his laden bicycle. Lowering his voice, Arthur Catnip revealed that his uncle had run away with one, after which the vegetable was banished from the house.

Once the *poulet à la moutarde* was served, the ticket inspector topped up her glass, and recounted the sights of the mysterious voodoo chickens he had seen while in Haiti with the Navy. Valerie Jennings took another sip of wine and found herself telling him about the cockerel owned by her godmother that had fallen in love with the kitchen mop, and tried to mount it each time the woman cleaned the kitchen floor.

As they were eating the *tarte tatin*, she muttered that she had been thinking about making cider from the apples in her garden in the summer, as they had never been good enough for baking. The tattooed ticket inspector said it was a great idea, and confessed to having once drunk so much of the stuff, he fell overboard and spent almost a week on a desert island before being spotted by his ship and rescued.

While they were drinking their coffee, one of the men they had seen earlier prodding the undergrowth with a stick put his head around the door and asked: 'You haven't seen a bearded pig by any chance, have you?'

They replied that they hadn't, and offered to keep a lookout on their way back, both thrilled at the thought of seeing a pig with a beard. But as they returned to the Lost Property Office, Valerie

144

Jennings forgot all about it as she only had eyes for Arthur Catnip.

*   *   *

That night, the ticking of the clock on the bedside table seemed much louder in the darkness. As she looked at the time, Hebe Jones wondered whether she would ever fall asleep. She moved on to her side, away from her husband's fitful slumber, and her mind turned to the evening they had just spent. Balthazar Jones had gone up to the room at the top of the Salt Tower as usual, without a word about what day it was, and she had remained on the sofa, pierced with shards of grief, wondering how he could have forgotten.

She remembered Milo's last birthday, when he had again requested a chemistry set. He had asked for one ever since his father first told him about Sir Walter Raleigh brewing his Balsam of Guiana in the Tower hen house. Much to her annoyance, he had filled the boy's head with wondrous tales of the Great Cordial, made with ingredients that included gold and unicorn, which had cured Queen Anne of a dangerous fever.

'Daddy said that the Queen was so impressed with it that she asked for some to save the life of her son Prince Henry,' the boy had said as his birthday approached. 'He said that they'd tried to cure him by putting dead pigeons on his head and two halves of a cock pressed against the soles of his feet. But once he'd swallowed the Cordial, he opened his eyes and sat up and spoke!'

Hebe Jones had continued peeling the potatoes. 'What your father failed to tell you was that he

145

died not long afterwards,' she replied.

But despite Milo's pleading, Hebe Jones refused to buy her son a chemistry set, fearing disaster, despite her husband's insistence that he would supervise each experiment. When the boy tore the wrapping off his present, he discovered a telescope that offered not the slightest possibility of eruption. His parents took him up to the Salt Tower roof, where Balthazar Jones showed him all the stars that the first Astronomer Royal who had lived in the Tower would have seen. 'If the ravens ever get in the way of your telescope, let me know and I'll fetch grandpa's shotgun,' the Beefeater promised. While Milo appeared delighted by the prospect of his father reducing the odious birds to a pile of black feathers, Hebe Jones knew that planet-gazing was no match for the experiments he had hoped to perform. Recognising her son's disappointment, she assured him she would buy him the present he had always wanted for his twelfth birthday. But it had never come. As she turned over to escape the memory of the promise she hadn't been able to keep, a hot tear slipped down her cheek.

When she woke several hours later, the room was still dark. Immediately sensing the absence of her husband, she ran a hand along the bottom of the sheet, and found that his side was still warm. Pulling back the shabby blanket, she got out of bed, and drew back a curtain. She gazed at the Tower, streaked with faint brushstrokes of light. Through the rain, which slid in greasy drops down the pane, she made out her husband slowly climbing the battlement steps, his wet nightclothes clinging to him. When he eventually returned, a new variety hidden in his dressing-gown pocket, he found that Hebe Jones and her suitcase were gone.

10

Unable to report for duty because of the weight in his chest, Balthazar Jones sat on the edge of the bed in a dry pair of pyjamas and picked up the telephone. As he called the office in the Byward Tower, his eyes followed each revolution of the dial and its laborious spin backwards.

'Yes?' replied the Yeoman Gaoler.

The Beefeater rubbed the shabby blanket between his fingers. 'It's Yeoman Warder Jones here,' he said.

'Good morning, Yeoman Warder Jones. The shrew's fine. It ate a cricket while I was in the shower this morning.'

'That's good.'

'Is it a he or a she, by the way?'

'I'm not sure. I'll find out.' Balthazar Jones cleared his throat, then added: 'I won't be reporting for duty today.'

'And why is that, may I ask?' the Yeoman Gaoler enquired, standing up and surveying the room for his packet of Fig Rolls.

'I'm not feeling very well.'

'Oh?' came the muffled reply as the Yeoman Gaoler peered inside a bin, looking for an empty wrapper.

There was a pause.

'I've had a surfeit of lampreys,' continued

147

Balthazar Jones, his mind drifting in the current of his despair.

'A what?'

The Beefeater tried to recall what he had just said, and suddenly realised that he had told the Yeoman Gaoler that he was suffering from an over-consumption of an eel-like fish that had caused the death of Henry I. But there was no going back.

'A surfeit of lampreys,' Balthazar Jones repeated as quietly as possible.

'Speak up, man!'

'Lampreys,' he muttered. 'A surfeit of them.'

There was a pause.

'Just a minute,' replied the Yeoman Gaoler, putting down the phone. He strode over to the bookcase next to the arrow slit, and pulled out a ring file in which absences were recorded. Returning to his desk, he sat down, picked up the receiver and selected a pen from an old Golden Syrup tin.

'And how are we spelling lampreys?' he enquired, finding his page. He twiddled his pen as he waited for a reply.

'I'm not sure,' replied Balthazar Jones, gazing at his wet dressing gown on the back of the door.

'Laammppreeez,' enunciated the Yeoman Gaoler as he noted down the affliction and filled in the date. He paused before adding: 'They must have been good.'

After putting down the phone, Balthazar Jones reached for the letter he had found on his pillow when he returned to bed earlier that morning, soaked with rain and reeking of the Thames. Despite the numerous times he had read it, he still

148

failed to find in it any hope that his wife would ever return. There was no mistaking her need to be away from him, her bitterness over his refusal to talk about Milo's death, and her despair over the erosion of their love.

As he stared at her name on the bottom of the page, he thought of the gust of serendipity that had blown him and Hebe Grammatikos together all those years ago. It was such a chance encounter, too random to be the reassuring hand of destiny, he had lived in terror of luck's capricious nature ever since, fearing that one day he might lose her.

For too long he had thought that he was never going to marry. An only child, he had been woken at night by the sound of laughter coming from his parents' bedroom above. Assuming that all relationships were of equal delight, his disappointment was bitter when the girls he met not only failed to make him smile, but induced in him the urge to weep. His parents assured him that his bride would eventually come, but as the years passed and their conviction failed to prove true, he decided to join the army in order to distract himself from his loneliness, opting to become a guardsman in the belief that it would present fewer opportunities to shoot someone. The day before he was due to leave, his hair shorn and packed bag waiting outside his bedroom door, he met the extraordinary creature in the corner shop.

About to buy some stamps for the letters he planned to write to his parents, he spotted the girl standing in an aisle holding a Battenberg cake, dark hair meandering down the front of her turquoise dress. She had the eyes of a fawn that

149

fixed on him as soon as he approached, and from that moment all sanity was lost. He walked up to her and informed her that the lurid yellow-and-pink checked cake had been invented by a distant relative of his in honour of the woman who had captured the man's heart. Unable to send her flowers because of her catastrophic allergies, he made her a cake of the most alluring colours he could find in his garden. The four coloured squares each represented an aspect of her that had so beguiled him: the paleness of her skin, her modesty, her wit and her piano playing. Each week, a carriage arrived at her home with a basket on the back seat bearing a cake. But the woman, who had been forbidden by her doctor from eating sugar, never tasted them. Instead, she packed up some of her china and kept the love tokens in her dining-room cupboards. When the man learnt of the secret stash, he started covering the cakes in marzipan to ensure their preservation. He continued baking them, and she continued keeping them, a habit they maintained up until their wedding, and the creation was named after the German town they visited during their honeymoon.

When Balthazar Jones finished his story there was a moment of pure silence. The Pakistani shopkeeper, as transfixed as Hebe Grammatikos, then declared from behind the till: 'It is true, madam,' simply because he wanted it to be.

The young couple sat on the wall outside the shop talking for so long that Balthazar Jones invited her for supper, to the initial devastation of his mother who wanted her son to herself on his last night. But it wasn't long before she was equally taken with Hebe Grammatikos, and she gave an extra serving of hogget to the tiny guest with the enormous appetite. When the girl's last train home had long departed, Mrs Jones made up the spare bed down the hall and retired upstairs with her husband. When all was quiet, Balthazar Jones eventually persuaded the extraordinary creature into his room, with the assurance of the most gentlemanly of behaviour. She sat on the end of his bed and asked why he was called Balthazar. He told her that he had been named after one of the Three Wise Men as he had been conceived on Christmas Day. In turn, she revealed that she had been named after the Greek goddess of youth. The pair talked until midnight when they were suddenly reduced to silence by the realisation that they would be parted within hours. So they stayed awake, knowing that sleep would hasten the unthinkable moment. As the ruthless dawn heaved away the night, Hebe Grammatikos kissed the tip of each of his slender fingers, which would have to get used to holding a gun. And when it was finally time to say goodbye, she stood on the doorstep next to his parents and joined them in waving him off, each with a stone in their heart.

The stamps he had bought were never stuck on letters to his parents, but used instead for those sent to the tiny creature he had met in the corner shop. But his writing on the envelopes was always so confused by love they took several weeks to arrive at the correct address. Kept awake by terrible snores coming from the bunk above him, he was in such distress over the time it took to receive a reply that he wrote more and more frequently, presuming that his letters were going

151

astray. Two years later, when he proposed, it was to the great relief of the postman whose back had long ago given way.

*　　　*　　　*

Balthazar Jones ignored the knocking on the Salt Tower door. He remained in the same position on the bed, clutching the letter as the wind blew its dank breath through the tiny gaps in the lattice windows. But the banging continued, and mounted with such urgency that the Beefeater, fearing the commotion would attract further attention, got up to answer it. He staggered down the stairs in his bare feet, heaved open the door, and shielded his eyes against the glare of the marble sky. Standing in front of him was Dr Evangeline Moore, carrying a black bag. 'I understand you're not feeling well,' she said.

Too troubled to think of a credible reason not to let her in, he stepped aside and followed her back up the stairs, feeling their chill on his soles, blackened from his nocturnal foray on the battlements. Once they had reached the living room, the Beefeater suddenly felt embarrassed at being caught in his nightclothes by the young woman. Taking refuge on the sofa, he warned: 'Mind where you're treading.' The doctor, whose copper ringlets glowed whenever caught by a freak ray of sunshine, promptly sidestepped Mrs Cook. She unbuttoned the jacket of her neat, brown trouser suit, and sat down on the armchair that failed to match the settee.

Taking out a file from her black bag, she opened it on her knees, and ran a finger down a page. She frowned, looked up, and said: 'According to the Yeoman Gaoler, you've had a surfeit of lampreys.'

Balthazar Jones gazed at the floor, and started digging at a threadbare patch of the emaciated carpet with a grimy toe. The only sound was a tiny creak as Mrs Cook stood up and started her day's journey across the floor. The Tower doctor looked at the tortoise while the Beefeater continued to look at the floor. She turned her eyes back to her patient, who had bored such a big hole that half his toe had disappeared.

'It's not that uncommon,' she suddenly declared. 'You'd be surprised. How many are we talking about? Half a dozen maybe? Well, however many it was, I'm sure it's nothing serious. Just take it easy for the rest of the day,' she concluded with a smile that he took to signify an end to the matter.

But just as Balthazar Jones thought that the doctor was about to leave, she suggested a quick examination. Too defeated to refuse, he stood up and the doctor proceeded to poke and hammer at him with a variety of implements that wouldn't have looked out of place at the Wakefield Tower's instruments of torture exhibition. When it was finally over, he retreated to the sofa, and immediately felt for the comfort of his beard as he watched the weapons being returned to the black bag.

'Everything seems to be fine. I'll let myself out,' announced the general practitioner, stepping over Mrs Cook and heading for the door. Reaching for the latch, she suddenly turned round and said: 'I'm sorry to hear about your wife.'

The silence that followed was eventually broken by the sound of heels descending the stone stairs.

The Beefeater, not in the least surprised that word had already got out, remained slumped on the sofa. Unable to bear the thoughts that threatened to engulf him, he stood up and made his way to the bedroom. Preferring to report for duty than to endure his own rumination, he slowly put on his uniform, wobbling as he clambered into his Victorian trousers.

*   *   *

Hidden from view, the Ravenmaster knelt down next to the bridge over the moat and took out his nail scissors. Carefully he snipped at the grass that grew around the tiny crosses marking the graves of long-departed ravens, a number of which had literally dropped off their perches. Despite the stories peddled to the tourists, the legend that the kingdom would fall should the ravens leave the Tower was utter poppycock. The kingdom had not so much as trembled when the birds were put into cages just before the start of the Second World War, and driven away at nightfall. Their unexpected holiday had been organised at the highest level to prevent them from receiving a direct hit, which would threaten the nation's morale. The same day, the Crown Jewels had also been secretly removed, transported in coffins by armed guards dressed as undertakers, and hidden in Westwood Quarry, in Wiltshire. The caged ravens were taken by ambulance to the terraced house of a Beefeater's aunt who lived in Wales, and smuggled inside. The pebbledash home in Swansea remained in permanent blackout, and the aunt was forbidden from opening her door lest word got out that the ravens had left the Tower. Not only was the woman paid to look after the birds, but she was also granted a stipend for the rest of her life to keep silent about their temporary removal.

When the war was finally over, it was not certain who had driven the other more mad. The wild-eyed aunt, desperate for human conversation, told anyone who would listen (as well as those who wouldn't) about her top-secret mission during the war. But even the local paper refused to believe her. And the generation of wartime ravens, a species noted for its talent at mimicry, never lost their Welsh accents during the remainder of their days at the fortress.

Satisfied that dignity had been restored, the Ravenmaster put his scissors back in his pocket and stood up. He then made his way to the entrance of the Tower, and stood on the bridge waiting to take the tourists on the last tour of the day. His black-gloved hands clasped in front of him, he watched the visitors who were on their way out, eyeing their rucksacks closely lest one tried to leave with a bird buried deep within as the ultimate souvenir. As one of the giraffes in the moat raised its head in search of a leaf, the tourists immediately pointed to it. A man with a video camera attached to his hat approached the Ravenmaster, and asked when the menagerie was opening.

'The day after tomorrow, if the Keeper of the Royal Menagerie gets his act together,' came the moustached reply.

'I heard there used to be a menagerie here years ago,' the Australian tourist continued.

'There was, until the 1830s when they finally realised it was a bad idea to have wild animals around the place. Still is, as far as I'm concerned,' said the Ravenmaster, turning his gaze back towards the giraffes.

'Was anyone killed?' asked the man, hopefully.

The Ravenmaster then told him the unfortunate tale of Mary Jenkinson, who lived with the lion keeper. 'One day in 1686, she was inside the den stroking one of the animal's paws when it grabbed her arm in its teeth and wouldn't let go. Her arm was amputated in an attempt to save her life, but she died several hours later.'

The tourist immediately related the tale to his wife, who beamed with equal satisfaction, and asked her husband whether they could come back when the menagerie opened.

The Ravenmaster looked at his watch, and called to the visitors waiting for the tour to step closer. He then threw open his arms, and announced in his best theatrical tones, employed to elicit tips from the Americans: 'Welcome to Her Majesty's Royal Palace and Fortress, the Tower of London! It is my pleasure to be your guide over the next hour as we look back over nine hundred years of history . . .'

An hour later, he stood at the door of the chapel as the tourists filed out, each pressing a coin into his hand. Once the last had left, he made his way to the ravens' pens and stood calling the birds' names one by one. They landed shambolically, then swaggered across the grass to their respective wooden homes, and flew up inside. Locking the doors after them to keep them out of the jaws of urban foxes, he looked at his watch, and smoothed

156

down his pigeon grey moustache with a leather-gloved hand. High with anticipation, he crossed the fortress to the Brick Tower, and, with the furtiveness of a horse thief, glanced behind him. Satisfied that he wasn't being watched, he unlocked the door. Closing it behind him, he reached in the gloom for the rope handrail, then suddenly remembered that he was still wearing a vest. Recognising instantly that it was not the correct attire for an illicit encounter, he unbuttoned his dark blue tunic, pulled off the undergarment and left it in a warm bundle on the bottom step to collect on his way out. Once he was dressed again, he continued up the stone steps. Finding the door of the first floor closed, he felt for the handle and pressed down on the latch. The sudden sound startled the birds, which created such an uproar that the Ravenmaster, who had completely forgotten about the new aviary, joined them with a squawk of terror. The birds continued their demented circular flight long after Ambrosine Clarke arrived, dressed in jeans and a jumper, the neckline of which revealed the tormenting depth of her cleavage. The Ravenmaster reached for her in the darkness, recognising instantly the smell of cooking fat. Once their clothes were shed, they sank to the floorboards, where they were covered in a drizzle of seed husks whipped up by the frantic flapping. The cook's eventual shriek of ecstasy was drowned out by the emerald hanging parrot's profanities, having been rudely woken from its upside-down slumber.

* * *

Balthazar Jones remained on the sofa in the same position since returning from an afternoon of patrolling the fortress. He hadn't bothered to close the curtains, and sat gazing at the night bulging up against the lattice windows that surrounded him. On the coffee table in front of him was the vest he had discovered on the bottom step of the Brick Tower when he went to check on the birds on his way home. He could find nothing to account for the gentleman's underwear, and when he pushed open the door to the aviary, he saw that its inhabitants, terrorised into a state of exhaustion, were huddled together on their perches to keep warm as they slept, while the emerald parrot hung below them, occasionally swaying while it dreamed. The only bird still awake was the wandering albatross, searching the cage for its companion, which was still at London Zoo as it didn't belong to the Queen.

It wasn't until the cold finally drove him to his feet that Balthazar Jones found the courage to go upstairs to the bedroom. He closed the curtains, the rings dragging sorrowfully across the poles, then undressed slowly to further delay the moment. Once in his pyjamas, he spent longer than usual in the bathroom, having decided that now was the moment to fix the tap that had dripped since the family arrived eight years ago. When, eventually, he could find nothing else to occupy him, he came back out and finally looked at the empty bed. Unable to get into it, he pulled on a jumper, turned off the light, and sat in the armchair next to the window. When, several hours later, sleep continued to evade him, he stood up,

158

drew back one of the curtains and opened the window. Leaning against the sill, he looked out over the fortress, gruesome in the moonlight, and breathed in the dank night. And out of the deathly silence came the mournful wail of the solitary wandering albatross that mated for life.

11

When Hebe Jones tried to leave the fortress in the early hours of the previous morning with her suitcase, the Beefeater on duty refused to unlock the small door inside the Middle Tower's vast oak gate. 'It's against regulations,' he replied to her protests. She sat on top of her case, coated in three years of dust, glancing at her watch with the impatience of a prisoner about to be set free. When six o'clock eventually came, and the ancient lock was finally turned, she got up and walked stiffly out with the intention of going to work. But as she stood in the crowded Tube carriage, subjected to more intimacy with strangers than she experienced with her husband, she soon realised that a day of attempting to reunite abandoned property with its absentminded owners was beyond her. She climbed the steps to the exit, and left a message on the office answering machine informing Valerie Jennings that she was unwell, and started walking the streets. After a while, she found herself by the entrance to Green Park, and slipped in to escape the relentless commuters marching to work, knocking her case against her shins as they passed. She spent much of the day on a bench, being pummelled by the wind as she wondered whether she was still a mother even though her son was dead.

When darkness started to seep around her, fear forced her to her feet. She returned to the warmth of the Underground, and rode the network wondering where women usually went when they left their husbands. Eventually, she made her way to Baker Street, and arrived at the Hotel Splendid, the only hotel she knew as she took Valerie Jennings there for lunch each year on her birthday. When the receptionist asked whether she required a single or double room, her eyes fell to the desk. 'I'm alone,' she replied, wondering whether the woman could tell that her marriage had just ended.

After being shown to her room by a Polish bellboy who insisted on carrying her case, she sat on the bed and her stomach reminded her that she hadn't eaten all day. She ordered a ham and mustard sandwich, and ate it at the dressing table still wearing her coat. Opening her case, she discovered that she had forgotten her nightdress, and she thought of it lying on the bed in the Salt Tower. Her mind turned once more to her husband, and she wondered whether there was anything in the fridge for his supper. Reluctant to sleep naked in such unfamiliar surroundings, she hung up her coat and skirt in the empty wardrobe and got into bed in her blouse and tights. She looked around at the cream swag curtains, the luxurious white bathrobes, and the vase of pink roses on the desk, and imagined the young honeymoon couples who had sealed their marriage in the room. And she wondered how many of them

160

were still together.

Between scraps of sleep, she spent the night listening to doors banging as guests returned, and the intermittent shrieks of laughter coming from the room above. The following morning, despite the grandeur of the dining room with its white linen napkins, polished silverware and uniformed waiters, Hebe Jones skipped breakfast, preferring the familiarity of people's lost possessions. After sliding her suitcase underneath her desk, she went to the original Victorian counter and opened one of the ledgers to the previous day. As her eyes fell down the entries, she saw that Samuel Crapper had been in to collect the same tomato plant that he had lost earlier in the month, a hand-written musical score had been discovered on the Hammersmith & City line, and a new wedding dress had been found on a bench at Tottenham Court Road station.

She sat at her desk, and was still looking at the phone directory in defeat when Valerie Jennings arrived and stood next to the inflatable doll, unbuttoning her navy coat. 'Feeling better?' she asked Hebe Jones.

'Yes, thanks,' she replied, immediately noticing something different about her colleague. Mascara had brought out her eyes from behind her glasses, an embellishment normally reserved for her birthday lunch at the Hotel Splendid. Instead of her usual flat, black shoes, her wide feet were wedged inside a pair of high heels. And instead of holding a white cardboard box from the high street bakery containing a little something for elevenses, Valerie Jennings was carrying a brown paper bag containing what looked suspiciously like fresh fruit.

'When are you seeing Arthur Catnip again?' Hebe Jones asked.

Valerie Jennings immediately looked away. 'I don't know,' she replied, hanging up her coat. 'I haven't heard from him.' She then unfolded her newspaper and handed it to Hebe Jones. 'Remember that man I told you about who came into the tea hut and asked whether we'd seen a bearded pig?' she asked. 'Apparently it escaped from London Zoo and it's still on the loose.'

Hebe Jones looked at the front-page photograph taken of the creature while still in its enclosure, its resplendent snout whiskers stretching across several columns. She handed it back to her colleague with a shudder, and returned to the directory. She peered at where she had left off, picked up the phone, and dialled the number.

'Is that Mrs Perkins?' she asked when it was finally answered.

'Yes.'

'This is Mrs Jones from London Underground Lost Property Office. Something has been handed in to us that relates to a Clementine Perkins who died last year. I was wondering whether you happen to have known her.'

There was a moment's silence.

'You've found it?' came the eventual reply. 'We haven't been able to rest since it went missing. My husband will be so pleased. I'm not sure how to get to you though, dearie. I'm not too good on my legs and my husband doesn't go up town any more. He says there are so many people he just ends up walking on the spot, and then it's time to come home again.'

162

'Would you like me to bring it round? It's not something I want to put in the post.'

'That would be very kind of you.'

It didn't take Hebe Jones long to find the house, which stood out from the others in the street due to its overgrown lawn. She pushed open the rotten gate, which felt rough under her fingers on account of the peeling paint. Warmed at the thought of having finally found the urn's owner, she walked along the concrete path, looked at the *No Hawkers* sign, and rang the bell. When there was no reply, she checked to see that she had the right house number. She rang again, and eventually an elderly woman wearing a pink dressing gown opened the door.

'Mrs Perkins?'

'Yes,' the woman replied, squinting in the light.

'I'm Mrs Jones from London Underground Lost Property Office. We spoke on the phone.'

'Oh, yes, I remember,' she said, stepping back. 'Come in, dearie. Cup of tea?'

While the woman was in the kitchen, Hebe Jones found somewhere to sit in the chaos of the living room, and gazed around at the slumped piles of free newspapers on the floor, the cabinets over-filled with cheap ornaments, and the unwashed dishes balanced on the mantelpiece.

Eventually Mrs Perkins returned with a tray, bearing two cups and saucers and placed it on the coffee table. 'Biscuit?' she asked, holding out a plate. When Hebe Jones declined, she helped herself, moved a pile of unopened letters from the armchair, and sat down. 'What did you say your name was again?' she asked.

'Hebe.'

'That's a nice name. I've got some in the back garden,' she said, nodding towards the French windows.

Hebe Jones picked up her cup and saucer and rested them on her knees. 'I was actually named after the goddess of youth, rather than the plant.'

There was a pause.

'I thought my parents had named me Flora after the goddess of flowers. Turns out I was named after the margarine,' Mrs Perkins replied, staring in front of her.

Hebe Jones looked down at her tea.

'What did you come about, again?' the old woman asked.

'Clementine.'

'Oh, yes. We loved her so much,' she said, reaching for a tissue in her dressing gown pocket. 'She was getting on a bit, and we knew she was going to pass away sooner or later, but it's always a shock when it happens. Even now I can't believe she's gone. I still keep imagining her walking in here through those doors, and sitting where you are now. We buried her in the back garden. It had meant so much to her. She was always out there, pottering amongst the rose bushes.'

'I see,' replied Hebe Jones, still holding her cup.

'My husband reckons it was one of those urban foxes that dug her up again. Attracted to the smell.'

'The smell?'

'Things start to rot, don't they? I told my husband not to use that cardboard box, but he insisted. I said Clementine deserved better, but he said I was being too sentimental. So I wrote her name on it to make it a bit more special,' said Mrs

164

Perkins, fiddling with a thread on the end of the armrest.

'When we discovered that she'd been dug up, we were heartbroken. Some people just couldn't understand. We expected her to turn up in one of the neighbour's gardens, but you said she was found on the Tube. That doesn't seem right to me. I reckon that lot next door had something to do with it. They never did like her. She kept widdling against their new conservatory. But cats won't be told,' she added, finally taking a bite of her Custard Cream.

*   *   *

After checking that the workmen had erected all the signs in readiness for the opening of the royal menagerie that afternoon, Balthazar Jones let himself into the Develin Tower. He caught the bearded pig in a state of unfettered ecstasy, its eyes shut and hairy nose pointed heavenwards as it rubbed its considerable flank against the corner of the stone fireplace. The Beefeater sat down on the straw, resting his back against the circular stone wall, and stretched his legs out in front of him. On seeing its keeper, the animal sent the battered grapefruit flying to the other side of the room, and charged after it. Once it had caught up, the pig turned its head towards the man with inferior whiskers. There was no response. Lobbing the fruit again with its snout, it galloped after it, its tasselled tail flying like a flag over its fulsome buttocks. It looked again at the Beefeater staring blindly ahead, but received not the least encouragement. The pig slowly made its way across the straw and lay down next to him, pressing its back against his thigh.

Oblivious to the damp seeping through his tunic, Balthazar Jones wondered again where his wife had spent the night, and hoped she hadn't been cold without her nightdress. Suddenly he felt a chill as he imagined her having all the warmth she needed in someone else's arms. He picked up a piece of straw and started to fiddle with it, remembering the day, all those years ago, when she had promised to be his forever.

Balthazar Jones invited Hebe Grammatikos to Hampstead Ponds two years after they met with the sole motivation of wanting to see her in her red bikini. When they arrived, she immediately took up a horizontal position on the bank in her new swimwear, her hair forming a black halo on the grass. When he tried to lure her into the water, she insisted that it was too cold. But the country was experiencing a record-breaking heat wave that had led to the dismissal of a weatherman for a prediction of continual clouds. Refusing to accept her argument, Balthazar Jones eventually talked her into the freshwater pond. It was only when the young soldier went to fetch his camera, and turned to look at her from the bank, that it occurred to him that she might not be able to swim. He watched as she disappeared without a sound into the dusty water shaded by the overhanging oak trees. Several seconds later, she rose again, her hair floating on the water like an oil slick.

When she immediately sunk again he thrashed towards her, and groped with desperate hands for her body. Unable to find her, he breathed in and dived underwater, but failed to see anything in the murky depths. It was only when desperation sharpened his vision that he saw a tendril of black hair floating on the top of the water in the distance. After grabbing her body, as slippery as an eel, he hauled her back to the bank. As he held her, her eyes rolling, he asked her to marry him, as he would rather be betrothed to the dying Hebe Grammatikos than to any other woman alive.

When she eventually came round in the hospital, a piece of pondweed still in her mouth, she was congratulated by the nursing staff for not only having survived, but also for being engaged to be married. During the sultry days of their engagement, while lost in the contentment of each other's arms, they often spoke of the proposal that had been so much more romantic than anything Balthazar Jones could have planned. Hebe Jones's only regret was that she had no memory of him asking her to marry him, as she recalled nothing after walking into the water in the hope that the ability to swim would suddenly come to her like a holy miracle. Each time she asked Balthazar Jones what her reply had been, he would quote back her words that evoked the Greek mysticism of her grandparents: 'It is better to tie your donkey than to look for it.'

*   *   *

The Beefeater was brought round from his memories by a sudden snort from the dreaming bearded pig. Getting up gently so as not to disturb it, he looked at his watch, brushed himself down, and hurried off to meet the man from the Palace before the menagerie opened.

When he pushed open the door of the Rack & Ruin, he saw Oswin Fielding already sitting at the table next to the framed signature of Rudolph Hess. He approached the landlady, and ordered an orange juice, despite his urge for a pint. He carried it past the tables occupied by numerous Beefeaters on their lunch break, and sat down opposite the courtier.

'I'm sorry to hear about your wife,' he said.

Balthazar Jones stared at him. 'How did you hear about that?' he asked.

'It was mentioned. You have my sympathies. My wife left me several years ago. You never get over it.'

Both men stared at their glasses.

'Anyway,' said the courtier eventually. 'Back to the matters at hand. All set for the opening?'

'Yes,' replied the Beefeater. 'Any news about the penguins?'

'Unfortunately not. Thankfully the Argentine Embassy hasn't been in touch, so it seems they're none the wiser. Let's hope they remain that way. We have, however, heard from someone in the Brazilian President's office. It was he who gave the Queen the Geoffroy's marmosets, if you remember. The chap wanted to know why they were flashing their private parts in those photographs taken with you, which, as he pointed out, were used all around the world.'

The Beefeater glanced away. 'Apparently it's something they do when they sense danger,' he muttered.

The equerry frowned. 'Really?' he asked. 'I wasn't entirely sure, so I told them it must have been your uniform.'

'My uniform? What did he say to that?'

'He said that he found it hard to imagine why monkeys would find the sight of a Beefeater in any way sexually alluring. I tried to explain that the Tower of London attracts more than two million visitors a year from all around the world, and they weren't just coming to see the Crown Jewels. "History's a big turn-on," I said.'

'What did he say to that?'

The equerry reached for his glass. 'I'm not entirely sure,' he said. 'It was in Portuguese. Then he hung up.'

*　　　*　　　*

When two o'clock struck, Balthazar Jones opened the gate that led to the moat, and a line of visitors who had been queuing for several hours immediately surged through. The Beefeater decided to follow them in case there were any questions, despite his fear that he would be unable to answer them. They stopped at the empty penguin enclosure and read the information panel that he had had erected, stating that the birds were not only amongst the smallest breed of penguin in the world, but also the most opportunistic. The tourists happily accepted the Beefeater's explanation that they were at the vet's, and then clattered their way along the boardwalk to inspect the President of Russia's gift. Stopping at a sign that said: 'Please feed me', they stood and stared at the small bear-like creature with yellow stripes running down its brown fur. After the recumbent glutton emitted an undignified belch, a young girl asked Balthazar Jones how much the creature ate.

'Even more than the Yeoman Gaoler,' he replied.

As the group headed towards the giraffes, the Beefeater immediately suggested that they go to see the Duchess of York before there was a queue. There was an instant murmur of agreement, and he led them to the Devereux Tower, which had been converted into a monkey house. Once the tourists had got over their disappointment that they were not actually in the presence of Princess Diana's former sister-in-law, but rather a blue-faced, snub-nosed monkey with titian hair, they got out their cameras declaring that the resemblance was nevertheless remarkable. The Beefeater offered to take them to see the birds next, but they were unable to move because of the crowds of visitors flocking up the stairs to see the Geoffroy's marmosets in all their glory.

*   *   *

Irritated by the sudden increase in tourists, the Yeoman Gaoler crossed Tower Green, stopping to point one of them in the direction of the Tower Café. After wishing her good luck, he continued on to the Chapel Royal of St Peter ad Vincula, wondering whether he would ever sleep through the night again. He had been woken in the early hours by the sound of leather boots striding back and forth across the dining room below. Instead of profanities about the Spanish, the house had been filled with poetic entreaties to a woman by the name of Cynthia. It hadn't been long before the stench of tobacco started to seep underneath his bedroom door, increasing his yearning for a cigarette. He remained in bed, his sheets drawn up

170

to his chin, fearing not only for his potatoes, but for the life of Her Majesty's highly strung shrew.

When he and his wife first arrived at the Tower, it had struck them as odd that such a large house was vacant. On learning that its previous tenants had moved to one of the smaller terrace cottages along Mint Lane, they assumed the family had been put off by the windows that were nailed shut, the blocked-up fireplaces, and the numerous locks on the doors. They prised out the nails, opened up the fireplaces, and only drew one bolt at night. Hand-in-hand they chose some new wallpaper, and started to scrape at the nicotine-stained walls, listening to records on the gramophone that had been a wedding present all those years ago. It wasn't long before they discovered the ominous warnings the children of the previous inhabitants had scrawled on the walls. Dismissing them as youthful fantasy, they continued redecorating as they swayed their middle-aged hips to the music they had danced to during their courtship.

Their happiness started to drift when the Yeoman Gaoler's wife accused her husband of having taken up smoking again, which he categorically denied. Each refusal to admit to having succumbed once more to the cursed habit only increased her fury. She named each relative whose life had been dramatically shortened by the vice, but still the smell of tobacco flooded the house each night. Convinced that her husband was going to meet a gruesome early death, she left the Tower in search of a new one, a task that didn't take long on account of her considerable charms.

Unable to bear his empty home where the sight of the gramophone reduced him to tears, the

Yeoman Gaoler spent his evenings in the Rack & Ruin. In between recounting their heroics while serving in the armed forces, the other Beefeaters would boast of their ghostly encounters in the Tower with even greater bravado. A number claimed to have heard the screeches of Margaret Pole, the Countess of Salisbury, who had been chased by a hacking axeman after his first blow failed to remove her head. Several insisted they had seen the white form of Sir Thomas More sitting on one of the chapel's chairs. And all of them were adamant that they had seen the terrifying vision of the Protestant martyr Anne Askew, the only woman ever to have been racked. The Yeoman Gaoler would listen intently, but never once did he reveal that the ghost of Sir Walter Raleigh had taken up residence in his home, something that terrified him more than anything he had witnessed on the battlefield.

The spirit had returned to the Tower to write the second instalment of his *History of the World*. The first, written while serving his thirteen-year sentence, had been an instant hit, outselling the collected works of William Shakespeare. He had assumed that the sequel would come to him with the ease of the first. But when he sat down at his old desk in the Bloody Tower, surrounded by globes and rolled-up maps, he was seized by the torment of second volume syndrome. As he nibbled the end of his quill with tar-stained teeth, desperately seeking the words that evaded him, he became convinced that the success of the first was simply the result of nostalgia for the man who had introduced to England the mighty potato. And not even the ale brought to him by the equally ghostly form of Owen the waterman could help him.

Pushing down the cold handle, the Yeoman Gaoler opened the chapel door and stepped inside. He found Rev. Septimus Drew bent double, trying to remove chewing gum from the bottom of a chair with furious pinches of his pink rubber gloves.

'I need your help,' the Yeoman Gaoler announced as he walked up the aisle.

The clergyman straightened, and rested his pink wrists on his hips.

'Birth, marriage or death?' he asked.

'Exorcism.'

*   *   *

When Hebe Jones returned from her wasted visited to Mrs Perkins, she stood in silence unbuttoning her turquoise coat next to the drawer containing one hundred and fifty-seven pairs of false teeth.

'Any joy?' Valerie Jennings asked.

'It was the wrong person,' she replied, taking the urn out of her handbag and returning it to her desk.

There was a moment of silence.

'Going anywhere nice?' Valerie Jennings asked.

'No. Why?'

'The suitcase under your desk.'

It didn't take long for the tears to come. Hebe Jones cried for her husband who, up until the tragedy, she still looked forward to seeing after three decades of marriage. She cried for Milo, all alone in heaven, whom she couldn't wait to join. And just when she thought she had finished, she cried for the stranger who had lost the remains of Clementine Perkins, whom she wasn't able to find. It wasn't until over an hour later, when Valerie Jennings had installed her in the armchair with the pop-up leg rest, and carried her suitcase to the spare room, that her tears finally stopped.

12

Rev. Septimus Drew strode across Tower Green, leaving large, dark footprints on the stiff, frosted grass. Much of the night had been spent agonising over Ruby Dore's affection for the creature not worthy of a mention in the Bible, and lamenting his failure to seduce her with his mother's treacle cake. By the time he woke, there had not even been time for the delights of Fortnum & Mason's thick-cut marmalade. He left the fortress as fast as his excessively long legs could carry him, ignoring the Yeoman Gaoler calling his name from his bedroom window. As he sat on the Tube carriage, heading for the shelter for retired prostitutes, his fingers worked their way into the cake tin on his lap, and he broke off a small piece of biscuit from the batch he had baked for them. Each had been shaped into the form of a disciple, their distinguishing features meticulously piped with white icing. As he nibbled, he hoped that none of the ladies would notice that Judas Iscariot's legs were missing.

By the time he arrived, the matron had already shown the new resident to her room with its single bed surmounted by a wooden cross. Sitting opposite her in the communal living room, the chaplain explained that she would be given free board and lodging for six months, during which time she would be helped to find alternative employment. In the meantime, she could, if she wished, assist the other women in the vegetable garden, which had become a labour of love. For, he explained, apart from prayer, there was nothing more restorative for the soul than growing something in God's good earth. He offered the woman the tin of biscuits, and she helped herself with painted fingernails. After brushing the crumbs from her red lips, she congratulated the clergyman on his talent for baking, and then politely enquired whether Judas Iscariot had really been disabled.

When the chaplain returned to the Tower, and stood at his blue front door searching in his pocket for the key, a tourist approached and asked whether he knew where the zorilla was kept. 'Down there, on the right,' the clergyman replied pointing. 'Follow your nose.' Once inside, he locked the door behind him, and headed up the battered wooden stairs to his study. Arming himself with his fountain pen, he started to compose a sermon of sufficient intrigue to keep the Beefeaters from sleeping slumped against the radiators.

The clergyman was so engrossed in his work that he failed to hear the first knock at the front door. He ignored the second one, fearing it was the chairwoman of the Richard III Appreciation Society. He had spotted her sitting on a bench by the White Tower on his return, and instantly recognised a woman burning with desire to impart the society's latest evidence that the maligned monarch had the most waterproof of alibis.

On the third knock, Rev. Septimus put down his pen with irritation, and stood with his forehead against the cold window as he peered down to see who was beating at his door. His heart tightened the moment he saw Ruby Dore blowing on to her hands and stamping her feet in the cold. He descended with such a commotion that when he opened the door the landlady enquired whether he had fallen down the stairs.

Panicked and delighted in equal measures at the surprise visit, the clergyman stood back to let her in. He indicated the way to the kitchen, not wanting her to see his melancholic bachelor's sitting room, particularly with its biography of Queen Victoria's rat-catcher on the armchair. But as he offered her a seat at the scrubbed-top table, he wondered whether he had made the right decision after all. There, on the counter, was the mournful teapot for one, with its matching single cup; sitting in the vegetable rack was a solitary carrot sprouting roots; and propped up on the window sill was an excessively thumbed edition of *Solo Suppers*. He busied himself filling the kettle to hide his unease, and eventually turned to face her again holding two mugs out in front of him.

'Tea or coffee?' he asked.

'Coffee, please,' she replied, taking off the lavender scarf she had knitted, and resting it on the table.

Once they were sitting opposite each other Ruby Dore covered her face with both hands and muttered through her fingers: 'I've got something to confess.'

The chaplain was about to explain that he didn't do confessions, and she'd be better off with the Catholics down the road, but the landlady continued. She had intended to return the cake that he had left behind in the pub, she insisted. But when she opened the lid and smelt it, she couldn't resist having a slice. She then had a second just to confirm that it was as good as she had thought. Deciding that she couldn't return a partially eaten cake, she promptly finished it. 'I had thought about blaming the canary, but I didn't think you'd buy that,' she admitted.

Rev. Septimus Drew dismissed the apology with a bat of a hand, insisting that her lack of resistance was a compliment to his mother, whose recipe it was. The landlady immediately asked for a copy, and he wrote it down with the flamboyant penmanship of a victim of love. As they drank their coffee, Ruby Dore told him of the latest object she had acquired for her collection of Tower artefacts: a pot of rouge said to have been used by Lord Nithsdale for his escape from the Tower in 1716 dressed as a woman. The clergyman replied that out of all the escapes, the bearded Jacobite's was his favourite, and that he hoped one day to visit Traquair House in the Scottish Borders where the woman's cloak he had worn was on display.

As the landlady got up to leave, Rev. Septimus Drew suddenly felt the bruise of loneliness. 'Do you fancy going to see the museum in Westminster Abbey this morning?' he suddenly found himself asking. 'The exhibits include what is probably the oldest stuffed parrot in the world.'

Once Ruby Dore had left to find someone to

take her place behind the bar, the chaplain fled upstairs. He took off his cassock, combed his hair hard, and returned to his place at the kitchen table hoping that she would be in luck. It wasn't long before she reappeared, having bribed a Beefeater's wife with a bottle of wine to stand in for her.

They squeezed their way out of the Tower through the tourists, and were equally taken aback by the length of the queue waiting to get in. Sitting opposite each other on the Tube, they discussed the extraordinary popularity of the royal menagerie, which had taken everyone by surprise. It wasn't until the chaplain had finished telling her of his affection for the Jesus Christ lizards that he noticed that he had forgotten to put on his socks before leaving.

When they arrived at the Abbey, Ruby Dore asked whether he minded if they had a quick look at the monument to Sir Isaac Newton, who had been Master of the Royal Mint, based at the Tower, for twenty-eight years. They stood side by side looking at the relief panel on the sarcophagus showing naked boys holding up a gold ingot, containers of coins, and firing up a kiln. Much to her delight, the chaplain then took her to Poets' Corner to show her the grey Purbeck marble monument to Geoffrey Chaucer, who had been Clerk of Works at the fortress from 1389 to 1391.

Stopping briefly to point out Britain's oldest door, thought to have been built in the 1050s, Rev. Septimus Drew led the way to the museum in the eleventh-century vaulted undercroft of St Peter. Ruby Dore gazed in wonderment at the collection of life-size effigies of kings, queens and society figures, most of them dressed in their own clothes, and all, except Lord Nelson, buried in the Abbey.

The clergyman explained that at one time the bodies of dead monarchs were embalmed and put on display for the funeral procession and service. Later, effigies were used instead due to the length of time it took to prepare for the ceremony. After 1660, effigies no longer formed part of the funeral procession, replaced by a gold crown on a purple cushion, but were used to mark the place of burial.

He showed her the cabinet bearing the oldest: Edward III made from a hollowed-out piece of walnut wood. The fourteenth-century curiosity had been analysed by an expert from the Metropolitan Police Laboratory. 'Its few surviving eyebrow hairs were found to be those of a small dog,' he added.

As they moved on to Henry VII, the clergyman pointed out that his face, with its lop-sided mouth, hollow cheeks, and tightly set jaw, was based on his death mask.

Ruby Dore wandered over to Nelson, bought in 1806 to attract people visiting his tomb in St Paul's Cathedral back into the fee-charging Abbey. Joining her, Rev. Septimus Drew pointed out: 'His left eye appears to be blind, instead of his right.'

Finally, the couple approached the Duchess of Richmond and Lennox, dressed in the robes she wore for the Coronation of Queen Anne in 1702. Ruby Dore immediately bent down to take a closer look at the historic stuffed parrot perched on a bracket next to the effigy, which for centuries had attracted a pilgrimage of myopic taxidermists from around the world, who knelt in reverence in front of the holy specimen.

As she contemplated the bird, Rev. Septimus Drew, whose fascinating insights into the collection had earned him a number of eavesdroppers, recounted the tale of the parrot and the Duchess. When Frances Stuart was appointed maid of honour to Charles II's wife, such was the teenager's beauty the King immediately fell for her. But he was not the only one to have noticed the considerable virtues of the girl, later used as a model for Britannia on medals. In an attempt to seduce her, an infatuated courtier gave her a young parrot as a love token, acquired from a Portuguese sailor who had been blown off course. The bird spoke nothing but Portuguese profanities, and Frances Stuart devoted so much time trying to coax out of it the simplest of English niceties that the King, jealous of the attention she gave the creature, attempted all manner of subterfuge to kill it. But the wily bird picked out the poisoned nuts from its bowl, instantly spotted the toes of the servants hiding behind the tapestries with nets, and immediately sensed when a hand approached not to tickle its throat, but to throttle it.

Frances Stuart eventually eloped and married the Duke of Richmond and Lennox. But when she returned to court, the King was just as bewitched, and his jealousy of the foul-mouthed bird was as fierce as his adoration for its mistress. At his darkest moments, he swore that the parrot had been his life's most confounding love rival. When, in 1702, the Duchess eventually passed away, the parrot mourned in the most eloquent of English, and then died six days later. The parrot was stuffed and displayed with her memorial effigy out of respect for its forty-year friendship. And the King, long since buried in the Abbey, was unable to overrule her instructions.

Ruby Dore was so delighted by the account, that on the way out she bought a postcard of the Duchess, which sadly lacked her much more famous pet. And, as she walked back to Westminster station with Rev. Septimus Drew, she wondered why so many men spun stories of their own brilliance, when women would much rather hear an intriguing tale about a stuffed parrot.

*   *   *

'A-four,' said Valerie Jennings, casting a furtive look at her colleague underneath her lustrous eyelashes.

Hebe Jones looked down at the grid she had drawn. 'Miss,' she replied. A moment later she announced: 'F-three.'

'Hit,' replied Valerie Jennings, frowning. 'C-five.'

'You've just sunk my destroyer,' Hebe Jones admitted, reaching to answer the phone.

Valerie Jennings had suggested a game of Battleship after noticing Hebe Jones gazing into the distance again, lost in a world that no longer existed. She handed her a piece of paper and challenged her to a game, hoping that it would distract her from her troubles. She had fully intended to let her houseguest win, but once they had drawn their grids and positioned their ships, Valerie Jones completely forgot about raising the other woman's spirits. Instead, she set about annihilating the enemy vessels with the ruthlessness of a pirate, brandishing her cutlass the moment she suspected that Hebe Jones had placed one of her submarines diagonally, which was in

181

strict contravention of the rules of the high seas.

Recognising she had now sunk Hebe Jones's entire fleet, Valerie Jennings decided to clean the fridge as a means of atonement. Squeezing her feet back into her high-heeled shoes that forced her toes into two red triangles, she stood up and armed herself with a pair of yellow rubber gloves and a damp cloth. As she bent over to see inside, several of her curls sprung from their mooring on the back of her head, and no matter how many times she pushed them away, they returned to obscure her vision with the persistence of flies. Infuriated, she looked around for a solution, and spotted a plastic Viking helmet on one of the shelves. She pulled it on, tossed its yellow plaits over her shoulders, and returned to her penitence. As she threw out an empty cake box, a relic of the glory days of elevenses, she bitterly regretted not having worn make-up for her lunch with Arthur Catnip.

When the Swiss cowbell rang, Hebe Jones instantly recognised an attempt at the Greek national anthem. She got up to answer it, stopping on the way to twirl the dial on the safe, as was the office custom.

As soon as she arrived, Thanos Grammatikos returned the bell to the counter and kissed his cousin on the cheek. Following her wasted trip to Mrs Perkins, Hebe Jones had given up the needle-in-a-haystack method, and asked him to stop by and look at the urn. While he had only a rudimentary knowledge of the dark art of carpentry, proven by his needing to have a finger stitched back on, Hebe Jones hoped he would be able to shed some light on the unusual wood.

'So how's everything?' he asked. 'I saw Balthazar's picture in the paper the other week. Why were all those monkeys flashing their bits behind him?'

'I didn't like to ask,' Hebe Jones replied.

He looked at the urn she was holding. 'Is this it?' he asked, taking it in his hands, and running his fingers over the cream wood. 'To be honest, I've never seen it before. Do you mind if I show it to someone?'

'You won't lose it, will you?' Hebe Jones asked.

'Name me one thing I've ever lost.'

'Your finger.'

'That was never lost. It was on the floor all the time.'

'Well, take care of those ashes,' she said. 'They've already been lost once.'

As Hebe Jones returned to her desk, her stomach emitted a low thunderous rumble. Like whales calling to each other, it was shortly answered by a similar sound coming from the figure stooped over the fridge. Hebe Jones recognised instantly the cause. The once sacred ritual of elevenses, a practice governed strictly by Valerie Jennings, had, since her lunch with Arthur Catnip, been reduced to a sliced apple and a cup of jasmine tea. As the pitiful sound started up again underneath her own blouse, Hebe Jones stood up and announced that she was just popping out for a minute.

As she stood at the head of the queue in the coffee shop round the corner, pointing the assistant's tongs to the largest flapjack in the counter, she suddenly felt a tap on the shoulder. She turned round and instantly recognised the

183

soft, dark eyes and neat hair marbled with silver.

'I thought it was you,' said Tom Cotton, smiling. 'I was the one who lost a kidney, remember?' He invited her to sit with him, and pointed to his table. Reasoning that a quick chat with him would give her sufficient time to eat her snack before returning to the office, Hebe Jones paid the assistant and followed him.

'Have you seen the papers today?' he asked as she sat down. 'Someone's spotted the bearded pig that escaped from London Zoo.' He held out his newspaper, and showed her the blurred photograph taken by a reader in Tewkesbury of a creature rampaging across the bottom of his garden.

'It doesn't look much like a pig to me,' she said, peering at it. 'It looks more like the Loch Ness monster.'

Tom Cotton opened a sachet of sugar and poured it into his coffee. 'That kidney you helped me get back saved a boy's life, you know,' he said.

Hebe Jones put down the paper. 'How old was he?' she asked.

'About eight, I think.'

Hebe Jones remained silent for so long, he asked her whether she was feeling all right.

'They couldn't save my son's life,' she said eventually, raising her eyes. 'The doctors insisted there was nothing they could do, but you never stop wondering.'

'I'm so sorry,' he said.

'Do you have any children?' she asked.

Tom Cotton picked up a spoon. 'Twins,' he replied, stirring his drink. 'They lived with their mother after we got divorced. It was really difficult

184

just seeing them at weekends. I can't imagine what you've been through,' he said.

Hebe Jones glanced away. 'Some people think they can,' she said. 'You'd be surprised how many bring up the death of their pet.'

They sat in silence.

'What was he like?' he asked.

'Milo?' she asked with a smile. 'I called him the apple of my eye, and he was.' She told him how she had fallen in love with her son the moment she saw him, and while younger mothers would complain about lack of sleep, she always looked forward to his cries in the night so that she could take him in her arms, rest her cheek against his velvet head, and sing him the Greek lullabies that had sent generations of her family to sleep. She told him that when she took Milo for his first day at school, dressed in the trousers that his father had insisted on making for him, she had cried more than all the children put together. She told him how terrified he had been when they first moved to the Tower, but he had soon grown to love it, which had made the place so much more bearable for her. She told him how he had wanted to become a vet ever since the family tortoise lost her tail, and despite his mystification when it came to science, she was certain he would have succeeded. She told him how his best friend had been a girl called Charlotte, who also lived at the Tower, and how she had hoped that one day the pair would marry as only his father had been able to make him laugh more than the girl did. And she told him how nobody had made *her* laugh more than her husband, but that those days were now gone because after they had lost Milo, they had lost each other.

*   *   *

When Hebe Jones finally returned to the Lost Property Office, Valerie Jennings had finished cleaning the fridge and was on the phone.

'We might have,' she replied evenly, casting a look at the magician's box. 'No, it doesn't sound like the one we've got . . . It was found about two years ago . . . I see, but if you lost it that long ago why has it taken you all this time to ask for it back? . . . What were you in prison for, if it's not impertinent of me to ask? . . . I see . . . No, no I quite understand, I'm useless with a saw myself . . . You have my sympathies. Glamorous assistants aren't what they used to be . . . Well, as I say, it doesn't sound like yours, but you're most welcome to come and have a look at it . . . Baker Street . . . For our more costly items we do like to see some proof of ownership—a receipt or a photograph, for example . . . Not at all. See you tomorrow then . . . Valerie. Valerie Jennings.'

Just as she put down the phone, the Swiss cowbell sounded. Offering to answer it, she stood up, and pulled her skirt down over her splendid thighs. On the way, she stopped at the safe, bent down, and turned the dial left and right, entering her vital statistics as all else had failed. Just as she straightened up, the heavy grey steel door swung open. Hebe Jones turned immediately on hearing the shriek.

The two women stood side by side looking down at the safe's open door.

'Go on then,' encouraged Hebe Jones. 'Have a

186

look what's in it.'

Valerie Jennings crouched down and reached inside. Out came bundle after bundle of fifty-pound notes, which she stacked on top of the safe around the kettle. She then put her hand in again, and withdrew a pile of documents. The two women stared at the money.

'How much do you think is there?' Hebe Jones whispered.

'Thousands,' Valerie Jennings whispered back. She looked down at the documents she was holding.

'What's in that folder?' Hebe Jones asked.

'It looks like some sort of parchment,' she replied holding it up.

Just at that moment the Swiss cowbell sounded again. Both women ignored the noise as they gazed at the fortune and then at the ancient manuscript. But the clanking continued. Valerie Jennings tutted, passed the papers to Hebe Jones, and went to answer it.

As she turned the corner, intoxicated with victory having finally opened the safe, she saw Arthur Catnip standing at the original Victorian counter. The ticket inspector appeared equally surprised to see her.

'I was just wondering whether I could take you out for lunch again,' he asked.

'That would be lovely,' she replied.

'How about tomorrow at twelve o'clock?'

'Splendid,' she said, and disappeared back round the corner to recover from her second shock. It was only when she was standing in front of the safe again and tried to relieve an itch on her scalp that she realised that she was still wearing the Viking helmet, from which hung two blonde woollen plaits.

*   *   *

Balthazar Jones sat alone at a table in the far corner of the Rack & Ruin, a hand round an empty pint glass. It had been a while since he had been in, as he had been trying to avoid the commiserations of the other Beefeaters over his wife's departure. Eventually, the ale lured him back, and he was relieved to find that the afternoon drinkers failed even to acknowledge his presence. Their arguments long forgotten, they stood captivated by the spectacle of Dr Evangeline Moore's first game of Monopoly. She had chosen as her weapon the landlady's alternative to the historic boot: a thrupenny bit her mother used to hide in the Christmas pudding, not so much to bestow good fortune on its finder as in the hope of choking her husband. The Beefeater sat shredding a beer mat, completely oblivious to the outrageous bets being laid around him. During the brief moments of respite from mourning his marriage, his mind filled with worries about the collection of royal beasts. While the animals appeared well enough—apart from the wandering albatross that had failed to settle—Balthazar Jones regarded the menagerie as a delicately balanced house of cards, susceptible to the faintest stirring of an ill wind. What he hadn't foreseen, however, was that it would be one of the Tower residents who would attempt to blow it down. Realising he could put off the moment no longer, he got to his feet, and on his way out, pinned a notice on the board stating that if anyone had lost a gentleman's vest they could collect it from the Salt Tower.

Resigned to yet another dressing down, he dawdled down Water Lane to his appointment with the Chief Yeoman Warder, hoping that a tourist would stop him to ask a question. But for once, it seemed that everyone knew the way to the lavatories. He knocked lightly on the office door so that he wouldn't be heard, but immediately a voice called to him to enter. Balthazar Jones stepped in and found the Chief Yeoman Warder sitting behind his desk, having just returned from a home-cooked lunch.

'Yeoman Warder Jones, have a seat,' he said, gesturing to the chair in front of him. The Beefeater took off his hat, placed it on his lap, and held on to its brim.

The Chief Yeoman Warder leant forward, resting his elbows on the desk. 'How is everything?' he asked.

'Fine,' the Beefeater replied evenly.

'Splendid. I thought you would like to know that the Palace has been in touch, and they're very pleased with the way the menagerie is shaping up. Visitor figures are up considerably compared to this time last year, and press coverage, both national and international, has been largely positive.'

The Beefeater remained silent.

The Chief Yeoman Warder then picked up a pen and started rolling it between his fingertips. 'There were, of course, those unfortunate pictures of you and the marmosets at the beginning. Hopefully the papers won't use them again now that we've allowed them to take photographs of the animals at the Tower. What was all that about, by the way?'

The Beefeater swallowed. 'They expose themselves when they feel threatened,' he said.

'I see.'

There was a pause.

The Chief Yeoman Warder glanced down at his file. 'Now,' he continued, 'there have been one or two complaints. And while I'm well aware that people are never happier than when they're moaning, they need to be addressed. The first one is the penguins. When will they be back from the vet's?'

Balthazar Jones scratched at his beard. 'Any day now,' he replied.

'Good. The sooner the better,' he said, tapping the desk with his pen. 'I don't like the look of that empty enclosure. It gives the impression that they've escaped like that bearded pig from London Zoo. Bunch of amateurs. Now, the second matter is a complaint from the Tower residents with regards to the wandering albatross. Apparently some of the Yeoman Warders can't sleep because it keeps wailing, which sets off all the other birds, and then the howler monkeys start up.' He sat back in his chair, his elbows on the armrests. 'Personally, I can sleep through mortar fire, but not everyone has my constitution.'

'I'll sort out the albatross,' said Balthazar Jones.

'Glad to hear it. Now keep up the good work. I don't want that lot at the Palace on my back if anything goes wrong.'

*   *   *

When Balthazar Jones returned to the Salt Tower,

190

he stood emptying his pockets of apples and sunflower seeds on to the coffee table. He didn't bother to turn on the light or draw the curtains, and sat on the sofa in the darkness. As he looked at the pale crease of the moon, he wondered again where his wife was. Eventually, he got up to make some toast, brought it back to the living room, and turned on the lamp. As he sat eating, his attention was caught by the front end of the pantomime horse, whose ears he still hadn't brought himself to sew back on. Looking away, he noticed the photograph taken of Milo holding the precious ammonite he had found while fossil hunting in Dorset. He lowered his eyes, but they fell to his wife's shoes.

Abandoning his supper, he scuffed his way up the cold spiral staircase, no longer caring that he was retracing the steps of a thirteenth-century Scottish king. He ran himself a bath, but as he lay back in the water he thought of his terrible secret, and what Hebe Jones would say if she ever found out. Too distressed to linger, he got out of the water.

After putting on his pyjamas, he looked at the armchair by the window where he had slept since finding his wife's letter the previous week. Unable to bear another night of crooked slumber, he climbed into his side of the bed and turned off the light. As sleep continued to evade him, he reached out a hand and felt around in the darkness. Eventually, his fingers found what they were searching for. Pulling the white nightdress towards him, he held it to his face and inhaled. He was still clutching it several hours later when he woke from a dream that Hebe Jones was lying next to him,

191

and the arrows of abandonment rained down on him once more.

He escaped to the bathroom, and sat on the side of the tub, putting off his return to bed. As he stared at the floor, he noticed a piece of brown lettuce on the carpet. Suddenly he realised that he hadn't seen Mrs Cook for a week, and a hand gripped his heart as he thought of the creature's exalted heritage.

Mrs Cook was no ordinary tortoise, but the daughter of a pet once owned by Captain Cook. The explorer had taken one look at her mother's alluring markings, and carried her on board the HMS *Resolution*, where she was given the run of the deck. In 1779, when the ship arrived in Hawaii during a festival of worship for a Polynesian god, a number of the locals mistook the Yorkshireman for a deity. In an effort to distract them from their conviction, he gave them his most treasured possession: the ship's mascot.

Almost a year later, the reptile, which had a natural propensity for absconding, was noticed on the beach by a seaman from a visiting ship. Convinced that tortoises were good omens at sea, he picked her up, and presented her to the crew with the fanfare of a showman once they had set sail. She became the pride of the vessel, and at night he would recount tales of spectacular fortunes enjoyed by crews with a tortoise on board.

But the ship was blown off-course, and soon the sailors had finished the rations. The starving men began to gaze at the creature with gastronomic longing. One of them stood up and announced that he was sure that it was black cats that were good omens for sailors. Another joined him, and eventually the entire crew agreed that the seaman had been mistaken.

The following day, pirates attacked the ship. When the seaman was taken by gunpoint on board the enemy vessel, he grabbed the bucket in which he had hidden the maligned mascot. Instructed to prepare the meals, he made sure that each was as near a culinary masterpiece as possible, given the limitations of ships' biscuits. When the vessel eventually docked at Plymouth, he was rewarded with his freedom and returned home to South Wales with his bucket. He presented the tortoise to his wife, who made a small fortune showing her to the good people of Gower, who refused to believe in the existence of a creature that carried its home on its back.

13

Balthazar Jones stirred, his bearded cheek pressed against his wife's cotton nightgown. As usual upon waking he felt the ache of her absence, but as he lay with his eyes still closed, he sensed that something else was wrong. As soon as he remembered the piece of withered lettuce on the bathroom floor his eyes opened.

Casting back the shabby blanket, he fed his feet into his tartan slippers. Tying his dressing gown across the gentle hillock of his stomach, he started to search for the creature that had been considered the matriarch of the family for generations of Joneses. First he looked in the bathroom airing cupboard, the door of which was kept ajar so that she could enter, lest the Salt Tower's bitter temperature condemned her to a permanent state of hibernation. He tried her lairs in the bedroom, peering down the side of the dressing table and behind the wastepaper basket. But all he found were the cobwebs the spiders had spun since Hebe Jones had left.

He descended the spiral staircase to the living room, and gazed down the gap between the back of the sofa and the circular wall. Something was there. But when he shone his torch into the dusty expanse, it turned out to be a ball. Moving aside his wife's easel next to the bookcase, he saw nothing more than an odd black sock. He then lifted up the front end of the pantomime horse, which offered the perfect place for concealment. But all he discovered were the ears that he hadn't brought himself to sew back on.

Head in his hands, he sat in the armchair trying to think when he had last seen her. He recalled the visit of the Tower doctor the previous week, and the arthritic sound of the animal's knees as she got to her feet, but couldn't remember seeing her since. He stood up, and retraced his steps, hunting for evidence of loose bowels. After searching underneath the bed for the seventh time, he sat on the floor with his back against the dresser feeling utterly alone in the world.

*   *   *

Rev. Septimus Drew worked a finger between each of his pale toes as he sat in bath water infused with tea tree oil. It wasn't a belief that cleanliness was next to Godliness that led to such meticulousness, but the conviction that prevention was better than cure. While he didn't get caught in the rain as often as the Beefeaters, he nevertheless feared succumbing to the fungus that flourished on the backs of their knees. As he lay back in the fragrant water, his mind turned to the invitation he had just opened, and he wondered again whether he stood any real chance of winning the Erotic Fiction Award. Having never come first at anything in his life, he put the possibility of victory out of his mind, and closed his eyes.

As he relived his trip to the Abbey's museum with Ruby Dore there was a knock on the front door. He rose with the thrust of a whale, slopping water over the side of the bath, hoping it was the landlady. Wrapping himself in a dressing gown, he made his way to one of the spare bedrooms at the front of the house, leant his forehead against the cold windowpane, and looked down. There, standing on his doorstep was the Yeoman Gaoler. The chaplain had been avoiding the man ever since agreeing to perform the exorcism. He was just about to hide behind the curtain when the Beefeater looked up and their eyes met. Unable to pretend to be out, as he had done on the three previous occasions, the chaplain heaved up the sash window and called: 'I'll be down in a minute!'

Dripping his way back to the bathroom, he took off his damp robe, and, as he dried his excessively long legs, wondered why he had always been so hopeless at exorcisms. It was a skill that would evidently be of great use to his congregation. While many of the Beefeaters boasted about the ghosts they claimed to have seen around the Tower, never once did they speak to anyone other than the chaplain about the spectral apparitions in their own homes, as they were a terror too far. Despite the number of times that he had been asked to perform one, he had never quite got the hang of the procedure, much to the Beefeaters' infuriation.

Once dressed, he idled his way down the stairs, stopping along the way to inspect a mark on the banister.

'Yes?' he said, opening the door.

'I was wondering if you'd come and sort out that little problem we were talking about,' the Yeoman Gaoler said, the shadows under his eyes even more noticeable in a freak ray of sunshine.

'What little problem?' the chaplain enquired.

The Yeoman Gaoler nodded towards his home. 'You know.'

'I do?'

'Odes to Cynthia? Smell of tobacco? Missing potatoes?'

'Oh, yes,' said the chaplain, starting to close the door. 'Just let me know when you're free and we'll arrange a time.'

The Yeoman Gaoler put a foot against the door frame. 'I'm free now,' he said.

There was a pause.

'Are you sure it's convenient?' queried the chaplain.

'It's been convenient ever since you agreed to do it last week.'

The chaplain followed him to number seven Tower Green, hoping to be waylaid by the chairwoman of the Richard III Appreciation Society. But the bench outside the White Tower was empty. The Yeoman Gaoler opened the door, and stepped back to allow him in. The chaplain immediately headed down the hall, calling out behind him: 'Shall we have a nice cup of tea before we get started? I haven't had my breakfast yet.'

The Yeoman Gaoler caught up with him and blocked the way to the kettle. 'I'd rather get on with it, if you don't mind,' he replied.

Rev. Septimus Drew peered at the cage on the table. 'What's that?' he asked.

'It's the Queen's Etruscan shrew.'

'Let's have a look.'

The Yeoman Gaoler picked up the cage and put it on the counter behind him. 'I'm sorry, it's of a nervous disposition. The dining room is through here,' he said, leading the way.

The clergyman followed and immediately went to inspect the Yeoman Gaoler's long-handled Tudor axe propped up in the corner, which he carried during special ceremonies. 'Your predecessors used this when escorting prisoners to and from their trials at Westminster, didn't they?' asked the chaplain, studying it. 'Am I right in thinking that if the blade was turned towards the prisoner, it meant that they had just been sentenced to death?'

'Aren't you meant to sprinkle some holy water around, or something?' asked the Yeoman Gaoler, ignoring the question.

'Quite right, quite right,' the clergyman replied, patting his cassock pockets for his vial. He then bowed his head, recited a quick prayer, and walked around the room scattering its contents.

'There we are,' he announced with a smile. 'All done!'

The Yeoman Gaoler looked at him,

dumbfounded. 'Is that it? Don't you have to ask it to leave or something?'

The chaplain covered his mouth with his hand. 'Do I?' he asked.

The two men looked at each other.

'No, no, that's so last century,' the clergyman announced, dismissing the suggestion with a bat of his hand. 'Right then, I'd better be off,' he added, heading for the front door.

As the Yeoman Gaoler watched the clergyman stride back across Tower Green, his red cassock flapping, he felt the unease of the duped. He walked back to the kitchen, opened the cage, and offered the Etruscan shrew another cricket, which it sniffed with its pointed velvet nose.

*   *   *

Hebe Jones found a note on the kitchen table from Valerie Jennings saying that she had gone to work early to sort a few things out. As she sat at the table eating a bowl of Special K, having found nothing more substantial in her colleague's cupboards, she looked around at the still unfamiliar surroundings and wondered how long she should stay. While Valerie Jennings had told her that the spare room was hers for as long as she needed it, and had done everything possible to make her feel at home, she didn't want to outstay her welcome. As she stood at the sink and washed up her dish, she decided it was time to dip into the money she had saved for Milo's university education and rent a flat until the tenants' lease was up on their home in Catford.

When she arrived at the Lost Property Office,

she thought she could smell wet paint. Assuming the odour was coming in through the open window, she put the thought out of her mind, and went to make them both some tea. As she waited for the water to boil, she looked down at the safe, firmly closed lest the cleaners made off with its contents, and hoped that her colleague would remember the combination of numbers.

'Did you find everything you needed for breakfast?' Valerie Jennings asked, emerging from the bookshelves.

'Yes, thanks,' she replied looking up. She was instantly reminded that her colleague was meeting Arthur Catnip for lunch again. Valerie Jennings had clearly searched deep within her wardrobe for something suitably flattering, only to retrieve a frock of utter indifference to fashion. There had been an attempt to tame her hair, which seemed to have been abandoned, and the fuzzy results were clipped to the back of her head.

'You look nice,' said Hebe Jones.

Both women sat down at their desks and got on with the business of reuniting lost possessions with their absentminded owners. It was only when Hebe Jones got up to make another cup of tea that she noticed the flagrant transformation. 'The magician's box is pink,' she said, a hand over her mouth.

Valerie Jennings turned round, one eye enlarged by the magnifying glass she was using to scrutinise the ancient manuscript. 'I thought I'd give it a bit of spruce up,' she said.

Returning to her seat, Hebe Jones studied the lotus leaf embroidery on one of the tiny pointed Chinese slippers, keeping her thoughts about her colleague's behaviour to herself. Valerie Jennings had been more than good to her by offering her the spare room when she was too ashamed to ask one of her sisters to put her up. Each evening, instead of asking her questions she couldn't bear to answer, she had simply installed her in the armchair with the pop-up leg rest with a glass of wine. And while she didn't cook their supper with the talent of her sisters, it was certainly with the love of one.

Shortly after elevenses, when Hebe Jones's stomach emitted a roll of thunder, she fetched her turquoise coat from the stand next to the inflatable doll, and announced that she was just popping out for something.

As soon as she was gone, Valerie Jennings slipped her hand into her black handbag, withdrew a paperback, and returned it to its place on the bookshelf. As she scanned the shelves for her next fix, the Swiss cowbell sounded. Irritated at being interrupted during her favourite part of the day, she turned the corner. Standing at the counter was a tall man wearing a black top hat, and a matching cape that flowed down to the floor. Tucked under his arm was a wand.

'I've come to see Valerie Jennings,' he announced, throwing one side of his cape over his shoulder, revealing the red silk lining.

'Oh, yes, I've been expecting you,' she said, opening the hatch. 'Come this way.'

She led him through the office and stopped in front of the magician's box that she had repainted that morning, so that Hebe Jones wouldn't be deprived of her sanctuary. The man ran a white-gloved hand along the surface. 'How strange,' he said. 'It's exactly the same as mine apart from the colour. It's even got the same marks on the wood where I didn't cut straight.'

Valerie Jennings folded her arms across her plump chest, and looked at the prop. 'I'm sure it doesn't help when the glamorous assistant starts screeching,' she said. 'It must be difficult telling whether she's just putting it on for the audience, or whether you're actually sawing her in half. Anyway, if it's not the right one, I'll show you out. If you'd like to follow me . . .'

When the Swiss cowbell sounded just before noon, Valerie Jennings's heart leapt. She covered her lips with another coat of Lilac Haze, and walked to the coat stand in shoes that forced her toes into two red triangles. But when she turned the corner, instead of the tattooed ticket inspector, she found a woman in a duffel coat and beret in tears. 'Has anyone handed in a boot?' she enquired, gripping the edge of the counter.

It was no ordinary boot, she went on to explain, as it had once belonged to Edgar Evans, the Welsh petty officer who had died while returning from the South Pole under the command of Captain Scott. The curator recounted how she had suddenly fled the carriage when she realised that she was travelling south on the Northern Line instead of north as the name suggested. It was only when the doors had shut that it occurred to her that she had left behind the historic footwear, which was to be triumphantly united with the explorer's other one, for decades the crowning glory of Swansea Museum, labelled simply as 'Evans's Boot'.

Hunting amongst the shelves, Valerie Jennings

eventually found it next to a pair of angling waders in the footwear section. When she returned with it to the counter, considerably hotter and crosser, the woman promptly burst into tears again and subjected her to an oral biography of Edgar Evans, warning her never to confuse him with Teddy Evans, Scott's second-in-command on the expedition.

'Good gracious me, I wouldn't dream of confusing him with *Teddy* Evans,' Valerie Jennings assured her, snapping the ledger shut to signal an end to the Antarctic ramble. Just as she was sliding it on to the shelf below the counter Arthur Catnip arrived. The battleground of his hair had been razed with the pomade that his barber had given him in retribution for the previous assault, and it now bore the shine of an ice rink.

Instantly regretting not having taken off her coat as she had started to sweat, Valerie Jennings accompanied him to the street, wondering where they were going. Eventually she found that they were in Regent's Park again, and the ticket inspector pointed to a bench by the fountain suggesting that they sit down.

'I've brought a picnic,' he announced, as he open his rucksack, and spread a rug on her knees. 'Let me know if you get cold.'

As Valerie Jennings helped herself to a roast pork sandwich, she told him that, according to the papers, there had been two further sightings of the bearded pig in Essex and East Anglia. Arthur Catnip replied that if he spotted it in his garden, he would never tell the press as the last thing he'd want would be a herd of journalists trampling all over his vegetable patch.

He offered her a pastry parcel, which Valerie Jennings eyed suspiciously. After her first mouthful, she congratulated him on his salmon en croute, and told him that she'd once gone salmon fishing with her ex-husband, and had been so bored that she threw herself into the river so that they would have to go home. Arthur Catnip helped himself to a tomato and replied that he had once thrown a sailor overboard after he made a comment about his then wife, but immediately dived in to rescue him as he realised that he had a point.

As the ticket inspector looked at the fountain, he recalled the time he poured car anti-freeze into the garden pond one winter, as his biology teacher had told him that the fish in Antarctica had anti-freeze in their blood so they wouldn't freeze solid. But when he went back to check on them, all his father's koi carp had died. Wiping a corner of her mouth on her napkin, Valerie Jennings told him how she had just handled a boot that had belonged to Teddy Evans, the petty officer who died on his way back from Scott's ill-fated trek to the South Pole. He was not, she pointed out, to be confused with Edgar Evans, Scott's second-in-command on the same expedition.

*　　　*　　　*

Once the Tower had closed, Balthazar Jones headed to the aviary, his nose numb with cold having led the last tour of the day. It had been a particularly busy afternoon, during which he had found time to take some of the tourists around the enclosures. His motivation was not so much to act as a guide—maps had been produced indicating where each animal was housed—as to keep an eye on his charges. He had already noticed that a number of the sightseers were off-loading their sandwiches and pastries bought in error from the Tower Café on to the glutton. But even the creature with the enormous appetite had refused them, and the waste was piling up in its pen.

As he climbed the Brick Tower's stairs clutching a Hamleys carrier bag, he thought again of the gentleman's vest he had found, and wondered why no one had come to claim it. As he pushed open the door, the King of Saxony bird of paradise jumped to a lower branch, its two blue brow feathers that stretched twice the length of its body looping gracefully through the air. The tiny hanging parrot opened one eye from its upside down slumber, and watched as the Keeper of the Royal Menagerie unlocked the wire door and entered the aviary. As he looked around, the female lovebird glided down from its perch and landed on his shoulder. Searching for a telltale pair of ugly feet, the Beefeater eventually found the wandering albatross sitting alone behind a potted tree, its black and white wings tightly drawn in. He sat down beside it, and pulled from his pocket his special purchase. Unwrapping it under the continuing one-eyed gaze of the emerald parrot, he laid the organic squid flat on his palm, and offered it to the melancholic bird. But the thinning creature refused to look at it. The Beefeater and albatross remained where they were, both staring into the distance, seeing nothing but their troubles. It was almost an hour later that the bird finally lifted its neck and nibbled at the gastronomic gift with its huge hooked beak, by which time the parrot had nodded off again. When it had finished eating, Balthazar Jones got to his feet, followed by the bird, which immediately shook its feathers and released a watery deposit. The Beefeater opened the carrier bag, drew out a white toy duck, the nearest thing he could find resembling an albatross, and placed it next to the creature before leaving.

He made his way through the gloom to the Salt Tower, and, after closing the door behind him, felt too defeated to climb the dank stairs to the empty living room. Sitting down on the dusty bottom step in the darkness, he rested his hairy white cheeks on his fists. His thoughts immediately found their way back to his wife, and he cursed himself for losing her. He wondered again about calling, but his conviction that he didn't deserve her chased away the thought. Eventually he stood up, and as he groped around for the light switch, his fingers brushed the door handle of Milo's bedroom, which he hadn't entered since that terrible, terrible day. Overcome by an urge to enter, he pressed down on the latch, the sharp noise echoing in the blackness. Pushing open the door, he ran a hand along the rough wall for the switch, and shielded his eyes with his hand until he got used to the light.

It took a while to take everything in. There on the wall above the neatly made up bed was the world map which had eventually replaced the dinosaur poster he had bought his son from the Natural History Museum to help him settle into his new home. He looked at the little black cross Milo had drawn marking the mouth of the Orinoco River where his favourite prisoner, Sir Walter

Raleigh, had started his search for El Dorado. On top of the chest of drawers stood the swing mirror that the Beefeater had spotted in the window of an antique shop and instantly bought, despite the imaginative price, to save him from trying to mount one on the circular walls. Next to it was a bottle of aftershave, despite the fact that the boy had been too young to need a razor, which Hebe Jones had insisted was proof that Milo was in love with Charlotte Broughton.

He approached the chest of drawers, picked up the brush and touched the dark hairs caught in it. He remembered telling Milo that he hoped he had inherited his mother's genes and wouldn't turn grey as early as he had. He stood in front of the bookshelf, and bent down to read the spines. Picking up a matchbox in front of the Harry Potter novels, he pushed it open and immediately recognised the fifty pence piece that had travelled through the boy's intestines to near lethal effect. He reached for the ammonite next to it, rubbing it between his fingers as he remembered Milo's delight at finding it. As he returned it to the shelf, he spotted a photograph between two books. He tugged it out and when he looked at the smiling picture of Charlotte Broughton standing on the battlements, he realised that his wife had been right all along.

Pulling back the chair, he sat down at the desk, and ran his palms over the wood, which his wife had kept dusted. He peered at the row of files, and took one out that he recognised. Glued to the front was a piece of paper, not quite square, on which was written: 'Escapes from the Tower of London'. Milo had got the idea for the history project after watching *The Great Escape* one Sunday afternoon with his father, after which the pair had rushed up to the Salt Tower roof with freezer bags, filled them with soil from Hebe Jones's tubs, and released them while walking nonchalantly around the moat, their hands in their pockets.

The Beefeater opened the file, remembering the time they had spent working on it together. They had gone to see Rev. Septimus Drew, an authority on the subject, and had sat in his kitchen eating jam tarts as he launched into his dramatic renditions of nearly forty escapes. Balthazar Jones glanced at the first page devoted to Ranulf Flambard, Bishop of Durham, the first prisoner at the Tower, who happened to also have been the first escapee. He read his son's account of how the Bishop had got his guards drunk and lowered himself down the outer wall on a rope smuggled to him in a gallon of wine.

Turning the page, he came across an essay on John Gerard, who asked his warder for oranges and wrote messages in their juice, legible when held against a candle, on seemingly innocent letters to his supporters. A plan was hatched and the Jesuit priest escaped with fellow prisoner John Arden by climbing along a rope from the Cradle Tower to the wharf. When the Beefeater had finished reading it, he recalled all the secret messages he and Milo had sent each other, much to the irritation of Hebe Jones, who could never find her oranges.

At the end of the folder, he came across several blank pages bearing just the name of a prisoner, and he thought about the distinction Milo would have received had he lived long enough to finish it. He picked up a pencil from a pot at the back of the desk and held it where his son's fingers had once been.

Walking across to the wardrobe, he pulled open the door. Milo's scent instantly hit him, and for a moment he couldn't move. Eventually, he raised both hands and pulled the hangers apart, remembering his son in each item of clothing. He then looked down at the shoes at the bottom of the wardrobe and thought how small they seemed. Unable to bear the familiar smell any longer, he closed the doors, switched off the light, and groping through the darkness, started the slow journey up to his empty home.

14

After one final catastrophic shudder that travelled down to his arthritic knees, the Ravenmaster collapsed on top of Ambrosine Clarke. As he lay breathing in the smell of suet from her hair, the birds continued to fly in hysterical circles in the aviary next to them, startled by the chef's cries of exhalation as she slid back and forth on the wooden floorboards with each thrust of his hips. Eventually the sound of frantic beating of wings subsided, and only the toucans continued carving their multi-coloured loops.

As he pulled on his black ankle socks, he glanced at the cook, rounding up her large, white breasts into her bra, the top of her hair still flattened where he had gripped her head for better purchase. Taken aback, as always, by how quickly the inferno of desire could be extinguished, he reached for his uniform, covered in seed husks. As he pulled on his trousers, his stomach turned at the thought of the torment that followed their clandestine meetings. Sure enough, as soon as they were both dressed, Ambrosine Clarke reached for her basket. Ignoring the Ravenmaster's protests that his appetite had deserted him, the chef unpacked its contents. As he cast an eye over the dishes, he saw that his penitence that morning was the full Victorian breakfast that she had been threatening for several weeks, which included kidneys, haddock in puff pastry, and jelly in the shape of a hare. And as the Ravenmaster forced it down, he was convinced that it was an even greater torture than that inflicted on William Wallace, whose pitiful moans from being racked were sometimes heard echoing through the Brick Tower.

The cook left first, taking care to look through the window before opening the heavy oak door. After pulling on his black leather gloves, the Ravenmaster followed her a few minutes later, the stench of the zorilla causing his stomach to turn again. As he crossed the fortress, which hadn't yet opened to the tourists, his anger at the Queen's animals being housed in the Tower smouldered more fiercely than his heartburn. The visitors had shown little interest in the ravens since the menagerie opened, despite the birds' reputed historic pedigree, and their intelligence that scientists had proved rivalled that of great apes and dolphins. He had frequently complained about the royal beasts in the Rack & Ruin, the sweetness of his orange juice no match for the bitterness spilling from his mouth. However, he rarely found the consensus that he sought. Despite their initial reservations, most of the Beefeaters had developed an affection for the animals, seduced by the glutton's breathtaking appetite; the softness of the reclusive ringtail possums that fell asleep in their arms; the showmanship of the fancy rats, which Ruby Dore had taught to roll tiny barrels along the bar; and the charm of the blue-faced Duchess of York, which clambered into their laps and searched their scalps with the ruthlessness of a nit nurse.

A downpour forced the Ravenmaster into an ungainly run, and he hunched his shoulders to prevent the rain going down his collar. Suddenly the sight of a body stopped him dead in his tracks. He stared in disbelief, then rushed over, emitting a low moan of dread. As the rain pummelled his back, he knelt down on the grass and picked up the raven from a pile of bloodied feathers, searching for signs of life. But its neck lolled backwards, and its glassy eyes failed to flinch despite the rain. He hurried with the creature back to his home, placed it on the dining-room table, and with frantic gasps began to administer the kiss of life.

*　　*　　*

As Balthazar Jones trudged through the rain, a common variety that fell in fat droplets from the brim of his hat, he noticed the Ravenmaster running in the distance, and wondered what he was up to. The previous night, when he had eventually got round to doing his laundry, he picked up the vest he had found and noticed the label of a certain gentlemen's outfitters which the Ravenmaster swore by. He stood next to the washing machine for a considerable time trying to work out how the man's undergarment had come to be on the Brick Tower steps, until the sight of a piece of shrivelled carrot on the floor distracted him, and he started another fruitless search for Mrs Cook.

Clutching a swede for the bearded pig, the Beefeater arrived at the Bowyer Tower to feed the crested water dragons. He was greeted in the doorway by one of the sullen press officers, who had been forced to abandon their comfortable office on the ground floor in order to accommodate the bright green reptiles. Their resulting loathing of the President of Costa Rica on account of his cursed gift had stretched to a ban on coffee drinking in their cramped new premises on the first floor. Not only had the three women suffered the indignity of shifting their desks, but they were now faced with almost constantly ringing phones on account of the number of enquiries from around the world about the new Tower menagerie.

'Ah, Yeoman Warder Jones, I was hoping to catch you,' the woman said, a pink cashmere scarf wrapped around her neck. 'We've had a call from one of the papers in Argentina. They're wondering where the rockhopper penguins are.'

The Beefeater scratched at his wet beard. 'They're at the vet's,' he replied.

'Still?' she enquired.

Balthazar Jones nodded.

'I told her that, but she didn't seem to believe

me,' the press officer said.

The Beefeater looked into the distance. 'Penguins won't be rushed,' he replied.

'I see. We've also had an enquiry from the *Catholic Times* wondering why the crested water dragons are also known as Jesus Christ lizards.'

'Because they can walk on water in emergencies,' he said.

There was a pause.

'The other thing is we've had a couple of calls about the giraffes,' she continued. 'Who were they from again?'

The Beefeater's eyes fell to the vegetable he was holding. 'The Swedes,' he replied.

* * *

Once he had fed the crested water dragons, Balthazar Jones headed through the rain for the Develin Tower, hoping the bearded pig would like its new ball. Just as he was passing the White Tower, he heard footsteps running up behind him. The next thing he knew he was pinned up against the wall by a hand round his throat.

'Which one of the animals did it?' demanded the Ravenmaster.

'Did what?' the Beefeater managed to reply.

'Savaged one of my birds.'

'I don't know what you're talking about.'

The Ravenmaster pressed his face up to Balthazar Jones. 'I've just found Edmund on the lawn. His leg and neck were broken. Which one was it?' he repeated.

'They're all locked up. Always have been.'

The Ravenmaster increased his grip on his neck.

'Well one of them must have escaped,' he hissed.

'Maybe it was a fox, or even the Chief Yeoman Warder's dog,' croaked Balthazar Jones.

'I know it was something to do with you,' the Ravenmaster said, pointing a black leather finger at him as he strode off.

Once he had caught his breath, Balthazar Jones readjusted his hat, and picked up the swede that had tumbled to the ground. While it went against the creature's nature, he wondered whether the bearded pig was responsible, as it was the only animal he hadn't checked on that morning. But when he reached the tower, he found that the door was still locked. Glancing over his shoulder to make sure that he wasn't being watched, he turned the key. As he entered the room, the animal bounded up to him, its tasselled tail flying like a flag over its fulsome buttocks. After scratching the pig behind its ears, the Beefeater presented it with the root vegetable, which it immediately knocked across the floor, and chased. He sat down on the straw, rested his back against the cold wall, and closed his eyes. Raising a hand, he felt his neck with the tips of his fingers.

After a while, he reached into his tunic pocket and drew out some of the love letters he had written to Hebe Jones all those years ago. He had taken them from her hidey-hole during the night while unable to sleep, but hadn't brought himself to read. He looked at the first envelope with its address confused by love, and took out the letter. As he began to read, he remembered the girl with dark hair meandering down the front of her turquoise dress, and her eyes of a fawn that had fixed on him in the corner shop. He remembered that first night together and their horror as they realised they would be parted in the morning. He remembered the first time they had made love during a weekend in Orford, when a power cut in the bar of the Jolly Sailor Inn, built from the timbers of wrecked ships, had driven them to their room earlier than expected. The light from the candle given to them by the landlady lit up the ancient murals of ships, their sails engorged with wind. And, after they had sealed their love, they promised to be with each other until they were so old they had grown a third set of teeth, just like the Indian centenarian they had read about in the paper.

As the bearded pig came to sit by him, resting a whiskered cheek on his thigh, the Beefeater unfolded another letter, feeling the creature's hot breath through his trousers. After reading the outpouring of devotion, he remembered the butterfly that had danced above the pews during their wedding, sending each member of the Grammatikos family into raptures over such a good omen. He remembered how they had vowed to stay together forever, despite what life threw at them, and how at the time it had seemed inconceivable to do otherwise. Looking down at his old man's hands holding the letter he had composed all those years ago, he saw the scratched gold band that had never left his finger since his bride slipped it on at the altar. And he decided to write her another letter.

Carefully locking the door of the Develin Tower behind him, he headed home, a wind of hope behind him. He climbed to the top of the staircase, pressed down on the latch and entered the room

214

where German U-boat men had been imprisoned during the war. Ignoring the chalk swastikas and portrait of Field Marshal Göring drawn on the wall, he pulled back the wooden chair, which scraped mournfully against the pitching floorboards, and sat down at the table he had found in a junk shop. He selected a piece of writing paper from one of the piles, and with the same penmanship that hadn't altered in three decades, wrote the words 'Dear Hebe'.

The outpouring of affection that followed was as fulsome as it was frantic. He told his wife how the seed of their love had been planted during their first night together when she kissed the top of each of his fingers that would have to get used to holding a gun. He told her how he had bitterly regretted having to leave her for the army in the morning, but that the shoots of their love had grown despite the distance between them. He told her how the butterfly had flown into the church and danced over their heads, attracted by their blossoming love. And he told her how Milo, the fruit of their love, had been his life's greatest joy, along with being her husband.

Pausing for a moment, he raised his eyes to the mantelpiece on the other side of the room, seeing nothing but their son a few hours old in his mother's arms, a moment for which they had waited so many years. But his thoughts suddenly turned to that terrible, terrible day, and the blade lodged in his heart plunged even deeper. Knowing his wife would never forgive him if she ever found out what he had done, he tore up the letter. And he sat at the table for the rest of the morning, head in his hands, bleeding with guilt as the rain

215

pounded the windows.

*   *   *

When the door of the cuckoo clock sprung open and the tiny wooden bird shot out to deliver eleven demented cries, Hebe Jones put out the 'Back in 15 minutes' sign, and pulled down the shutter. She waited at her desk, hoping that her colleague's resolve had finally cracked. But when Valerie Jennings stood up from rummaging in the fridge, instead of the butter-rich dainty Hebe Jones was hoping for, she drew out the same green apples that she had had to endure longer than she cared to believe.

Despite the fact that Valerie Jennings had already told her every detail of the picnic lunch, Hebe Jones listened to her reminiscences, sipping her jasmine tea. She heard again about the rug Arthur Catnip had handed her to keep out the cold. She heard again about the glasses he had brought for the wine, which were real crystal rather than plastic. And she heard again about the hours he must have spent the previous night preparing all the food, and how it was only polite of her to have tried his rhubarb and custard, despite her regime.

When elevenses were over, Hebe Jones stood rinsing the cups, remembering how her husband had always offered her a rug to defend her against the cold in the Salt Tower, and while he had never subjected himself to the torment of making pastry, he had been an expert at making tomato chutney, until the Chief Yeoman Warder spotted the plants he and Milo were growing up the side of their

216

home and ordered their destruction.

As she hauled up the shutter, one of the ticket inspectors was already waiting at the counter. Standing next to him was a wooden sarcophagus with a chipped nose.

'Anything in it?' asked Hebe Jones, looking it up and down.

'Just a bit of old bandage,' he replied. 'The mummy must have got out at an earlier stop.'

After noting it down in the ledgers, Hebe Jones helped him carry it down the aisle to the Egyptology section, a troublesome journey due to their vastly differing heights.

Back at her desk, she picked up the phone and called the Society of Woodworkers, having been assured by Thanos Grammatikos when he returned with the urn that morning that it was made from pomegranate wood. She spoke to the chairman, hoping he could put her in touch with someone who specialised in it. But he didn't know of anyone, and promised to send her a list of members who took on commissions to help her in her search. After hanging up, she glanced at her colleague to make sure she wasn't looking, and opened the gigolo's diary.

'The treachery of the Swedes,' Valerie Jennings suddenly announced.

'Pardon?' asked Hebe Jones, who had been engrossed in an encounter with an ice cube.

'The treachery of the Swedes,' she repeated, closing the Latin dictionary she had borrowed from one of the bookshelves. 'That's what *perfidia Suecorum* means. It's one of the few things I can make out on this manuscript. Terrible handwriting.'

Hebe Jones stopped to peer at it over her colleague's shoulder on her way to answer the Swiss cowbell. As she rounded the corner, she saw Tom Cotton in his blue uniform standing at the counter. She raised a hand to her mouth and asked: 'You haven't lost something else, have you?'

'I was just wondering whether you fancied a coffee,' he said.

*　　　*　　　*

While Tom Cotton stood in the queue, Hebe Jones chose the same table at the back of the café where they had sat the previous time. As she waited, she looked at him trim in his uniform talking to the girl behind the counter, and wondered why his wife had let him slip through her fingers. She lowered her eyes as he approached with a tray.

'So,' he said, sitting down and putting a cup and plate in front of her. 'Anything interesting been handed in recently?'

Hebe Jones thought for a moment. 'A tuba, which my colleague plays during moments of despair, and a sarcophagus,' she said.

She took a bite of her flapjack. 'Saved any lives recently?' she asked.

'It's the donors and doctors who save lives. I just fetch and carry,' he insisted, raising his cup to his lips.

Hebe Jones looked at the table. 'We didn't donate any of Milo's organs,' she said, eventually raising her eyes. 'They took his heart to be examined by a specialist. It was weeks before we got it back. I couldn't stand the thought of him

218

being without it.'

There was silence as both of them looked away. Eventually Tom Cotton spoke: 'You haven't lost Milo completely, you know. I lost my sister when we were both very young. We always carry a part of those we loved tucked inside us.'

After she had dried her cheeks on the soft, white handkerchief that was offered to her, she looked at him through a shimmering kaleidoscope of tears. 'Thank you,' she whispered, placing her tiny hand on his.

*   *   *

Balthazar Jones hadn't intended to go out once he had finished work for the day. But the top floor of the Salt Tower no longer felt like the sanctuary it once was, and after sitting slumped on the sofa in the darkness for an hour, he left to walk the battlements. As he strode, his hands sheltering in his pockets from the cold, he found that his problems had followed him. He stopped for a moment and gazed at Tower Bridge, lit up like a fairground attraction in the darkness, but his troubles rose around him like a fog, and he was forced to move on. No matter how fast he walked, he was unable to shake them off.

Eventually, he sought refuge in the Rack & Ruin. Pushing open the great oak door, he stood for a moment on the worn flagstones, wondering whether he could bear the company of so many people. Spotting an empty table next to a cabinet of Beefeater souvenirs, he ordered a drink, hoping that no one would notice him. But as he waited to be served, one of the Beefeaters standing at the bar turned to him and said: 'Sorry to hear about your wife.'

He took his pint to the table, where he sat, head slumped in his hand, drawing lines in the condensation on his glass. The sound of the chair opposite him scraping against the flagstones suddenly interrupted his rumination. He looked up to see Rev. Septimus Drew sitting down, and placing his glass of red wine on the table. With the wild enthusiasm of a man who had just unearthed the Holy Grail, the clergyman started telling him about his amazing discovery. It had taken him many months of endeavour, he explained, but finally he had managed to prise the archives from the covetous fingers of the Keeper of Tower History. He had spent night after night bent over the age-stained pages looking for a hint of an explanation, and had been about to give up, when suddenly he found what he was looking for: the scandalous story behind the bullet hole in the bar.

Balthazar Jones's eyes dropped to the table in disinterest, but the clergyman continued. One night in 1869, two Beefeaters got so drunk in the Rack & Ruin that the landlord was unable to rouse them after calling time. Leaving them to sleep with their heads collapsed on the tables, he retired upstairs. During the night, one shook the other awake, convinced that he had seen the ghost of a Jesuit priest. The Beefeater told his terrified colleague that he must have been dreaming, returned his head to the table, and went back to sleep. But the man went to the bar to retrieve the landlord's pistol, and sat with his back against the wall, waiting for the apparition to return. The Tower chaplain, who was always armed at night in case one of the Beefeaters attempted to steal his bells, crept into the tavern to help himself to the gin. At the same time, the landlord appeared on the bottom step brandishing his wife's pistol, roused by the noise downstairs.

'Suddenly a shot was fired!' Rev. Septimus Drew cried, gripping the Beefeater's arm as he worked himself up to his explosive denouement. But before the clergyman could reveal who shot whom, the door to the Rack & Ruin burst open, and the Yeoman Gaoler stormed in.

'Where's Yeoman Warder Jones?' he demanded.

The Beefeater stood up.

'I've just seen the Komodo dragon running past the White Tower!' the Yeoman Gaoler shouted.

The Keeper of the Royal Menagerie was followed out of the door by the rest of the drinkers, who immediately abandoned their pints in order to see the spectacle. As soon as they reached the White Tower, they discovered that the giant lizard wasn't the only creature to have escaped. Two howler monkeys were running across Tower Green, and judging by the stench that flooded the air, the zorilla was also on the loose. As he started after the monkeys, Balthazar Jones noticed that the door to the Brick Tower was wide open. Charging up the spiral steps, he reached the aviary and found that it was also open. All the birds had vanished, apart from the wide-eyed albatross, sitting alone in the middle of the enclosure, its white head sunk into its body. The Beefeater ran down the stairs, and searched the night sky. But all he saw was the sugar glider's pale stomach as it sailed over his head like a tiny furry kite. Spotting the Duchess of York in the distance,

221

he immediately headed after her. But as he turned into Water Lane, sprinting on their hind legs towards him were the Jesus Christ lizards. He stopped for a moment, resting his hands on his knees as he caught his breath, watching the golden monkey turn into Mint Lane. As he shot clouds of panic-fumed breath into the night, the Komodo dragon lumbered past him, flicking its forked tongue. Turning to see where it had come from, he spotted the reclusive ringtail possums lying motionless on the cobbles. He ran over, and knelt down beside them, taking each one in his arms. But no matter how often he ran a trembling hand across their silken heads, not one of them could be roused.

15

It wasn't until the watery glow of a new morning appeared that Balthazar Jones finally scuffed his way up the Salt Tower's spiral steps. Despite not having eaten since the previous lunchtime, he fetched just a glass of water from the kitchen before making his way upstairs. Too defeated for a bath, he lay on his side of the bed still in his uniform and closed his eyes. But he was kept from his dreams by images of the last frightful few hours he had spent trying to get the animals safely back into their enclosures.

He had gone after the howler monkeys first, unable to stand their demonic shrieks that pinned the Beefeaters' wives to their beds in terror. He cornered the first one with the help of a sentry, whom the beast was attempting to scale, lured by his bearskin hat. The other three ran to Rev. Septimus Drew's house, which he had forgotten to lock when he rushed back to fetch a torch. The Beefeater was relieved that the chaplain hadn't been there to witness the destruction. The teapot for one was smashed, four dining-room chairs upended, and neat piles of documents in his study took to the air in a paper blizzard that momentarily suspended pursuit until vision was finally restored. After a diversion involving a freshly laundered cassock, the monkeys finally sprinted out of the front door, only to be corralled outside the Rack & Ruin by a number of Beefeaters who had joined the chase. The creatures were eventually coaxed back to the Devereux Tower with the help of cheese-and-pickle rolls scavenged from the pub.

Balthazar Jones then went to the aid of one of his colleagues who was in a standoff with the Jesus Christ lizards on Tower Green. Sensing a crisis as he approached, the creatures suddenly stood up on their hind legs and ran past the two men, their hands stretched out either side of them as they sought to maintain their balance during their ungainly green sprint. The pair chased them past Waterloo Barracks. They were eventually caught by two Beefeaters coming in the opposite direction in pursuit of the female lovebird, which had just hunted down its mate and savaged it, sending clouds of peach and green feathers drifting into the night. As ladders were erected to bring the sugar glider down from one of the White Tower's window ledges, Balthazar Jones went in search of the zorilla, which, judging from the smell, was somewhere nearby. He found it asleep outside the Tower Café, its rank odour mingling with the stench of the discarded food in the bin outside. He then watched the Geoffroy's marmosets, which had gathered on top of a cannon, declare a state of emergency as a group of Beefeaters smelling fiercely of beer slowly approached them with outstretched arms. The monkeys continued exposing themselves long after the men had fled, crimson beneath their beards.

As far as the birds had been concerned, it was a game of patience. After considerable effort, Balthazar Jones persuaded the Yeoman Gaoler to surrender his dripping. The man returned from his house with pieces of bread covered with mean scrapings, which Balthazar Jones scattered on the ground underneath the trees. The first to give in was one of the toucans, which he swiftly captured with a fishing net. And after one final lap of victory around the White Tower, even the female lovebird succumbed to the fatty temptation.

But the hanging parrot, lit up by the moon, refused to abandon its position on one of the plane trees, where it swung upside down with the nonchalance of a trapeze artist. As the rest of the Tower residents headed to their beds in defeat, Balthazar Jones tried a succession of succulent titbits in an attempt to coax it to the ground. When they failed to work, he finally reached into his pocket and sacrificed the Fig Roll he had taken from a packet in the Yeoman Gaoler's kitchen when visiting the Etruscan shrew. But not even a biscuit made from sun-ripened Turkish figs could make the tiny bird surrender its illicit perch.

Eventually, he gave up on gastronomic

entrapment, and rested a ladder against the trunk of the tree. The bird watched him with one eye as he made his way up the rungs with the surefootedness of a rum-soaked sailor climbing a mast. Just as he came within arm's reach of the bird, the creature performed a spectacular double somersault and dropped to the branch below. The Beefeater descended several rungs, and stretched out his slender fingers. But the bird shut both eyes and plunged to the floor with the weight of a corpse. Just before hitting the ground, it snatched the Fig Roll and flew up to the White Tower roof, where it sat on a gold weathervane, swinging in the breeze as it showered Balthazar Jones with crumbs.

*   *   *

The Beefeater didn't remember turning off the alarm clock when it rang several hours after he finally got to bed. The first thing he was aware of was the phone ringing on the bedside table next to him. He ignored it at first, pulling the covers over his head. Eventually it stopped, but started up again seconds later. He stuck out a hand from underneath the shabby blanket and picked up the receiver.

'Hello?' he croaked.

'Good morning, it's Oswin Fielding. I'm at the Rack & Ruin. It's already twenty past. You were meant to be here at nine.'

Assuring him he was on his way, the Beefeater flung back the bedclothes and found his way to the bathroom. As he battled against the might of constipation, he remembered the forlorn bodies of the reclusive ringtail possums, and he wondered how he was going to explain their deaths to the equerry.

He had no doubt who was responsible for letting the animals loose: the same person whose white vest was hanging in his airing cupboard. His anger rose as he remembered the Ravenmaster pinning him up against the White Tower. He hadn't trusted the man since their confrontation over the loss of Mrs Cook's tail when the family first arrived at the Tower eight years ago. Neither did he like the way the man treated his wife, a woman as thin as parchment who was so rarely seen in the Rack & Ruin that Hebe Jones once declared: 'He shuts her up in a walnut.'

On his way out, Balthazar Jones looked at his creased uniform in the bedroom mirror, and regretted not having taken it off before going to sleep. He pulled on his hat over his tumultuous hair, and headed down the stairs, apprehension turning his empty insides.

Shielding his eyes from the glare of the alabaster clouds on his way to the Rack & Ruin, he opened the tavern door and found relief in the beer-scented gloom. He ordered a cup of tea from the landlady, who refused to serve alcohol before ten o'clock, a custom started by one of her ancestors to ensure that all Tower residents were in charge of their faculties when emptying their pisspots. Muttering his thanks to her for rounding up the fancy rats, he carried it past the empty tables to Oswin Fielding, who was peering at a file.

'There you are,' said the equerry, looking up. 'I hear there was an incident last night.'

The Beefeater remained silent as he sat down

226

opposite him.

'When I came in this morning I spotted the possums sitting in one of the trees. The Chief Yeoman Warder informed me of the carry on. The only saving grace seems to be that none of the animals in the moat escaped, so the public should be none the wiser.'

Balthazar Jones thought of the pile of bodies on the cobbles of Water Lane. 'I thought the Komodo dragon had killed the possums,' he found himself saying.

'They must have been playing dead. They're fit as a fiddle now,' Oswin Fielding replied. He took off his spectacles and started cleaning them on a blue handkerchief.

'The Chief Yeoman Warder wondered whether you'd forgotten to lock the enclosures, but I told him that a man who hadn't lost his tortoise in all these years wouldn't be that careless.'

Balthazar Jones looked at the table.

'Any idea who let the animals loose?' the equerry continued, returning his glasses to his nose. 'I don't for a minute think that they managed to escape by themselves.'

The Beefeater sat back. 'I've got my suspicions,' he said.

'Care to tell me who?' he asked.

'I haven't got any proof.'

'Well, we'll conduct a thorough enquiry to flush out the culprit,' said the equerry, turning a page in his file. 'At least all the animals have been recaptured.'

The Beefeater's thoughts immediately turned to the occupant of the White Tower weathervane, and he raised his cup to his lips.

227

'Now,' continued Oswin Fielding. 'The reason why I called this meeting is to let you know that the Prime Minister of Guyana has just dispatched some giant otters to the Queen, which is rather annoying I must say.'

Balthazar Jones stared at the courtier. 'But we haven't got any room for giant otters,' he protested.

'No one is happy about it, I can tell you. We'll just have to put them in the penguin enclosure for the time being. Make sure you look after them. They're an endangered species, like that Komodo dragon. How is it, by the way?'

'It's fine. Just a little plump, that's all.'

The equerry looked down at his file. 'As long as it hasn't eaten a small child, I wouldn't worry about it.'

The Beefeater gazed out of the window wondering when was the last time he had seen the Chief Yeoman Warder's dog.

'Now, there's one other thing I wanted to mention,' Oswin Fielding said.

Balthazar Jones started fiddling with a beer mat.

'There's a story in the Swedish papers this morning about the giraffes being a gift from the King of Sweden,' the equerry continued. 'What I can't understand is that the Press Office said that they got that information from you.'

The Beefeater looked away. 'I happened to be carrying a swede at the time,' the Beefeater muttered.

'A Swede? Anyone in particular?' asked the equerry.

'The vegetable, not a Scandinavian.'

The man from the Palace squinted at Balthazar

Jones. 'Couldn't you have just picked a country in Africa?' he asked. 'We've already had a call from the King of Sweden's office. I told them that the Press Office had got their wires crossed, so I'd avoid those ladies for a while if I were you. They're not very happy.'

The courtier closed his file, and sat back with a sigh. 'How's Mrs Jones?' he asked.

There was no reply.

'Still hasn't come back?'

Balthazar Jones looked out of the window. 'No,' he replied eventually.

'Shame. My wife never did either.'

*   *   *

Once the two men had left, Ruby Dore cleared the table of their empty cups, and gathered up the pieces of shredded beer mat. She vowed to go to bed early that night, having been up long past midnight finding the last of the fancy rats. She had almost given up hope when Rev. Septimus Drew ran up to her as she was looking in the bin outside the Tower Café, saying he had just seen two running past the Fusiliers' Museum. More than an hour later, they had chased them through the doors of the Chapel Royal of St Peter Ad Vincula, left open by one of the Beefeaters during the mayhem. The rodents immediately darted underneath the organ, and the pair sat down on the front row of seats in despair. When the vermin reappeared in front of them, and proceeded to shamelessly sink their teeth into the white linen altar cloth, the chaplain went to fetch that most unholy of lures: peanut butter.

229

Once the creatures were safely back in their cages in the Well Tower, Ruby Dore invited the clergyman into the Rack & Ruin, locking the door behind her lest the Beefeaters expected to be served. She reappeared from the cellar with a bottle of vintage champagne, which she had been saving for a special occasion that had never arrived. As she poured them both a glass, Rev. Septimus Drew looked at the canary asleep on its perch and said that he had always thought it such a shame that Canary Wharf had not been named after an infestation of tiny yellow birds as one might assume, but after the Spanish islands whose fruit had arrived there by the boatload. As she handed him his drink, the landlady knew that the special occasion had finally come.

Once she had finished her first glass, she revealed that she was studying for an Open University degree in history. She hadn't told anyone, she said, watching his reaction closely, as she didn't want people to think that she had ideas above her station. She had taken over the pub from her father, without having given much thought to another career. But she had come to the conclusion after almost two decades behind the taps that there must be more to life than pouring Beefeaters pints.

Rev. Septimus Drew replied that he thought it a splendid idea, and had considered reading history at university himself, but theology had been a stronger calling. The landlady refilled his glass and as they sipped their champagne, they discussed the lives of several European monarchs including Ethelred the Unready, Pippin the Short and George the Turnip Hoer.

When the bottle was empty, Ruby Dore finally found the courage to ask him the question that had recently perplexed her: why he had never married. Rev. Septimus Drew replied that he had only once met a woman who he wanted to spend the rest of his life with, and who would find living in the Tower a privilege rather than a curse.

'What happened?' she asked.

'She doesn't know,' he admitted. And he held Ruby Dore's gaze for so long, she lowered her eyes to the bar with a blush.

*   *   *

Ruby Dore yawned as she stood at the sink washing Balthazar Jones and Oswin Fielding's cups. As she looked down, she wondered when people would start to notice that she was pregnant. She had already decided to rebuff any enquiries about the father with the simple explanation that they were no longer together. It was a line she used when she broke the news to her parents. Her mother had remained silent for so long that she wondered whether she was still on the line. Barbara Dore then told her the truth: 'I'm not ready to be a grandmother, but then again I wasn't ready to be a mother.'

It was her father's reaction that she had been more concerned about. Once again there was a moment's silence on the line, this time as Harry Dore worked out that his daughter must have fallen pregnant while in Spain, having honed his mathematical skills during decades of Beefeaters attempting to defraud him. Swallowing the questions he wanted to ask, he offered her his

231

congratulations and shouted to his second wife the exalted news that he was going to be a grandfather. When, several minutes after hanging up, the full ramifications of the situation dawned on him, he immediately called his daughter back. 'For God's sake, don't let the Tower doctor handle the birth,' he urged. 'I don't think the kitchen lino is up to it.'

Ruby Dore fetched the broom from the cupboard under the stairs, and started working it in between the bar stools. When she opened the pub door to sweep out the dust, she noticed the mess left by the howler monkeys when they had been cornered the previous night. They had grabbed what they could as they fled from the home of Rev. Septimus Drew. She picked up a large sock bearing a snowman, a clerical collar, and then reached for the crumpled pieces of paper. As she walked back inside, she was struck by the familiarity of the handwriting. She smoothed down one of the pages on the bar, and it wasn't long before she recognised the hand that had written out a recipe for treacle cake. But what she couldn't understand was why the chaplain would be writing about the glory of rosebud nipples.

*   *   *

Hebe Jones set down her suitcase in the hall. Slipping the keys she had just collected from the lettings agency back into her coat pocket, she set about exploring her new home. As she wandered from room to room she discovered to her dismay several things she had failed to notice when she agreed to rent the flat. As she stood in the living room that overlooked a main road, she realised how loud the traffic was. While the kitchen was much bigger than the one she was used to in the Salt Tower, the cooker was electric rather than gas, and the insides of the cupboards were covered in grime. She went into the bathroom and saw that the carpet curled up in discoloured corners under the sink. As she sat down on the lumpy bed used by countless strangers for the most intimate act of all, she wondered whether she would ever get used to sleeping alone.

She looked at the shabby 1970s dressing table in front of her, which she would never have chosen. Already missing the comfort of Valerie Jennings's over-heated flat with the frilly tissue-box covers, she reminded herself that this would only be temporary. When the tenants' lease ran out, she would be able to move back into their home in Catford where the carpeted stairs rose in a straight line, the rooms were square rather than circular, and the neighbours didn't even know her name, let alone her business.

However the thought of returning home was not enough to defend her against the tide of misery that rose up around her, and she picked over the flotsam of her marriage. For years she and her husband had remained in a state of blissful delusion, seeing many more virtues in each other than really existed. While some spent the silences of their marriage imagining being in another's arms, Hebe and Balthazar Jones had maintained a lifetime of conversation, each entirely convinced that they had picked the right one. But after the tragedy, a corrosive despair had worked its way into the bolts of their affection until the mechanics of their colossal love was unable to turn. And all she had left was its echo.

Eventually, the unfamiliarity of her surroundings drove her to her feet, and she walked back to the hall. She opened the front door and pulled it behind her. As she headed down the steps for the Lost Property Office, the harsh sound of it slamming followed her.

*   *   *

When Hebe Jones arrived, Valerie Jennings emerged from behind the shelves and asked how the flat was.

'It's lovely,' Hebe Jones replied. 'Thanks again for letting me stay with you for so long.'

She sat down at her desk and, working a silver letter-opener across each of the envelopes' spines, opened the post to distract herself. The only things of interest were yet another thank-you letter from Samuel Crapper—this time for having reunited him with his corduroy jacket—and a list of members of the Society of Woodworkers who took on commissions. Hebe Jones glanced through the numerous pages, her heart sinking. When she thought of the stranger who had lost the urn, it sank even further, and she dialled the first number. After the initial disappointment, she dialled again, then continued down the list, enquiring whether they had ever worked with pomegranate wood. Just as she had reached the bottom of the first page, she heard the clanking of the Swiss cowbell. Irritated at being disturbed, she looked over to see whether Valerie Jennings was going to answer it. But she caught a glimpse of her disappearing down one of the aisles carrying a set of golf clubs, listing like a ship with uneven ballast.

Standing at the original Victorian counter was a man in a long black leather coat. His hair had been grown to counteract its unequivocal retreat from the top of his head, and was fashioned into a mean ponytail that hung limply down his back. Blooms of acne highlighted his vampire-white skin.

'Is this London Underground Lost Property Office?' he asked.

'Can I help you?' Hebe Jones asked.

The man placed his hands on the counter. 'I left a diary on the Tube about a month ago. I've only just found out that this place exists and was wondering whether you've got it. It's got a black, hardback cover and is written in green ink.'

'Just a minute.'

Hebe Jones rounded the corner, and swiftly returned with the gigolo's diary, which she slid across the counter with a fingertip.

'You didn't read it, did you?' the man asked, putting it into his pocket.

'Heavens no,' she replied.

After washing her hands thoroughly, she returned to her desk, picked up the phone and called the next number on the list. 'Is that Sandra Bell?' she asked.

'Yes.'

'My name's Mrs Jones. I was wondering whether you've ever worked with pomegranate wood?'

'I have done, as a matter of fact, but unfortunately I don't have any left.'

Hebe Jones explained where she was calling

235

from and that she was trying to trace the owner of an urn made from the curious wood.

'I did make someone a box out of pomegranate, but I've no idea what it was for,' the woman replied. 'The gentleman just gave me the measurements and I got on with it as soon as I'd tracked down some wood. It's not easy to come by. But I can try and get in touch with him, if you like.'

'God delays, but does not forget,' thought Hebe Jones as she put down the phone. She looked over at Valerie Jennings who was standing next to the inflatable doll putting on her coat.

'I'm just going to the Danish Church,' she said, doing up her buttons.

Hebe Jones had suggested the place as a possible lead after Valerie Jennings had come to a dead end in her attempts to trace the owner of the safe. All the documents she had found inside had been signed by a Niels Reinking. When she called the shipping firm whose address was on the top of them, she was told that he had left and it was against company policy to give out personal details. After she tried the phone book in vain, Hebe Jones pointed out to her that Reinking was a Danish name.

'I don't think I've ever met anyone Danish,' Valerie Jennings had said.

'Nor me,' Hebe Jones replied, adding that her mother had never allowed Danish bacon into the house as Denmark had surrendered to the Nazis after just two hours of occupation. Then she suggested trying the Danish Church up the road in Regent's Park. 'You never know, someone might have heard of him.'

Before leaving the office, Valerie Jennings gave

her lips another coat of Lilac Haze in the hope that she would bump into Arthur Catnip on her way out. But it was disappointment rather than a tattooed ticket inspector that accompanied her to the street. Wondering again why she hadn't heard from him since their second lunch, she thought what a fool she had been to mix up Edgar and Teddy Evans during her tale of the lost Antarctic boot. As she approached the church, she cursed herself, explorers, and finally their forsaken footwear.

Reasoning that if God understood Danish, he would also understand the anguish of constricted bunions, she took off her shoes and left them next to the umbrella stand. She padded up the cold aisle, grateful that neither big toe had bored through her tights. Standing at the altar, she looked around, but failed to find any sign of life, so she sat down on one of the pews to rest her feet. Opening the pamphlet she had picked up from the table at the entrance, she started to read about the services the church offered to Danish sailors. But her thoughts immediately turned to Arthur Catnip, and she wondered whether he had ever visited English chapels overseas, if such things existed, during his years in the Navy. Just as she was trying to find the resolve to stand up again, a side door opened and the pastor came out wearing a pair of jeans and a red sweater.

'You're in luck, we're not usually open at this time of the day. I've just popped in to catch up on some paper work,' he said, coming to sit beside her. He looked down at her feet. Valerie Jennings followed his gaze, then quickly explained that she worked at London Underground Lost Property

237

Office and had found something belonging to a Niels Reinking. 'I was wondering whether you might know him,' she said.

The pastor gazed at the ceiling as he thought. 'The name doesn't ring a bell,' he said. 'But I'll ask around. I'm better at faces than names.'

He walked her to the door and watched as she forced her feet back into her shoes.

'Maybe I should try Jesus sandals,' Valerie Jennings muttered, and reached for the door handle.

Back in the Lost Property Office, she put on the kettle and updated Hebe Jones on her progress with the safe while waiting for the water to boil. As she reached for the teacups, the Swiss cowbell sounded. Valerie Jennings was round the corner as fast as her footwear could carry her. But instead of the tattooed ticket inspector, she discovered a woman wearing a mac, clutching a large plastic carrier bag.

'I've just found this on the District Line, and thought I'd bring it in,' the customer said, pushing the bag across the original Victorian counter. Valerie Jennings reached in and drew out its contents. First came a black cloak, followed by a breastplate, a plastic light sabre, and finally a black helmet with a pronounced mouthpiece.

After thanking the woman, and wishing that everyone was as honest as she was, Valerie Jennings noted down the items in the ledgers. Once she was certain that she was alone, she picked up the helmet and pulled it on. As she was holding the light sabre in front of her with both hands, she looked up and saw through the eye slits someone standing in front of her. She turned her head slightly, and instantly recognised the confused features of Arthur Catnip.

'Is that Valerie Jennings?' he asked.

'It is,' came the muffled voice.

'I was wondering whether you would like to go to dinner tonight,' he said, keeping his distance from the weapon.

The black helmet nodded.

'Would eight o'clock at the Hotel Splendid be OK?'

There was another nod.

The ticket inspector hesitated for a moment then turned to leave. 'May the Force be with you,' he called over his shoulder.

*　　　*　　　*

The bathroom curtains drawn tightly against the night, the Yeoman Gaoler hauled himself out of the tub. He stood on the mat rubbing his back with his towel, his japonicas swaying underneath the full moon of his belly. Once in his pyjamas, he brushed his teeth, and such was his contentment he even gave them a floss to please his dentist.

Climbing into bed, he turned off the lamp, and released the contented sigh of a silver-muzzled dog as he waited for the blissful uninterrupted sleep he had enjoyed ever since the chaplain had worked his magic. He had had little hope in the abilities of Rev. Septimus Drew, and had only asked for his help in an act of desperation. But the exorcism had been such an emphatic success that the Yeoman Gaoler, who had previously deemed religion to be a form of witchcraft, had even considered turning up for the chaplain's service on

Sunday.

The explosion sounded some time after midnight, terrifying the odious ravens to such an extent that they simultaneously discharged a hail of droppings. The Yeoman Gaoler woke from his dreams, convinced he was in the grip of the heart attack the Tower doctor had warned him about. When the painful beating finally slowed, he swung his legs out of bed, and staggered to the window. Rubbing a hole in the condensation with his fingers, he cupped his hands against the pane, and peered through. Unable to make out anything in the darkness through the streaks, he hauled up the sash window and saw the shimmering form of a converted hen house, minus its front door. Lying flat on his back amongst the splintered wood was a man in a plumed hat and velvet breeches, his face covered in soot. It took a while for the ghost of the doomed explorer to come round following the botched experiment. He slowly sat up, lamenting the state of his pearl-encrusted jacket. He then got to his feet, dusted himself down and set about mending the door.

'That bastard Raleigh,' raged the Yeoman Gaoler, and slammed down the window. He unhooked his dressing gown from the back of the bedroom door, and pulled it on. As he tied it around his waist, he cursed the useless chaplain, with his skinny white ankles, who had simply transplanted the problem outside his house. Gripping the wooden handrail, he made his way down the narrow stairs in his bare feet, and headed along the hall to the kitchen to check on the Etruscan shrew after the commotion. He found his glasses, opened the cage, and carefully took the lid off the plastic house. But no amount of nudging the creature's tiny ribs with his plump finger could make it reveal its pointed velvet nose.

16

Balthazar Jones carefully placed the Egyptian perfume bottle inside the cabinet, and stepped back to admire it. It was a particularly fine sample, he thought as he stood in his pyjamas, taken from a light shower that had fallen the previous night. Giving the display a careful wipe with a duster, he ran his eyes over the other varieties, reading their labels with a collector's fixation.

Closing the door on the wartime graffiti, he was halfway down the stairs thinking about breakfast when the phone rang. He picked up speed, his hand burning on the filthy rope handrail. But when he answered it, instead of his wife, he found a salesman on the line trying to sell him the genius of double-glazing.

He hung up, and sat down heavily on his side of the bed. While he knew that Hebe Jones wasn't coming back, he still had the tormenting hope that she would get in touch. At one stage he had become obsessed with the thought that she would write, insisting that she had made a mistake in leaving. Several times a day he called in at the Byward Tower to check his pigeonhole, certain that if the letter hadn't arrived with the postman, it would be hand-delivered. But as the weeks continued without a word, he became convinced that the only letter that would come would be from her solicitor. From that moment on, he refused to collect his mail, and so much built up that the Chief Yeoman Warder threatened to dispose of it if he didn't take it away.

Sheltering his hands between his thighs from the draught, he looked around the room wondering what to do with his wife's belongings. There, on the dressing table, was the colourful pot he had bought her on their honeymoon in which she kept her earrings. Hanging from one of the knobs on the chest of drawers were her necklaces that once swayed across her neat chest as she walked. And on top of the wardrobe was the box containing her wedding dress that she had refused to leave in the loft in their house in Catford, insisting it was the first thing she would grab in the event of a fire. Deciding that everything belonged exactly where it was, the Beefeater put on his uniform, and left the Salt Tower without breakfast, not having the stomach for it alone.

Entering the enclosure on the grass next to the White Tower, he looked for the reclusive ringtail possums that had gone into shock the night they were released. As he hunted for them amongst the leaves, his mind turned to the man responsible for the treachery, whose vest was still hanging in his airing cupboard. Without any proof of his culpability, he doubted whether the Ravenmaster would ever have to account for his actions.

Eventually he found the secretive animals hiding at the back of their enclosure, only their magnificent coiled tails visible amongst the foliage. Satisfied that they had fully recovered from the trauma, he opened the wire door that led to the tiny sugar glider, a gift from the Governor of

242

Tasmania. The pearl grey creature, which suffered from depression when left alone, immediately opened its huge brown eyes. After teaching it to climb the little ladder he had made for it, he tickled its fur with a feather shed by one of the toucans. And after engaging in a mutually enjoyable game of hide-and-seek, he fed it pieces of fresh fruit to satisfy its addiction until it fell asleep in his hands.

Leaving the nocturnal creatures to their dreams, he headed for number seven Tower Green, and looked up at the White Tower weathervane. He stared at the emerald dot still swinging upside down in the breeze, and turned away in frustration. At the same moment, he felt what he recognised as a parrot indiscretion land on his shoulder. Furiously wiping his uniform with a tissue, he pressed on through the crowds of tourists that had started to seep in. After knocking on the pale blue door, he stood surveying the clouds as he waited. Several moments later, he rapped again. Suspecting that the Yeoman Gaoler was in, he took off his hat, bent down and looked through the letterbox. The man was sitting on the bottom of the stairs in his pyjamas, his head in his hands. Slowly his fingers opened, and two eyes looked at Balthazar Jones.

'Open the door. I've got some more crickets for the Etruscan shrew,' the Beefeater called.

The Yeoman Gaoler approached the letterbox, and bent down.

'Just pass them through,' he replied.

As the Beefeater began to feed the plastic bag through the door, he was suddenly gripped by suspicion. Snatching it back out again, he declared:

'I think it might be easier if I just give it to you. It doesn't seem to fit.'

The Yeoman Gaoler opened the door just wide enough to get his hand through. Ignoring the plump outstretched fingers, Balthazar Jones leant a shoulder against the wood and pushed. 'If it's all right with you, I think I'll just check on the shrew while I'm here.'

Once Balthazar Jones had got past the Yeoman Gaoler, a feat that required an ungentlemanly tussle, he walked straight down the hall to the kitchen. Placing his hat on the table, he opened the cage, reached inside, and lifted the lid off the tiny plastic house. He gave the creature a gentle prod. It failed to stir. He poked it again, but it was useless.

Turning to the Yeoman Gaoler he asked: 'Any idea why it's not moving?'

The Yeoman Gaoler's eyes slid to the other side of the room then returned to his visitor with a look of infinite innocence. 'It's having a nap?' he suggested.

The Keeper of the Royal Menagerie reached inside, drew out the creature by its tail and held it up in front of him, where it swung as lifeless as a hypnotist's watch.

'So when did it die?' Balthazar Jones demanded.

Sitting down, the Yeoman Gaoler ran a hand through his hair, and confessed that it hadn't stirred for almost a week. The two men looked at the stiffened corpse in silence.

'We'll just have to tell everyone it's gone into hibernation,' Balthazar Jones decided. 'And in the meantime you'll have to find another.'

The Yeoman Gaoler looked at him in defeat. 'I

don't think they have Etruscan shrews in England,'
he pointed out. But Balthazar Jones ignored him,
and let himself out.

As he walked towards the moat to feed the rest
of the animals, the Beefeater remembered
collecting the Queen's gift from the President of
Portugal, and their pitifully slow journey across the
city together listening to Phil Collins' *Love Songs*.
He thought of the night it had spent on the old
dining table on the top floor of the Salt Tower,
unknown to Hebe Jones, while he tried to think of
the best person to look after it. And he
remembered its pointed velvet nose that no longer
quivered as it swung by its tail before the Yeoman
Gaoler. He passed through Byward Tower, and
stood on the bridge over the moat. But not even
the sight of the enormous queue outside the
fortress waiting to see Her Majesty's collection of
exotic beasts lifted his mood.

*   *   *

Rev. Septimus Drew filled up the orange watering
can in the bathroom, then carried it to his
workshop dedicated to the extermination of *rattus
rattus*. It had been several weeks since he had sat
at the table with the Anglepoise light, toiling until
the early hours on his latest apparatus that aimed
to bring a swift and irrevocable end to a life
nourished by his tapestry kneelers. The change
had not come about because of a decrease in the
whiskered population—which continued to
discharge its droppings throughout the chapel
without the slightest blush—but out of respect for
Ruby Dore's unfathomable affection for the

245

vermin.

As he watered the anaemic spider plants, in a state of collapse from lack of attention, his thoughts turned again to the landlady's sudden froideur. After the hours they had spent together in the Rack & Ruin following the recapture of the fancy rats, he had returned home high with exaltation. It wasn't the vintage champagne that had put him into a state of grace, though the year was certainly exceptional, but the conviction that Ruby Dore was without a doubt the most sublime woman he had ever met. As they had sat alone in the tavern, the canary's head long tucked under its wing, the landlady had told him the most fascinating tale about Thomas Hardy's heart, which he had never heard before despite his lifelong passion for Westminster Abbey. As the landlady poured him another glass, she revealed that the author had stipulated in his will his desire to be buried in his home county of Wessex. However, after his death in 1928, the government had insisted that the national treasure be buried in the Abbey alongside the other famous poets. An undignified row broke out, after which Hardy's heart was removed to be buried at Stinsford, and given to his wife. The rest of his body was cremated and ceremonially entombed in the celebrated Abbey. However, legend had it that the heart was placed in a biscuit tin and put in the garden shed for safekeeping, only to be found by the household cat, who consumed the delicacy. It was said that, on discovering the atrocity, the undertaker promptly wrung Cobweb's neck, and placed its body in the casket before it was buried. When the landlady had finished her tale, it was all the chaplain could do to stop himself picking up her soft, pale hand and kissing the back of it in admiration.

But despite those intimate early hours spent with only the sticky wooden bar top separating them, the following evening Ruby Dore had acted as if they were little more than strangers. Every day since, no matter when he arrived at the bar, he would find himself the last to be served, the greatest indignity to befall an Englishman. Whenever the Beefeaters moved away to find a table, he would linger to talk to her, but the landlady would either pick up her knitting and start thrusting her needles, or disappear to change the barrels.

As he watched the soil greedily soak up the water, he wondered again what he had done to offend her, but was at a loss as to what it might be. Unable to stand the uncertainty any longer, he descended the battered wooden stairs, returned the watering can to the cupboard below the kitchen sink, and drew back the net curtain. As he feared, the chairwoman of the Richard III Appreciation Society was sitting like a sentinel on the bench by the White Tower, her knees pressed tightly together and the breeze lifting her gunmetal hair. Nevertheless, the clergyman grabbed his keys, and strode out of the house.

He made it as far as the Bloody Tower before he felt a tap on the shoulder. He turned round, and before the woman had a chance to speak, he held up his hand and told her that there was nothing she could say to convince him of the merits of the hunchback king. 'If it's a Richard III apologist you're after, try the Yeoman Gaoler. He's convinced that the Duke of Buckingham murdered the two little princes. He lives over there,' he added, pointing in the direction of number seven Tower Green.

As he continued towards the tavern, he felt a second tap on his shoulder. Assuming he still hadn't shaken off the chairwoman, he turned swiftly to tell her that he was engaged in a matter of utmost importance. But standing next to him was the Keeper of Tower History, wringing his covetous fingers.

'Have you seen Yeoman Warder Jones?' he asked.

'Not today,' the clergyman replied.

'Well, if you do see him, tell him that a couple of oryx have just arrived,' he said.

Rev. Septimus Drew continued easing his way through the tourists. Passing the 'Private' sign at the top of Water Lane, he pushed open the door of the Rack & Ruin. A crowd of Beefeaters was stood in captivated awe around a table at which Dr Evangeline Moore and the Ravenmaster were engrossed in a game of Monopoly started the previous evening. Since the game's ban had been lifted, the Tower doctor hadn't lost a single game, all of which she had played with the thrupenny bit. After each win, during which the general practitioner would seize property with the ruthlessness of a bailiff, her next opponent would insist on playing with the coin that still bore the scars of having been lodged inside a flaming plum pudding. But nothing could convince the doctor to surrender the thrupenny bit.

The chaplain approached the bar, and, when he was finally served, ordered a pint of Scavenger's

Daughter. But his choice of beverage did nothing to mellow the landlady, who silently slid his change towards him through the puddles of beer on the bar. She returned to her stool, picked up her knitting and lowered her head. Rev. Septimus Drew watched as each furious stitch was dispatched on to the other needle the instant it was formed. He set down his pint, looked around him, and leant forward. 'May I have a word with you in private?' he muttered.

Ruby Dore looked up, said nothing for a moment, then replied: 'I'll meet you in the Well Tower in a minute. You'd better go before me or the gossip will be unbearable.'

As the chaplain waited in the gloom with his back to the fancy rats, he tried to keep his mind off the gruesome scrabbling by thinking about the magnificent carrots the retired ladies of the night were growing in the kitchen garden. It wasn't long before the landlady entered, closing the door behind her with such force that the rodents fled to their burrows. She reached inside her jeans pocket, pulled out a piece of paper and offered it to him. 'I think you might have lost this,' she said. 'One of the howler monkeys got hold of it when they ransacked your house, and dropped it outside the pub.'

Rev. Septimus Drew unfolded it and started to read. Instantly recognising his own prose, he quickly folded it up again, and pushed it deep into his cassock pocket. He then told her of his passion for creative writing, inspired by his widowed mother's love affair. He explained that he had attempted all other literary genres, but the country's leading publishing houses had banned

249

him from any more submissions. And he added that every penny he received went to a shelter he had set up to help prostitutes find a more wholesome means of employment, and stop peddling their self-destructive love.

But the succulence of the ladies' cabbages was not enough to appease Ruby Dore. She informed him that as a clergyman he had no place to be writing about rosebud nipples, and that not only was he putting the reputation of the Church in jeopardy, but also that of the Tower.

'Why aren't men ever who they say they are?' she finally hurled at him as she headed for the door, her ponytail swinging. As he stood alone in the dark, her words echoed with such volume that he no longer heard the gruesome sound of gnawing coming from the enclosure behind him.

*   *   *

From under her lustrous lashes, Valerie Jennings watched as Hebe Jones turned the corner to answer the call of the Swiss cowbell. She got to her feet, hoisted up the waistband of her floral skirt, and walked over to the bookshelves. As she searched the titles of the obscure Edwardian novelist Miss E. Clutterbuck for something with which to escape the world, it struck her as strange that the only ticket inspector ever to discover the books was Arthur Catnip. Her mind turned once more to the last time she had seen him: on the steps of the Hotel Splendid where he had risen to his toes and given her a goodnight kiss.

There had been no time after work to go home and change for dinner. Instead, she had made her way to the dress section of the Lost Property Office, and rummaged through the racks with frantic fingers. Eventually, she found a black frock with three-quarter-length sleeves still with a label on, which she immediately snipped off. She then hunted in the handbag section for something to match it, and eventually found a black clutch with a large diamante clasp that closed with a satisfying snap. Scrabbling through the drawer of abandoned perfumes, she deliberated over Evening Sensation and Mystic Musk. Unable to choose between the two, she decided on both, and stood with her eyes closed as the heady precipitation descended upon her in a fragrant confusion. She opened the drawer below, and found amongst the necklaces a string of cream pearls. Noticing that the diamante clasp matched the one on the bag, she put it on with tremulous fingers. In front of the lavatory mirror, she released her dark curls from their usual mooring at the back of her head, and they tumbled to her shoulders.

Standing on the meticulously swept steps of the Hotel Splendid, pitched forward by the shoes that forced her toes into two red triangles, she adjusted her freshly polished spectacles as she waited. When the tattooed ticket inspector arrived, she almost failed to recognise him as his hair had been shorn into what appeared to be a crop circle.

As they entered the dining room, she saw that it was even grander than the hotel's Victorian conservatory filled with orchids where Hebe Jones took her for lunch on her birthday. As the waiter pulled back her chair, she noticed that theirs was the only table with yellow roses. Arthur Catnip sat down opposite her, and commented on how lovely she looked, and she no longer felt the humiliation of wearing a stranger's dress that didn't quite fit.

When their starters arrived, the ticket inspector looked at Valerie Jennings's oysters and pointed out that one of the few things he remembered from science lessons was that the shellfish could change sex several times during its lifespan. Valerie Jennings replied that the closest she had ever got to a sex change was going to a hospital to distribute Christmas presents dressed as Santa, and having to use the gents' lavatory so as not to confuse the children.

As the main courses were served, Valerie Jennings glanced uneasily at Arthur Catnip's goose, and told him how one had attacked her while she was feeding the ducks in the park. The ticket inspector recalled the time when he was six and ate all the bread his mother had given him for the ducks. His brother subsequently pushed him into the pond, and the park keeper had to pull him out by his hair when he sank.

While Valerie Jennings was waiting for her Danish apple cake, Arthur Catnip mentioned that if she ever fancied getting out her Santa suit again, Denmark was the place to go as it held an international Father Christmas convention every summer. As they sipped their dessert wine, Valerie Jennings replied that she would never go to Denmark as they had surrendered to the Nazis after just two minutes of occupation during the war.

The couple only realised it was time to leave when the waiter approached and told them that the restaurant would shortly be closing. They stood on the immaculate steps, oblivious to the bitterness of the night as the uniformed doorman hailed them both a taxi. When the first cab pulled up, Arthur Catnip wished her goodnight, then rose several inches and planted a kiss on her lips. It sent her into such a state of rapture she remembered nothing about her journey back home.

Cursing herself for muddling the time Denmark had taken to surrender, Valerie Jennings selected a book, returned to her desk, and slipped it into her handbag. As she sat down, the phone rang. 'London Underground Lost Property Office. How may I help you?' she said in the voice of a 1930s radio announcer.

A heavily accented voice asked whether he was speaking to Valerie Jennings.

'You are indeed.'

The parson of the Danish Church explained that it had taken a bit of work, but he had managed to track down someone by the name of Niels Reinking. 'I have no idea whether he's the man you're looking for, but I have his address. Maybe you could write to him,' he added.

'What a good idea,' she replied. 'I've always thought it such a pity that the art of letter writing is no longer revered. What is it?'

Valerie Jennings had no intention of wasting time subjecting herself to the vagaries of Royal Mail. As soon as she put down the phone, she reached for her *A to Z*, and fetched her navy coat from the stand next to the inflatable doll.

Less than an hour later, she was standing outside an Edwardian house that rose gracefully to the sky, its front door flanked by two laurel bushes. She pressed the bell, and glanced through the bay window as she waited. A blue-eyed man with a

253

snowdrift of hair answered the door.

'May I help you?' he enquired, wiping his fingers on a rag covered in paint smudges.

'Are you Niels Reinking?' she asked.

'Yes.'

'I'm Valerie Jennings from London Underground Lost Property Office. I was wondering whether you might have lost something.'

Niels Reinking put his hands on his hips. 'I'm always losing things. Usually it's my glasses, which my wife points out are on the top of my head. You haven't found my chequebook by any chance, have you?' he asked, looking hopeful.

'It's actually something a bit larger than that. It's a safe.'

He looked at her for a moment, unable to speak. 'I think you'd better come in,' he said eventually.

Valerie Jennings sat on the leather sofa in the drawing room looking at the curious paintings on the walls, while Niels Reinking disappeared into the kitchen. He returned with a pot of fresh coffee, which he poured with trembling fingers, then sat back in the matching armchair. Several years ago, he explained, the house was burgled and the thieves managed to make off with the safe. He should, of course, have followed the manufacturer's instructions and bolted it to the wall, but he had never got round to it. Although he had reported the break-in to the police, he had heard nothing about it since, and had completely given up hope of getting the safe back. 'And now you say you've found it?' he asked.

Valerie Jennings pushed her glasses up her nose. 'A safe was left on the Tube a number of years ago, and we've just managed to open it,' she said. 'But

254

in order to verify that it's yours, I need to ask you what was in it.'

Niels Reinking looked at the cream rug in front of him. 'Well, it was a while ago,' he said, 'but I suspect there would have been some documents relating to the shipping company I once worked for. I've been wondering where they'd got to. There was some cash in there too, which my wife quaintly referred to as her running away fund. Needless to say, we're still together. But I'm not bothered about any of that. What I'd like to know is whether there was a manuscript inside.'

'There was something of that nature in it,' Valerie Jennings replied.

The kiss that subsequently landed on her cheek startled her to such an extent that the coffee she was holding slopped into its saucer. Niels Reinking returned to his seat then told her the story of the manuscript, which was of such historical significance to his home country that he had been unable to insure it. Back in the seventeenth century, one of his ancestors called Theodore Reinking had been so incensed by Denmark's diminished fortunes following the Thirty Years' War that he wrote a book entitled *Dania ad Exteros de Perfidia Suecorum,* or *From the Danes to the World on the Treachery of the Swedes.* The defamed country promptly arrested him, and after many years in prison, offered him the choice of decapitation or eating his work. He made the book into a sauce, duly consumed it, and his life was spared. Once released, he returned home. But while thin, bearded and foul smelling, victory was all his. The author produced from his mouldering stocking the most damnable section of his work, which he had torn out and stuffed down his undergarment. The relic was not only highly revered by his kingdom as testament to the superior cunning of the Danes, but also for being part of the only book in the world ever to have been cooked and consumed, which, explained Niels Reinking, was a great source of national pride.

*　　*　　*

When Hebe Jones arrived at the coffee shop, Tom Cotton was reading a newspaper on the front of which was a grainy photograph purporting to be of a bearded pig taken in the Scottish Highlands. She took off her turquoise coat and sat down, asking how his day had been.

'I had to go to Birmingham by helicopter to deliver a heart to one of the hospitals,' he said, folding his paper.

She tore open a sachet of sugar and poured it into the coffee he had ordered for her. 'Whose was it?' she asked, looking at him as she stirred.

'A man who'd died in a car accident.'

Hebe Jones lowered her eyes. 'At least they know why he died.' There was a long silence.

Eventually, when she found her voice again, Hebe Jones recounted that terrible, terrible day. The night before her world ended, she had gone into Milo's room to wish him goodnight as usual. He was lying in bed reading a book on Greek mythology that had belonged to his grandfather. After placing it on his bedside table, she pulled the duvet up to his chin, and kissed him on the forehead. As she walked to the door, he asked who her favourite Greek god was. She turned, looked at her son, she replied in an instant: 'Demeter, goddess of fertility.'

'What's Daddy's?' Milo then asked.

Hebe Jones thought for a minute. 'I suppose it would have to be Dionysus, god of wine, merriment and madness. What about you?'

'Hermes.'

'Why?'

'One of his symbols is a tortoise,' replied the boy.

The following morning, when Milo still hadn't appeared for breakfast, she walked down the spiral staircase and opened his door. 'A hungry bear doesn't dance,' she said.

When he failed to stir, she approached his bed, and gave him a gentle shake. But still he didn't wake. She then shook him more forcefully, which was when she started shouting for her husband. When the paramedics arrived, they had to pull him away, as he was still trying to revive the boy. They followed the ambulance to hospital, the only time in her life that she had ever seen her husband jump a red light.

It was a young Indian doctor who had told them that he was dead. After Hebe Jones collapsed, she came round in one of the cubicles, where the doctor informed her that she had to stay until she was fit enough to leave. And when she returned to the Salt Tower no longer a mother, she lay on her son's bed for the rest of the day weeping as the ashes of her life rained down on her.

An expert pathologist examined Milo's heart to find out why he had died. When the man stood up at the inquest, he announced that in about one in every twenty cases of sudden cardiac death no definite cause of death could be found, despite a specialist having examined the heart. This was called Sudden Arrhythmic Death Syndrome. He cleared his throat and said that a cardiac arrest was brought on by a disturbance in the heart's rhythm. In some cases such deaths were caused by a group of relatively rare diseases that affected the electrical functioning of the heart, which could only be detected in life and not post mortem. Some had no symptoms, he said, while others had blackouts. Some youngsters died in their sleep or on waking, others while exerting themselves or suffering from emotional stress. Before he sat down he added that twelve young people died from sudden cardiac death each week.

When the coroner had heard from all the witnesses, he raised his eyes from his paperwork and announced that Milo Jones had died from natural causes. It was then that Hebe Jones stood up and screamed: 'What's so natural about a child dying before his parents?'

17

As Balthazar Jones walked past the White Tower, he picked off an emerald feather that had landed on the front of his uniform. Refusing to look at its upside-down owner, he continued his journey across the fortress to number seven Tower Green, ignoring the common variety of sticky drizzle that had started to fall. He knocked on the door, and, as he waited for it to open, he scratched the back of his left knee ravished by fungus.

258

When the Yeoman Gaoler eventually answered the door, Balthazar Jones immediately detected the amber notes of gentlemen's aftershave. As he followed him down the hall, he looked through the open door of the sitting room and spotted the chairwoman of the Richard III Appreciation Society perched on the edge of the chaise longue, a teacup clutched to her knees and her gunmetal hair in uproar.

The Yeoman Gaoler carefully closed the kitchen door behind them. He approached the table, opened the cage, and with the flamboyance of a stage magician took the lid off the tiny plastic house. Balthazar Jones peered inside. For a moment he was unable to speak. 'But it's twice the size of the old one,' he said, incredulous.

There was a pause.

The Yeoman Gaoler scratched the back of his neck. 'It was all I could get my hands on in the circumstances,' he said. 'There are only so many hedgerows a man can frisk.'

There was silence as the two men stared at the creature's colossal hips.

Eventually Balthazar Jones sighed. 'If anyone asks, you'll just have to say you overfed it,' he said, and walked out, slamming the door behind him.

As he passed the scaffold site on Tower Green, the Beefeater looked at his watch. There was still a while to go before the tourists would be let in. He made his way to the Brick Tower, squinting to keep the rain out of his eyes, and climbed the spiral staircase wiping his face with his handkerchief. He sat down next to the wandering albatross that mated for life, took off his hat, and leant against the cold wall. The movement caused

259

a cloud of white feathers to take to the air, and they pirouetted on their way down, eventually settling on his navy trousers. The melancholic bird, which was losing its shimmering plumage, moved its ugly feet several paces sideways towards the Beefeater. It sat pressed against his thigh, protecting its pink patches from the draught skimming across the floorboards.

With the back of his fingers, the Beefeater stroked its head as soft as silk. Savouring the time that he had his charges all to himself, he looked up at the King of Saxony bird of paradise, whose blue brow feathers were used by grey songbirds to decorate their courtship bowers. His eyes turned to the female lovebird, its green and peach feathers still puffed up in victory after savaging its mate, and his thoughts turned to the Yeoman Gaoler's dishevelled lady guest who must have stayed the night to be at the fortress so early. And he knew he would never want to wake up with anyone other than Hebe Jones.

As he continued to stroke the albatross's head, he gazed at the rectangle of dirty sky in the window opposite him, and wondered who was holding the hand of the woman he no longer deserved. He hoped that whoever it was appreciated her many virtues that he had spent most of their marriage counting, and that he realised that her great obstinacy was something to be admired rather than judged. But he knew that no one would be able to love her as much as he did.

The Beefeater jumped at the sound of the oak door opening, and the toucans instantly took to the air, carving multicoloured circles with their alluring beaks believed by the Aztecs to be made from rainbows. He turned his head to see Rev. Septimus Drew standing in the doorway.

'There you are,' the chaplain said, peering at Balthazar Jones through the fencing. 'I thought you should know that a herd of wildebeest has just arrived. The Chief Yeoman Warder has called Oswin Fielding to get him to take them away.'

There was a pause as both men looked at each other.

'Can I come inside?' the clergyman asked.

'As long as you don't make any sudden movements. It frightens the birds.'

The chaplain opened the wire door with his long, holy fingers, and carefully closed it again behind him. He gazed up in wonder at the birds with the colourful bills and deafening shrieks beating crazed circles in the air. Eventually, there was a thud of scaly, grey feet as they landed next to the lovebird, its jewel-coloured head cocked to one side as it peered at the clergyman with the scrutiny of a judge.

Balthazar Jones took a handful of sunflower seeds out of his tunic pocket and offered them to the chaplain. 'If you hold these next to your shoulder, the lovebird will come and sit on it,' he said.

Rev. Septimus Drew took the seeds, and sat with his back against the opposite wall, his excessively long legs stretched out in front of him. It wasn't long before the lovebird landed on the clergyman's shoulder in a flash of green and peach, and started to feed in nervous beakfuls. Once it had finished, it inched its way towards the chaplain's face and proceeded to rub its head against his neck.

'It likes you,' the Beefeater said.

'At least somebody does,' Rev. Septimus Drew replied. 'What's wrong with that one?'

The Beefeater looked down at the albatross. 'It doesn't like being separated from its mate,' he replied.

There was a long silence as each man's thoughts were blown into the same dark corner.

'How long has Hebe been gone? A month?' asked the chaplain.

Balthazar Jones nodded.

'Is she coming back?'

'No.'

There was silence.

'What have you done to try and persuade her?'

The Beefeater didn't reply.

'Isn't it worth trying to change her mind?' Rev. Septimus Drew asked. 'If she were my wife, I'd spend the rest of my life trying to get her back.'

The Beefeater continued to look at his hands. Seduced by the intimacy of the birds, he eventually replied: 'I don't know how to love any more.'

There was a pause.

'Try showing her some of the love you give to the animals,' the clergyman said. There was a flutter of wings and the green and peach bird returned to its perch. Rev. Septimus Drew looked at his watch, got to his feet, and dusted himself down. As the chaplain opened the aviary door, the Beefeater turned his head and asked: 'So whose bullet was it in the Rack & Ruin's bar?'

The clergyman stopped and looked at him. 'I don't know, I was making it up as I went along. I was trying to cheer you up,' he replied, and the only sound that followed was the echo of his large feet on the ancient spiral staircase.

*   *   *

Hebe Jones pulled down the shutter marking the sacred hour of elevenses feeling the weight of dread in her empty stomach. Over the weeks she had considered bringing in her own snack to head off the mid-morning thunder that rolled beneath her blouse. But she had dismissed the idea as too cruel to a woman whose marvellous girth prevented her escaping the day's torments by clambering inside the magician's box. Bracing herself for another quartered apple, she wiped off the dust that had settled on the urn. Valerie Jennings approached with a cup and saucer, giving off the undeniable bergamot and citrus scent of Lady Grey. She returned with a small plate bearing a homemade rock cake of sufficient heft to start a landslide. Once she had finished staring at it, Hebe Jones looked over at her colleague, who had returned to her seat. Not only was she also drinking proper tea, but she had in her hand a rock cake of similar bulk. She glanced at her again and noticed that she was no longer wearing makeup. Her eyes then travelled down to the woman's footwear, and she saw that she had returned to wearing her flat black shoes.

Hebe Jones had avoided all mention of the tattooed ticket inspector as each day passed without word from him. Initially she had shared Valerie Jennings's optimism whenever the Swiss cowbell rang, and they would both look at each other in silent hope that it was him. Eventually a black cloud of despair drifted into the office and

263

remained over Valerie Jennings as a result of so many disappointments. She had begun to show such reluctance to go to the counter that Hebe Jones had taken it upon herself to answer the clanking as often as she could.

'Lovely rock cake,' Hebe Jones said.

'Thanks.'

'Any idea how you're going to spend the reward that the owner of the safe gave you?'

Valerie Jennings looked at the cheque propped up against the Oscar statuette that Niels Reinking had given her when he came to collect the safe. 'I haven't really thought about it,' she replied.

When elevenses were over, Hebe Jones suggested a game of Battleship to help get them through the morning, and handed Valerie Jennings a piece of paper with two grids already drawn on it before she could refuse. By lunchtime she found herself in the extraordinary position of having sunk her colleague's entire fleet. She then fetched her the box set of theatrical facial hair. But not even the sudden arrival of her favourite Abraham Lincoln beard could tempt Valerie Jennings into trying it on.

Not knowing how else to cheer her, Hebe Jones looked at her watch and got up to meet Tom Cotton. As she stood buttoning up her coat, the phone rang. She turned round, hoping that Valerie Jennings would answer it so she wouldn't be late, but saw her disappearing down one of the aisles carrying a violin case. She sighed and picked it up.

'Is that Mrs Jones?' came a voice.

'It is.'

'This is Sandra Bell. You called me about an urn made from pomegranate wood.'

Hebe Jones immediately sat down. 'Did you manage to find the man's number?' she asked, fiddling with the telephone cord.

'I did, but unfortunately I haven't been able to reach him. Maybe he's gone away. Would you like his number so you can try yourself? I've got his address too, if you need it.'

Once she had hung up, Hebe Jones put the urn into her handbag, and left a note for Valerie Jennings explaining where she was going. With the hint of a stoop she had acquired from the weight of her son and husband's absences, she walked to the Tube station and managed to find an empty seat in the carriage. She spent the journey clutching her handbag, hoping that she would finally be able to reunite the urn with its owner.

Eventually she found the house, built in the 1950s to fill in the gap that the Blitz had left in a row of Victorian terraces. Pushing open the metal gate, she looked at the daffodils flanking the path, and wondered whether those on the Salt Tower roof had flowered. She reached up and pressed the bell with a gloved hand, and felt the cold pierce her tights as she waited. When there was still no answer, she cupped her hands against the window and peered inside. There, in an armchair, was an elderly man asleep in front of the television. She knocked gently on the pane, causing the man to jump. He looked at her and she offered him a meek smile. Hauling himself to his feet, he came to open the door.

'Yes?' Reginald Perkins asked, his thin lips just above the steel door chain.

Hebe Jones looked at the old man, willing him to be the owner. 'My name's Mrs Jones, and I work at

London Underground Lost Property Office. We've found a wooden urn with a plaque bearing the name Clementine Perkins. I was wondering whether it might be yours.'

He remained silent for so long, Hebe Jones wondered whether the man had heard her. A solitary tear shone behind his smudged spectacles.

'You've found her?' he eventually managed to say.

While Hebe Jones unzipped her handbag, Reginald Perkins fumbled with the chain and opened the door. Reaching out hands that trembled like sparrows, he took the urn, and raised it to his lips that had no one left to kiss.

As he made tea in the kitchen, Hebe Jones waited on the sofa, grateful for the warmth of the gas fire. The living room had passed unscathed through decades of decorating fashions, and retained the timid wallpaper it had first been dressed in. On the mantelpiece was an old black-and-white photograph of a young couple whose smiles bore the invincibility of new love as they stood in the church doorway fresh from the altar.

Hebe Jones spotted traces of Clementine Perkins around the room: the framed tapestry of a vase of flowers she had made hanging on the wall; a pink button in a china ashtray that she had not got round to sewing back on; and a coaster bearing her initial, which had since been used by her mourners.

Passing Hebe Jones her cup, Reginald Perkins lowered his brittle frame into his chair, placed his hands on the armrests, and began to tell the tale of Clementine Perkins's extraordinary journey.

They had first met as children while queuing for their ration of sugar just after the war. Their mothers forged a friendship as they waited, bonded by the unforeseen difficulties of suddenly having their husbands home. The youngsters were left to play with each other when the women met to swap stories about the stranger in the house who the children had long forgotten and now had to call Daddy.

Years later, the mothers lost touch when the Perkins family moved. But the distance was not enough to fell the friendship that had developed between their offspring. Unwilling to suffer the delays of the postal service, the teenagers sent each other notes via the milkman, who, recently married himself, understood the agonies of the love-afflicted. All went well for a while, until he started to confuse the notes given to him by the two lovers with those from his other customers. Before long housewives for miles were cursing the besotted milkman with his scribbled outpourings of devotion left on their doorsteps with the wrong order, while the lovers struggled to understand the romantic subtext of a request for an extra pint of milk.

The wedding was a small affair, and by the end of the year Clementine Perkins was pregnant. Two further children followed, and they lived a life of suburban contentment. Eventually, they both took early retirement in order to spend more time together, and their biggest pleasure was taking day trips to see England's historical treasures. But as old age approached, Reginald Perkins was seized by a secret dread of being separated from his wife, and he would look at her in the garden from the living-room window, wondering which would be worse: dying first or second.

He still hadn't made up his mind when he found her collapsed in the bathroom during a holiday to Spain, which they had taken to lift her spirits during the gloom of winter. He flew home in silence, his wife's remains in his blue holdall on the empty seat next to him. For months he refused to leave their home, and no amount of begging by his children could prise him from her ashes.

One afternoon, as he was sitting in his armchair, he could no longer stomach the poison of loneliness. So he went into the kitchen, made some fish paste sandwiches, and put them into his holdall, along with the urn. He then made his way to Hampton Court Palace, the next stately home he and his wife had planned to visit.

It was the first of many places that he and Clementine Perkins visited following her death, and suddenly his life had meaning again. But, while returning from a trip to Kew Palace, he fell asleep on the Tube, lulled by the heat and the rhythm of the carriages. When he woke, he discovered someone had taken the bag containing his wife's remains, and he had sunk into a decline.

'My greatest fear was having to face her in heaven, knowing what I'd done,' he said, a tear running down his sunken cheek. 'Where was it found?'

Hebe Jones put down her tea that had gone cold as she listened. 'On the Central Line,' she replied. 'It's not unusual for thieves to abandon things once they realise they're of no value to them. Why, if you don't mind my asking, was your wife's death not registered?'

Reginald Perkins took out a white handkerchief and wiped his cheek. 'We registered it in Spain,' he said, returning it to his trouser pocket. 'You don't have to do it here as well. What am I going to do with a certificate telling me she's dead?'

There was a pause.

'The wood's beautiful,' said Hebe Jones.

His eyes returned to the urn. 'They gave me such a wretched thing to carry Clementine home in. I couldn't bear the thought of her being in it, so I had something special made for her. It's pomegranate wood. The fruit is a symbol of ever-lasting life.'

They sat in silence as the gas fire hissed.

Reginald Perkins suddenly turned to his visitor. 'I think I'd better find Clementine a resting place before I lose her again. Would you care to help me?' he asked.

Hebe Jones followed him into the back garden, where he stood, a trowel in one hand, contemplating the borders. He knelt down stiffly on his worn-out knees, and dug a hole in the earth. Picking up the urn that had spent so many weeks on Hebe Jones's desk, he gave it one final kiss, then placed it inside, and covered it with dark, moist soil. She helped him to his feet, and he stood surveying his handiwork.

'She'll get the sun there,' he said with a smile. When there was no reply, he turned and looked at his visitor.

'Let's get you inside, luvvie,' he said when he saw the tear fall.

When Hebe Jones was back on the sofa, warming her fingers on a fresh cup of tea, she told Reginald Perkins about the terrible, terrible day. When she had finished, she added: 'We still haven't even scattered his ashes. We couldn't

269

decide where. Neither of us could bear to talk about it.'

'Where are they now?'

'Still in the back of the wardrobe.'

It was Reginald Perkins who was left holding a cup of tea that had chilled as he listened. He put it down on the table, and sat back. After a while he said: 'At least you've still got your husband. That should be some comfort.'

Hebe Jones stared at the ball of sodden tissue in her hand. 'I haven't,' she replied, and she told him how she had walked out with her suitcase, and hadn't spoken to him since. 'What I can't forgive is that he's never even cried.'

The old man looked at her. 'We might love each other in the same way,' he said, 'but it doesn't mean that we grieve in the same way.'

Hebe Jones looked at him through a veil of tears. 'It makes me wonder whether he ever loved him.'

Reginald Perkins held up a crooked finger. 'Did you ever wonder whether he loved the boy when he was alive?' he asked.

'Never.'

'There's your answer, luvvie,' he said, lowering his hand.

* * *

Sitting in his white wrought-iron chair, Rev. Septimus Drew gazed out over the fortress from his rooftop garden. Through four varieties of sage ravished by winter he watched a group of tourists standing in contemplation at the scaffold site, and another wandering out of Waterloo Barracks mesmerised by the shimmering vision of the

Crown Jewels. His eyes turned towards the chapel, and he thought again of what Ruby Dore had said to him in the Well Tower. Was he really fit to call himself a servant of God? It was a question that had plagued him since his literary career took off, but the transformation of the ladies, who nurtured the kitchen garden with more tenderness than they had ever shown themselves, had always chased away his doubts.

Filled with regret that his relationship with the landlady was over before it had begun, he saw himself in years to come still sitting on the sofa with the unruly spring in his melancholy bachelor's sitting room. Unable to bear the vision any longer, he rose to his feet, and trudged down the stairs. Opening the door to his study, he sat down at his desk to write a sermon. But inspiration evaded him. He got up and looked for it out of the window, then studied the floorboards that he started to pace. When it still failed to arrive, he sat in his worn leather armchair with his eyes closed, waiting for it to descend from heaven. But the only thing that dropped was a dusty spider, its legs clutched neatly together in death. He got to his feet and stood on the singed rag rug before the hearth, gazing up at the portrait of the Virgin Mary, the brushwork of which had seduced his father into buying it for his bride on their honeymoon. But the memories of his parents' happy marriage immediately drove his thoughts back to Ruby Dore, and his torment increased. His gaze came to rest on the white embossed invitation to the Erotic Fiction Awards, propped up on the mantelpiece. He picked it up and looked at it, the gold edging glittering in the embers of the afternoon light. In a moment of utter lunacy, which he later put down to acute stress, he took off his cassock and dog collar, put on his coat, and headed out of the Tower to buy himself a wig.

It was easier than the chaplain had imagined to transform himself into Vivienne Ventress. He had known exactly where to go, having passed the shop on numerous occasions on his way to his favourite butcher's. The Spanish salesman, dressed in a frock that did nothing for a figure destroyed by *patatas bravas*, immediately came to his rescue. After picking out a shoulder-length brunette wig, the assistant riffled through his racks for something smart enough for dinner, but discreet enough not to attract attention. Rev. Septimus Drew contemplated each option with mounting horror, and refused to try any of them on. The salesman returned to his racks, and with the furious quick movements of the piqued, selected a second batch. Amongst them the clergyman spotted a long-sleeved plain black dress, which he was willing to take into the changing room. And not even the act of clambering into it with his excessively long legs snapped him out of his madness.

When he drew back the curtain, his wig in place, the assistant clasped his hands together, and ushered him to the mirror in the middle of the shop. Both men cocked their heads to one side, and knew instantly that nothing could trump the long black frock with the charming row of pearl buttons. After broaching the delicate matter of underwear, the assistant disappeared into the back, and returned with a large cardboard box. He opened it with a flourish, revealing a pair of black court shoes of such colossal size an entire colony of rats could have set sail in them. By the time the assistant had finished his terrifying assault with the weapons in his make-up bag, Rev. Septimus Drew looked at his reflection, and was convinced that he looked even more alluring than the bearded Lord Nithsdale when he escaped from the Tower in a skirt in 1716.

Wearing his heavy overcoat, he stood on the opposite side of the road to the Park Lane hotel where the ceremony was being held, feeling the wind through his tights. When he had gathered his courage, he crossed the road with the cumbersome gait of a man not used to the feminine pitch of heels. Not daring to raise his eyes from underneath his crow's wing lashes, he flashed his invitation at the woman on the door, and slipped into the ballroom where the guests were already seated around tables set for dinner. Standing at the back, away from the candlelight, he refused each invitation to sit down, having caught the attention of a number of single gentlemen. As the ceremony began, he resisted the urge to offer up a prayer for victory, and resorted instead to evoking the pagan god of good fortune by crossing his fingers. With his back against the wall to ease the ache caused by his footwear, he watched as each winner was called one by one to the stage, his only consolation being the conviction that his was the most elegant gown.

When the master of ceremonies left the stage, and the waitresses filed in with the first course, the clergyman slipped out through the nearest door and found himself in the bar. He sank into an armchair and only remembered to close his legs when the waiter approached to take his order. He remained where he was for over an hour, distracted from the pinch of his shoes as he sat under the rockfall of failure. He was eventually brought round by the waiter asking him whether he wanted another drink, and he got up to go home. As he passed the door to the ballroom, he glanced in and saw that the master of ceremonies had returned to the stage.

'And now,' the man said, leaning towards the microphone, 'the moment you've all been waiting for. It gives me great pleasure to announce the overall winner . . .'

Rev. Septimus Drew crept in for his final moment of humiliation. The man in the bow tie then opened an envelope, looked up and announced two words that sent the chaplain into a state of shock. He failed to hear the subsequent praise for Vivienne Ventress's unique prose: the teasing chinks left for the reader's imagination; the moralistic voice never previously heard in the genre; and her absolute belief in the existence of true love which gave her work an extraordinary quaintness that rivals had tried to imitate without success.

It was the sight of his publisher getting to his feet to accept the award on Miss Ventress's behalf that catapulted the chaplain towards the stage. He glided up the steps with his head bowed and received the award with a flutter of his crow's wing eyelashes. Despite the loud chorus of 'speech!', he left the stage without uttering a word. And he maintained his demure silence all the way to the door, through which he escaped at speed clutching his shoes before his publisher could shake his hairy hand.

*   *   *

Rev. Septimus Drew was already snoring, the award standing on the bedside table next to him, when Balthazar Jones took to the battlements to exercise the bearded pig. Halfway through their moonlit walk, he stopped and lowered himself to the ground. He leant against the cold, ancient wall, hidden from the sentry, grateful for the warmth of the creature resting its head on his thigh, sending clouds of turnip-scented breath into the diamond-studded sky. Fingering its lead, he thought once again about the chaplain's words in the Brick Tower. Eventually, when he had made his decision, he gently shook the pig awake, and, making sure they wouldn't be spotted, returned to the Develin Tower so it could continue its dreams.

As he headed home, he heard the mournful cry of the wandering albatross across the darkened fortress. Making his way to the Brick Tower in order to comfort it, he was joined by a group of Beefeaters returning home from the Rack & Ruin, having been asked to leave by the landlady for conspiring to seize the thrupenny bit. They stopped outside the White Tower, where the men complimented him on the success of the menagerie, and each told him their favourite animal, which they admitted to visiting with a tasty little something when the tourists had left.

Suddenly the wind picked up and the hanging parrot, giddy from a series of furious revolutions as it clutched the weathervane above them,

275

opened its toes. And as it plunged headfirst towards the ground, it let out a lusty moan that reduced the Beefeaters to silence, followed by the words: 'Fuck me, Ravenmaster!'

18

Sitting bare-chested on his side of the bed, Balthazar Jones fed his pale feet into his crimson tights. He stood and hauled them up over his thighs and stomach, performing a low plié in order to raise the gusset. Striding across the room, the nylon hissing between his thighs, he pulled open the wardrobe door in search of his matching breeches. But the sudden movement caused it to collapse, having never fully recovered from being dismantled when it was first brought up the spiral staircase eight years ago.

Swearing in Greek, a habit picked up from his wife, the Beefeater hunted amongst the ruins for the rest of his red state dress uniform which Oswin Fielding had advised him to wear when he rang moments earlier, requesting that he come to the Palace at once. Placing the tunic and breeches on the bed, he rushed to the trouser press and extracted his white linen ruff, which scalded his fingers. After attaching red, white and blue rosettes to his knees and his shoes, he reached for his Tudor bonnet from the top of the wardrobe, and fled down the stairs.

He spent the journey in the cab, pitched forward so as not to crush the back of his ruff, gripped by fear. Had the Portuguese found out about the death of the Etruscan shrew, or had someone discovered the bearded pig? Maybe the Queen had suddenly realised that no one had ever given her four giraffes, and had decided to hand his job to someone else? By the time he arrived at the Palace, he had worked himself up into such a state that he could barely talk.

After being shown into a side door by a police officer, he was met by a silent footman whose polished buckled shoes were equally as silent as they passed along the corridor of dense blue carpet. He escorted the Beefeater to Oswin Fielding's office, and knocked. Given the order to enter, he opened the door and stood back to let in Balthazar Jones. The equerry immediately rose to his feet. 'Yeoman Warder Jones! Do have a seat,' he said, gesturing to the chair in front of his desk.

Balthazar Jones silently took off his Tudor bonnet and sat down, holding on to the brim.

'What we need is a cup of tea,' the equerry announced, picking up the phone. After requesting that some be brought, he added hastily: 'No shortbread.'

He then sat back in his chair, crossed his fingers over his runner's stomach, and asked: 'So, all well with you?'

The Beefeater ran his palms down the armrests to dry them. 'Fine,' he replied.

'And the boy? How's he?'

'What boy?' he asked.

'You said you had a son. What's his name?'

There was a pause.

'Milo,' Balthazar Jones replied.

'Nice name. Italian?'

'Greek.'

'Has your wife . . . ?'

'No.'

At that moment the door opened and the mute footman appeared with a tray. He served in silence, then retreated, closing the door behind him. Oswin Fielding helped himself to some sugar, and finally got to the point. 'I have some news, Yeoman Warder Jones.'

'I thought as much,' the Beefeater replied evenly.

'As you know, things have been going rather well with the menagerie. Very well, in fact. The Tower has been enjoying its highest visitor numbers for years. Her Majesty is immensely pleased.'

Balthazar Jones continued to look at him in silence.

'However, as you also know, a number of giant otters arrived from Guyana not so long ago, followed by a pair of oryx from Qatar, and a herd of wildebeest from the President of Tanzania. Quite what that man was thinking of, I have no idea. Then this morning we heard that the Americans are sending over a couple of grizzly bears. At best these people are being generous. At worst they're just PR stunts.'

The man from the Palace adjusted his rimless spectacles. 'The Queen's very great fear is that, the longer the menagerie stays open, the more it will encourage foreign rulers to send her increasing numbers of animals,' he continued. 'Before we know it, the Tower will be a veritable Noah's ark.'

The equerry leant forward. 'Between you and me, when she heard about the grizzlies she hit the roof. If you thought her shortbread was misshapen

278

last time, you should have seen what came out of the oven earlier. Unrecognisable.'

Balthazar Jones swallowed.

'Her Majesty has made the decision to transfer the animals back to London Zoo before things get out of hand,' said the equerry.

'What do you mean?' asked the Beefeater.

'The menagerie is going to have to close, I'm afraid.'

Balthazar Jones was unable to reply.

'The Queen's decision in no way reflects upon the efforts you have made, Yeoman Warder Jones. On the contrary,' the equerry continued. 'She very much appreciates the care and attention you have shown to the collection of royal beasts, and wanted to tell you in person, but she was suddenly called away. She has decided that you will remain Keeper of the Royal Menagerie, even though it will be just an honorific title. It will add a little intrigue for the tourists too. We're sure that the renewed interest in the Tower will continue, what with all the coverage it's had around the world. In appreciation of what you have achieved, Her Majesty has decided to make a small, but significant increase to your salary.'

'But what about the animals?' asked the Beefeater, clutching his armrests. 'They're all settled in. The Duchess of York is looking even better than when she first arrived. You should see the gloss on her coat. The fancy rats have learnt all sorts of tricks. And the Komodo dragon has just laid some eggs. It was a virgin birth. They can do that, you know.'

There was silence.

'And I've just put the glutton on a diet.'

The equerry closed the file in front him, and sat back. 'I'm afraid the decision is final,' he said. He studied the penholder on his desk, while the Beefeater stared at the floor.

'So when are they going back to the zoo?' Balthazar Jones asked.

'Tomorrow.'

'Tomorrow?' he asked, looking up. 'That's a bit soon, isn't it?'

'The sooner we act, the sooner it will put a stop to this nonsense.'

Balthazar Jones brushed the black crown of his Tudor bonnet with his fingertips. Eventually, he stood up. 'Make sure you don't use the same removal people who lost the penguins,' he said, and headed for the door.

*   *   *

The following morning, the Beefeater flung back the waxy sheets that he hadn't washed since Hebe Jones left, already feeling the blade of abandonment. He dressed as quickly as possible, clambering over the ruins of the wardrobe as he hunted for a clean pair of socks. Gripping the filthy rope handrail, he fled down the stairs to feed the animals one final time, and to say his goodbyes in private.

By the time he came out of the Brick Tower, a number of vans and lorries were already parked inside the fortress, and he spotted Oswin Fielding pointing at one of the towers with what looked to be a new silver-handled umbrella. As the animals were herded into the vehicles, the Beefeater stood issuing a stream of instructions to ensure their comfort, and making sure that they had plenty of water for the journey. The equerry asked him to leave, insisting that he was getting in everyone's way.

Unable to sit down, he paced the moat, and came to the spot he had once shown Milo where two medieval lion skulls had been unearthed in the 1930s. He sat down on the damp ground, and, as he fiddled with a piece of grass, he remembered the time he had told his son of the original menagerie's demise.

By 1822 the collection had dwindled to an elephant, a bird or two, and a bear, Balthazar Jones explained to the boy as they sat on deck chairs on the Salt Tower roof. That year, Alfred Cops, a professional zoologist, was appointed keeper, and he became the first to actively purchase animals for the menagerie, rather than relying on gifts to the king or souvenirs from explorers. A collector himself, he also exhibited his own animals alongside the royal beasts. Six years later, it had over sixty species and nearly three hundred animals. As well as kangaroos, mongooses, and dog-faced baboons, it boasted a five-fingered sloth, a pair of black swans from Van Dieman's Land, a kangaroo rat from Botany Bay, a boa constrictor from Ceylon, a crocodile from the River Nile, and a Malayan bear from Bencoolen presented by Sir Thomas Stamford Raffles. Visitors were charged no extra to watch feeding time at three o'clock, lion cubs were allowed to wander loose amongst the crowds, and there was always a long queue to see the female leopard with an appetite for umbrellas, muffs and hats.

'So then why did they close it, if everyone wanted to go?' Milo asked.

'Unfortunately, the menagerie's popularity was not enough to save it,' the Beefeater explained, resting his feet on one of his wife's flower tubs.

After George IV's death in 1830, the Duke of Wellington, an executor of his will and Constable of the Tower, set in motion a plan to transfer the one hundred and fifty royal animals to the gardens of the Zoological Society of London in Regent's Park, which later became known as London Zoo. The new king, William IV, who had little interest in the menagerie, gave his approval in 1831 and the move went ahead.

'But how did they get there?' asked Milo, feeding Mrs Cook a fuchsia.

The animals made the long journey across London on foot, Balthazar Jones told his son, herded by the Beefeaters carrying the small birds and pheasants in baskets. The elephants were placed at the front in an effort to prevent injuries, but the five-fingered sloth suddenly snapped out of its life-long stupor and darted ahead, producing the first casualty. Despite the bags of flour that had been placed inside their pouches to slow them down, the kangaroos arrived way ahead of the rest. They were closely followed by the ostriches, one of which kicked a zebra. A stampede broke out, which the Beefeaters struggled to contain. By the time the serpents turned up, many of their undercarriages had been rubbed raw, and for the next three months they continuously shed their skins. The last to arrive—two days after the storks—was the pair of black swans from Van Dieman's Land, smelling strongly of ale. Issued with leather booties to protect their feet during the mammoth trek, they had been invited into numerous taverns along the way by drinkers seduced by their footwear. They didn't refuse a single invitation, and a number of public houses across the country changed their name to the Black Swan in the creatures' honour.

'So what happened to the keeper?' asked Milo.

Alfred Cops also sold some of his own animals to the Zoological Society, Balthazar Jones replied, but continued to show the rest at the Tower, and the entrance fee was dropped from one shilling to sixpence to continue luring the crowds. Following the escape of a wolf, and a monkey biting a member of Wellington's garrison on the leg, in 1835 the keeper closed the attraction in accordance with the King's wishes. The remnants of his collection were disposed to an American gentleman and exported to America. Six hundred years of keeping wild animals at the Tower of London finally came to an end.

Milo picked up the tortoise. 'Was he a good keeper, Daddy?' he asked.

'Yes, son, a very good keeper. He loved the animals very much. Hardly any of them died. Unfortunately the secretary bird, which had a particularly long neck, stuck it into the hyena den, and that was the end of it.'

There was a pause.

Milo turned to his father. 'A bit like Mrs Cook's tail?' he asked.

'Exactly. Wouldn't have felt a thing.'

*   *   *

Standing alone on the wharf as the early morning light flickered on the Thames, Balthazar Jones watched as the first vehicle slowly left the Tower, carrying the giraffes that had never been a gift from the King of Sweden. Next came the Komodo dragon with its eggs, the result of an immaculate conception. The reclusive ringtail possums followed, dreaming with their tails perfectly coiled below them, along with the sugar glider that had been given one final tickle with a toucan feather. Sitting in the lorry's footwell was the cage containing the male lovebird, its leg still in a splint following the assault by its partner. Sensing an emergency, the crested water dragons rose on to their back legs and started running back and forth inside their van, their hands stretched out either side of them to keep their balance. Then came the glutton, which, despite having been put on a diet, had managed to hide a number of raw eggs within its fur. The giant otters, which he had never got to know, were in the truck behind, and, judging by the smell, the zorilla left next. The monkeys followed them in a vehicle with blacked-out windows lest the Geoffroy's marmosets felt threatened during the journey. And finally came the birds, which were flying from one end of their lorry to the other, headed by the wandering albatross exposing its pink patches. The only creature that failed to take to the air was the concussed hanging parrot, which clutched its perch with its toes for the entire length of its upside-down journey.

Feeling a chill as he watched the last vehicle leave, Balthazar Jones turned and walked to the van he had hired for the day, and drove out of the

Tower headed for the zoo. Next to him on the passenger seat was the cage containing the common shrew, which had finally squeezed its colossal hips out of the door of the tiny house.

Arriving at the wrought-iron gates that had nearly decapitated the giraffes, he parked at the entrance and carefully carried the cage inside, putting the creature's breathtaking girth down to a diet of Fig Rolls fed to it by the equally corpulent Yeoman Gaoler. He checked to see that all the animals had arrived safely, and stood watching as they rediscovered their enclosures. After witnessing the extraordinary sight of the reunion between the wandering albatross and its mate, he gave a toucan feather to the sugar glider's keeper, who looked at it in confusion. Returning to his van, he stood on the pavement checking each direction. Once he was certain that he wouldn't be seen, he slid open the door, and bowled a grapefruit along the ground through the main gates. The bearded pig hesitated for a moment, then bounded after it, its tasselled tail flying at full mast over its generous buttocks.

*   *   *

When Rev. Septimus Drew pushed open the heavy oak door of the Rack & Ruin, one of the Beefeaters was standing on his head performing an ambitious impression of the hanging parrot's historic cry as it dropped from the White Tower weathervane. On recognising the chaplain's skinny ankles, the Beefeater immediately turned himself upright, and apologised for his rendition of the unholy avian profanity. It wasn't the first time that the clergyman had heard it: the parrot's lusty shriek had been repeated around the Tower with unreserved enthusiasm whenever the Ravenmaster passed, much to the man's humiliation.

The chaplain approached the birdcage and looked at its yellow occupant, which suddenly started to disgorge a melody. Bending down to watch the creature empty itself of its cursed notes, he kept an eye on Ruby Dore. As soon as the landlady was free, he approached and asked whether he could talk to her in private. She looked up and hesitated. 'They locked the Well Tower again after they took away the fancy rats,' she replied. 'I'll meet you in Wakefield Tower in a couple of minutes.'

After looking at the small oratory where the imprisoned Henry VI was said to have been murdered while knelt in prayer, he joined the tourists heading to the lower chamber, which housed the instruments of torture exhibition. He listened to their murmurs of disappointment as they read the information panel stating that torture had been rare in England, and that there were only eighty-one documented cases of prisoners enduring it at the Tower. Their mood lightened, however, as soon as they saw the rack with its tantalising rollers that turned in opposite directions, the manacles from which prisoners would hang from their wrists, and the scavenger's daughter with its gruesome metal bars that compressed the body into an agonising kneeling position.

When the landlady appeared, apologising for having taken so long, the clergyman guided her towards the shadows at the back of the room. He glanced behind him to make sure that he wouldn't be heard, and told her of his decision: 'I'm going to leave the Church,' he said, looking at her through the gloom.

The chaplain explained how he thought he could do more of God's work at the shelter than at the Tower, whose congregation only seemed to come to his sermons to warm themselves against the radiators. His publishers had offered him another six-book deal with an even bigger advance than the first, which meant that he could rescue many more ladies than he could at the moment. Not only that, but the succulence of the vegetables they grew was such that they had just secured a contract to supply a local restaurant.

There was silence.

'Where will you live?' Ruby Dore finally asked, fiddling with the end of her scarf.

'I'm going to rent a little place near the shelter. I don't need much.'

Ruby Dore glanced away. 'I haven't been entirely truthful with you, either,' she admitted. 'I'm not going to be able to hide it forever, so I may as well tell you. I'm going to have a baby.'

It was Rev. Septimus Drew's turn to be silent, and both of them looked at the floor. The landlady eventually broke the silence. 'I'd better get back to work,' she said.

As she turned to leave, the clergyman suddenly found himself asking: 'Do you fancy visiting the Florence Nightingale Museum some time? One of the exhibits is her pet owl called Athena.'

Ruby Dore stopped and looked at him.

'She rescued it in Athens, and it travelled everywhere in her pocket. She loved it so much she had it stuffed when it died,' he added.

*   *   *

Valerie Jennings lay on her back in the empty sarcophagus breathing in the dusty remains of an ancient Egyptian. She closed her eyes in the cedar-scented gloom, having just discovered that her favourite obscure nineteenth-century novelist had remained a spinster for all her life.

Not even the sudden appearance of Dustin Hoffman at the original Victorian counter that morning had managed to lift her mood. She had simply asked for some identification, and, without a word to Hebe Jones about the exalted presence at the counter, collected the Oscar that had been standing on her desk for the past two years. She handed it to the actor with the same disinterest as reuniting a member of the public with a lost set of door keys.

Opening her eyes, she stared at the underside of the lid, its decoration visible in the light that came in courtesy of a hardback placed under the lid to prevent suffocation. Once again she thought how ridiculous she must have seemed to Arthur Catnip, whom she hadn't heard from since their dinner together. And she bitterly regretted having worn someone else's dress to dinner with him.

Suddenly there was a polite knock on the sarcophagus's lid. It had taken a while for Hebe Jones to find her colleague. She had walked the aisles of mislaid possessions piled up on metal shelves stretching far into the distance, until she came across a pair of flat back shoes with rubber soles. She looked around, turning three hundred and sixty degrees in the process, but it seemed that Valerie Jennings had vanished. Eventually her eyes fell to the sarcophagus, and she spotted the book wedged underneath the lid.

Hearing the knock, Valerie Jennings sat up like Dracula rising from his coffin. Smelling strongly of cedar wood, she clambered out, made her way silently back to her desk and opened a packet of Bakewell slices.

Hebe Jones followed her and sat down. 'I just asked one of the ticket inspectors why we haven't seen Arthur Catnip, and he said that he hadn't been to work for ages,' she said. 'Nor has he called them to explain why he hasn't come in. Someone went to his house, but there was no reply and his neighbour hadn't seen him either. They're really worried about him.'

Valerie Jennings remained silent.

'Why don't you try and find him?' Hebe Jones suggested.

'I wouldn't know where to start,' she replied.

'If you can find the owner of the safe after five years, you can find a tattooed ticket inspector.'

Valerie Jennings looked at her. 'Do you really think something's happened to him?' she asked.

'People don't just disappear like that. Especially him. He never even liked taking his holidays. Why don't you ring round the hospitals?'

'Maybe he just got sick of the job.'

'They said all his stuff is still in his locker.'

Unconvinced, Valerie Jennings reached for the phone book. A few minutes later she replaced the receiver.

'Well?' asked Hebe Jones.

'They don't have a patient there by that name.'

'Try the next one. The tree wasn't felled by one stroke,' she said.

Less than half an hour later, Valerie Jennings moved aside a discarded copy of the *Evening Standard*, and sat down heavily in a Tube carriage. She failed to notice the front-page story about the miraculous return of the bearded pig to London Zoo following its journey around Britain, and stared blindly ahead of her as the train started to rattle its way out of the station.

When she arrived at the hospital, Arthur Catnip was lying in a four-bed ward in much the same state that she had imagined. Despite his powers of intuition, he had not had the slightest premonition that he was going to suffer a heart attack more catastrophic than the first shortly after kissing Valerie Jennings on the well-swept steps of the Hotel Splendid, an oversight he later put down to being befuddled by love.

The sight of her in her navy coat, smeared glasses and flat black shoes immediately set his monitors shrieking. When the nurses finally calmed him, Valerie Jennings was called from her seat outside the ward and permitted to approach the patient. She sat by the bed, took his cold hands in hers, and told him that when he was discharged he could convalesce on her armchair with the pop-up leg rest, and she would lend him the works of Miss E. Clutterbuck to keep up his spirits. She told him she would help him regain his strength by taking him for walks around the local park, despite the geese, and if he fell into the duck pond she would pull him out herself, no matter how little hair he had left. And she told him that when he had fully recovered, she would pay for them to go on a cruise with the reward she had been given by the owner of the safe he had found on the Circle Line five years ago, and he could show her the island on which he had been marooned after falling overboard sodden with cider while in the Navy.

By the time she had finished, the warmth had returned to Arthur Catnip's hands. As she began to walk out of the ward he finally opened his eyes and turned his head. 'I like your shoes,' he said.

*   *   *

Hebe Jones opened the drawer containing one hundred and fifty-seven pairs of false teeth, and dropped another neatly labelled pair inside. Returning to her desk, she looked again at the bouquet of flowers from Reginald Perkins, and she thought of his wife tucked up safe and warm amongst her daffodils. Just as she put the tiny Chinese slippers into the mailbag, she heard the Swiss cowbell. Turning the corner, she saw Samuel Crapper standing at the original Victorian counter, the tips of his ochre hair standing up in triumph.

'Someone handed in your briefcase yesterday. Sorry, I meant to ring you,' she said.

'Did they?' he asked. 'I didn't know I'd lost it. I've come because I've actually found something for a change.' He then picked up a large Hamleys carrier bag, and put it on the counter. 'It was on the seat next to me on the Bakerloo Line and was still there when everyone got off. I forgot to bring it in, so it's been sitting at home for a few days, I'm afraid. I can't for the life of me work out what it is.'

Hebe Jones pulled the object out of the bag and looked at it. Eventually she was able to speak. 'It's a cabinet of rain samples,' she said.

19

Balthazar Jones stood on the bridge above the raven burial ground, where a tiny freshly dug grave contained the remains of an Etruscan shrew. As he watched the workmen dismantling the enclosures in the moat, he was struck once again by how empty the place seemed without the animals. Unable to watch, he made his way up Water Lane, passing the Bloody Tower with its red rambling rose, said to have produced snow-white blossoms before the death of the two little princes. No longer bothering to look around him in case he was being watched, he unlocked the door to the Develin Tower, and started to sweep up the straw that had once warmed the belly of the bearded pig. As he worked his brush into the corner next to the vast stone fireplace, he discovered Hebe Jones's mouldering grapefruit.

Under an endless cinder sky, he crossed the fortress and made his final journey up the Brick Tower's spiral staircase. The workmen had already taken away the aviary fencing, as well as the trees in their pots and the artificial perches. All that remained of its previous occupants were the seed husks covering the floor, dried droppings, and the white feathers shed by the wandering albatross. As he began to sweep the floor, he remembered the conversation he had had with Rev. Septimus Drew amongst the birds, and his subsequent decision to try and get his wife back. But despite the samples he had left on the Tube hoping Hebe Jones would come back, she had never got in touch, and the blade in his heart turned once more.

Picking up his black rubbish sack, he was about to leave when something on the windowsill caught his eye. He walked over and recognised one of the King of Saxony bird of paradise's prized brow feathers that stretched twice the length of its body, a sight so extraordinary that early ornithologists dismissed the first stuffed specimen as taxidermic trickery. He picked up the bewitching blue plume, and studied it in the light. After drawing it slowly through his fingers, he curled it up and put it in his pocket.

As he walked back to the Salt Tower, he was stopped by an American tourist who asked him whether he was the Keeper of the Royal Menagerie.

'I am,' the Beefeater replied.

'It's such a shame that they took the Queen's animals back to London Zoo,' the visitor said, adjusting his baseball cap. 'By all accounts, the Geoffroy's marmosets were a sight to be seen.'

Balthazar Jones put down his bag. 'Maybe it was for the best,' he said, and he told the man about the wandering albatross which mated for life, and had lost too many feathers mourning for its companion which had remained at the zoo.

'I guess home is where the heart is,' the American said with a smile. But the Beefeater was unable to reply.

Picking up his bag, he crossed the lawn in front of the White Tower, and looked at the marks left by the enclosure that had housed the reclusive ringtail possums and the sugar glider. Hearing a shout, he turned to see the Ravenmaster standing in front of the odious birds' pens, calling mournfully to his charges so that he could say his goodbyes. It hadn't, in the end, been the Chief Yeoman Warder who had asked him to leave the Tower. He had refused to take the hanging parrot's words as any proof of wrongdoing, and had threatened anyone repeating the historic cry within earshot of the tourists with the sack. It had, in fact, been the Ravenmaster's wife who insisted that their days at the Tower were over, recognising instantly the footprint of infidelity in the emerald shriek. She had suspected her husband's affairs over the years, and had done nothing about them, reasoning that the more of his awkward intimacies he shared with others, the less she would have to endure herself. But the public exposure of his philandering by a parrot had been a humiliation too far. Waiting until their daughter was out of the kitchen, she turned round from the sink and informed him he would have to choose between her and the Tower. The Ravenmaster instantly picked his wife, as he knew he was nothing without her. Leaving her husband to do the packing, she took the opportunity to go shopping, and eventually found the precise weapon she had been searching for in an antiquarian bookshop. And, as she watched the sales assistant wrap up the 1882 first edition of *Vice Versa or A Lesson to Fathers* by F. Anstey, she very much hoped that her husband would find it as hilarious as the Victorian novelist Anthony Trollope had. For, while laughing at a family reading of it, the author had suffered a stroke and died the following month.

When Balthazar Jones was called into the Chief Yeoman Warder's office in the Byward Tower earlier that morning, he had assumed he was going to have to account yet again for his lamentable record in catching pickpockets. Instead, the Chief Yeoman Warder had offered him the position of Ravenmaster. But the Beefeater immediately turned it down, keeping to himself his thoughts on the birds' villainous character. Still gripping the brim of his hat, he took the opportunity to ask if he could nevertheless move into the Ravenmaster's superior quarters to escape the Salt Tower's wretched damp, the mournful sound of chiselling, and the smell of Catholic priests' mouldering sandals. For a moment the Chief Yeoman Warder didn't reply, and engaged instead in a short burst of drumming with his embalmer's fingers. It was eventually followed by a sigh and the words: 'If you must.'

Balthazar Jones threw the black rubbish sack into the bin by the Tower Café, and turned to see Rev. Septimus Drew striding past on his way to the Rack & Ruin, his nibbled red cassock billowing in the wind. The Beefeater immediately ran to catch him up and asked whether it was true that he was leaving the Tower. The chaplain invited him to the tavern, where they sat at the bar waiting to be served while the landlady confiscated the thrupenny bit from the Tower doctor. He listened with regret as the clergyman told him that he would be gone by the end of the month.

'But what about our bowling?' Balthazar Jones asked.

Rev. Septimus Drew emptied his glass and put it on the beer mat in front of him. 'Everyone has to move on eventually,' he said. He then looked at his watch, and apologised for not being able to stay any longer as he was taking Ruby Dore to see a little stuffed owl called Athena. He then put a hand on his old friend's arm and asked whether he had done anything to persuade Hebe Jones to come back following their talk in the aviary. Balthazar Jones nodded.

'Any joy?' the chaplain asked.

The Beefeater's eyes dropped to the bar.

'At least you tried,' said the clergyman, filling the silence.

After finishing his pint alone, the Beefeater wiped his moustache on the back of his hand, and headed for the Salt Tower. As he climbed the spiral staircase, he heard the phone ringing, and burst into the living room to answer it. But it was only the man from the Palace, and he sunk to the sofa.

'I thought you'd like to know that we've got the rockhopper penguins back,' the equerry said.

The Beefeater leant back. 'Where were they?' he asked.

'They'd got all the way to Milton Keynes. A police officer noticed them on a roundabout in the early hours of yesterday morning.'

Once he had put down the phone, he made his way upstairs. Unable to bear the smell of Hebe Jones's absence any longer, he stripped the bed, leaving her nightdress on his pillow. As he opened the airing cupboard to fetch a clean set of sheets, he noticed the gentleman's white vest, and dropped it into the bin.

Confronted once more with the ruins of the wardrobe, he set about reassembling it. Once it was back on its feet, he picked up the clothes, and started to hang them back up. Amongst the pile he found several of his wife's jumpers, and as he folded them he discovered Milo's urn. He picked it up, and sat on the bed looking at it. He thought about all he had had in life, and all he had lost, and concluded that he had never deserved any of it in the first place. He dusted the urn gently with his handkerchief, stood up, and placed it on the windowsill.

Lying down on the clean bedclothes, he hoped to get some rest before resuming his duties. But he was unable to get comfortable because of the ache of solitude in his bones, and he immediately sat up again. He descended the stairs to the living room, but was unsettled by the sight of the front end of the pantomime horse. He wandered into the kitchen, pulled out a chair, and sat at the table. But he soon got up again when he spotted the picture above the sink of three smiling figures, two large, one small, standing next to a colourful blob. Crossing back through the living room, he walked down the corpse-cold stairs.

He pushed open Milo's bedroom door, and pulled back the curtains he had made all those years ago, filling the room with March's brutal light. He sat on the bed, and ran a hand over the soft pillow where his son's head had once rested. He looked around at his possessions that he would soon have to pack. Picking up the matchbox from the bookshelf, he slid it open, and looked at the fifty-pence piece. He reached for the ammonite and ran his thumb over its contours. Opening the book on Greek gods on the nightstand, he flicked through the pages, stopping to look at a picture of Hermes and a tortoise. He didn't know how long he had been there when he suddenly heard a sound. When he looked up with eyes as pale as opals he saw Hebe Jones standing in the doorway with her suitcase.

Neither said a word. Eventually, she put down her case and came to sit next to her husband. Balthazar Jones spoke first. 'It was me who killed Milo,' he said, looking at the floor.

Hebe Jones raised a hand to her mouth. 'What are you talking about?' she demanded, her eyes upon him.

The Beefeater haltingly told her about the argument he and Milo had the night he died over the homework he had failed to finish, and his threat not to take him to the Science Museum at the weekend if it wasn't done in time.

'What's that got to do with anything?' she asked.

He reminded her of the words of the expert pathologist, spoken at the inquest for all to hear, that some children suffered sudden cardiac death after emotional stress.

Hebe Jones rested her hand on his thigh. 'Is that what you've been thinking all these years?' she asked, searching his face. She then reminded him that the pathologist had also said that some died in their sleep, when they woke up, or while exercising, and Milo had been up and down the wretched stairs all evening.

She then gazed ahead of her in silence. At last she spoke: 'If anything weakened that poor boy's heart it was the love he had for you.'

His tears fell and fell and fell. And when they

298

both thought it was finally over, they fell some more.

*   *   *

After they had finished talking, Hebe Jones unpacked her suitcase, checked on the daffodils blooming in her tubs on the roof, and discovered her nightgown on her husband's pillow. While it was still light, they descended the spiral steps, and walked to the Tower wharf. Standing next to each other, they looked out across the stretch of the Thames where Henry III's polar bear used to fish for salmon while tied to a rope. When finally she was ready, he slowly took off the lid and turned the urn on its side. They watched as the ashes fluttered away with the breeze and came to rest on the water's silver surface. As they began their journey out to the sea, Hebe Jones reached for the hand she would hold forever. When they had disappeared from view, Balthazar Jones told her about the house he wanted to buy in Greece to escape the English rain when he retired, which would be on the coast so they could be with Milo forever.

Later that night, as they lay in the sanctuary of each other's arms, the magnificent blue brow plume used by grey songbirds to decorate their courtship bowers hung on the wall above their bed. And such was their contentment, neither of them heard the creaks as Mrs Cook returned from her travels, an odious black feather still caught in her ancient mouth.

299

Author's Note

Gifts of live animals given to Her Majesty The Queen, and placed in the care of London Zoo, have included a canary from Germany following a state visit in 1965; jaguars and sloths from Brazil in 1968; two black beavers from Canada in 1970; two giant tortoises from the Seychelles in 1972, and an elephant called Jumbo from the President of Cameroon in the same year to mark the Queen's Silver Wedding Anniversary; and two more sloths, an armadillo and an anteater from Brazil in 1976.

The most recent animals received by the Zoological Society of London from the Queen were six red kangaroos, which were kept at London Zoo, and two cranes sent to Whipsnade Zoo. They were presented by Melbourne Zoo in 1977 to mark Her Majesty's Silver Jubilee. One of the cranes is still alive.

The Needs of Children

Mia Kellmer Pringle

The Needs of Children

A personal perspective prepared
for the Department of Health
and Social Security

HUTCHINSON OF LONDON

Hutchinson Educational Ltd
3 Fitzroy Square, London W1

London Melbourne Sydney Auckland
Wellington Johannesburg Cape Town
and agencies throughout the world

First published in this edition June 1975

Printed in Great Britain by litho by The Anchor Press Ltd
and bound by Wm Brendon & Son Ltd
both of Tiptree, Essex

ISBN 0 09 124411 0

Contents

Contents

Contents

Foreword

By the Secretary of State for Social Services (1970-4)

I have long been concerned that crippling social, material and emotional deprivations and miseries continue to be passed on from generation to generation. This problem has remained despite the continuing development of our health, education and social services and the devoted work of those who provide them. I suggested in a speech almost two years ago that a cyclical process might be at work, which I called 'the cycle of deprivation'. Modern methods of academic research, I ventured to think, might be able to test this hypothesis, whilst concerted drives within the services concerned to try to intervene in such a process might, on the basis of existing knowledge, lead to progress in practice.

I know there are some who see the solution simply in terms of alleviating material deprivations – poverty and poor housing. I applaud and share their urgent desire to do this. But I am not shaken from my view that there is another dimension to the problem and that one of the ways of tackling it is likely to be by promoting wider understanding of the emotional needs of children and of the importance from the earliest years of the quality of the relationships between a child and those who are responsible for his care. The two approaches are not mutually exclusive.

For the past eighteen months my Department has been exploring with the Social Science Research Council the concept of an inter-generational process of transmission of deprivation, and the possibilities of investigating this concept, and the Council will be mounting a major research programme for this purpose. As a separate initiative Mrs Thatcher and I held meetings with a wide range of voluntary, professional and other organisations to discuss ways in which people might be better prepared for parenthood, and we received many very valuable suggestions; we also held an academic seminar at Oxford where people from a number of academic and professional disciplines were invited to discuss the dimensions of parenthood with which their specialisations made them familiar. Accounts of these consultations and of the seminar have been published as the first two volumes in a series entitled 'The Family in Society'.* We are now trying out in experimental projects some of the suggestions we have received.

At the same time we asked Dr Kellmer Pringle, Director of the National Children's Bureau, to prepare an account, based on knowledge already available to the Bureau, of what is understood about the needs of children, and requested the Bureau, as a second exercise, to undertake an extensive review of the literature on the subject. This book is the outcome of Dr Kellmer Pringle's work. I believe that it provides a valuable basis for further thinking about development of our strategies for family support and I hope many parents, and others caring for children or training to do so, will read it and find it, as I did, a compelling and fascinating book.

Keith Joseph.

---

* *Preparation for Parenthood* and *Dimensions of Parenthood*, H.M.S.O. Publications, 1974.

Editorial Foreword

This book by Dr Mia Kellmer Pringle is the first in a new series entitled 'The Contexts of Human Change'. The unity of the series will derive from the fusion of two perspectives. First, it will be concerned with human development. Inevitably, there will be some emphasis upon development during childhood and adolescence since these are the periods of most rapid and important change in terms of the life-style and adjustment of individuals.

Important as these formative years are, however, we cannot be unaware of changes occurring later in life which significantly alter the pattern of living for individuals and for groups. The series, therefore, will be concerned with human development over the whole span of life from earliest infancy to old age.

The second perspective, which adds another dimension to the concept of development, is the context in which any changes occur; hence the title of the series. Most advances in our knowledge and understanding of human development stem from work in particular and specific disciplines: psychology, sociology, education, paediatrics, social medicine, geriatrics and so on. This is inevitable but it has one severe limitation. The blinkers of professional training tend to produce different vocabularies and different concepts, which often lead the specialists in these fields either to ignore entirely the common ground between them, or else to neglect opportunities for establishing fruitful links. In a sense our knowledge about people tends to be structured vertically in the conventional academic disciplines, whilst people themselves are structured horizontally. That is to say, a person's intellectual functioning is inextricably bound up with his emotional life, with the social contexts in which he operates and with his physical health.

In this series, then, an attempt will be made to forge links between the disciplines. Authors will be chosen who are prepared to lower their professional blinkers and actively to seek out and develop the relationships between their own fields and relevant aspects of other areas of knowledge.

So much for the two main perspectives of the series, which might be summarised as: human development seen in an interdisciplinary context. However, the human life cycle is a broad canvas indeed. The series will therefore be given a sharper focus. Within the life cycle, there are particular phases, or circumstances, which may be important, even critical, in influencing the subsequent course of events. Some of these periods have been well documented, although often narrowly treated; others have received relatively little attention. The middle years of childhood, for example, have largely escaped scrutiny when compared with the pre-school period and adolescence.

A second marriage is becoming a more common phenomenon in Western societies as attitudes to the institution of marriage change and divorce becomes more accepted. What are the psychological and social repercussions of this situation? Changing family structures and increased life span add new perspectives to human development in the declining years. These are examples of some of the topics which may be explored in the series.

It would be difficult to think of a more appropriate topic with which to launch the series than 'the needs of children'. It would be difficult to think of a more appropriate author to tackle this formidable task than Dr Mia Kellmer Pringle. Dr Pringle is an educationalist and a child psychologist, but both she and the National Children's Bureau, which she has directed since its establishment in 1963, are committed to an interdisciplinary approach. Her breadth of vision shows through every page of this book. She brings together insights from many different fields and presents a coherent picture of the present state of our knowledge about children's needs and what happens when these needs are not met. She does not shrink from radical or controversial solutions to the problems which arise. I am sure that the book will have a major impact on our thinking and on our policies in relation to children's welfare, health and education.

It is intended to form a small Editorial Board for the series but events in a number of directions moved so rapidly that this first book was in the printer's hands before the composition of the Board could be finalised. However, I am delighted to say that Professor G. M. Carstairs, Vice-Chancellor of the University of York, and Professor D. V. Donnison, Director of the Centre for Environmental Studies, have agreed to join the Board.   R.D.

Preface

This work, which has been commisioned by the Department of Health and Social Security, is not meant to be either a systematic research review or a theoretical critique. Rather, the Department wishes to have available a source document when it comes to take, or encourages others to take, new initiatives or to develop existing ones in connection with Sir Keith Joseph's twin themes of breaking the 'Cycle of Deprivation' and 'Preparation for Parenthood'. The Department intends to draw on the document in formulating possible measures for disseminating knowledge about child development and parenthood in a broad general context.

The actual terms of reference were as follows:

To prepare a comprehensive document about the developmental needs of all children, about the ways in which these needs are normally met, and about the consequences for the emotional, intellectual, social and physical growth and development of children when, for one reason or another, these needs are not adequately met.

The present report was to be based on the results of the Bureau's work as well as on my own experience and knowledge. It will be followed by a comprehensive review of the literature, also commissioned by the Department, which will take about two years.

To help make the task of preparing this document somewhat more manageable in the brief time available, I decided that it would be concerned only with conditions in developed Western societies; that the main emphasis would be on children's psycho-social needs; and that the development and needs of the younger age groups would be given the major attention. Finally, the views expressed are my own and not necessarily those of the Bureau.

ACKNOWLEDGEMENTS

While many people gave generous help, any omissions, weaknesses or inconsistencies which remain are mine alone.

First of all I must thank the Department of Health and Social Security at whose instigation this book was written. To the extent to which it will be found to meet a real need, to that extent the credit is entirely theirs. I am grateful too for the many helpful suggestions made by the Department, the Department of Education and Science, and other Government Departments who read through the first draft.

Next, four 'official' readers were invited, jointly by the Department of Health and Social Security and myself, to go through and comment on the text. They were Professors David Donnison, Michael Rutter, Gordon Trasler and Bill Wall. All of them did so with the greatest care and I am deeply grateful for their constructive and detailed comments and criticisms, which led to many improvements.

On hearing of the preparation of this book, many friends and colleagues expressed an interest and offered to read the manuscript. In particular I am grateful to Mrs L. A. Hersov, Mr A. Jacka, Mrs S. Kitzinger, Mr and Mrs A. Rampton, Miss J. Rowe, Baroness Serota and Dame Eileen Younghusband for their many suggestions.

Also all my colleagues in the National Children's Bureau were offered the opportunity to comment on the manuscript. Many of them devoted a great deal of time and thought to doing so. Their help is much appreciated, particularly the constructive comments made by Miss D. Birchall, Professor R. Davie and Dr R. Pearson.

The final version was typed and collated with great care and intelligence by Miss Ruth Francis and Mrs Margaret Green, of whose painstaking work I cannot speak too highly.

Invaluable support and encouragement were given to me by my husband Len Hooper throughout the period of writing, rewriting and checking the final proofs. He read and re-read every draft, commenting critically and constructively on matters of both substance and detail. If the book is judged to be intelligible to a lay readership, then a great deal of the credit must go to him in helping me to make it so. He also willingly shared with me the giving up of leisure time in the evenings and weekends to make possible the completion of the task in the required time.

M.K.P.

1. Some Basic Concepts

Children's physical, emotional, social and intellectual needs must all be met if they are to enjoy life, develop their full potential and grow into participating, contributing adults. At present only physical needs are being satisfactorily met, at least to any considerable extent. Hence, the main emphasis in this book will be on psycho-social needs.

Five basic premises underlie the discussion and these are briefly outlined in this section. They are: that the environment is of over-riding importance; that it is the early years of life which are particularly vital to later development; that there are marked individual differences in the extent and pace of children's growth; that vast improvements could be brought about in their emotional, social, intellectual and educational achievements; and that the strategy so successfully used in the health field may well be appropriate also to these aspects of development.

THE NATURE-NURTURE ISSUE

The first premise is that, for all practical purposes of social action and policy, the environment is of overriding importance. Human capacity to learn is such that the new-born child can adapt to widely different environments. Since, to begin with, he has a rather limited range of innate behavioural mechanisms, this very limited capacity makes him entirely dependent on his environment: having only the potential for becoming human, he must needs have a human environment to do so.

This is clearly shown by two phenomena; first, by the extremely circumscribed development of children who lack the necessary sense organs to perceive, communicate and interact with their environment, such as the deaf-blind (Helen Keller being the most famous example of success in overcoming these obstacles); secondly, by the fortunately rare cases of children who spent their early years in extreme isolation: by the time they were rescued, aged six years or more, they had acquired few truly 'human' characteristics. The same need for an appropriately nurturing environment is illustrated by the fact that even great gifts, such as the ability to compose music, might not be realised, or even discovered, in a culture without music.

Somewhat less extreme examples of the environment's overriding influence relate to sex-typing – the teaching of the socially expected sex role – which normally begins at birth. One of the first questions asked about a baby is whether it is a boy or a girl and from then onwards parental attitudes and expectations become different according to the answer given: both in major and minor ways, the child will be treated, and expected to behave, differently. Clothes, toys, subtle differences in words, play, hugs, rewards, punishments and parental example, surround the child with a world which clearly distinguishes behaviour expected from boys and girls.

Those psychological characteristics considered appropriate will be developed by about the third year of life; and throughout childhood the 'assigned' sex role will be practised in social relations, in play and in fantasy, and be continually reinforced by the responses and expectations of others. Finally, it will be reinforced at puberty by the various physiological changes.

In the past, the consistency and reliability of the sex role performance had been thought to be due to its innate basis. Now many studies have shown the immense influence of psychological and social factors in determining sexual attitudes and behaviour. Furthermore, studies of children born with the same defect of physical sexual development have illustrated that they can be raised either as boys or as girls. With very few exceptions, they grew up to behave in accordance with the sex role to which they had been – almost arbitrarily – assigned (Hampson and Hampson, 1961; Kagan and Moss, 1962; Money, 1963).

These findings suggest that children learn to behave in 'masculine' or 'feminine' ways through being treated as such; in other words, the gender role is psychologically determined first by parental and then by wider society's expectations.

This conclusion is in line with other recent findings relating to educational achievement. These showed the influence of parental attitudes and expectations on scholastic progress (Douglas, 1964 and 1968). Another study demonstrated that children 'demoted' to lower streams were soon conforming to the lower standards prevailing in them (Lunn, 1970).

There is another developmental area where this is still a controversial issue, namely the question of the relative contribution made to intellectual development by the genes and the environment respectively. This has been debated, with greater or lesser heat, for many years. Following Jensen's much-quoted article (*Harvard Educational Review*, 1969), it has once again become a topical controversy.

The current debate differs in two ways from that which raged in the 1930s. On the one hand, few would now deny that environment plays a part in shaping a child's intelligence, even if they believe heredity to have a much greater influence; the pure environmentalist has been discredited too. On the other hand, more explicit racial implications have now been added to the previous political overtones. This has increased the bitterness of the argument as well as its implications for current political and educational thinking.

Though a belief in the interaction of heredity and environment is the most generally accepted standpoint, available research findings allow a wide range of possible interpretations. The debate about measuring the relative importance of the two is likely to remain rather sterile, since it is doubtful whether conclusive evidence can ever be provided. This situation is only too familiar to the farmer: to obtain a good crop of wheat, he needs not only good seed but also good soil and appropriate moisture, temperature and fertiliser to nourish its growth. However, all of these can be controlled and varied in a way which would be neither acceptable, nor indeed possible, in relation to the genetic and environmental components of human beings.

Yet the mistaken belief about reliable measurement is most clearly shown in relation to the I.Q. The credibility of most educational testing – whether concerned with assessing attainments, aptitudes or intelligence – depends largely on a tautology: the validity of the tests is demonstrated by their ability to predict performance at school; yet such performance amounts to an ability to perform well on tasks similar to those in the tests. This has led to the false impression that doing well in tests necessarily means a greater competence in coping, later on, with life in general. Hence there is a 'grave danger of perpetuating a mythological meritocracy' (McClelland, 1973).

The solution is not – as some would have it – simply to abandon testing; if for no other reason than that subjective judgements are considerably less reliable. Instead, three changes are required: first, the search for innate factors, such as intelligence, should be abandoned to be replaced by measuring instead improvement resulting from new experiences and from deliberate teaching. Secondly, currently used items, consisting of very artificial word and number games should be replaced by issues and problems occurring in everyday social and occupational life. Thirdly, rate of progress over time should become the yardstick for learning potential instead of the static concept of the I.Q.

Genetic-environmental interaction starts in utero and hence 'pure' inborn abilities and characteristics can never be assessed. For example, the development of the nervous system in the foetus and new-born is affected during pregnancy and parturition by adverse conditions, e.g., malnutrition or exposure to certain diseases, heavy manual work or extreme anxiety. Thus a child may be born with a brain which is incapable of normal development, not because of defective genes but because of pre-natal conditions or birth injury. On the other hand, inborn temperamental differences inevitably affect the environment; for example, a hypersensitive, irritable baby is likely to call out irritability in his mother which in turn only serves to increase his own irritability.

In growth of all kinds, the interaction of powerful genetic forces and powerful environmental forces is at work cumulatively over long periods of development. In optimum environments, genetic factors will appear predominant and environment will appear less important because its influence is roughly constant. In sub-optimum environments, environmental effects will appear more obvious (Clarke and Clarke, 1972).

The weight or influence exerted solely by the nurturing process could only be determined by a study of identical twins who alone are perfectly matched genetically. However, ethical reasons preclude the deliberate and extreme environmental manipulation which would be needed to make possible a systematic exploration of the effects of very different experiences on subsequent development.

There is one well-documented and detailed study of two pairs of identical twins who were reared apart from early infancy and did not meet again until they were in their late twenties (Hudson, 1970).

The two girls had been adopted into very different homes and hence their upbringing and education had also been markedly different. By the age of thirty-five, there were even marked physical differences: the one who had had the much easier life was, for example, better preserved, apparently physiologically younger and an inch taller; there were also marked differences in ability, attainments, personality and overt behaviour. The two boys, on the other hand, were adopted by families who were of absolutely the same social and economic status and these twins led extremely parallel lives. By adulthood, the similarities between them were quite striking in almost all areas of development and physically they had repeatedly been mistaken for each other by strangers.

No doubt the controversy regarding the relative contribution of heredity and environment (including the intra-uterine) to children's abilities, attainments and adjustment will continue. That genetic and physical factors play some role, if only in setting limits to potential development, is widely accepted. At the same time, all available evidence confirms that, from a practical viewpoint, the most important element in shaping behaviour and development is the environment in general and other people in particular. Hence, from the point of view of action – whether preventive or remedial – this is where intervention should be concentrated.

Genetics, after all, describes only the raw material on which a particular culture acts. As educational systems evolve, so too do the skills of the individuals within them. Logically, we can set limits to children's capacity to learn only if every permutation of their environment, every method of nurturing and teaching them, has been exhausted. This is a task we have scarcely begun; and which, even in principle, we could never finish (Hudson, 1972).

EARLY EXPERIENCE, DEVELOPMENTAL PACE AND
SENSITIVE PERIODS

Longitudinal research is beginning to provide an understanding of the pattern of human growth. Three quite specific features have emerged which have important practical implications for child rearing. First, the development of various basic characteristics does not proceed in equal units per unit of time, i.e., growth does not take place at an even pace.

Secondly, for most aspects, the period of most rapid growth takes place in the early years (i.e., from conception to six years or so) and is then followed by periods of less and less rapid growth with a 'spurt' at puberty; for some characteristics there is as much quantitative growth in a single year of a child's life as there is in eight to ten years at other stages in his development.

Thirdly, available evidence suggests that environmental influences have the greatest effect during the most rapid periods of growth. From this it follows that it is experiences and opportunities during the early years of life which are particularly vital to later development. This is the second basic principle adopted in this document.

A few examples are given as illustrations. These are drawn from the Bureau's National Child Development Study; the Berkeley Growth Study (Bayley, 1964); the longitudinal studies of the Fels Institute (Kagan and Moss, 1962); the writer's own research; and the evidence synthesised by Bloom (1964).

Physical development

Height is the most extreme case of the first generalisation referred to above. During the nine months from conception to birth, growth is of the same absolute magnitude as it is during the nine years from three to twelve; and from conception to the age of about two and a half years, half the full adult stature is attained. Hence, one would expect that it is pre-natally and during early infancy that the environment has the greatest effect, for better or worse. Available evidence shows this to be so.

Intellectual development

As much development takes place in the first four years of life as in the following thirteen years. It has been estimated that about 50 per cent of intellectual growth takes place between conception and the fourth year, and about 30 per cent between the ages of four to eight years. Unlike physical development, however, it continues well into adulthood, but the pace becomes very much slower after eighteen years or thereabouts.

With regard to vocabulary, by eight years of age, about 50 per cent of the level attained by eighteen years will have been reached. So again, early environmental influences have a marked effect on measurable cognitive functioning. Recent studies suggest that social class differences, affecting language development, emerge during the first year of life and become unequivocal by about the age of three (Kagan, 1971).

Emotional and social development

Precise and objective evidence remains very inadequate in this area. Paradoxically, less is known about the development of normal than of deprived, disturbed or delinquent children. Two aspects of personality have, however, received particular attention, partly because of their central significance in personal relations and partly because they are more readily observable than other characteristics. These are aggressiveness and dependence on others for support and direction.

Differences between boys and girls in the development of these aspects can be noted early and the 'sex-appropriate' behaviour becomes well established during the pre-school years. This suggests that for personality development, too, the early years are of great importance.

With regard to behaviour and adjustment, problems are already apparent among children in infant schools, by which age some 14 per cent show considerable difficulties in school (Chazan, Laing and Jackson, 1971; Pringle *et al.*, 1966). The lower the parental occupational status, the lower tends to be the proportion of well-adjusted children (Davie *et al.*, 1972).

Educational development

Available evidence suggests that of a child's general attainment at the age of eighteen, approximately half has been reached when he is about nine years old. However, the capacity to respond to, and benefit from, education inevitably depends on the level of a child's intellectual, language and emotional maturity. Therefore, it is again experience during the pre-school years which has a vital influence on later scholastic progress.

Findings from the National Child Development Study show that even as early as the age of seven years there are marked differences in scholastic attainments between children coming from each of the five occupational groups into which the Census divides the total

21

population; during the following four years, these differences in attainment continue to widen. With regard to children removed from their families, their educational difficulties were found to be more severe, the earlier the child's first separation from home and the less contact his parents had maintained with him subsequently.

Differential growth, which takes place during early childhood, is presented below in summarised form for the six aspects of development just discussed. It is based on the assumption that growth is more or less complete by the age of eighteen to twenty years. What is shown is the age by which – according to Bloom's synthesis of available knowledge – the half-way stage of development is reached for each aspect.

	Age in years
Height (from conception)	$2\frac{1}{2}$
Intelligence	4
Vocabulary	8
Aggressiveness in boys	3
Dependence in girls	4
School attainments	9

'Sensitive' periods

It is evident then that normally more progress, change and development take place during the first few years of life than in any comparable time thereafter. This is true too of the post-natal growth of the brain itself, which is more rapid in the first two years. In the case of young birds and mammals, the existence of 'sensitive' and 'critical' periods over a very wide range of development is incontrovertibly established; during these periods, there is greatly heightened susceptibility to specific experiences, such as stimulation or isolation, which may have a lasting and irreversible effect.

Whether in children's development there are also such 'sensitive' periods during which responsiveness to the environment is maximal – and hence learning optimal – has not yet been quite so clearly demonstrated. The evidence suggests they do occur but that they are not as 'critical' or fixed as, say, the result of 'imprinting' is in birds. However, there are definite indications that children, too, respond more readily to various environmental opportunities at certain periods: strong emotional relationships, particularly with their mother, are developed during a relatively circumscribed period (from about six to twenty-four months); and skills such as walking and talking are usually acquired at roughly similar ages by most children. Conversely, if a child has not learned to speak at all by the age of five years or to read by the age of ten (despite normal opportunities to do so and in the absence of sensory handicaps), then it is most unlikely that quite normal speech or reading ability will ever be achieved.

At the same time, not only are these sensitive or optimal periods of longer duration among the human young but also later learning can and does take place, although it is slower and more difficult then.

That early childhood experiences have great potency is quite beyond doubt; so is the fact that their consequences are often long-lasting and may be very difficult to alter. Of course, this does not mean that experiences later in a child's life may not also have a similarly marked or lasting effect on subsequent development.

As in most other fields, prevention is undoubtedly better than cure. Hence, the attention and emphasis now being given to the earliest years, indeed months, of life is entirely justified. What is not justified is the pessimism which has followed, both from this new insight about the probable existence of 'sensitive' periods and from recent only partly successful attempts to reverse the effects of a deprived early environment.

Reversibility and recovery

This pessimism has a three-fold basis: first, the growing evidence that the effects of early disadvantage or deprivation are multiple and cumulative; secondly, that the provision of more educational opportunities during the past twenty-five years has least benefited those most in need of them; and thirdly, the rather disappointing long-term results produced by pre-school intervention programmes, such as Headstart in the USA.

In fact, the first and second arguments are linked. The belief that formal education could itself bring about the desired changes can now be seen to have been unrealistic in the light of more recent understanding of the nature of emotional, social and intellectual development. With regard to intervention programmes, those devised so far have all been too short-term; they have been further handicapped by too narrow a framework, too late a start, too limited a methodology and insufficient theoretical knowledge about early learning. Also, most of them failed to involve the parents; there is now some evidence that concurrent maternal participation can lead to substantial improvement (Bronfenbrenner, 1973; Halsey, 1972; Midwinter, 1972).

In fact, there is cause for optimism regarding the possibility of recovery and reversibility of even severe and early deprivation. First, work with mentally subnormal patients over the past fifteen years has shown that some degree of recovery can be achieved even in adulthood (Clarke and Clarke, 1973).

The second source of evidence comes from the study of children who have suffered prolonged and extremely severe social isolation in early life. Unfortunately, in most of these cases, their subsequent history has been inadequately documented. Inevitably, what happened during the period of isolation could only be pieced together retrospectively; also, details of the rehabilitation process itself have been inadequate but for a few exceptions (Mason, 1942; Davis, 1947; Koluchova, 1972). These suggest that considerable improvement, if not complete recovery, is possible, given a carefully devised and prolonged programme of rehabilitation.

When labour was cheap, and fulfilment of potential the prerogative of a minority, waste of human abilities was not seen as a problem. Now this is fortunately no longer so. A beginning has been made with exploring systematically both available and new psychological, educational and social methods for preventing or reducing the loss of human potential; and for undoing and, if possible, reversing the effects of early neglect or damage.

INDIVIDUAL DIFFERENCES

In the physical field, it is readily accepted that large individual differences may exist, even among children in one family. When a healthy, well-nourished child is nevertheless of small stature and rather slight build, this may cause comment, even regret perhaps, but neither concern nor reproach. Although theoretically there is a similar understanding in regard to intellectual, educational, emotional and social development, yet in practice, parents, and to some extent professional workers too, react with less tolerance and understanding.

Slow intellectual and educational progress are readily attributed to 'laziness' with disapproval and punishment being meted out in the hope of bringing about improvement. A similar attitude is taken to emotional and social 'deviation', such as timidity or shyness. This then is the third basic principle: that there are as marked individual differences in the extent and pace of children's intellectual, education, emotional and social development, as there are of physical development.

Recent evidence indicates how very early individual differences in behaviour and 'cognitive style' can be observed. 'New-born infants write their signature with their sucking rhythm, showing a constant individual pattern in the number of sucks and intervals between sucks per minute' (Lipsitt, 1972). Though this is congenitally determined, nevertheless the baby learns very quickly to modify his sucking pattern in response to the way he is fed.

The next example of early individual differences shows the equally early interaction between nature and nurture: 'Stable individual differences were found in motor activity [of new-borns] both in hospital and at home... The mothers of the more active infants were more demonstrative towards their children and appeared to form a stronger and earlier attachment to the baby' (Campbell, 1972). Here is the beginning of an egg-and-chicken question: a more active baby probably calls out stronger maternal feelings and a more 'motherly' mother is likely to encourage the baby to be more active and responsive.

A third example of individual differences relates to the respective development of boys and girls. There is considerable and consistent evidence showing boys to be much more variable and vulnerable from birth onwards. For example, their morbidity and their accident rate is generally higher; their speech, language development and level of reading attainment are poorer, at least during the first ten years of life; a much higher proportion show emotional and behaviour difficulties, ranging from enuresis and school phobia to delinquency and crime; the majority of drop outs are also male. Girls, on the other hand, 'are born with slightly more mature skeletal and nervous systems and gradually increase their developmental lead (in absolute terms) throughout childhood' (Tanner, 1974).

Various hypotheses have been put forward to account for these sex differences. Most suggest a combination of and interaction between genetic, biological and environmental factors. Some consider that boys' greater deviancy may be a function of a Y chromosome and hence largely genetically determined (Birley, 1973). Cultural, social and family influences are stressed by others and motivational aspects are also thought to play a part; for example, most parents are more ambitious career-wise for boys than girls. On the other hand, fathers cannot so readily serve as models for their sons; not only do most of them spend the major part of the child's waking life away from home, but also they do work which their sons can neither observe nor clearly comprehend. Also, in Western society a boy is expected to be more active, outgoing, aggressive and less home-centred – not only in childhood but in his future work and leisure interests too – than a girl. Peers too exert greater pressures on boys than girls by their competitive self-assertiveness, in particular in relation to games and physical prowess. Additionally, the roles which boys are expected to play are less consistent than those demanded of girls: for example, the greater stress laid on boys' educational progress means that they must be more studious and intellectual which inevitably conflicts with being more active physically and more outgoing; also physical prowess is not necessarily allied to educational abilities. Such conflicting expectations may to some extent at least account for the greater deviancy found among boys. Though all these expectations may now be changing, or at least becoming modified, such change is unlikely to bring rapid results.

It follows that methods of child-rearing must take individual differences more into account than at present. The practical implications would seem to be three-fold. First, only a few directions or antidotes can be of universal application; and it is the quality of understanding – often intuitive, rarely fully explicit – which can best guide parents in applying their knowledge of developmental needs to the upbringing of a particular child. An understanding of his physical and mental equipment at any given stage, and hence his readiness at a given time to respond and to adapt, is the most reliable gauge of whether parental expectations are appropriate. From a general knowledge of the principles of child-rearing parents need to fashion a method 'tailor-made' for each particular child at each particular stage of his development and suited to his particular environment.

The second implication is that it is never possible to treat two children in the same family alike if the aim is to treat each appropriately. Nor is 'the same family' psychologically the same for each child: partly because of the interaction between the parents' personalities and that of the child; partly because the family constellation itself is different in respect of each member of the family – the parents' age and the child's position in the family (first-born, middle one, etc.) are just two examples.

The third implication lies in making allowance for the fact that just as physical endowment ranges from the resilient to the delicate, so children differ genetically in their intellectual and emotional constitution and susceptibility to stress. At the same time, environmental influences come into play at birth and in some respects from conception onwards; and they have potentially a far greater effect than has hitherto been generally realised.

THE POSSIBILITY OF IMPROVEMENT

While no-one would question that it is possible to bring about vast improvements in children's physical health and educational achievements, there is less agreement in relation to intelligence and still outright scepticism about emotional and social aspects. Nor is there agreement about how any such improvement might be brought about. Nevertheless, that the possibility exists in all these areas is the fourth basic assumption made in this book.

One reason for doubt may be that much more is known about deficiencies and failure than about 'optimal' or even normal growth. For example, there have been many studies of delinquent children or poor readers but there is little detailed understanding of how language or reading skills are acquired; or, even more important, what enables a child to develop normally despite an adverse emotional or social environment.

The whole issue is further complicated by the fact that society rarely asks – and certainly has no answer to – the question: into what kind of people do we want today's children to grow? Even to pose the question could give a new slant both to child-rearing methods and to research.

Physical development

The past forty years or so have seen in this country what amounts to a revolution in children's health: they are taller; they mature earlier; and certain diseases have been virtually eliminated (Tanner, 1974).

Even so, there remains room for improvement: for example, poor nutrition and inadequate housing are known to affect the health and growth of the mother and thus her capacity to bear healthy children; stress or malnutrition during pregnancy influences the baby at the time and subsequently; extreme parental rejection may lead to 'deprivation dwarfism'; and chronic malnutrition in early childhood has been linked to mental retardation.

Intellectual development

Now it is no longer held that functional intelligence is entirely innate. Like physical growth, it needs appropriate nourishment for its development. Moreover, 'man has by no means reached the limits of his mental powers; there is immense room for improvement at the lower end of the scale, and the possibility of more effective "techniques" at the top end' (Vernon, 1972).

As for translating this comparatively new knowledge into practice, there has as yet been little general or systematic attempt to do so. The exact contributions made respectively by genetic and environmental factors are still under debate; as is the question of whether 'thinking' needs to be taught as a separate skill (de Bono, 1972). Nor is there agreement on the optimal time, the most effective methods or the respective roles of home and school in fostering intellectual growth.

Educational development

That there is much room for improvement in this area is unanimously accepted. Evidence showing that this is indeed so is reliable and plentiful. There is less agreement on the causes of scholastic shortcomings or on the most appropriate methods for helping children to overcome them. Some concepts continue to be controversial, such as under-achievement, educational subnormality and dyslexia; there is also disagreement about basic teaching methods for, say, reading; about the effectiveness of different remedial treatments; about the merits of segregating handicapped children; and about many other basic educational issues, such as streaming, examinations and corporal punishment.

Extreme solutions, such as free schools, schools without walls, making education optional at an earlier age than at present, or abolishing compulsion altogether, have so far met with limited support.

In the United States the most consistent attempts to provide alternatives within the state school system are the voucher experiments, already under way in a few areas. By channelling public money for education through the parents in the form of vouchers, it is hoped to introduce a much more diverse range of options. While a similar scheme is unlikely to be introduced in this country, there is scope within the system for providing real choices. These could be initiated by existing schools, or groups of teachers, or parents or older students. They would offer a range of small-scale experiments whose importance, however, might well be out of all proportion to their size as a testing ground for real alternatives to formal schooling, especially at the secondary level. In that way they would come to fill the innovative role which progressive independent schools used to perform in the past.

Emotional and social development

These aspects of growth are the least explored and the results of available studies are usually neither clear-cut nor conclusive. This is demonstrated in a recent review of the short- and long-term effects of 'maternal deprivation' (Rutter, 1972).

It had been thought that rising standards of health and material prosperity would reduce the incidence of backwardness, maladjustment and delinquency. There is evidence to suggest that to some extent, this has already happened. For example, children whose parents have been re-housed do better at school than those who remain in over-crowded conditions; and the delinquency rate is higher in slum areas than on well-established housing estates.

Yet it has become evident that the problems of emotional, social and educational malfunctioning will not be solved by improvements in health and in standards of living alone; these make satisfactory family and community life more likely but do not ensure it. Few would deny that there is much room for improvement at a time when vandalism, violence, drugs and crime are causing widespread concern.

Yet there has been no attempt to raise the general level of emotional and social resilience; indeed considerable resistance and suspicion surround even the discussion of this possibility, fears being voiced of brain-washing, social engineering and political manipulation. Instead, we must face the fact that these processes have been at work from time immemorial. Our various prejudices – be they about race, colour, class, sex or religion – are witness to that. The cost of refusing or neglecting to tackle directly the fostering of social and emotional maturity and resilience has been and continues to be very high in terms of human fulfilment and effectiveness.

MEANS OF BRINGING ABOUT IMPROVEMENT

At present, very considerable resources are being devoted to the treatment or containment of the disturbed, backward or delinquent; and when two out of every three known burglars are under twenty-one years old, there is clamour that more ought to be done. Yet neither child guidance clinics nor schools for the maladjusted have as yet produced convincing evidence of long-term success. Similarly, the success or failure rate of approved schools (measured in terms of recidivism) did not suggest that their style of treatment had found the answer.

It is evident that as yet we know little about why one child becomes delinquent when another in apparently similar circumstances does not; more is known about the general social and emotional conditions in which anti-social behaviour is likely to arise, and it is realised that its roots often go back into childhood (Robins, 1966; West, 1969 and 1974).

In the past twenty-five years many of the physical illnesses of childhood have been virtually eliminated. Tuberculosis of bones, joints, glands, digestive tract and meninges have almost disappeared with the control of bovine tuberculosis and the sterilization of milk supplies. Diphtheria and poliomyelitis have yielded to immunization of the child against the infecting organism. These victories, and a host of others, have been made possible because painstaking research has revealed eradicable causes of these diseases.

But a less encouraging picture is presented when we assess accomplishments in the field of mental and social health of the child. Here, there are to be heard no jubilant strains of victory; indeed, no unbiased observer can fail to be impressed with the poverty of achievement. Research in the mental, behavioural and social sciences has hitherto attracted too few of our best brains and attracted far too little financial encouragement (Cohen, 1965).

Thus, our state of knowledge in these areas is akin to that which prevailed in the health field some forty years ago. Might not the strategy, so conspicuously successful in that area, be appropriate also to other aspects of development? This is the fifth basic concept propounded in this paper. Spectacular progress began to be made when it was accepted that 'the treatment of established disease is a most inefficient way of ensuring that we survive in good health... it is good preventive medicine and improved hygiene that does so, through the unostentatious departments of public health' (Malleson, 1973).

By providing maternity and child welfare clinics, by ensuring that children and pregnant mothers received the care and nourishment needed for proper growth, a virtual revolution was brought about within a generation. For example, fifty years ago, some 80 per cent of children in London's East End schools had signs of rickets and hence remained stunted in stature. Now the disease has almost been eliminated.

Just as it proved possible to vaccinate and inoculate successfully against whooping cough or poliomyelitis without necessarily understanding why a particular child was more liable to contract the disease or how to cure it, so there is now an understanding of the broad preventive measures likely to raise the general level of children's intellectual, educational, social and emotional development.

The developmental sciences offer evidence in, as yet, rather broad terms, which enables the environmental circumstances favouring or disfavouring the full development of human genetic potential to be, in an actuarial sense, prescribed. One of society's problems is to learn how to use this knowledge, particularly since evidence points to the crucial importance of long-term domestic environments over which, unlike schools, society exercises little control (Clarke and Clarke, 1972).

It might well be more economical and effective, in human as well as in financial terms, to apply these measures 'across the board' rather than merely on a highly selective basis, concentrating either on individual children and their families, or on particularly 'vulnerable' or disadvantaged groups. Then within such a framework of universality, positive discrimination can give additional help in areas of high need. Similarly, it is reasonable to assume that inter-

31

vention is likely to be more effective and least costly – in terms of personnel, time and techniques – not merely during the earliest years but the earliest weeks and months of life; and most effective if a start is made with today's children – the parents of tomorrow.

2. The Needs of Children and How They Are Met

It used to be thought that developmental needs come into play in a hierarchical sequence, the most basic being those necessary for sheer survival (such as the need for food and water); and that only when these have been satisfactorily met do the higher needs emerge (such as the need for a loving relationship). Now it is held that all human needs are inter-related and inter-dependent in a subtle, complex and continuous way. For example, an unhappy baby may reject food and, even if he takes it, he may fail to thrive; or a child may fight sleep for fear that his mother or father may leave home.

It was also believed that the infant's attachment to his mother arose from her providing him with nourishment. Evidence has shown that this 'cupboard love' theory is not justified either, not even among monkeys. Similarly, emotion and learning were considered to be separate, distinct aspects of development; indeed this view is still widely held, particularly in relation to older children.

In fact learning (in the widest sense of the word) and emotion, the cognitive and affective aspects of development, intellect and feelings, are so closely interwoven and from so early an age as to be almost indivisible. Given inborn potential for development; given the impetus of maturation; and given environmental opportunities of an appropriate kind and at the appropriate time – what can still be missing is the willingness or motivation to learn and make progress. The essential driving force of the will to learn has its roots in the quality of relationships available to the child right from the beginning of life.

While parental love, and mothering in particular, has always been held to be important for children, social scientists continue to fight shy of the concept of 'mother-love', regarding it as unmeasurable, sentimental or both. Partly in consequence, practitioners have also undervalued it, if not in their daily attitudes to children and their

B

families, then certainly in their staff training procedures. In 1951 a milestone was reached when Bowlby put forward the view – argued much earlier by Pestalozzi, Froebel and then Spitz – that 'mother-love in infancy and childhood is as important for mental health as are vitamins and proteins for physical health'. Now widely accepted by 'tender-minded' theorists and practitioners, its vagueness continues to arouse unease, even hostility, among the 'tough-minded'; so much so, that the word 'love' either appears in quotation marks or other terms, such as 'warmth' or 'attachment', are substituted.

Admittedly 'love' is not readily defined in scientific terms nor easily measurable. However, the elements which go to make up good parental care can be readily defined and many of the aspects of parent-child interaction can be assessed and evaluated. Much is now known about the ways in which the quality of family relationships affect children's development; and even more is known about the probable consequences when they are unsatisfactory or completely absent.

The position taken here is that even at its lowest the term 'maternal love' is a convenient shorthand; and, within the context of what follows, the role it plays in meeting children's developmental needs will become readily apparent. Since physical ones are not only more clearly understood but also more easily and now more generally met, the emphasis will be on psycho-social needs. These have been enumerated in lists, varying in length from as few as two to as many as sixty.

For practical purposes, a four-fold classification seems sufficient: the need for love and security; for new experiences; for praise and recognition; and for responsibility. These needs have to be met from the very beginning of life and continue to require fulfilment – to a greater or lesser extent – throughout adulthood. Of course, their relative importance changes during the different developmental stages as do the ways in which they are met.

THE NEED FOR LOVE AND SECURITY

The need for love

This need is met by the child experiencing from birth onwards a stable, continuous, dependable and loving relationship with his parents (or permanent parent-substitutes), who themselves enjoy a rewarding relationship with one another. Through this relationship – first with his mother, then his father and gradually an ever-widening circle of other people – the child comes to a realisation of personal identity and worthwhileness. It forms the basis of all later relationships, not only with the family, but with friends, colleagues and eventually his own family. On it depend the healthy development of the personality, the ability to respond to affection and, in time, to become a loving, caring parent.

The basic and all-pervasive feature of parental love is that the child is valued unconditionally and for his own sake, irrespective of his sex, appearance, abilities or personality; that this love is given without expectation of or demand for gratitude; and that the constraints imposed upon parental freedom of movement, upon time and upon finance are accepted without resentment or reproach. (Occasionally begrudging these constraints is, of course, different from a permanent sense of resentment.) Parents communicate this unconditional affection through all their relations with him: from physical care and handling to responding to his first smile and sounds; from protecting him from, and then gradually initiating him into, the social world; and from restraining to eventually punishing him for going beyond the limits they have set for acceptable behaviour.

The greatest impact of such love is on the self. Approval and acceptance by others are essential for the development of self-approval and self-acceptance. Whether a child will develop a constructive or destructive attitude, first to himself and then to other people, depends in the first place on his parents' attitude to him. During the earliest months of infancy and biological helplessness, the mother acts as insulator and filter, protecting the baby from the impact of his new environment. For example, a loud noise startles a baby far less, or a mild digestive upset will be endured more easily, when he is in his mother's or father's arms. Throughout the early years, close physical contact continues to be protectively reassuring, as well as an expression of parental affection. This is probably why, during the war, children who remained with their parents during bombing attacks coped better with anxiety than those who were evacuated to safer areas.

During this time, few demands are made on the infant and all his wants are met. It is he who at this early stage provides both the impetus and directive for maternal behaviour: she responds not only because of her concern for him but also for her own comfort, as his crying is painful to her. Following this period of total ego-centricity the initiative passes to the mother: the baby is expected to begin to give up instant gratification, to accept postponement and to respond to the requirements of others; this sets him on the way – slowly and often painfully – to becoming integrated into a wider social world. From now on the relationship becomes and continues to be a reciprocal one.

Though able to respond to sights and sounds within the first forty-eight hours of life, the first truly social step is the infant's smile responding to a smiling face. This happens in about the second month of life; only several months later does he become able to identify and differentiate his mother's face from that of others. This is an important milestone: it marks the emergence of his awareness of his mother as a separate person, 'outside himself' as it were, and thus the beginning of his identity or self-concept; it also marks the growth of his first and vital emotional attachment or bond. To reach this stage, he has had to accomplish a vast amount of learning so as to be able to distinguish between a host of sensory impressions.

From this first reciprocal love relationship flow three further consequences of vital importance to development: first, the baby enjoys the mother's presence, even if he can only hear her moving about, and he becomes concerned when she disappears. Secondly, the loving mother who watches and encourages each step forward is likely to accelerate progress by her anticipatory interest and delight in the earliest signs; these 'reward' the baby for his efforts and spur him on to continue making them. Hence he may learn to walk and talk earlier than a child whose mother has not the time or inclination for such close involvement in his progress. Conversely, she conveys disappointment and disapproval of behaviour which she wishes to discourage.

The third consequence is that the child is enabled through mutually rewarding relationships, first with his mother and then with others who become significant to him, to learn self-control and to acquire moral values. This he accomplishes by imitation or 'modelling'. Mothering mediates between the child's inner subjective and the outside 'real' world; it recognises and establishes his personal identity and individuality; and her loving care is unique in the sense that it is adapted to his very special, individual needs which are recognised as being different from those of any other child.

Such love is extremely difficult to replace and hence it makes the child vulnerable when it is lost to him, temporarily or permanently. In most cases 'The best that community care can offer is impartiality – to be fair to every child in its care. But a developing personality needs more than that: it needs to know that to someone it matters more than other children; that someone will go to unreasonable lengths... for its sake' (Newson, 1972).

The need for security

First and foremost, this need is met by giving the child the security of stable family relationships where attitudes and behaviour are consistent and dependable; the security of a familiar place; and the security of a known routine. All these make for continuity and predictability in a world in which the child has to meet and come to terms with so much that is new and changing.

Because he is so small and so ignorant, much that is later taken for granted is seen as threatening; for example, such simple things as the water running out of the bath. Similarly, the unpredictability of objects can be frightening, such as glass breaking when dropped. Perhaps most of all, the nature and strength of his own feelings threaten his security from time to time. If the whole framework of his life is secure, it provides him with the needed reassurance to venture out, knowing that he can again return to its comforting safety.

It is the quality of family relationships which is of basic importance to the child's psychological development. This applies not only to the mother's and father's relations with him, but also to those between the parents themselves, as well as to the child's with his siblings and other close relatives. Parental expectation and discipline which are consistent – whether tending to be strict or lenient – enhance his sense of security, providing a dependable predictable framework. So does a familiar place, as is clearly shown by the contrast between a young child's usual behaviour in his own home and in a strange place. Keeping close to his mother or a familiar person, refusing to speak or eat, are all signs of insecurity. A familiar object gives reassurance, as witnessed by a cherished possession – often something cuddly such as a rag doll or blanket – from which he will not be parted at bedtime or in a stressful situation.

The extent to which a known routine helps the growing child is shown by his insistence that certain everyday events are followed in exactly the same manner and sequence; bedtime rituals and the way stories must be told in the self-same words are just two examples. Parents are in a unique position to know about the particular objects, rituals and situations which foster a particular child's sense of security. By allowing them expression (and time where need be), his right to individuality and to a measure of self-determination is acknowledged, which contributes towards building up his feeling of worth.

There are two further aspects to allowing him the right to certain idiosyncrasies within the home: first, the fact that the child can revert to more immature behaviour becomes a valuable safety valve in the face of the constant and increasing demands on him for greater maturity and control; and secondly, he begins to learn that different standards of behaviour are permitted within the privacy of his family, which will help him later to understand and cope with this fact in relation to school and other social settings.

The need for security is closely related to the standards of behaviour being set by the parents. Knowing what is expected of him and, as soon as he can understand, the reasons why, makes growing up a less difficult business. Inevitably the child will transgress, will be disobedient – partly because he needs to test the consequences of doing so, partly because he is liable to forget rules – but knowing the limits of what is permitted provides the reassurance of both reasonableness and predictability. In contrast, when the same behaviour gives rise to widely different reactions, with the same parent at different times or in either parent, then the child's concept of acceptable conduct becomes linked to individual whim rather than to general principles.

Lastly, but perhaps most important, stable family life also provides the child with a sense of personal continuity, of having a past as well as a future. By relating to him events of his early life, backed up by photos and other evidence, and by looking ahead to likely developments in his life, he acquires a coherent self-image which is essential for a well-adjusted personality. Children love hearing stories about their own doings. These together with comments made casually in conversation about other members of the family all serve to accumulate a store of memories which put his own life into long-term perspective. 'When you were younger' and 'when you are older' are phrases which may well at times irritate children by the very frequency with which they are used; yet they contribute to building up a mental concept of his continuing self within the larger family context. It is through human ties that personal identity comes to be established.

Teacher–pupil relations

Since the relationships available to the child are of paramount importance, one would expect the teacher to become one of the most influential adults in the child's expanding world – after all he stands *in loco parentis* during a large part of the day; so much so, that a deprived child will often address a teacher to whom he becomes attached as 'mummy'.

In a review of some fifty studies, carried out in recent years, on the way in which teachers' behaviour affects the achievements of their pupils, two aspects were consistently found to be important: teacher enthusiasm and warmth (Rosenshine, 1971). These not only elicit greater response from each individual but they also create for the whole class a climate of involvement reflected in the attitudes of pupils to each other, to the teacher and to learning.

Disapproval and discipline

Once a child has learned through a loving mother's response to him that he is valued and cherished, this satisfying experience is 'ever afterwards craved and so constitutes a powerful driving force of human nature' (Moore, T. V., 1948).

Disapproval is felt as a temporary withdrawal of affection and is sensed long before the child can understand speech or talk himself. Even later, speech is not necessary: facial expressions – a frown, a smile or even a raised eyebrow – can at times be more eloquent and effective than words. Indeed, such non-verbal communication remains a potent means of conveying displeasure way beyond childhood. Thus if his mother is displeased with him, the child becomes anxious.

Later the disapproval of others, who are emotionally significant to the child, will also induce anxiety. In this way, the loving relationships formed in early infancy provide the most effective and basic motivation for a child to respond increasingly to adult expectations. Throughout his childhood, he will adapt to parental training, demands and guidance because he wants to retain their love; transgression means the interruption of this valued relationship, because feeling disapproved of is painful to his self-image and because anxiety is such a disturbing emotion that he endeavours to avoid behaviour likely to arouse it.

The fact that during adolescence many youngsters rebel against parental standards and seek to find their own way of solving problems in no way changes the need for parents to make clear what they regard as desirable or acceptable standards. The more loving and warmer the home, the easier it is for the child to discriminate between a continuing basic affection and what feels like its temporary loss (i.e., disapproval), because the signs or cues are quite distinct; this helps him to understand what is expected of him and facilitates his response. Inconsistent, erratic parental handling makes this more difficult since the cues will be contradictory and hence confusing. The situation is most difficult for the child who is rejected or being brought up in the more impersonal atmosphere of a children's home, since the cues will be blurred, if they exist at all; disapproval only confirms his feeling of being unloved. When he has no permanent parent figures, he has no hope of gaining or regaining their affection.

It is through a caring adult then that the child learns to care. To begin with, neither words nor actions are inherently right or wrong – it is the response they evoke which teaches him how they are regarded. It is not only consistency of response but also whether the adult himself provides a consistent model for the child, which will influence how readily he comes to understand what is expected of him. Since parents provide not only the first but also the most intimately observed models, their standards, values and disciplinary approach lay the basis for the child's eventual conduct; in particular, whether it becomes inner- or outer-directed.

In common usage, the term 'discipline' has become practically synonymous with punishment, and often has overtones of severity. Perhaps because of this, 'methods of child rearing' is a preferable term, though, in fact, the original definition of discipline is equally neutral, namely training which develops self-control and the capacity to cooperate. The more child rearing methods are based on reasoning and discussion, the more readily understanding develops of parental standards and expectations. This lays the basis for moral insight as a guide to behaviour rather than 'blind obedience' induced by either fear of punishment (whether physical or verbal lashings) or by the 'emotional blackmail' of withholding affection.

When behaviour is inner-directed, the child comes to feel shame and guilt when he is doing something which he knows his parents would disapprove of. To begin with, anxiety about parental displeasure and, later on, understanding of parental precepts induce him to adopt socially and morally acceptable behaviour by exercising self-control. In this way he eventually develops a 'conscience' through anticipating and internalising likely parental (and then increasingly other people's) expectations and reactions so that he will behave in an increasingly mature and self-directed manner, independent of the parents' physical presence.

Consistent and reasonable expectations which are appropriate to the child's age and level of understanding; punishments which are similarly consistent and logically related to the 'offence' (from having to forgo a treat to having to make restitution; and from being scolded to being temporarily isolated because of anti-social behaviour); and an open and 'democratic' family climate in which explanations are readily given; all these are conducive to emphasising the value of internal controls.

In contrast, outer-directed behaviour operates largely on an *ad hoc* basis, where 'love-orientated' methods of discipline cannot come into play, either because there is no continuing, warm relationship or because there is no consistent and appropriate pattern of parental expectation. Outer-directed behaviour relies heavily on rewards and punishment; is orientated towards the present; and adapted to the standards and expectations of a particular person or situation at a particular time.

Autocratic discipline, which is imposed from outside rather than accepted through identification with a loved person, has to rely more on punishment, fear and external control; it is these which come to regulate behaviour and ensure conformity. To evade detection and beat the system then become a challenge to the child.

THE NEED FOR NEW EXPERIENCES

New experiences are a prerequisite for mental growth as essential to the mind's development as food is for the body's. From birth onwards, tasks appropriate to each particular stage of growth are presented to the child, and their mastery provides in turn the stepping stone towards more difficult achievements: for example, from having learned to grasp and hold an object, he proceeds to learn to feed himself. If denied the opportunity of new experiences, no learning can take place. For example, in a non-speaking environment, the child will not acquire speech even though his hearing and speech organs are quite normal.

The small child has a strong urge to explore, and everything that goes on around him becomes an absorbing new experience as soon as he is able to perceive it; so is every one of his earliest accomplishments, be it the ability to move his limbs at will or to examine the texture, taste and shape of materials and objects. Similarly, learning to crawl, walk, run and climb are new experiences in themselves, in addition to opening up an increasingly wider world for first-hand exploration. Later still, the challenge will be the mastery of reading, riding a bicycle or climbing a mountain. All these, and many more, provide new fields to be conquered, making life for the normal active child a series of rewarding adventures.

Once interest in novelty appears, then it becomes increasingly important as a source of motivation for further exploration and thus for learning. In Piaget's words, 'the more an infant has seen and heard, the more he wants to see and hear'. At the same time, there can be too much or too little stimulation or 'input'; the former gives rise to withdrawal and fear, the latter to boredom and apathy. It is one of the skills of child-rearing to be able to judge accurately the optimal level which will foster the cognitive development of a particular child at any particular stage of his growth.

New experiences enable the child to learn one of the most important, because basic, lessons of early life: learning how to learn; and learning that mastery brings joy and a sense of achievement. This is demonstrated by the exultant cry of 'I can do it myself', which also illustrates the link between emotion and learning, between cognitive and affective experiences. Competence brings its own reward while the mother's or other adults' pleasure in the child's newly acquired skill further reinforces his willingness to seek new fields to conquer.

In contrast, the child whose exploratory activities are disapproved of, discouraged or punished – whether this is because they disorganise a tidy, smooth-running, adult-centred household, or because the potential hazards worry an anxious mother, or because in over-crowded conditions a harassed, over-burdened mother cannot provide either the time or space – such a child will develop quite another attitude to learning: its likely features will be passivity, fearfulness, frustration or irritability, and there will be little joy or satisfaction.

In this way, educability – a child's responsiveness to all the growth tasks to which education, in the very widest sense of the term, exposes him – depends not only on his inborn capacity, but on environmental opportunity and encouragement. The emotional and cultural climate of the home, as well as parental involvement and aspirations, can foster, limit or even impair intellectual growth. Potentialities for learning may be developed to the full, be disorganised or remain unrealised according to the nature of the child's environment.

Just as an appropriate diet is essential for normal physical growth, so it is for mental development. The most vital ingredients of this diet are play and language. Through them, the child explores the world and learns to cope with it; this is as true for the objective outside world as it is for the subjective internal world of thoughts and feelings. Thus too are motor skills, perception and concepts developed.

The functions of play

The phrase 'he is only playing' is still far too often heard, implying that play is only slightly superior to doing nothing at all. In fact, it is an intensely absorbing experience and even more important to the child than work is to the adult. Hence it ought to be treated with similar respect. It fulfils a number of different though related functions, and takes many forms.

Perhaps the earliest play occurs at the breast with the baby's exploratory touching of the mother. If breast-fed babies thrive better – as is believed by many – it may be not only for nutritional reasons but also because, in addition to body contact, it provides the first mutually enjoyable play opportunity. Possibly too

an appreciation of the value of play begins at this stage and not simply later when the toddler is fitting blocks into holes. The middle class mother encourages the latter but may find it difficult to tolerate the time-wasting involved in the former. The peasant mother, and this includes some immigrant mothers, may be particularly responsive to the former, but cannot see the importance of a toddler's exploratory activities unless she is taught the why and how of play (Kitzinger, 1973).

Play also enables the baby to acquire control over his body. Through moving his limbs and exercising his muscles, coordination develops and in playing he sets himself increasingly difficult tasks; for example, from crawling to walking and running; and from jumping to hopping on one foot, and eventually to playing complex games.

Next, children play with sounds, words and objects in a very similar way, partly to practise newly developing skills, partly to acquire new knowledge and partly for the sheer joy of it. The babbling baby who tries to imitate the sounds his mother makes has his counterpart in the older child who chants difficult words which intrigue him; while the chanting of nonsense rhymes and jingles is fun, as well as giving a sense of power over words. Playing with materials such as sand and water, he learns about their different properties, just as he does when accidentally dropping a saucepan or jam jar on a hard floor.

For creative play, both words and objects are used. Pounding clay, smearing paint, erecting a brick structure, taking an old clock to pieces, playing a musical instrument or writing a poem, all these provide both a means for self-expression and for learning about and remaking the world as he experiences it. These activities also help to lay the cornerstone of his feelings about himself in relation to that world; while the foundation for later imaginative and artistic pursuits and appreciation is laid through music, movement and nursery rhymes.

There is yet another aspect of play. It provides not only an outlet for feelings but a means of coping with them. For example, the angry child has made a step forward when he kicks his teddy bear or a ball instead of the baby or the furniture; the next step is the child telling the teddy that it is naughty to kick and that he must learn more sensible means of containing his anger; when much later the child himself is able not only to control but to use his anger constructively – be this through hammering nails into wood to make a toy or by writing an essay attacking unduly repressive ways of disciplining children – then he is well on the way to maturity.

Two further aspects of play deserve mentioning, namely role-playing and make-believe. The former enables a child both to 'practise' his future identity as an adult man, father and worker; and to feel himself in imagination into the parts played by others, be it his mother, his teacher, the milkman or an astronaut. By learning to put himself 'into their shoes' he will become more adept later at cooperating with others. (Incidentally, it can be a salutary experience to realise through watching a child's expression and voice how he perceives the adults around him.)

One reason why boys show a higher incidence of emotional difficulties, not only in this country but in all developed countries which publish statistics, may be because it is less easy for them to observe, identify with and practise role-appropriate behaviour. The mother's home-making work is much more 'visible' to the young child than the father's job; this is true too for the early school years when boys are usually taught by women.

Make-believe games allow the child to anticipate through the medium of fantasy impending, and possibly frightening, experiences, such as having to go into hospital. He is enabled to assimilate new experiences by re-living them, such as after a visit to the zoo, when he will pretend to be each of the various animals he has seen. Perhaps most important of all, he can find temporary relief and refuge from being small, inexperienced and without any real power, by creating in his imaginative play a world where he is king, where his deepest wishes are fulfilled, and where it is he who makes and breaks the rules. In short, make-believe assists the child in working through and coming to terms with the frustrations and conflicts which are almost inseparable from growing up in a complex and fast-changing society.

Last, though by no means least, play is enjoyable not only for the child but also the adult. Partly because of the somewhat belittling attitude towards play referred to earlier and partly just because they enjoy it, some parents tend to feel that it must take very much second place to all the other tasks of home-making and family life, from shopping and cooking, to gardening and servicing the car. Yet if play is to provide the wide range of opportunities for learning, which it potentially can do, then adult involvement is essential.

Choosing toys, materials and equipment which are appropriate to the child's age and level of maturity requires care and understanding. Decisions need to be made not only as to quantity but also regarding the balance between 'raw' (i.e., clay or paints), constructional (i.e., bricks or Lego) and 'finished' (i.e., dolls or trains) materials.

Similarly, the balance between completely 'free' play, which is entirely of the child's own choosing and under his sole direction, and 'guided' activities, where the parent or teacher suggests, participates, contributes or even teaches and corrects, is an important matter. Moreover, for some children, the right atmosphere needs to be created for dramatic and spontaneous play; yet it may be inhibiting if the guiding adult injects or imposes the logic of objective reality or the pattern of adult imagination.

In summary, play can be seen to meet the need for new experiences in two major ways: by enabling the child to learn about the world he lives in; and by providing a means for learning about and resolving complex and often conflicting emotions, i.e., by fantasy being allowed to over-ride reality and logic. Thus a synthesis is brought about between the inner and outer world, between rational and non-rational processes, new understanding being absorbed through the child's individual prior store of ideas, images, feelings, wishes and conflicts.

The functions of language

The child who asked, 'How do I know what I think till I hear what I say?', neatly summarised the central role of language for intellectual functioning; indeed, thought itself has been defined as 'internalised speech'. The young child uses monologue a good deal, in a kind of running commentary on what he is doing. Whether this reflects his egocentricity at this stage (as Piaget suggests) or whether it is a sort of self-directive communication (as Vigotsky maintains) remains to be established as do many other aspects of speech.

Once a detailed understanding is achieved of exactly how language is acquired, then more substantial progress will be made with programmes designed to foster and enrich its growth. Meanwhile, there is no doubt that language development is basic to an effective cognitive life, because it makes larger areas of rational thought possible.

Language development follows a regular sequential pattern, from babbling to short words and finally to sentences, which will increase in length and complexity. The child who is 'bathed in language' – whose mother talks while she plays with and does things for him, who tells him nursery rhymes, stories, sings and converses – such a child will be attuned to sounds from an early age. In turn, the first sounds he himself makes, which vaguely resemble real words, will be greeted with such pleasure by parents aware of the importance of early vocalising, that he is likely to repeat them more often until he does in fact connect the word with its object.

Being able to name things extends the child's power over his environment – he can identify and demand things instead of having to rely on his mother's guesswork of what he might be wanting. Vocalising also seems to bring its own reward; how else can one explain that babbling continues when the child does not want to communicate with anyone nor has an interested audience? Playing with words at an older age may well be a counterpart of this early activity.

Once the child has acquired some language and understands that words refer to things, child-rearing becomes easier. Communication is improved and speech also provides the child with increasing control over himself as well as his environment. For example, the word 'no' makes it possible for him to reach out to touch something hot and then to control the impulse himself by the incantation of the parental prohibition, which had checked him on previous occasions.

Thus language plays a part not only in learning self-control but in the formation of conscience. Also, with increasing age the child comes to appreciate that verbal aggression is socially more acceptable than its physical expression and that it can be equally effective, even if not quite as immediately satisfying. Similarly, through words he begins to form concepts and to generalise; for example, he will learn to distinguish between cats and dogs, and to comprehend that both are animals. Gradually, with increasing linguistic facility, the higher mental processes of reasoning and judgement will begin to develop.

Though there are wide individual variations among children, eight-year-olds have on average acquired 50 per cent of the vocabulary they will have at the age of eighteen. Generally speaking, girls are ahead of boys in language development – until the age of eight years, if not later – whether the yardsticks used for assessment are speech sounds, articulation, vocabulary or sentence structure.

Also, at every age, children from middle class homes are ahead of those in working class homes. It is not simply a question of the latter reaching the same level but at a somewhat later age; rather, the whole mode of language differs, from a smaller vocabulary to the use of shorter, simpler and often incomplete sentences; also, subordinate clauses, adjectives and adverbs are employed less imaginatively and frequently. Language, furthermore, shapes both thought and behaviour.

The most systematic study of children's thinking has been made by Piaget who demonstrated that cognitive development passes through stages of increasing complexity, the sequence of which is not readily altered. The 'sensory-motor' period is the first and lasts about two years. At this stage, the infant's knowledge of the world depends on his bodily interaction with and his actual handling of objects.

Next comes the period of 'pre-operational thought' which lasts until about seven years. During it, the child is beginning to think symbolically, with speech playing an increasing part. For example, when he pretends to be driving a car, while sitting in a cardboard box, he symbolises his past experience and relates it to the present. These two stages are dominated by his immediate perception, and thinking is on what Piaget calls the 'intuitive level'.

The third stage, which lasts until about eleven years, he calls the period of 'concrete operations' and the final one, which is accomplished by about fifteen years, the period of 'formal operations'. During the former, most of the child's thinking is still based on concrete objects or specific situations; he cannot as yet transfer what he has learned in one physical context to another. For example, the concept of 'conservation' of volume requires the understanding that certain properties (in this case the volume) of objects remain constant even when other properties (e.g., the shape) are changed. Most eight-year-olds know that pouring water from a tall thin container into a short broad one does not change the amount of water; but only by about eleven years will there be the ability to comprehend that the volume of the two containers is also the same. In other words, the capacity for hypothetico-deductive reasoning is reached in the period of 'formal operations'. It is only then that abstract thinking becomes possible.

By his work, Piaget has shown that children's thinking is qualitatively different from adult thought; however, his studies are not concerned with age-related norms and considerable variability has in fact been found among children. Also, he argues that there is constant interaction between emotions and intellect so that during stress a child will regress to an earlier level of thinking. Presumably, too, emotional difficulties may prevent a child from ever reaching a higher level of logical functioning, so that unresolved emotional conflict at one level of development will hinder thinking at the next level.

Here then is one link between language, thought and behaviour. Others are even more important because more generalised and pervasive. The use of simpler, less individualised language – more habitual among working class homes – is likely to mean that small or subtle differences between objects, people and situations are ignored; also, the nuances of wishes and feeling will be more difficult to convey with more restricted speech. In consequence, children will grow up less sensitive to their own emotions and those of others; less able to distinguish the finer shades of meanings; and in their thinking they may well remain at the 'concrete' level, never passing to the level of 'formal operations'.

In summary, language helps children to learn to reason, to think and to understand the world around them; speech facilitates the making of relationships, both with adults and with contemporaries; and verbal communication is and remains a vital means of coping and coming to terms with life. Eventually, the child's response to school and the progress he is able to make will depend in no small measure on his ability to express himself, and on his mastery and enjoyment of the spoken word.

Social class differences

Why should speech and thought processes of children from working class homes tend to be more limited in range, subtlety and sensitivity? Two main hypotheses have been put forward to account for this differential language development (Bernstein, 1961; Hess and Shipman, 1965; Newson, 1972). First, middle class children generally live in a verbally much richer environment where they are encouraged to listen and respond to increasingly more mature speech patterns; where stories, nursery rhymes and word games are an important part of daily routine; and where conversation is freely engaged in, for example at meal times, during shopping and at bedtime, rather than being regarded as time-wasting chatter.

Secondly, working class and middle class homes tend to differ in their style of child rearing, the former favouring an 'authoritarian' and the latter a more 'democratic' form of discipline. In democratic homes, the reasons for expected behaviour and for rules are explained, verbal means of control are preferred to physical, and the child's views and wishes are taken into account in decision making. So in addition to the greater inclination for verbal interchange, there is also a greater need for it in 'democratic' homes. This means that there are more frequent, prolonged and reciprocal interactions between parents and children. These foster two other aspects of behaviour: a readiness to approach new problems with an open mind and a sense of personal independence (Wall, 1973; White, 1971).

On the other hand, less conversation is needed in the 'authoritarian' home since mainly non-verbal means of prohibition and punishment are employed, and words are used more to threaten and enforce obedience rather than to make the child understand the rationale behind social behaviour. It may well be that cuffs and blows are resorted to more often by working class parents partly because they are less able to put their feelings into words. The use of actual physical violence in socially impoverished or disturbed homes is likely to produce poorly socialised children who will then carry the same behaviour into the next generation.

Thus these two different ways of upbringing – conveyed through language – generate a different family 'climate' which in turn shapes behaviour and personality. On going to school, the child is expected to adopt the language of mainly middle class teachers and to cope with a largely middle class curriculum. Whether this necessarily creates difficulties will be discussed later (Chapter 5, p. 101).

The teacher's role

Going to school is itself a major new experience, which opens up a larger and more impersonal world. Fortunate is the child who can be introduced gradually rather than having to adapt suddenly to spending the greater part of his day away from his mother, in unfamiliar surroundings with a strange adult for whose attention he has to compete with many strange contemporaries. In addition to this unaccustomed sharing, it may also be a new experience for him to have to compare himself with his peers.

Inevitably his previous attitudes to new experiences will be reflected in his response; his mother's attitude to 'losing' him as well as her views of education in general, and to his school in particular, will also affect his own expectations and adjustment. Since the regime of most infant schools is child-centred and 'discovery' orientated, at least during the first year, most children show little difficulty in coping with this major change in their lives, provided that their curiosity and exploratory activities have previously been fostered.

The child's progress will come to be powerfully affected by his teacher's attitudes, values and beliefs; some of these will be overt and deliberate; others may be implicit and incidental; still others may well be unconscious but just as powerful in influencing his learning. Wide interests, enthusiasm for things of the mind and receptiveness to new ideas – all these are infectious. Many a child has had new doors opened by, and chosen his life's work because of, an inspired teacher.

However, as he advances up the educational ladder, he is likely to find school becoming increasingly 'achievement' orientated, subject-centred and competitive. Indeed, the progressive ideas of primary education, with their stress on stimulating inquiry and discovery by pupils through largely self-chosen activities, have aroused considerable doubts, both among secondary schools and the public at large; yet there is no necessary incompatibility between these ideas and high standards of attainment.

Schools can be genuinely concerned with gaiety and joy and individual growth and fulfilment, without sacrificing concern for intellectual discipline and development. They can be simultaneously child-centred and knowledge-centred. They can stress aesthetic and moral education without weakening the three R's (Silverman, 1970).

Perhaps the most important role of the teacher in opening up new worlds to the child is by being a bridge-builder. Four aspects will be singled out. The first concerns the relation between emotion and learning. Schools have for far too long over-emphasised the place of cognitive abilities and underestimated the importance of motivation. Instead, it needs to be recognised that the major determinant of educational success lies in bridging the two. To do so requires teachers to have an optimistic attitude; to accept that wanting to know and to seek evidence, and knowing how and where to find information, are more important and lasting than mere rote learning; to adopt teaching methods which maximise the strength and minimise the weakness of each pupil; and to devise a curriculum which is relevant to his interests and stage of development. Because neither interest nor stages are watertight entities, rigid boundaries between

51

different subjects, and between nursery, primary, middle and secondary schools are inappropriate.

Next, the school should bridge the world of the child's home and the community at large. The teacher, by involving himself, as well as his pupils, in outward-looking activities, which include both the parents and the neighbourhood, will discover unsuspected resources of ingenuity and initiative. Current thinking on bringing parents into much closer relationship with their children's schooling and making the premises a focal point of neighbourhood life, to some extent also aims to foster greater parental and community involvement. By providing a better understanding of the purpose of new methods of teaching and learning, parental interest may be enlisted; this in turn is likely to influence the children's attitudes and achievements. However, neither project work nor group teaching nor community use of premises is feasible in traditional classrooms; hence, these must become a thing of the past in primary and secondary schools alike.

Thirdly, the teacher is best placed to build bridges between education and the other professions most closely concerned with the development and well-being of children. In order to promote greater inter-disciplinary cooperation at the 'grass roots', people need to come together from different professional fields and from the statutory and voluntary services, in a variety of activities based on the school as a neighbourhood resource centre. Then education could be carried on 'against a relevant and recognisable background of human interaction and responsiveness rather than in an over-protected, over-regulated institution in danger of losing touch with its changing purposes' (Cooksey, 1972).

The fourth aspect of bridge-building relates to being an innovator. Perhaps the best teacher has always tried to be ahead of his time, recognising that education should be for tomorrow; it is stagnant if it prepares only for today and fossilised if appropriate mainly for yesterday's world. This is why society must be prepared to support and even encourage what Schon has called 'the vanguard role of the teacher' (5th Reith Lecture, 13 December 1970). This means openness and flexibility on the teacher's part: learning himself as he adopts the new methods and new techniques which educational technology has to offer; retaining what he finds valuable in traditional approaches; and discarding what fails to fulfil its promise in the new ways. Just as children become truly considerate only when shown consideration by their parents and teachers, so it is only the teacher whose own thinking is flexible who will succeed in imparting a receptive and adaptive attitude of mind.

By these various means, teachers will be able to preserve or to rekindle the curiosity and joy in learning shown by the young child which stand in such stark contrast to the frustrated boredom of not a few secondary school pupils.

THE NEED FOR PRAISE AND RECOGNITION

Because growing from a helpless baby into a self-reliant adult requires an enormous amount of emotional, social and intellectual learning and because it is inevitably beset by difficulties, conflicts and setbacks, a strong incentive is needed. This is provided by the pleasure shown at success and by the praise given to achievement by the adults who love the child and whom he in turn loves and wants to please. Encouragement and a reasonable level of expectation act as a spur to perseverance. Too little expectation leads the child to adopt too low a standard of effort and achievement; too high a level makes him feel that he cannot live up to what is required of him which produces discouragement and again diminished effort. An optimal level of expectation needs to be geared to each individual's capabilities at a given point in time and stage of growth, at a level where success is possible but not without effort.

Mistakes and failure should be regarded as an integral part of learning for which he is neither disapproved of nor scolded. Of course, this does not mean a child should never be reproved, be required to make restitution, or be punished; refusal to do something he is capable of doing, deliberate disobedience or destructiveness are quite different from mishaps, like breaking an ornament because of not yet being able to discriminate between breakable and unbreakable objects, or mistakes due to lack of knowledge, such as spelling errors. The child who is made to feel anxious because of his mistakes, often becomes more concerned about avoiding anxiety which is painful, than about analysing and profiting from the reasons for his failure. Also, he needs to feel that learning is unhurried and that successful accomplishment is largely a matter of time.

Teachers also play a key role – for better or worse – in meeting the need for praise and recognition: they are the only profession in close and continued contact with all children for at least eleven years; and from the age of five years at the latest, every child spends about half his waking life in school. This provides an unrivalled opportunity not only to establish a favourable attitude to learning in general and scholastic progress in particular; but also, where necessary, to improve or entirely rebuild the foundation for a child's self-esteem and hence his attitude to learning.

To succeed in this, a teacher has to act on the assumption that every pupil possesses an as yet unrealised potential for development; that an appropriate 'diet' can succeed in improving intellectual or emotional 'under-nourishment;' and that rather than accepting previous assessments or test results or even the parents' judgement of the child's abilities, the teacher should try to 'beat prediction' even though he may not always succeed.

Such a positive and optimistic attitude communicates itself very readily. Even such minimal 'signals' as raised eyebrows, smiles, nods and encouraging 'hms' effectively influence (or 'reinforce') attitude and performance. After all, a child's self-concept is developed through the views others hold of him. If he is called slow, he feels stupid – his yardstick can only be that of the adults who matter to him. Even very bright children may think of themselves as failures if their ability remains unrecognised; the number of such 'able misfits', as I have called them, is by no means negligible – thousands pass through our schools each year.

A child's attitude to himself and to learning will determine how effectively he learns, as much as, if not more than, his actual abilities. Recognition from his teacher and his peers assumes increasing importance with increasing age, the influence of the latter reaching a peak during adolescence. Eventually, a job well done becomes its own reward but that is a very mature stage, not usually reached before adolescence; and even the most mature adult responds, and indeed blossoms, when given – at least occasionally – some praise or other form of recognition by those whose views he values.

If the school environment provides the individual with evidence of his adequacy over a number of years, especially in the first few years of school, supported by consistent success over the next four of five years, we believe that this provides a type of immunisation against mental illness for an indefinite period of time. Such an individual should be able to surmount crises and periods of great stress without suffering too much. His own sense of adequacy and his personal and technical skills (some learned in school) should enable him to use realistic methods in surmounting these crisis' situations (Bloom, 1974).

THE NEED FOR RESPONSIBILITY

This need is met by allowing the child to gain personal independence, to begin with through learning to look after himself in matters of his everyday care, such as feeding, dressing and washing himself. Because he is constantly modelling himself on his parents, he wants to imitate what they can do. Despite the difficulties and frustrations arising from his immaturity and lack of control, he demands the chance to struggle on; hence 'me do it' is the constant refrain of the two-year-old. This need is met too through having possessions, however small and inexpensive, over which the child is allowed to exercise absolute ownership.

As he grows older, increasing independence means permitting, indeed encouraging, increasing freedom – of physical movement; of taste in food, play and clothes; and, perhaps most important of all, of choice of friends, studies, hobbies, career and eventually marriage partner. Giving such independence does not mean withholding one's views, tastes and choices, or the reasons for them; nor does it mean opting out from participating and guiding the lives of children; nor, indeed, condoning everything they may do.

On the contrary, children need a framework of guidance, of limits – knowing what is expected or permitted and what the rules are – together with the reasons and whether these are in their interests or in the interests of others. This means that it is important to distinguish clearly between disapproval of their behaviour, on the one hand, and on the other rejection of the child himself; and that the only lasting and effective force for influencing their beliefs and behaviour is the model we ourselves provide: it is what we really are and how we behave which matters, not what we say or believe we are. By sharing our everyday lives, children learn about our values, standards, concerns and ambitions in a subtle yet pervasively influential way.

Young people also need

experience in coping with egalitarian relationships with their immediate peers and contemporaries apart from the normal setting in which they are invariably subordinate to adults. Having learned in

55

association with parents, teachers and older kinsfolk to come to some kind of terms with authority and to adjust to externally imposed codes of behaviour, they need a period in which they relate to others as equals and so learn to stand on their own feet. Only in age-homogeneous peer groups can true equality be found and thus it is as members of such youth groups that vital steps towards ultimate autonomy and independence have to be made. So the college sorority, the street corner gang, the orthodox youth club, the students' union, the spontaneous sports team, the 'click', personal friends, mates or pals fulfil an important social and psychological function which must necessarily to some extent make their members feel themselves distinct from other groups and generations. A great amount of emotion is usually invested in peer-group and friendship relationships at the adolescent stage. The group solidarity and companionship often generate a warmth and romanticism which give youth an almost transcendental glow and rapture never to be regained (Mays, 1974).

How can responsibility be given to the immature and to the irresponsible? There is no way out of the dilemma that unless it is granted, the child cannot learn how to exercise it. Like every other skill, it needs to be practised under adult guidance which then gradually diminishes during adolescence and adulthood. That it is worth taking the risks involved has been shown by the work of those who make this a central issue of their care for deprived, disturbed or delinquent young people.

Yet to some extent, family, school and society may be failing to provide sufficient and sufficiently graded training for responsibility and autonomy. It has been suggested

That the road to maturity lies through the construction of four selves – social, sexual, vocational and philosophic ... in these four areas adolescents are driven to make a series of responsible choices which – if they are real and stable ones – no human being can take for another; they are also matters where knowledge and information are essential to wise decisions; because so often the consequences of choice look so irrevocable, and the young feel themselves so inexperienced, the very need to choose may provoke acute anxiety or even panic (Wall, 1968).

The task of training adolescents for responsibility is a complex one. Help needs to be given in defining the problem, providing the necessary information (or where it can be found), and assisting in the process of weighing up and predicting the likely consequences of alternative choices. Next, the decision must really be the young person's who consequently must also be allowed to cope with its outcome. Then the adult should not interfere even if he disagrees with the choice made (unless the wrong decision would really be quite disastrous); at the same time he should be prepared to stand by the adolescent if things do go wrong and give what help he can in putting things right.

Just as at present too many children grow up without insight into their own feeling and motives, so many get the opportunity too rarely to make their own decisions with a clear awareness beforehand of what is involved and with the responsibility afterwards to accept the consequences. Yet only such understanding and such practice will eventually enable them to deal competently with their own emotions and with their own decisions.

Schools have a vital contribution to make here. In the conventional classroom setting, where both work and discipline are laid down by the teacher, there is relatively little room for allowing each child a measure of responsibility for his own actions and learning. A more pupil-centred regime gives children a sense of involvement and participation in planning their own activities according to their different interest and ability levels; while rules evolved jointly with the teacher help to make the reasons for necessary constraints understood and hence more readily accepted by the pupils.

Research has shown that schools which emphasise cooperation rather than competition, which neither stream nor use corporal punishment, have a lower incidence of bullying, violence and delinquency, without any lowering of academic standards. Also, fostering emotional and social potential may prove more conducive to improving a child's rate of learning than concentrating more directly but narrowly on educational progress itself (Gooch and Pringle, 1966).

Many non-academic adolescents have for long felt that schooling is not sufficiently about life as they know it. This feeling has increasingly come to be shared by their grammar school peers and was well expressed by the sixth-former who edited *Youth Now* (Hadingham, 1970) when he wrote: 'Education is not simply a matter of passing exams and reaching university, but of playing a responsible, active part in social and political life.' This desire for a closer contact with 'real life' is a vital ingredient in the process of growing towards moral and emotional maturity. Young people are involved in a number of different and often interacting social groups – family, peer groups, school and society. Secondary schools could be playing a major role in helping adolescents to interpret themselves in relation to these groups and these groups in relation to themselves.

An appropriate curriculum should both transmit 'an organised body of knowledge and skill to a new generation, and also seek to achieve five goals' (Bruner, 1965). These are: giving pupils respect for and confidence in the powers of their own minds; giving them respect for the powers of thought concerning the human condition, man's plight and his social life; providing them with a set of workable models that make it simpler to analyse the nature of the social world in which they live and the condition in which man finds himself; imparting a sense of respect for the capacities and plight of man as a species, for his origins, for his potential, for his humanity; and leaving the student with a sense of the unfinished business of man's evolution.

Such a curriculum synthesises cognitive, emotional and moral aspects. Its appropriate setting is a school community in which the same principles of relationship and responsibility obtain as those included in the curriculum. To combine an appropriate curriculum with an appropriate school community opens up for the adolescent a rich developmental experience with which he can identify because he recognises what it offers as the means to his personal fulfilment (Hemming, 1974).

3. The Parental and Family Role

The multi-generation family, which included a large number of children as well as grandparents – and possibly some other relatives – is held by many sociological, anthropological and historical writers to have been the pre-industrial, near-universal model. However, a recent study argues that the large extended family has in fact never been the norm, either in this country or in Western society (Laslett, 1972). It suggests that the large family is part of a kind of 'Golden Age ideology', which nostalgically prefers a mythical past to what society and life were actually like. From the late Middle Ages onwards, 'The nuclear family household constituted the ordinary, expected, normal framework of domestic existence ... It is simply untrue, as far as we can tell ... that the complex family was a universal background to the ordinary lives of ordinary people.'

What has perhaps changed is that most people no longer live near relatives and friends most of their lives, so that they are not surrounded by a network of kinship and neighbourhood, all within walking distance. Increased mobility has made for greater isolation, almost anonymity, in high density conditions of modern urban life. In what follows the parental role in the modern nuclear family will be considered within the context of Western societies.

Basically this consists of meeting the developmental needs of childhood – which vary, of course, with age – to ensure optimal growth of all a child's potentialities. Comparative studies of child-rearing methods have shown that the quality, type and amount of contact with parents and with other children all have a differential effect on development.

To begin with, it is primarily the inter-action between mother and infant which satisfies the basic physical and psychological needs. Evidence suggests that, to be maximally effective, it has to be a two-way process: not only does the child imitate the mother but the mother also imitates the child (Bell, 1968; Bronfenbrenner, 1970).

59

Thus, it is the one-to-one relationship and its continuing and reciprocal nature which promote maximal learning and progress.

Preparing the child for life outside the family home is one of the major social functions of the parental role. The quality of family relationships exerts a profound and lasting influence on children's psychological development. The family which is able and equipped to carry out its parental tasks consistently and successfully gives a sense of security, of companionship and belonging to each of its members; it also bestows a sense of purpose and direction, of achievement and of personal worth. For the child it is of unique importance because it mediates between him and the world at large, providing what might be called a buffer, a filter and a bridge. It thus fulfils the irreplaceable function of laying the basis for the adjustment of the individual within society. The capacity for integration, cooperation and creativity has its roots in family living.

PARENTING – A SHARED TASK

Lip service has for long been paid to the concept of parenting being a shared task. In practice it is, however, the exception rather than the rule for fathers to feel actively involved in pregnancy, labour, childbirth and the first few months of the baby's life. Indeed, even psychological preparation for motherhood is still uncommon though relaxation classes – which may include talking about or demonstrating various tasks of mothering, such as bathing a baby or how to sterilise its bottle – have become increasingly widespread. Yet these months of waiting may well be an emotionally most receptive time for both partners. Surely the shared task of parenting could and should begin right at the beginning?

Pregnancy and birth involve developmental crises, not only for the woman but very often for the man too (as well as for the larger family of which they are a part). It is a key point in their individual life cycle and in the cycle of their relationship, whether or not the couple are married. Education for childbirth and parenthood can help the prospective parents towards maturation ... it can help towards a deeper understanding of relationships – between the couple and in-laws, between the parents and child – in the family and in the wider society (Kitzinger, 1973).

The next phase of parenting when sharing becomes particularly important is the post-natal period. A great deal of attention, joy and interest are focused on the mother and her new baby, but these tend to wane just when she is likely to be in greatest need of support, namely two or three months after the actual birth. By that time, the father is beginning to realise more fully the extent of his wife's preoccupation with the baby and its effect on their relationship. The young mother may be growing exhausted from her new responsibilities and anxieties, broken nights and perhaps feeding difficulties, made worse by feelings of social isolation and post-natal depression. These may engender anger, or even hatred and rejection, of the baby which in turn lead her to fear that she might do it some harm. It then becomes vital that she has support, understanding and counselling available to her, not only from her partner, relatives and friends but also from professional helpers.

THE PATERNAL ROLE

The father's part in fostering the child's development is primarily a two-fold one: firstly, it provides the child with a second adult model so that he can identify with a member of his own sex, if a boy, and also learn at first hand about the behaviour and attitudes of the opposite sex, if a girl. Secondly, better developmental progress appears to be made when praise and recognition come not only from the mother but from another person, preferably of the opposite sex (Bronfenbrenner, 1970).

There is a third likelihood for which there is not yet research evidence: the mother herself probably receives reassurance in her maternal role from her husband's support so that he 'reinforces' not only the child's but her own feelings of adequacy and self-esteem; this in turn increases her confidence in her mothering which communicates itself to the child. The same may well be true in relation to the mother, conveying both to father and child the value of the paternal role.

There is also some evidence that children's sense of responsibility develops best not in a matriarchal or patriarchal family structure, but where both parents participate actively in child rearing with somewhat different roles: the father increasingly becoming the principal companion and disciplinarian for the boy as he grows older and the mother for the girl. The father's absence – particularly where it is for long periods or permanent – has been shown to have an unfavourable effect on the child's psychological development, especially when it happens during the pre-school years; the influence of the father's absence on the mother will also affect the child, both directly and indirectly.

Being a readily replaceable cog in the industrial machine deprives many a man of a sense of identity and personal value. To a considerable extent this loss could be restored to the breadwinner by the family. Fathers can make an indispensable contribution to the psychological development of their children, daughters as well as sons. The importance of the mother-child relationship has been so much stressed in recent years that it almost seemed fathers need merely to provide material things for their offspring.

Work with handicapped children has shown how mistaken this view is. Where the father shares responsibility for upbringing and care, there is a much better chance of the child's triumphing over his disabilities than if the mother is left to cope by herself. The same is now seen to apply also to the normal child. 'For optimal development bonds need to be formed with people of both sexes and it is very likely that early attachments will influence the kind of close relationships which are possible later' (Rutter, 1972).

Through a true partnership with their wives, fathers can give a living example of democratic cooperation which their sons may then emulate and their daughters may seek in their future husbands. By taking an active part in his children's everyday care, finding time to play and later to share interests with them, fathers can enjoy and get to know them from their earliest age. Delegating it all to the mother until the children are older prevents the building up of those early relationships which are of such vital importance.

In short, a three-person model, including two adults of the opposite sex, appears to be more effective for socialisation than a two-person mother-child model...The fact that the structure most conducive to a child's development turns out to be the family is hardly surprising. The family is, after all, the product of a million years of evolution and should therefore have some survival value for the species (Bronfenbrenner, 1973).

SHARING THE PARENTAL ROLE

Can parental care be given in settings different from conventional family life as we know it? Communes have not been established long enough to assess their effects on child development. The Israeli

Kibbutz is the only Western child-rearing pattern which is markedly different. Upbringing is shared from the earliest months of life between parents and professional educators, the latter undertaking the major part of the daily care, training, teaching and disciplining.

Parental concern and involvement remain nevertheless paramount; the choice of the caring personnel, as well as the pattern of care, are decided by, and remain under the close surveillance of, the parents themselves; also each child spends three or more hours daily with his parents. During this time, they are free from all other responsibilities to devote their whole attention to playing with, talking to and enjoying their children. This is very different from the kind of half-attention given for part of or throughout the day in our society to pre-school children by mothers, busy with cleaning, shopping and cooking; and very different, too, from maternal or paternal separation.

Though it is nonsense to equate Kibbutz methods of child upbringing with maternal deprivation, this claim has nevertheless been made from time to time. In fact, it is a very specific way of dividing the parental role which is unique in developed societies. It is worth noting that over the years increasing responsibility has been given to mothers in most Kibbutzim for the care of their infants. For example, they now have six weeks off from work to nurse their newborn babies; and then they work half-time or less for a further six months, devoting the rest of the day entirely to the baby, since all work is done communally.

The evidence regarding the effects of a Kibbutz upbringing remains contradictory. There is said to be virtually no juvenile crime, few serious sexual difficulties, no homosexuality and practically no illegitimacy; also a disproportionately large number achieve high political office and high rank in the armed forces. So far, the Kibbutz has produced few major artists, writers or musicians; and, by American standards, young people are said to be over-dependent on the approval of their peers.

It is worthy of note that among the first generation of children, now themselves becoming parents, many wish their children to live in their own homes. Greater affluence makes this possible by simply enlarging the living space of each family. Youngsters themselves also want to sleep most nights with their own families, at least up to the age of twelve to fourteen years; then they begin to opt increasingly for sharing sleeping quarters with their contemporaries in the children's house.

SHARING MATERNAL ATTENTION

The only, as well as the first-born, child has an exceptional position in the family. On the one hand, he is more likely to be over-protected because his parents are relatively inexperienced; over-anxiety about development and progress may also be more common for the same reason. It is possible, too, that first-borns tend to be more competitive because they internalise their parents' high hopes for them; and jealousy of subsequent arrivals may also express itself in a desire to excel and beat competitors (including younger brothers and sisters).

On the other hand, the first-born does not have to compete for attention with siblings, at least to begin with; he is conceived and reared at a time when parental vigour, both physical and intellectual, is likely to be at its height; and the parents, but particularly the mother, have more time and energy to devote to him throughout the time during which he remains an only child. Any of these factors may be expected to promote the fullest realisation of a first child's potentiality, not least because he is given a headstart during his early life.

There is agreement in the literature that 'the dice are loaded in favour of the first-born' (Hudson, 1970). That this is so has been demonstrated again by a recent study of infants during their first year of life, and also by the Bureau's *National Child Development Study*. The former compared the effects of being reared in three different environments in Israel, namely family, Kibbutz and residential institution. Attention was concentrated on only children and the youngest child in a family. The same type of behaviour, namely vocalisation and smiling, was observed in both the infants and in those looking after them.

As one would have predicted, the adults spoke and smiled least in the institutional setting, and most often in the family; only children were spoken to and smiled at markedly more often than the youngest in the family; in the Kibbutz, the frequency was comparable to that of mothers in the family in relation to the youngest child. All these differences were mirrored in the infants themselves (Gewirtz and Gewirtz, 1969).

Since results from the Bureau's *National Child Development Study* will be quoted from time to time by way of illustration, a brief description of its design and aims might be useful. It is based on the Perinatal Mortality Survey, the subjects of which consisted of a whole week's births, some 17,000 babies in all, born in the week 3–9 March 1958, in England, Scotland and Wales. An unparalleled amount of sociological, obstetric and medical information was collected concerning the mother and the course of her pregnancy and labour, as well as detailed information on the baby at the time of delivery; a record was also made of the infant's weight, progress and any illnesses in the first weeks of life (Butler and Bonham, 1963; Butler and Alberman, 1969).

In 1965 (and also in 1969 and 1973) it proved possible to trace and study again the children who as babies had been the survivors of the Perinatal Mortality Survey. This longitudinal follow-up investigation is called the *National Child Development Study*. At each follow-up, detailed information is gathered from four main sources. First, a comprehensive picture is obtained from the schools of each pupil's abilities, behaviour and adjustment as well as about the school itself and about the contact between school and home.

Secondly, mothers, and sometimes fathers too, provide information about the home environment as well as about the child's development and behaviour. Thirdly, from a special medical examination, data are gathered on the children's height, weight, speech, hearing, vision, coordination and laterality. And fourthly, each child is given a number of tests and assessments (Pringle, Butler and Davie, 1966; Davie, Butler and Goldstein, 1972; Donnison, 1972).

In addition, children with special needs or problems, such as those who are born illegitimate, adopted, handicapped, socially disadvantaged or gifted, are being studied (Crellin, Pringle and West, 1971; Seglow, Pringle and Wedge, 1972; Hitchfield, 1973; Wedge and Prosser, 1973).

The *National Child Development Study* explored the question of shared maternal attention in two ways: firstly, in relation to family size, and secondly in relation to working mothers who have to make alternative arrangements for their child's care during part of the day. The results of the former investigation show that even at birth family size begins to exert an influence, high perinatal mortality being associated with high parity. By the age of seven or eleven years, the overall picture clearly indicates that children from large

c

families are at a considerable disadvantage physically, educationally and in terms of social adjustment.

For example, not only are children with many siblings shorter than those with few, but the arrival of each additional child also appears to act subsequently as a check to the growth of all preceding, i.e., older children; so, when there are younger siblings, the first-born does not reach the height of an only child at the age of seven or eleven years. In reading, the difference in attainment between the first and the fourth, or later born children was equivalent to sixteen months of reading age, and two or more younger children had an additional 'effect' of seven months. Conversely, those in one- or two-child families were about twelve months advanced in reading compared with those in families of five or more children (Davie, Butler and Goldstein, 1972; Prosser, 1973). These findings are very much in line with those of previous studies of the effects of family size.

It is not solely a question of low income, and thus a lower standard of living, since these effects of family size upon development were found to operate irrespective of social class. Obviously one explanation is that when parental time, attention, and maybe also patience, have to be shared, less is available for each child; this appears to be as true in respect of psychological resources as it is in terms of the family budget.

The child of the working mother shares the mother's attention with whatever paid responsibility she undertakes. To the extent that she has less time available to interact with and stimulate him, one might have expected a similar 'effect' to that of family size. However, this was not found to be so to the same extent (Davie, Butler and Goldstein, 1972; Wedge, 1973).

For example, after allowing for social class and family size, the average reading level of those whose mothers started work before the commencement of compulsory schooling was only three months below those whose mothers did not work; and where mothers started work after the child went to school, the difference shrank to six weeks. The effects were rather less if the work was on a part-time basis. In any case, it is likely that it is not so much the mother's working outside the home which affects the child's development as the quality of the substitute care which she is able to arrange.

PARENTS' INVOLVEMENT WITH THEIR CHILDREN

Relatively limited evidence is available on this aspect of parenthood. Much remains to be learned about the influence of the home background and of family relationships on child development; and about exactly how parental behaviour and expectations interact with the growing personality. Considerably more is known about the consequences of inadequate than of satisfactory parenting, most likely because 'happy families have no history' (Tolstoy, *Anna Karenina*).

While there is general agreement that the child's relationship with his parents is of vital importance, there have been a few voices of dissent regarding the most propitious nature of this relationship. For example, Musgrove (1966) argues that if it is

close, warm and affectionate, the child is likely to be handicapped for life...The boy's long-term interests are best served by an inadequate and feckless (if 'demanding') father...to be left alone is perhaps one of the most urgent needs of children in a child- and home-centred society.

In fact, among the upper middle classes in Britain in the nineteenth and early part of the twentieth century, parental involvement with children was quite circumscribed, being delegated first to nannies and then to boarding schools. That this markedly affected emotional and social development is strongly suggested by available evidence which, however, is mainly biographical and autobiographical. There is even less evidence on the effects of the nanny's modern substitute, the *au pair* girl; it may well have even greater disadvantages, since she lacks both training and permanency. Furthermore, many know very little English, at least to begin with. Most are themselves young and may have little understanding of a small child's needs. Perhaps worst of all, since they usually stay for a few months only, the child suffers the bewildering, if not traumatic, experience of being looked after by a succession of such girls who inevitably bring with them the differing expectations and habits of their own national cultures.

Musgrove's views, however, have received little supportive evidence and are diametrically opposed to conclusions based on examining child-rearing practices in the United States as well as those based on cross-cultural studies (Bronfenbrenner, 1970; Devereux, Bronfenbrenner and Rodgers, 1969). There has been, it is argued, 'a decrease in all spheres of inter-action between parents and children ... Over recent decades, children have been receiving progressively less attention ... As parents and other adults have moved out of the lives of children, the vacuum has been filled by the age-segregated peer group.' It might also be that the radio and, even more, television have played a part in filling this vacuum, both here and in other developed countries.

Bronfenbrenner contends that in this trend of decreasing inter-action are to be found the roots of the growing alienation of children and youth in American society; and that, as a matter of urgency, policies and programmes should be planned to upgrade the role and functions of parenthood, to foster community involvement, to re-integrate children and schools into the life of the neighbourhood and to give genuine responsibility to youth for the care of the young. These proposals are very much in line with suggestions which have also been put forward in this country in recent years (Halsey, 1973; Kogan and Pope, 1973; Leissner, Herdman and Davies, 1971).

THE PARAMOUNTCY OF 'BIOLOGICAL' PARENTHOOD AND THE MYTH OF MATERNAL FULFILMENT

On this question of paramountcy, society's attitude in this country is ambivalent and contradictory. Both in law and in practice we often act as if the blood tie and natural parenthood ensure satisfactory parenting. Yet, on the one hand, we fail to provide sufficient community support to enable parents to look after their children in times of difficulty; for example, every year several thousand pre-school children suffer the distress of coming into local authority care because their mothers are giving birth to another baby.

On the other hand, we so over-value the child's ties with his natural family that we let him remain with patently disturbed or rejecting parents. For example, a baby who has been assaulted and injured is allowed to return to his home in the hope that social work support will avoid a recurrence, when both common sense and research indicate that there is a high chance of it happening again. All the more so since social services are rarely, if ever, in a position to provide the daily surveillance required if a recurrence is to be prevented.

To argue that the parent needs the baby for his or her own recovery is to sacrifice the child's welfare to that of the adult. It is estimated that at least 700 infants die every year in England and Wales as a result of being brutally assaulted by their parents (D.H.S.S., 1970); and there is every reason to believe that several thousand children under the age of four years are victims of what is now euphemistically being called 'non-accidental injuries', some suffering permanent brain damage or crippling disorders. 'The depth of suffering is extreme and, tragically, is perpetuated from generation to generation. Battered children grow up to batter their own babies' (Jobling, 1973). Those who come to official notice may be only the tip of the iceberg. Moreover, excessive stress is not invariably the cause as tends to be claimed. (Smith, Honigsberger and Smith, 1973; Oliver and Cox, 1973; Smith, Hanson and Noble, 1974).

There is also a contemporary myth about the effects which fulfilling the maternal role has upon a single girl who has herself been rejected in childhood. It is argued that she should not be offered birth control facilities or later advised to have her baby adopted despite her own immaturity and emotional inadequacy. Rather, it is said that when her need to have something which belongs to her is fulfilled by having a baby, she will grow to greater maturity and stability.

In fact there is no evidence whatever to support this assumption of a therapeutic effect. On the contrary, available clinical and case-work material shows that there is a high probability of the baby's coming into care within the first year or two of its life; even if he returns to his mother from time to time, or remains with her, his chances in life are unfavourable practically from conception onwards (see Chapter 6, p. 125).

Again, the child's welfare is being sacrificed to that of the adult. It is a disturbing reflection of current attitudes to parenthood that a recent study found one third of pregnancies among women who enjoy a stable relation with a man to have been unwanted; and that half of these unwanted pregnancies remained regretted (Office of Population Censuses and Surveys, 1973).

If the quality of children's lives is to be improved, then several notions need to be dispelled which have no foundation in fact: that having a child is the sole or most important or easiest way to feminine fulfilment (many a dissatisfied woman is doomed to disappointment and, worse still, may then come to resent the baby for failing to bring this fulfilment); that a baby completes a family, rather like a

T.V. set or fridge; that it will cement a failing marriage; and that a child belongs to his parents like their other possessions over which they may exercise exclusive rights. At most, he is theirs only on temporary loan, as it were. There needs to be a shift from stressing the importance of parental rights to an emphasis on parental duties; and from the child being regarded as a chattel to a recognition of his right to loving care. The current idealised picture of parenthood needs to be replaced by a realistic and perhaps even daunting image of the arduous demands it imposes on one's emotions, energy, time and finance, as well as the inevitable constraints on personal independence, freedom of movement and indeed one's whole way of life.

It is evident that the ability and willingness to undertake all these responsibilities is neither dependent, nor necessarily consequent, upon biological parenthood. Rather it is the single-minded, unconditional desire, together with the emotional maturity to provide a caring home, which is the hallmark of good parenting.

4. Behaviour Problems and Learning Difficulties

Growing up is a difficult, and at times rather unhappy, business because of the child's very lack of experience: the younger he is, the more exclusively he lives in the present and the less he can draw comfort from a sense of perspective as well as from the knowledge, which time alone can bring, that most anxieties and problems are transitory.

However much parents try to protect their child from frightening situations, however reasonable and loving they may be, however child-centred a school they choose for him, growing up is inevitably beset by difficulties. Learning to manage feelings, learning to make sense of a bewilderingly complex world and learning to find one's own identity, bring both joy and sadness. Hence, all children find it difficult from time to time to adjust to the demands and expectations of the adult world. What then is the difference between children with problems and problem children?

THE CONCEPT OF MALADJUSTMENT

Hard and fast distinctions between 'normal' and 'abnormal' behaviour are artificial since the difference is one of degree and not of kind: the maladjusted child closely resembles the normal child in the way he reacts to insecurity, jealousy, rejection, inconsistent handling, or whatever it may be; but he shows these reactions in an intensified form.

All children pass through phases of temporary maladjustment. Transient problem behaviour is so common as to be normal and it has in fact been argued that a child who has never shown any difficulties should be considered abnormal. The negativistic three-year-old who has made 'no' and 'shan't' his most frequently used phrases; the seven-year-old who is anxious about going into the big junior school; the thirteen-year-old who is moody and inconsistent –

these reactions are characteristic of a particular age and stage of development.

CRITERIA POINTING TO MALADJUSTMENT

Five criteria might be found helpful when considering problem behaviour. The first criterion is chronological age, which means viewing a child's behaviour in the light of developmental norms. Frequent temper tantrums are quite common in a four-year-old, are unusual in a seven-year-old, but are so rare in an eleven-year-old that at that age they are likely to indicate serious disturbance.

The second criterion is intelligence. Age alone is insufficient for judging the significance of behaviour which deviates from what is usual for a particular age group. For example, the eight-year-old who prefers his own company or that of adults to his contemporaries; who refuses to learn by rote; who will not admit defeat and cries angrily when unable to solve a problem he has set himself; who refuses to go to sleep because he never has enough time to complete what he wants to do; who is insatiably curious and bitterly resents interruptions; such a child is clearly out of step with those of his own age. However, when it becomes recognised that his intelligence (or, as some people prefer to call it, his educable capacity) is similar to that of the average twelve-year-old, then his behaviour is seen to be part of a general developmental acceleration rather than symptomatic of emotional disturbance. Of course, high intellectual ability and maladjustment are not mutually exclusive.

The third and fourth criteria are the intensity and the persistence of a particular symptom. For example, a good many children have fears, tell lies and steal. Emotional difficulties must be suspected when a child is so full of fears that no sooner does one disappear than another takes its place; or when he persists in fabricating, and believing in, fantastic stories long after most children have learned to distinguish between fact and fiction.

An example showing the significance of the intensity of a symptom might be nailbiting. Research has shown that the great majority of children bite their nails at some time or other. However, few do it to the extent of drawing blood. Such a degree of intensity indicates emotional disturbance rather than just a bad habit; another example is the child who seems quite unable to tell the truth, even when it would be to his advantage.

The fifth criterion is a child's home background, including its cultural and social setting. For example, Jean lived in a high-delinquency area; her family had a criminal record, unusually consistent even in such a district (both parents, three brothers and one sister having been in prison, borstal and approved schools respectively); by coming into conflict with the law, Jean followed the family pattern. Her delinquencies were unlikely to be symptoms of maladjustment but rather reflected a lack of moral and social training. This in no way implies that such antisocial behaviour should be condoned; rather that the measures needed for re-education and rehabilitation will be different from those appropriate for the maladjusted child. In contrast, when twelve-year-old John, the son of a headmaster, spent his leisure time breaking open gas meters, this activity was the outward expression of strong inner conflicts, since such behaviour was out of keeping with his family's standards and the social and moral training given to him.

On the one hand, just as nature allows wide individual variations in physical stamina, so it probably does with respect to emotional stability. For example, individual differences in such traits as fear and affection are quite evident in the first year or two of life. Even the Dionne quins, who were biologically similar and brought up almost identically, showed individual differences in social development by the time they were two years old.

On the other hand, there is ample evidence – from clinical, sociological and psychological work – that a great deal of emotional maladjustment is related to, if not caused by, an unfavourable home or school environment. Lack of sufficient insight and support on the part of parents or teachers may be decisive factors in whether or not a child is able to cope with stressful situations. The belief that 'there are no problem children, only problem parents or teachers' is supported by the fact that emotional difficulties may clear up completely after help has been given.

Since there is constant interaction from conception onwards between hereditary and environmental influences, it is quite impossible in any given case to attribute difficulties solely to one or the other, or to apportion the extent to which either factor is responsible. For example, a boy may have inherited his father's quick temper and irritability; excessive aggressiveness may, however, equally well be due to being continually subjected to outbursts of temper, coupled with the fact that boys tend to identify themselves with their fathers. In practice, emphasising the influence of heredity may well become a self-fulfilling prophecy.

A more constructive attitude lies in placing the main emphasis on the positive influence which environment can exert at any stage of a child's development. This means acting on the assumption that problem behaviour is due to adverse factors in the family or social environment or in the child's own make-up; but that, given help, at least some readjustment can take place by redirecting such behaviour into more constructive channels.

CONFLICT AND LEARNING

'Children must be allowed to do as they please, as conflict causes problem behaviour.' This fallacy is unfairly attributed to the teaching of modern psychology. Conflict is essential to growth. It only becomes harmful when it poses a problem which is insoluble or which is inappropriate to the child's age and ability.

Indeed, for any development to take place, the child must learn to give up more primitive behaviour for new, more mature satisfactions. For example, the two-year-old has to give up the comfort of being carried about, for the pleasure of independent locomotion; the five-year-old must inhibit the inclination to grab what he wants, for the advantage of playing cooperatively with others; the thirteen-year-old must resolve the conflict between joining the leisure activities of his friends and doing homework, which will earn him the approval of parents and teachers or better marks or whatever satisfaction is most desired at the time. Of course, a conflict will not invariably be solved in the more mature direction but then progress rarely proceeds in a straight line.

The harm comes from inappropriate or insoluble conflict, the more so if it is chronic. A two-year-old cannot be expected to give up grabbing for the sake of sharing with others nor can the five-year-old be expected to choose doing homework instead of playing; and there is no satisfactory solution open to the child who is unwanted or whose loyalties are being competed for by warring parents who openly disagree about his upbringing. Such conflicts undermine a child's sense of security and impede healthy growth because no constructive alternatives are available.

THE MEANING AND SIGNIFICANCE OF SYMPTOMS

Just like pain, symptoms of maladjustment are a danger signal, a call for help; they indicate that there is intolerable tension between the personality and the environment. Withdrawal is as urgent a danger signal as aggression although the latter is more likely to be heeded because it constitutes a threat to adult authority. The range of possible symptoms is wide but basically they fall into two broad categories: aggression or withdrawal, fight or flight. Some children habitually choose one mode of reaction, others oscillate between retreat and attack.

To some extent, habitual behaviour is determined by personality type. The emotionally robust, confident and outgoing child is likely to adopt outgoing, aggressive methods whilst the gentle and retiring one is likely to choose retreat. To begin with, a child will try out various means of meeting a difficult situation. Experience then teaches him which is the most effective or least painful way.

Thus the relative success of aggressive or withdrawn behaviour influences which facet of the child's personality subsequently finds predominant expression. If he gains his ends more readily by one mode, he will persevere with this behaviour pattern. Hence, the way in which the earliest attempts at non-conformity and independence are handled has a vital influence on shaping later reactions to adult authority. By the time a child begins school the decisive choice between aggression and withdrawal has usually been made and the same choice is likely to be made in the school situation. This is one more reason why purely educational or purely emotional problems are rarely found in practice.

In practice, nuisance value or social unacceptability still tend to be used as the main criteria of problem behaviour. This leads to two undesirable consequences: the aggressive child who hits back arouses aggression in the adults concerned; this leads to a vicious circle of increasingly severe punishment calling out increasing aggression in the child who grows hardened to punishment, so that it loses its effectiveness. Secondly, the withdrawn, over-conforming child, though receiving gentler handling, tends to be overlooked. His real needs are likely to remain unmet since the understanding that a child can be 'too good' is still slow in coming.

No generally acceptable definition exists of a mentally healthy child; however, there would probably be general agreement that a confident, enquiring attitude of mind and the ability to make mutually rewarding relationships, both with adults and peers, are essential characteristics. Viewed in this context, the anxious, timid, always obedient child must cause concern. In fact, fight or flight, aggression or withdrawal, need to be regarded as equally significant danger signs, indicating that a child's emotional, social or intellectual needs are not being adequately met.

Symptoms of maladjustment are perhaps most appropriately likened to a fever: a sign of malaise, of disease, indicating the need for careful examination and diagnosis but by itself providing little clue to what is wrong or to effective treatment. Knowing the symptoms does not provide the key to the underlying causes; nor does knowing the underlying causes make it possible to predict likely symptoms.

Take, for example, stealing: parental rejection was the underlying cause with Ann; her parents wanted a boy and instead had a girl, and a rather timid and plain one at that. Peter, on the other hand, subjected to harsh discipline by his ex-sergeant-major father, expressed his defiance by stealing; and in Edward's case, stealing was not so much a symptom of maladjustment as due to a feckless home where he lacked moral guidance. Thus the same symptom may have a variety of causes. Hence action appropriate in one case would be inapplicable, ineffective, and possibly even harmful, in another.

Conversely, the same underlying causes may find expression in different symptoms. For example, Alan, jealous of his brilliant, popular brother, reacted by over-conformity, timidity, bed-wetting and underfunctioning at school; while Jennifer, faced with the same problem of jealousy, was spiteful and disobedient at home, but at school was over-ambitious and extremely hardworking. Thus the actual symptoms shown were almost diametrically opposed.

THE CONCEPT OF UNDERACHIEVEMENT

The term 'backwardness' relates educational attainment to chronological age, and hence to the level of work reached by the majority of a child's contemporaries; underachievement or underfunctioning relate it to the capacity of the individual pupil. In the one case a group norm serves as the yardstick, in the other it is the learning ability of the particular child in question.

The needs of children who are either educationally backward, slow learning or both, have received considerable attention in recent years. Though provision to meet their needs still remains inadequate, at least they are fairly well understood. This is by no means the case with regard to underachievement. Far too often it is still thought – by parents and even by teachers – that if a child does badly at school he must be either stupid, lazy or possibly both; large classes and inexperienced teachers are also made to take a share of the blame.

That intellectually able or very able children may in their schoolwork not reach the level of their own potential, or fail to achieve even the level of the majority of their own age group, is an idea which has been particularly slow in gaining acceptance despite available evidence (Pringle, 1970).

Exceptionally intelligent children can hardly be expected to function at a level commensurate with their mental age. For one thing, it is unlikely that they will be taught at so advanced a stage; for another, it is by no means established that the teaching appropriate for the average fifteen-year-old is equally suitable – qualitatively or quantitatively – for the ten-year-old who has a mental age of fifteen years. Moreover, for the most outstandingly gifted, such as a mathematical genius, the commonly used standards of attainment are anyhow unlikely to be applicable. Be that as it may, the education of able children generally, and the needs of able underfunctioning children in particular, have so far received only limited consideration in Britain.

CAUSES OF EDUCATIONAL DIFFICULTIES

Because of the close link between emotion and learning, scholastic failure is often accompanied by behaviour difficulties of one kind or another (Burt, 1937 and 1946; Chazan, 1963; Pringle, 1965 and 1970). Since the basis of all learning is laid in the home during the earliest years of life, the chances are high that, in many cases, the roots of educational difficulties may also be found there.

These conclusions have been confirmed once again by the findings from the *National Child Development Study*. For example, the incidence of maladjustment at the age of seven was four times higher among poor readers than among the rest of the cohort. By seven, children have been at school long enough for backwardness in reading to be reliably assessed but not so long that their difficulties are likely to have led to maladjustment in any but a few cases, particularly since most infant schools do not 'label' or otherwise penalise the slower learner. This strongly suggests that maladjustment is often a cause or at least an accompaniment of backwardness rather than a result of it (Davie et al., 1972).

The parents' attitudes to the child, to achievement in general and to scholastic success in particular, as well as their own level of education and the cultural stimulation they provided during the pre-school years and thereafter, play a major part. The child's own personality and how it interacts with all environmental influences will determine his readiness, adaptation and responsiveness to the school situation.

This in turn may be favourable or inimical to his particular needs. If he is fortunate it will build on and supplement what his home has given him so far, thus extending his range of emotional relationships as well as his intellectual horizons. At worst, it may extinguish his curiosity and his delight in learning, because of an uninspired teaching approach, because there is failure in personal relations, or because of a combination of these.

The teacher who sees his role in a wider framework than the inculcating of skills and the purveying of information is in a position of great influence. He can counteract, or at least mitigate, some of the consequences of an emotionally or culturally unfavourable home background; he can rekindle the child's curiosity, harness his emotional energies by giving praise and recognition, and compensate him for emotional deprivation by offering affection, albeit of a less 'exclusive' and close nature than parental love. Of course, the larger the class and the more deprived the child, the more difficult it is for the teacher to give the necessary time and attention to an individual pupil. In most cases, it would also be essential to involve the parents and influence their attitudes.

The environmental factors leading to under-achievement or indeed 'over-achievement' will repay closer scrutiny and study. A genetically potential I.Q. of 150 is of little value to society if largely unused. Real equality of educational opportunity is a will-o'-the-wisp while inequality remains in the home. And by inequality in the home we do not especially imply an inequality in material factors but also, and perhaps more powerfully, an inequality in attitudes to the child, attitudes to education and attitudes to life which in combination appear to exert continuous and long term influences upon psychological growth. These inequalities do not merely reflect the differing practices of different social classes but also occur within classes, and indeed also appear to occur within families (Clarke and Clarke, 1972).

MULTIPLICITY OF CAUSATION

Perhaps most fundamental of all is the fact that rarely, if ever, are either problem behaviour or learning difficulties due to one single cause or circumstance. Rather there is a multiplicity of inter-related and inter-acting factors, so that there is unlikely to be a short cut either to diagnosis or to treatment. The health, appearance, intelligence and whole personality of the child; the economic, social and cultural standing of his parents; the relationship between them and between all the other members of the family; the child's experiences at school and in the neighbourhood – all these and many more factors may play a part. Their combination and impact are unique for each child. Thus the relative importance of a particular set of circumstances differs for each child, even in the same family, as does the aspect most likely to respond to intervention or therapy.

Frequently one is faced with the apparent paradox of one child who has survived an extremely unfavourable environment, apparently unscathed, while another has succumbed to far less adverse circumstances. The answer lies probably in the fact that the constitutionally most stable and resilient are capable of overcoming even intense and prolonged stress. Yet, everyone has a breaking point. The child's more malleable personality is more vulnerable and hence more likely to become irreparably warped than that of the mature adult. In addition to inborn differences in temperamental stability and intellectual potential, every child's development is helped or hindered by the opportunities afforded by his home and school to make appropriate choices and to cope with resolvable conflicts.

Perhaps an analogy might help to illustrate the way in which multiple causation accounts for learning and behaviour difficulties in childhood. Cars come in all shapes and sizes: some, like Land Rovers, can negotiate the roughest ground: others are so flimsily made that even relatively minor bumps in the road will soon lead to trouble; others yet are excellent of their kind, such as the Rolls-Royce, though not designed to travel over unmade country roads. Secondly, roads themselves not only differ, but become unexpectedly hazardous from time to time, due to floods, subsidence or other 'acts of God'.

Thirdly, drivers differ not only in their actual driving skills but also in their understanding, and indeed interest in, what makes the engine tick; some will do reasonably well given straightforward weather and road conditions; some will excel whatever the conditions; and others will be a hazard to themselves and other road users because of poor road sense, too slow or too fast reactions and a lack of understanding of what it is reasonable to expect from the particular model they are driving. Indeed, the majority of accidents are caused by human short-comings rather than by faults in the car's design, performance or capability.

For cars now substitute children: some are born sturdy and resilient; others are vulnerable, perhaps due to genetic factors or some slight neurological impairment but more often because of unsatisfactory life experiences which leave them inadequately equipped to cope with subsequent stress; a small minority are born actually damaged. For the road substitute life, which for the majority will be reasonably smooth with only occasional 'bumps' but for some may bring difficulties if not disaster.

Lastly, for the driver substitute parents and teachers. No one questions that the best made, reliable car can become a menace in the hands of an inexperienced, vacillating, selfish, impulsive, aggressive, neglectful, or simply stupid and generally inadequate driver. Nor that the highly skilled, responsible motorist takes his task seriously, devoting time and thought to obtaining the best performance his vehicle is capable of, and giving constant care to appropriate handling and servicing.

Of course, neither parents nor teachers deliberately mishandle children – the vast majority are deeply caring and concerned. But why is it assumed that because we have all been children, we know how best to foster the development of our own offspring? Most people would not accept the similar argument that because we have all been to school we could therefore be adequate teachers without the need for lengthy professional training. Though analogies must not be pushed too far, does some preparation for parenthood not seem desirable to enhance our knowledge of the developmental needs of children?

5. Consequences of Failure to Meet Children's Needs

If one of the basic needs remains unmet – or inadequately met – then development may become stunted or distorted. In practice it is likely that if one need fails to be met, others will be affected too, but· in what follows the likely consequences will be discussed separately. It is also probable that there is an optimal level of need fulfilment so that 'too much' may also be harmful. This question will also be considered, but more briefly.

'We've tried everything'. . .'We treat them all alike'. . .'We've given the child everything he wants'. These three remarks are frequently heard when parents ask for help with a difficult child. The first suggests inconsistent handling, with swings between strict control and weak indulgence...The second overlooks the fact that siblings are not 'all alike' but vary in age and personality – and therefore in their individual needs...The third remark suggests that the parents have tried to compensate in irrelevant, extravagant material ways for their difficulty in meeting the child's emotional needs (Berry, 1972).

THE NEED FOR LOVE AND SECURITY

When this need is not met adequately, then the consequences can be disastrous later on, both for the individual and for society. Prisons, mental hospitals, borstals and schools for the maladjusted contain a high proportion of individuals who in childhood lacked consistent, continuous and concerned care, or, worse still, were unloved and rejected. Their number is high too among the chronically unemployable and among what I have termed 'able misfits' (Pringle, 1970).

Such young people are one example of the fact that parental rejection is neither the prerogative of any social class nor necessarily linked with socio-economic disadvantage. The existence of an unwanted child may more readily come to light in families whose other problems have already necessitated some involvement of one helping agency or another. In the affluent middle or upper class home, emotional deprivation is rarely suspected or detected; to the discerning teacher the signs are quite evident yet not infrequently it is the child himself who is blamed for his difficult behaviour and lack of progress, being labelled 'uncooperative', 'disruptive', 'lazy' or 'backward'.

Anger, hate and lack of concern for others are probable reactions to being unloved and rejected. Vandalism, violence and delinquency are not infrequently an outward expression of these feelings. In embryo these reactions can be seen when a young child, who has been scolded or smacked, kicks his teddy bear or the table. Through a loving relationship, children learn to control their anger and later to use it constructively during adolescence and adulthood; without affection, it remains primitive and grows more vicious and vengeful with increasing strength.

Can too much love and security be given to a child? There is a sense in which this may be so where a parent builds such a close and exclusive tie that eventual emancipation from it or even sharing it may not come about. As a result, the chance of future emotional independence may be jeopardised, together with the establishment of mutually satisfying sexual and parental relationships. Too much security – being as it were wrapped protectively in cotton wool – may make a child too fearful to venture out and face the uncertainties of a less safe and protective world.

Not so long ago it was believed that children became attached to their mothers chiefly because they provided nourishment. This theory of 'cupboard love' has been disproved by the work of the Harlows with monkeys and by Bowlby's studies of attachment behaviour. Now the pendulum may have swung so far in the other direction that there is a risk of the importance of nutrition being overlooked within this context. Recent evidence suggests that impaired food intake is probably an important contributory cause of dwarfism in children from neglectful or rejecting homes.

The concept of maternal deprivation

Bowlby's monograph, prepared for the World Health Organisation in 1951 on maternal deprivation, was a major landmark and his subsequent work has continued to shed light on the nature of mothering. The numerous studies carried out since then, both with humans and animals, bear witness to the remarkable influence of his thinking.

The contention, which Bowlby made his own, that the nature of the child's earliest emotional relationship to his mother is of vital importance; that he needs to establish a lasting 'bond'; and if it is irrevocably broken or has never been satisfactorily established, then subsequent physical, intellectual and social development may be seriously and lastingly affected, is now generally accepted; as is the evidence that if a child has not had the opportunity to become closely attached to one and the same mother-figure during the first three years of life, he may become a psychopath or 'affectionless character'.

Controversy has, however, continued to surround his views. Three aspects in particular have been challenged. First, that deprivation of maternal care inevitably causes permanent damage; for example, it is argued that mental retardation can be mitigated by appropriate training in later childhood despite severe deprivation in infancy (Clarke and Clarke, 1973). Secondly, it has been questioned whether all children are equally vulnerable to the distorting effects of such deprivation; indeed, Bowlby himself said that only some children are gravely damaged for life. There are likely to be innate differences in responsiveness to stress; equally important, there is evidence that the child's age and stage of development, as well as the degree and duration of maternal deprivation, are of crucial importance (Pringle, 1971).

Thirdly, it has been argued that the term itself is imprecise. It suggests that there has been a loss, when in many cases the child has never experienced continuous, loving care, i.e., he has always lacked it; in other cases the quality of care has been insufficient or distorted; if a relationship was established, it may have been interrupted for longer or shorter periods. Each of these situations is likely to have different effects on development; as is also the nature of the mother-child relationship prior to the separation experiences.

Incidentally, the question of love and security is invariably discussed within the context of the mother-child relationship because this is the usual situation in developed countries. However, there is no evidence that – if the mother went out to work – the father could not meet this need and bring up children equally well, given appropriate attitudes, both on his and on society's part. One would then expect prolonged paternal deprivation early in a child's life to have similar consequences to maternal deprivation.

In his recent reassessment of 'maternal deprivation', Rutter (1972) suggests that the concept

should now be abandoned. That 'bad' care of children in early life can have 'bad' effects, both short-term and long-term, can be accepted as proven. What is now needed is a more precise delineation of the different aspects of 'badness', together with the analysis of their separate effects and the reasons why children differ in their responses.

Whether it is wise to give up this concept until there has been the further research that Rutter pleads for and until more discriminating terms become available, might be questioned.

In the writer's opinion it is more urgent to dispel two misconceptions which have had very unfortunate consequences. Both are based on misinterpretations of Bowlby's views. His stress on the need for a warm, intimate and continuous relationship has been taken to imply that the same person must provide care uninterruptedly for twenty-four hours a day. In fact, he has always held that it is wise to accustom even quite young babies to being looked after by someone else occasionally; yet some mothers continue to feel guilty about seeking a temporary and brief 'escape'.

The second misconception is seen in the dictum 'better a bad family than a good institution'. While there is no evidence to support this assertion, it has led to some official reluctance to remove children even from appallingly bad homes. This view ignores the most crucial factors in mothering, namely its quality, stability and intensity. Instead it postulates a powerful bond, commonly referred to as the 'blood tie'. Again, there is no evidence for this myth. Rather, present knowledge indicates that good mothering (or fathering for that matter) is neither dependent on, nor necessarily consequent upon, biological parenthood.

That this is so is shown by the generally very satisfactory outcome when children are placed in adoptive homes. Moreover, there is much evidence that this is the case even when a child has, prior to placement, been subjected to potentially damaging experiences, such as prenatal stress, early institutional care, parental neglect, ill-treatment, or even a combination of these (Kadushin, 1970; Pringle, 1966; Seglow, Pringle and Wedge, 1972; Skeels, 1966; Skodak and Skeels, 1949).

The effects of maternal deprivation

Inevitably, the evidence for the relationship of maternal care to children's mental health comes primarily from two sources: from the clinical observations of those concerned with emotionally disturbed children; and from retrospective psychological studies which compare the development of family-reared children with those growing up deprived of a loving and secure home. Methodologically it would certainly be more conclusive if objective studies of intra-family behaviour in the 'natural' environment of the home were possible; clearly they are not. Controlled experiments to explore the effects of various types of maternal deprivation on human babies are, of course, quite unacceptable.

Just such experiments, however, have been carried out on baby monkeys. The results are clear cut, startling and convincing. Several generations of monkeys were raised under a wide range of depriving conditions: partial or complete deprivation of maternal care; rearing in complete isolation; rearing with other motherless infants; and varying the onset of these abnormal situations. This work was continued long enough to see whether infant experiences have effects lasting into adulthood (Harlow and Griffin, 1965; Harlow and Harlow, 1969 and 1970).

The results suggested that bodily contact (and not food) is the single most important requirement for the infant's attachment to its mother. Much more important, however, was the finding that 'monkeys which have known no affection can never develop either normal sexual behaviour or normal maternal behaviour and are bound to live out their lives as social failures'. This applied equally to male and female monkeys. Those females who did become pregnant – thanks to the persistence of normally-reared males – turned out to be 'hopeless, helpless and heartless mothers': either they ignored their babies or else they abused them brutally.

Studies with other animals, such as rats and goats, have produced similar results. These findings are striking enough to lend strong support to the hypothesis that being deprived of love and security in early life may well have similar long-term consequences in man; however, their exact nature must await the findings of further research.

Impaired family relationships

The importance of relationships to the child's optimal development has been implicit in much that has already been discussed. Here a closer look is taken at what is known about the long-term effects when relations are severely or chronically disturbed, whether at home or in school.

The emotional climate of the home depends largely on the success of the parents' marriage, and temperamental, intellectual or sexual incompatibility often leads to a tense atmosphere, if not to open quarrels. Even when the child is not deliberately drawn into these, his own adjustment is likely to be affected. Similarly, if one parent is inadequate or mentally ill, it will affect not only the marital situation but also the parenting capacity of the affected partner.

A child from a discordant home is liable himself to become emotionally disturbed or antisocial, and not infrequently educationally backward too. A quarrelling, inadequate or disturbed parent makes a poor adult model. Evidence is now accumulating that parental hostility has a particularly harmful effect on a child's later development, especially on his ability to give as an adult unselfish loving care in the parental relationship. Thus parental hostility perpetuates itself from one generation to another in what is literally an extremely vicious circle.

Several studies both in this country and the USA show that parents who assault or otherwise injure their babies share a number of characteristics: the parents had been treated similarly themselves; even if they had not suffered quite the same violence, they had all been deprived of good mothering and been subjected to constant parental criticism. As adults they have quite unreasonably high expectations of their baby: his inability to conform with demands for obedience is seen as wilful and deliberate defiance; the baby's crying is interpreted as his refusal to love the parent; a punitive self-righteousness results in severe measures to 'discipline' him at a totally inappropriate age. Often too the battering parent is socially isolated and failing to find in the marriage partner the fulfilment of unmet needs (Kempe, 1962; Hughes, 1967; Helfer and Kempe, 1968; Court, 1969; Skinner and Castle, 1969).

Inevitably treatment of such a parent is both complex and lengthy. This poses extremely difficult issues. These are, at present, generally speaking, not being faced realistically; also they are considered more from the point of view of the battering parent than that of the infant, and his long-term welfare. Surely, the future safety of the injured child ought to be of paramount importance? Punishment of the parent helps neither him nor the child; yet returning the baby to a dangerous home where there is a high risk of further attack and injury, both physical and emotional, seems even less justifiable.

Preoccupation with inter-personal stress and (for the child) insoluble conflict tend to interfere with successful learning. Also unsatisfactory relations with parents may make the establishment of good relations with other authority figures more difficult; this is likely to apply particularly to teachers in so far as the child perceives them to be *in loco parentis*.

Parental mental disorder is most likely to be followed by behavioural disturbance in the children when the parent exhibits long-standing abnormalities of personality...The involvement of the child in the symptoms of the parental illness does seem to be crucial...Children in families where both parents are ill or where the parental illness is accompanied by break-up of the marriage seem to be especially at risk (Rutter, 1966).

Of course, genetic factors predisposing to mental illness in the adult may also play some part in the child's disturbance but available evidence suggests that this is not a major factor.

There is evidence too, that in homes where the father has been absent for long periods or permanently, boys are at greater risk of becoming delinquent and girls of having an illegitimate baby; but little is known as yet about the age at which absence is particularly harmful or relatively least damaging. The death of a parent appears to have a delayed or 'sleeper' effect: children bereaved in early childhood (but not infancy) seem most at risk but often emotional disturbance does not develop until adolescence. This is particularly so when the parent of the same sex has died, perhaps because this deprives the child of a model for adult behaviour as he reaches maturity (Rutter, 1966).

It looks as if there is a particularly close link between the home background, the child's educational achievements and antisocial behaviour (West, 1969; West and Farrington, 1974). In two long-term studies in which quite large groups of juvenile delinquents were followed up, respectively for eight and thirty years, it was found that seriously antisocial youngsters and especially recidivists showed these tendencies while still quite young; that a high proportion came from neglecting, disrupted and broken homes; that the majority had fathers who did semi-skilled or unskilled work; and that the children themselves had low ability and even lower educational achievements (Robins, 1966; Wolfgang et al., 1972).

Affection for and acceptance of children are not, of course, the prerogative of any social class; nor are impaired family relationships confined to any stratum of society. However, they may come to light more readily when a family is beset by social and economic problems, which come to the attention of the helping services. Since impaired relations are almost inevitably more frequent where there are such problems, children from socially and economically deprived homes are at greater risk.

They are also at greater risk educationally.

Even in these latter days when so much has been written and so much is known about the causes of social and personal maladjustment, school often proves, for some unlucky youngster, to be a painful and sometimes a permanently damaging experience...Neither delinquency nor maladjustment are solely products of school life yet strain and tension induced by formal education could produce such results in children who are particularly stress-prone or who are already emotionally disturbed...How much misery is still inflicted upon children in school (and in their own homes, too, for that matter) it is quite impossible to estimate (Mays, 1974).

The major harm is probably done by teachers who undermine a child's confidence by constant disapproval and by irony; and who kill his joy in learning by dreary teaching, a permanent preoccupation with marks and rigid streaming, and by being interested in him only as a pupil rather than as an individual. Secondary schools are more likely to inflict such harm than primary schools, since, in the former, teaching is usually subject-orientated rather than child-centred.

THE NEED FOR NEW EXPERIENCES

Both under- and over-stimulation can have damaging effects, even on adults. One of the worst punishments is solitary confinement which deprives the individual of social interaction and severely restricts sensory and intellectual stimulation; even a monotonous or restricted environment is difficult to endure (as shown by polar expeditions as well as by research in the armed forces), producing depression, anxiety, irritability and a disruption of the ability to think clearly. Very similar consequences may well result from over-stimulation.

The exact difference which an enriching or depriving upbringing and home background can make, needs a great deal more research.

However, a conservative estimate of the effect of extreme environments on intelligence is about 20 I.Q. points. This could mean the difference between a life in an institution for the subnormal or a productive life in society. It could mean the difference between a professional career and an occupation which is at the semi-skilled or unskilled level (Bloom, 1964).

Under-stimulation

The more uneventful and dull life is, the more readily boredom, frustration and restlessness set in. This is shown clearly by the contrast between the eagerness, alertness and vitality of normal toddlers whose life is filled with new experiences and challenges; and the aimlessness and boredom of adolescents with nothing to do and nowhere to go. The urban environment – in which the majority of the population now live – is hostile to the young; there is little freedom or safety to explore or experiment, particularly without adult supervision.

Too small houses or flats, small, formal gardens or playgrounds (if any) and dangerously busy roads severely restrict the space and freedom for unsupervised play. Conversely, children who are allowed to roam about freely, find themselves far too readily in conflict with the law through curiosity and a sense of adventure. Yet making adequate provision for both indoor and outdoor play and leisure facilities is still considered an unjustifiably costly 'frill'. Even adventure playgrounds, which in any case are few and far between, are fixed in location and duration as well as being circumscribed in providing scope for real discovery.

In seeking – legitimately – the excitement of new experiences where few are to be found or attainable, the forbidden, risky or dangerous are liable to acquire an aura of daring and excitement. What may start as a lark – an expression of high spirits and the desire for adventure – can all too readily turn into vandalism and other delinquency.

It does not seem fanciful (though it remains to be proven) to suggest that some adolescent escapades which result in crime are child's play conducted with adult means, that the exaggerated need to identify with a group is a reaction to a depersonalised and incomplete experience of a human community...yet active challenge is comparatively rare, in spite of the attention it gets from the courts and the press; even juvenile delinquents amount to less than three per cent of the age group (Wall, 1968).

In the young child, insufficient sensory stimulation can retard or even impair development, including intellectual growth.

During recent years, the concept of infant intelligence has in fact assumed a new look. Marked individual differences have been observed quite early during the baby's first year of life and there is evidence that they are likely to be due to the effects of social stimulation (Kagan, 1971). If further studies confirm this, are remedial procedures required before the child has even left the cradle?

Probably the single and in the long run most crucial factor which promotes intellectual growth is the quality of the child's speech environment: not merely how much he is talked to, but how relevant, distinctive and rich the conversation is. The most essential element is the reciprocity of speech between child and adult, the latter initiating or responding to conversation. Hence, the mere presence of adults or just listening to conversation (on T.V. for example) is insufficient.

That this is so is shown by the comparatively more limited verbal ability of canal-boat and gypsy children as well as those reared in large families or those where language skills are very limited (Davie, Butler and Goldstein, 1972; Douglas 1964; Douglas, Ross and Simpson, 1968; Prosser, 1973; Rutter and Mittler, 1972). Such children have more contacts with other children than with adults; their language environment is less rich and possibly also less clear – because there is competing noise, whether from other children or the constantly switched on radio or television; and there is less likely to be an active enjoyment of language as a means of thought and communication. In consequence, the acquisition of verbal ability is adversely affected; this in turn affects the ability to respond to formal education, in particular to learning to read and write – the key skills to further scholastic progress.

Language has two main roles. It is a communication system – a way of sharing ideas and information with others; its second and probably more important role lies in controlling thought and, through it, behaviour. This is not to say that there can be no thought without language. Rather, thought remains markedly impoverished without language, perhaps in a real sense sub-human. Language is to thought what a catalyst is to a chemical reaction: it sets it off, speeds it up and facilitates it. Exactly how children learn to internalise language into thought remains to be explored in detail (Russia's A. R. Luria being one of the leaders of such studies); some linguists, it should be added, question the validity of these psychological theories.

Cultural and linguistic disadvantages

During the past ten years language development has grown to be a topic of central interest to educators, psychologists and sociologists; the concept of cultural and linguistic disadvantage, however, has become an issue of intense political controversy. In the fifties (and to some extent still now, *vide* Jensen, Shockley and Eysenck), theories of intelligence and intelligence testing were the focus of similar debates. The increasingly accepted current view is that tests are among the most useful tools for assessing a child's present level of functioning in the areas of performance for which the particular test has been designed – no more and no less; a minority continue to see them as an evil instrument of capitalistic or middle-class elitism and hence argue that they should be abolished.

It has been known for at least thirty years that children growing up in unstimulating environments – whether these be their own homes or institutions – often have limited language skills. But the sixties saw an upsurge of interest in linguistics and the birth of a new hypothesis, namely that language shapes not only thought but also (via various other processes) social class (Bernstein, 1961 and 1972). This goes much further, of course, than saying that language indicates social class. It postulates that the different language modes, characteristically used by the middle and the working classes, initiate and then reinforce different patterns of behaviour and personality. Thus they are held to perpetuate the structure of society itself. They have been respectively termed 'restricted' and 'elaborated' codes: the former is a stereotyped, condensed way of speaking, with short, simple and often incomplete sentences, generally rather limited in range and detail; whereas the middle-class language is held to be just the reverse. 'As the child learns his speech, so will he learn his social structure: and the latter will become the substratum of his innermost experience.'

Some recent American studies reached similar conclusions. For example:

Given these two kinds of communication networks within the family, repeated thousands of times in many different situations in the pre-school years, children from the two kinds of families can hardly fail to enter school with quite different capabilities for receiving and processing information...for defining the world, understanding it, or developing strategies for ordering it (Hess and Shipman, 1965).

Also the ability to motivate children to be attentive is important in developing intellectual capabilities to the full (Stinchcombe, 1969). If these views are accepted, they would seem to provide the answer to the question which has increasingly exercised educators: why do so many working-class children fail in school despite the fact that the British educational system has become increasingly open?

There is a four-way and largely ideological split about how to solve this problem. First, the politically committed, radical spokes-man argues that these views on the role of language serve to protect the privileges and power of the ruling middle-class elite, particularly within the educational system. Moreover, he is highly critical of the theory itself on a number of grounds; these include that far too little is known about working-class language and its relationship to class, Bernstein and others notwithstanding; that the research methodology of recorded interviews with mothers itself militates against obtaining the richness of the vernacular culture of the street, resulting instead in atypical inarticulate responses; that the influences of other powerful agencies of socialisation, besides the home, school and peer group, are being ignored, from the mass media to non-conformist chapels and brass bands; and that much of middle-class speech is anyhow turgid, redundant, empty and lacking in vitality (Baratz and Baratz, 1970; Barnes, Britton and Rosen, 1971; Labov, 1971).

Secondly, some educational reformers, who believe in working from within the system, refute the accusation that teachers are aiming to impose middle-class values on working-class children; in any case, they believe that middle-class values encompass two different systems, one of status-striving and the other based on intellectual interests: often they go together since academic achievements are among the main means for improving status, but there is no inevitable or intrinsic link between them.

Instead, they argue that the teacher's task is to widen the horizons of the children whose homes are insufficiently stimulating and to initiate them into more subtle and complex ways of thinking and reasoning. The aim is to free them from the mental confines of their environment and to extend their range of values – which they may or may not accept subsequently. They hold that to preserve the social status quo or to introduce a kind of educational apartheid with popular education based on the folk culture of the working class would mean insulating class cultures from each other; either aim serves to dampen down working-class aspirations to an intellectually and materially richer life which compensatory education seeks to encourage.

Thirdly, the progressive humanist and environmentalist sees compensatory education as a means of overcoming 'cultural', 'social' or 'linguistic' disadvantage or deprivation; the earlier it is provided and the more the family, and in particular the mother, can be involved, the more likely it is to be successful. Fourthly, the conservative and reactionary believer in heredity uses impoverished language development as the justification for maintaining two separate systems of education, one rigorously academic, the other vocational and practical.

Bernstein himself (1971) seems to be speaking with two voices, as is demonstrated by the following quotations from the same book:

the normal linguistic environment of the working class is one of linguistic deprivation [page 66];...The concept of 'compensatory education' implies that something is lacking in the family, and so in the child...the school has to 'compensate' for the something which is missing...and the children become little deficit systems...Once the problem is seen even implicitly in this way, then it becomes appropriate to coin the terms 'cultural deprivation', 'linguistic deprivation', etc. and then these labels do their sad work [page 192].

Confusion becomes worse confounded when Bernstein's use of the term 'working class' is examined. On the one hand, he says his concept of linguistic deprivation applies only to the unskilled working class, but on the other he claims that these constitute 29 per cent of the population. Yet according to the Registrar General's classification of occupations, unskilled workers comprise 8 per cent and semi-skilled 20 per cent of the population. Nor are all, or even the majority, of children from unskilled working-class homes either linguistically or educationally deprived by any definition.

This was again shown by the results of the *National Child Development Study* (Davie, Butler and Goldstein, 1972): regarding oral ability some 40 per cent, and in reading attainment some 48 per cent, of children whose fathers are unskilled were said by their teachers to be below the average (and 10 per cent and 7 per cent respectively markedly poor); the proportions were somewhat lower for children whose fathers are semi-skilled. In other words, Bernstein's conclusions would seem to apply at most to some 10 per cent rather than almost 30 per cent of the population. Nor are such learning difficulties confined to any one class; even in Social Class I and II, some 15 per cent of the children were found to have below average oral and some 13 per cent below average reading ability (but only about 2 per cent were markedly poor).

In my view, insufficient intellectual and language stimulation is as real a problem as under-nourishment used to be. And, in a similar way, such mental under-nourishment is likely to be the result of an unfavourable total environment – poor housing, low income, poorer physical care, an unstable family structure and a culturally impoverished home leading to intellectual malnutrition.

On the one hand, the consequences of such complex and interacting patterns of disadvantage cannot be remedied by the school alone; on the other hand, many secondary schools compound the damage by their subject-centred organisation which makes for minimal personal interaction between teacher and pupil, and by a curriculum which too often has little relevance to their interests or future lives.

With regard to American 'enrichment' or 'compensatory' programmes, they were launched with too high hopes (also they were often too 'symptom specific'). Now they are being dismissed with similarly unwarranted disappointment. It was unrealistic to expect a few extra hours of schooling, available for a year or two, together with a few excursions to tip the scales against such powerful factors as poverty, ignorance, disease and despair, to which the children had been exposed for years and in which they continued to live.

These special programmes did not succeed in enabling disadvantaged children to catch up in those academic skills which can be measured, in particular in respect of intelligence quotients which often were the sole criterion used. Nevertheless, as the massive Coleman report (1966) concludes, there were some gains, such as a more favourable attitude to school. Indeed, any broadening experience must be counted as a net gain.

The urban aid and educational priority areas programmes in the UK appear to have made somewhat greater impact but it is too early to judge their long-term effectiveness in stimulating intellectual and language development (Halsey, 1972). A real breakthrough will require a multi-pronged and sustained approach, including parental support and involvement; even then, dramatic or quick changes are highly unlikely.

Over-stimulation

In the young child, over-stimulation may lead to uncontrollable excitement, tenseness, exhaustion and disturbed sleep. In the adult, too, the ability to cope may become impaired if he has to grapple with unfamiliar or unpredictable events, relationships or objects at too great a pace. This is shown, for example, by the traveller who suffers from 'culture shock' when plunged into an alien environment without adequate preparation. The need to adapt rapidly and repeatedly to changing conditions produces disorientation and distortion of reality, anxiety or extreme irritability; eventually fatigue, apathy and withdrawal may set in.

Sensory bombardment can have as devastating effects as deprivation (and is used for similar purposes in political brain-washing). In the early months of life, one of the functions of good mothering is to act as a filter or barrier to avoid over-stimulation; yet later on some young people seem to seek a surfeit of sound and movement in discotheques, perhaps because there is not enough stimulation in their everyday life.

Similarly, on the cognitive and decision-making level, attention wanders and performance deteriorates at school or at work, when there is insufficient challenge; yet if there is too much to learn or understand – or if in the factory the conveyor belt moves too fast – then confusion, mistakes, tenseness and frustration result. Research has shown that, whatever the task, there is for each individual an optimal level of stimulation and a marked excess leads to stress and maladaptation (Miller, 1964; Sargeant, 1963; Selye, 1966).

Recently the thesis has been put forward that contemporary society is plunging headlong into accelerating and unmanageable change; and that unless measures are taken to prepare the young – and the community at large – to cope with it, a condition termed 'future shock' will result (Toffler, 1973). This is defined as 'the distress, both physical and psychological, that arises from overload of the human organism's physical adaptive systems and its decision-making processes . . . it is the human response to over-stimulation'.

Arguing that ours is becoming a 'throw-away society' in which things, people and organisational forms are becoming disposable, Toffler suggests that children are being trained from early on for 'turn-over and disaffiliation', due to frequently moving home and losing friends, and to the high rate of turnover among teachers. At the same time, 'our time perspective on education is unbalanced. At school we go heavily into the past, minimally into the present and zero into the future'. The accelerating rate of change is enforcing a new life pace where mastery of new situations becomes essential in ever shorter intervals. For some this 'overload' leads to confusional breakdown; signs of this, in Toffler's view, are the spreading use of tranquillisers and drugs; the rise of mysticism; the revolt of the young; the recurrent outbreaks of violence and vandalism; and the politics of nihilism and anarchy.

The so-called 'rat-race' probably plays a major part in the alienation and opting-out of the young from apparently 'good' middle-class homes. Pressurised by status and achievement-orientated parents towards what is seen by them as success without being given much of their parents' time or indeed affection; with few other values or ideals being put before them, either at home or at (usually boarding) schools; is it surprising that such young people prefer a future different from that mapped out by their parents?

When we consider together the urge of youth to rebel – to escape, to be adventurous – and the current openings for unconventional life-styles, what is remarkable is how strong the pull towards conformity remains. The picture of youth as in total revolt is a quite false presentation. For every out-and-out rebel, whether of the blatantly destructive or of the intelligently critical kind, there are many others in the same age-range and situation who accept without question the expectations of those in authority... The number of conformist adolescents puts in question the popular assumption of an exceptional 'generation gap' today. That such a gap exists between some young people and some adults is obvious. Communication may break down completely. But in other families the communication and cooperation are of a frankness and friendliness which seem to be far in advance of the norms of 1910, or even 1930, when, for the most part, no communication between the generations on personal matters was expected, and the role accorded to young people was not to discuss but to obey (Hemming, 1974).

THE NEED FOR PRAISE AND RECOGNITION

Unfortunately, praise and recognition are almost invariably given for achievement and not for effort. In consequence, this need is most readily and often satisfied in the case of intelligent, healthy, adjusted and attractive children (who are even praised merely for their pleasing appearance!).

In contrast, the intellectually slow, the culturally disadvantaged, the emotionally neglected or disturbed get far less, if any, praise and recognition. Yet their need is very much greater. Whatever small successes they achieve inevitably demand far more effort and perseverance; yet they receive less reward because they achieve less. Worse still, those who are rejected by their parents, and regarded as failures by their teachers, are wholly deprived of the satisfaction of this need by adults.

Even ability and talent well above the average may never declare themselves if adequate nurture or emotional support is lacking. The quality of family relationships, the emotional climate of the home, together with parental interest and encouragement, are of paramount importance also in helping able children to realise their potential (Pringle, 1970). Reviewing the causes of failure among gifted children, Burt (1962) concluded: 'Many of the parents appeared entirely indifferent to the child's success either in school or even in later life.'

Of course, no environment guarantees high achievement or consigns children irrevocably to low achievement. But a much higher proportion with unrealised potential will be found among certain economic sectors, social classes, ethnic groups and geographic areas than in others. Recent years have seen a conflict of viewpoint between those who argue that everyone must be given an equal educational opportunity and those who advocate that special attention ought to be devoted to the abler child. The former make a case for positive discrimination in favour of the socially and culturally disadvantaged child; whereas the latter claim that a country's ability to compete successfully in a scientific and technological age depends on the fostering of excellence.

The conflict between these two standpoints is, however, more apparent than real. It springs from the mistaken belief that all men are equal despite the enormous disparity found in physical and intellectual potential in all walks of life. To be given equality of opportunity is the right of every child; to expect equal capacity to make use of this opportunity runs counter to common sense and experience. Indeed, it has harmful consequences because such expectation is bound to engender a sense of failure.

Instead, we must act as if all children were equal and then respect, as well as accept and cater for, their differences. This means giving recognition to and developing all the different abilities and talents a child may have. Within such a framework, it is legitimate both to provide a democracy of opportunity while at the same time to strive for excellence so as to ensure an aristocracy of achievement.

Can the need for praise and recognition be 'over-satisfied', as it were? There seem to be two different ways in which this may happen. First, when praise and recognition are given too readily, then the child will not be encouraged to give of his best but be satisfied with the results of too limited an effort; or he may ignore such undeserved praise altogether because it has become devalued in his eyes, so that once again it will be ineffective as an incentive.

Secondly, when parents make achievement almost a condition of their love, then this may lead to the development in the child of an abnormally strong drive for success, esteem and power. Perhaps this is the driving force behind some of the strikingly successful people in business, sport or the arts, who seem to be spurred on by an almost insatiable need for praise and recognition which to them probably spells 'love'.

If this need is inadequately met or remains unsatisfied, then in the long term the effects are destructive of self-respect and of confidence in tackling new situations, tasks or relationships.

The role of competition

Another and linked difficulty relates to the belief – which is probably based on our puritan tradition – that the spur of competition leads to greatly increased effort; in this context, even the idea that all children must experience a measure of success is suspect. In fact, one of the most difficult challenges to parents and teachers is how, despite differences both in ability and in emotional development, all children can be helped to achieve some success.

The intensely competitive climate of our society, which is mirrored in the family and in the educational system, gives rise to two difficulties. First, if all children had equal ability and opportunities, then competition would be a measure of effort made. Because they have not, the same group remains comparatively unsuccessful. (The belief that the intellectually or verbally less competent are better with their hands is not corroborated by evidence.)

If a goal is felt to be unattainable, effort diminishes, partly because the cumulative effect of failure leads to a sense of hopelessness and partly because feeling rejected as being 'no good' arouses anxiety which further inhibits learning. Under-achievement, like envy, seems to feed on itself. A poor start in school snowballs into chronic failure and the teacher's understandable disappointment with poor progress only serves to lead to further discouragement in the pupil. And so both are caught in the vicious circle of discouragement, disapproval, unresponsiveness and further failure. The more competitive the system, the greater the proportion of children who are doomed to failure since only a select few can succeed. Moreover, an emphasis on competition tends to lead to an emotional climate where winning becomes the most important goal; learning for its own sake takes a back seat.

The second difficulty lies in the fact that an emphasis on competition interferes with the development of cooperative attitudes. Both experimental and clinical studies have demonstrated the disruptive effects of competition. If cooperative behaviour has survival value, then the skills of cooperation are far more basic to successful living than those of competition. Yet many children are exposed by their parents to a very competitive climate, siblings and other children being held up to them as examples, even when emulation is beyond the child's capacity. Similarly, parental expectations and pressures bear a measure of responsibility for the competitive atmosphere which prevails in many schools. (After all, some mothers start being competitive by comparing their babies' bladder control!)

Undoubtedly, children themselves create many competitive situations and test their abilities in countless ways of their own; these provide a means of realising their strength and discovering their limitations. When the yardstick is his own previous level of performance, maturation and experience alone will assure success; adding the incentive of recognition and encouraging the child to aim at surpassing his own past achievement are the surest road to progress and to establishing his self-esteem. These will then in turn act as powerful incentives to further effort.

How effective is group work compared with individual work? A lot of research has been done on this aspect of teaching and the general conclusion is that individual work is more fruitful when dealing with simple techniques where there is nothing to be gained from an exchange of views.

But there is general agreement that more advanced intellectual operations benefit from group work. This seems to be because more suggestions are put forward; the quality of the work tends to be set by the level of the most able members of the group; since they will be judged by their peers, the individuals are keen to cooperate and to show up well; ideas proposed are subjected to immediate approval or criticism (Hotyat, 1974).

The teacher's role

Because the school is more overtly concerned with standards of attainment and assessment of performance than the home, success and failure inevitably assume a major role. Streaming, marks and examinations are all means of publicly, as it were, recognising achievement or the lack of it. What has just been said about the role of competition applies with even greater force to the class-room: it is primarily achievement which calls forth recognition, the more so the older the child; and because the teacher is in a much better position than the parent to view a child's performance in relation to that of his contemporaries, disapproval and failure acquire an additional dimension.

Yet praising for achievement instead of effort has very harmful effects on the slower learner as well as on the child with emotional or physical handicaps: he has no chance of shining and always finds himself near the bottom. Such constant failure inevitably damages self-esteem and motivation. Nor do able children benefit from a highly competitive school regime, because they can do better than average without necessarily giving of their best or even trying very hard; this tends to breed arrogance and complacency, neither of which are conducive to effort or a spirit of cooperation. The teacher who believes that what matters most is the effort a child makes, and who praises whenever there is progress, however slow and limited, provides an appropriate incentive for all pupils, whatever their abilities.

The recent evidence that the foundation for intellectual and emotional growth is laid long before the start of compulsory schooling might have a rather depressing effect on teachers. They might reason that if parental attitudes to education are so vital to the child's response to education, if home circumstances outweigh the effect of schooling, then what hope is there that schools can bring about any radical improvement? Such a defeatist attitude on the part of the teacher would inevitably be transmitted to a pupil without its being spelt out; in turn it would affect his own attitude and hence his level of progress, as much if not more than his actual ability.

However, some even more recent research justifies a much more optimistic attitude on two grounds: it has shown just how potent are parental participation on the one hand, and the expectations of teachers on the other in influencing children's progress (Meyers, 1973; Pidgeon 1970; Wall 1973; Wieseman 1972). One example must suffice. Pupils with similar attainment levels were given intelligence tests and then their teachers were told that some had better learning potential than expected, whereas others were slow learners. A follow-up examination showed that those pupils, who the teachers had been led to expect could do better, were in fact doing better than the others, although the two groups had been matched for ability at the outset (Rosenthal and Jacobsen, 1968).

This finding underlines the truth of the saying 'give a dog a bad name'; labelling a child 'slow' (or 'bright') becomes a self-fulfilling prophecy. And this is as powerful in affecting the teacher (and parent) as it is in affecting how the child feels about himself, whether he thinks he is stupid or capable, and how hard he tries: self-confidence and motivation are fostered or extinguished by the way teachers think about and treat their charges.

Work experience

When a young person starts work, he is once again in a situation in which his self-respect may become enhanced or diminished. In our competitive society, exams and certificates have practically become the hall-mark of success; not only for climbing up the economic ladder but even for finding employment when the need for un-skilled labour is contracting. Hence for those who have done badly in the educational system, the chances are high that they will only be able to obtain jobs which carry the lowest level of recognition in terms of both prestige and pay. Technical advances, together with automation, are making even undemanding jobs scarce so that opportunities for unskilled teenagers have greatly diminished. Also the less able, educationally backward school leaver is particularly hard hit by a high level of unemployment.

Enforced idleness, boredom and little money in his pocket tend to undermine further what limited self-respect is left to the adolescent who has for years been caught in a web of multiple disadvantages, including being denied the satisfaction and spur of praise and recognition. Feeling that society disowns him may well engender a feeling that he in turn owes nothing to society.

THE NEED FOR RESPONSIBILITY

Society is ambiguous and ambivalent about granting responsibility and independence, particularly during adolescence. This is reflected in the way in which various adult rights – such as to enter a public house, to consume alcohol, to drive a car, to vote, to work part- or full-time, to marry without parental consent – are conceded at different ages. Parents and teachers differ even more widely in the amount of independence they are prepared to allow or to tolerate and in the extent to which they expect responsible behaviour without at the same time granting the right to make responsible decisions.

To thrust too much responsibility onto a child or to do so too early may have harmful effects. Without the necessary under-standing of what is involved and of the probable consequences of a particular decision or choice, responsibility will be perceived as a burden. He may nevertheless be prepared to shoulder it but at a high cost in terms of anxiety; or he may refuse to accept it, spending much time and ingenuity in devising ways of avoiding responsibility, perhaps wishing and dreaming but rarely doing.

The child who is denied opportunities to exercise responsibility will fail to develop a sense of responsibility for himself, for others or for material objects. When this denial has gone hand in hand with a lack of training in self-control and in planning ahead, then such youngsters will tend to be impulsive, unwilling to postpone immediate gratification of impulses, and contemptuous of the rights of others – in short, irresponsible.

It is likely that the self-same youngsters will later on find themselves in jobs which give them little, if any, responsibility. Work which fails to fulfil the need for involvement is likely to heighten the sense of alienation and irresponsibility which is bred by being made to feel an educational and vocational reject. Work which is repetitive, undemanding and frequently carried on in noisy or otherwise unpleasant conditions, is likely to induce both boredom and frustration. Whether at school or at work, these probably account for the craving of so many young people to find, in their spare time, excitement and an outlet for bottled-up needs and energies.

Practice in decision-making

The freedom to make decisions is part of exercising responsibility. The steadily lengthening process of compulsory education means that young people remain financially dependent on their parents longer and dependent on their teachers in relation to a major part of their waking day. Yet as soon as they leave school, young people are faced today with a wide variety of choices and decisions. There is a bewildering range of jobs, of life-styles and of religious, political and social beliefs. Choices are particularly difficult and complex in two areas which involve the deepest and most personal feelings.

First, most adolescents are trying to grapple with questions relating to their eventual social and sexual adjustment in the adult world. Secondly, they are searching for some interpretation of life, however vague or tentatively formulated - perhaps no more than a *modus vivendi*, 'do as you would be done by' or some simple code of fair play – which would give some meaning and direction to their own behaviour and to that of others.

For many, little guidance is available either in their homes or at school. Perhaps this is because there is now a lack of certainty, of moral imperatives, of ready answers and traditional religious beliefs.

In this situation, it is tempting to evade the issues altogether. May it be that this evasion creates its own problems? Determined not to inculcate values, we instead almost avoid discussing them altogether, thus providing no reference points for the many decisions later demanded by life itself? Is it because we have failed to provide appropriate nourishment for the imagination of many young people, and adequate support in their search for meaning, that they are seeking it in the hallucinations of drugs or are opting out altogether? Or because they feel the standards of the previous generation to be irrelevant or even immoral in the context of today? It is vital for youngsters to consider 'preferable futures'. Some may at present spend ten or more years in school without ever being encouraged to look at their value-systems and to ask themselves: 'What kind of life do I want to lead?' or 'What kind of person do I want to become?'

Preparation for parenthood

A strong case could be made out for including three new areas of knowledge in the curriculum of all secondary schools: first, an understanding of human psychology; second, preparation for parenthood; and thirdly, education for leisure. A knowledge of human psychology would include the dynamics of human conduct, the roots of prejudice and the ways in which people interact at a great variety of levels. This might contribute to an understanding or consciousness of one's self which is different from self-consciousness. Though difficult to acquire, it is probably more essential than sex education or a knowledge of how the body functions; yet in practice it receives far less, if any, attention. Of course, schools alone cannot in any case be expected to bring this about.

To be effective, a programme of preparation for parenthood would have to adopt a wide base. 'Education' is too narrow a connotation, suggesting classes and instruction on the model of sex education; also, it conveys too formal a framework and too intellectual a conception, suggesting that 'knowing' is enough. What is required is neither a narrow course, seen as a branch of biology or home economics, nor a very wide, general one in citizenship; equally, it should not be confined, as it tends to be at present, to girls and the less able ones at that. Some first-hand experience of babies and young children should form an integral part of such a scheme.

Included too should be an appreciation both of parental rights and responsibilities. At present, the father's role is rarely mentioned, while home-making and motherhood are undervalued. So much so that the housewife with small children, whose working hours are often twice as long as that of the thirty-five-hour-a-week clerk, is described and treated as not being gainfully employed.

Education for leisure is important because, at any rate in the foreseeable future, many young people will be working at dull, repetitive jobs. This may be so even for university graduates, according to a recent forecast (Holloway, 1973). It predicted that in ten years' time, only half the men leaving universities and one woman in five would be able to obtain intellectually demanding jobs. The rest would have 'to dirty their hands'. Until and unless available employment opportunities improve and working conditions become more satisfactory, leisure pursuits are likely to provide the major source of personal fulfilment. Shorter working hours are already on the way with increasing technological advances, particularly automation.

Again, courses should be widely based, covering the many possible forms of physical recreation as well as an appreciation of what they can offer by way of a healthy mind in a healthy body. Also crafts of various kinds and in particular the cultivation of an appreciation of the arts and, better still, the confidence to participate creatively in at least one of them – can make a vital contribution to the development of emotional maturity and to the growth of a compassionate understanding of man's predicament. Giving young people the basis for an enjoyable use of leisure may, moreover, make it more likely that later on they will be prepared to seek opportunities for further education. If their memories of secondary education are happy, then one important step towards lifelong education – considered by many to be a necessary goal in a rapidly changing society – will have been taken, namely preventing a reluctance to go on learning.

Will-power or determinism

If the basic psychological needs remain unfulfilled, is a child doomed forever? And if he is not, what determines whether or not he succeeds in overcoming the ill-effects of early and cumulative deprivation? At present, no precise answers are available but opinions cover the whole range from determinism to the belief that everyone, given the will, can 'win through'.

Advocates of determinism run the risk of conveying to young people that a deprived early life is an excuse, indeed almost a justification, for subsequent violent, lawless or otherwise deviant behaviour. This belief is unwarrantably defeatist. Advocates of will-power are, however, unwarrantably optimistic since no one is entirely 'master of his fate', least of all those who – even from before birth – have been beset by a pattern of complex and continuing disadvantage.

The truth lies somewhere between these two extreme positions. In practice, we cannot but act as if it were never too late, as if rehabilitation and treatment always have a chance of success. Unless we do so, we shall not improve upon available methods. Even more important, applying therapeutic and remedial measures without real confidence in them is the surest recipe for failure.

6. Children Who Are 'Vulnerable' or 'At Risk'

The myth of childhood being a carefree, happy time persists despite scant evidence to substantiate it. On the contrary, there is much that frustrates, frightens and baffles the growing child just because of his inevitable lack of experience and power. The younger he is, the more he lives solely in the present and his time perspective is limited so that he does not even have the consolation that anxieties and unhappiness will pass. Nor does he know that his frequent feelings of uncertainty, his lack of confidence and his failure to understand adults' reactions, are shared by many, if not most, of his contemporaries. This awareness comes largely with maturity except for the fortunate minority whose parents and teachers have the gift of remembering these feelings and, by using their memories, enable the young to cope with them more easily.

In one sense, then, all children are vulnerable and likely to experience unhappiness and stress. In addition, certain groups are made doubly vulnerable because of the presence of specific, potentially detrimental personal, family or social circumstances. It is such children who should be regarded as being 'at risk'. The idea that certain individuals or groups may be at high risk of future misfortune or malfunctioning has for long been accepted and acted upon in the world of life or accident insurance. The concept of being 'at risk' psychologically, educationally or socially is beginning to gain currency, following its successful application in the medical field.

The Perinatal Survey (Butler and Bonham, 1963; Butler and Alberman, 1969), emphasised the danger signs which place a baby at high risk of dying. These were shown to be not only abnormalities of pregnancy and complications of labour, but also biological factors, such as extremes of maternal age, and social circumstances, such as low socio-economic status. Moreover, adverse social and biological characteristics tended to reinforce one another. There is evidence too that an unfavourable socio-economic environment continues to exert an adverse effect on the growing child. That this is so, at least until the age of eleven years, has been shown by the *National Child Development Study.*

To ensure the earliest diagnosis of defects, local health authorities were encouraged to keep 'at risk' registers of those babies thought to be vulnerable because of adverse circumstances before, during or after birth. Though some doubt has recently been cast on their effectiveness, there is evidence that they can be of considerable value (Davie, Butler and Goldstein, 1972); this is particularly so if it leads to the differential allocation of resources between 'high' and 'low' risk children – in other words, positive discrimination in favour of the most vulnerable.

Whether it is either desirable or practicable (or both) to keep a register of children who are psychologically, educationally or socially at risk is a controversial question. Undoubtedly, such a suggestion is fraught with difficulties, not least because of its political implications. Also knowledge regarding likely physical consequences is much better established than the understanding of psychological concomitants.

In essence, the issue is this: if later malfunctioning or handicap can be predicted early with a satisfactory degree of probability, then three consequences could follow as a matter of practical politics: first, to assess, and where necessary to refine, methods for identifying 'vulnerable' or 'at risk' groups at the earliest possible time; secondly, to devise procedures to prevent the harmful effects altogether if possible, or else to mitigate their severity; and thirdly, to evaluate the short- and long-term effectiveness of any interventionist procedures.

There are five groups of children who are particularly 'vulnerable' or 'at risk' of becoming stunted or damaged in their psychological development because of personal, family or social circumstances. They are: children in large families with low incomes; children with physical or mental handicaps; those in one-parent families; children who have to live apart from their parents for longer or shorter periods; and those belonging to some minority groups. There are, of course, other stressful circumstances such as living in a home where there is a chronically sick or disabled parent or a step-parent; or where the father is unemployed or follows a criminal career, spending long periods in prison; or where the child has been in a natural disaster. However, these five groups have been chosen because they include the great majority of children 'at risk'.

The various kinds of potentially harmful circumstances are not, of course, mutually exclusive. The exact proportion of children affected by one or more of them is not known. It could well be as high as 15 or 20 per cent but the proportion depends to some extent on the definitions and borderlines which are chosen.

It must also be stressed that none of these circumstances inevitably leads to psychological damage. To some extent, the concept of vulnerability is a statistical one, being rather like an actuarial prediction: it is concerned with likelihood, not certainty, in respect of any individual child. Indeed, there are many who triumph, apparently unscathed, over severe and prolonged environmental handicaps.

LARGE FAMILIES WITH LOW INCOMES

In Great Britain at least three million children – or nearly a quarter of the child population under the age of fifteen years – are growing up in families of four or more children. As a group, they tend to be on average, relatively under-privileged whatever the socio-economic level of their parents. Some of the likely reasons for this have already been considered (see Chapter 3, page 66) but here we are concerned with families of limited means.

Some of the measurable effects

The most recent evidence from the *National Child Development Study* demonstrates that the handicapping effects begin before birth and affect subsequent physical, psychological and educational development. This was so both at the age of seven and eleven years (Davie, 1972; National Children's Bureau, 1972; Prosser, 1972; Wedge and Prosser, 1973).

Family size was found to have an adverse effect on both height and educational attainment. For example, the difference between a child who has no older siblings and one who has three or more was 2.8 cm height and fifteen months of reading attainment at the age of seven years. By the age of eleven years the difference had increased to 4.0 cm for height and twenty-nine months for reading. These findings applied irrespective of the father's occupation, the mother's height or the number of younger children in the family. It used to be thought that children's social adjustment in school was better when they came from large than from small families; more recent evidence, including the above study, has shown the opposite to be the case.

Children from large families with low incomes may also be at greater risk right from conception onwards because of their mother's smoking habits. It is now widely accepted that maternal smoking during pregnancy is associated with both a reduction in birthweight and an increase in perinatal mortality. In the *National Child Development Study* a higher proportion of mothers from working-class homes were smoking during pregnancy and, irrespective of social class, more mothers with large families (three or more children) were doing so while pregnant. After allowing for these factors, this had a measurable effect both on height and on educational attainment. Its size was the same at the age of seven and eleven years, namely 1.0 cm and four months in reading (Butler and Goldstein, 1973).

There are likely to be additional disadvantages since large families tend to occur more often in the lowest socio-economic groups. For example, in the *National Child Development Study* 5½ per cent of children in Social Class I and 32 per cent in Social Class V came from families with five or more children. Irrespective of family size, the income of semi- and unskilled workers is substantially lower than that of the other socio-economic groups (Central Statistical Office, 1972). Hence financial hardship is virtually inevitable despite various allowances and benefits where there is a large family. According to official figures (D.H.S.S., 1971), there were 135,000 families with four or more dependent children, where the wage earner was in full-time employment, whose income was less than five pounds above the Supplementary Benefit level, allowing for housing costs.

The disadvantages of belonging to a large, low income family are further magnified by the consequences of suffering from other associated shortcomings. The parents' own education, parental interest shown in the child's scholastic progress, housing, play space, household amenities such as indoor sanitation or running hot water – all these and many other circumstances are more frequently unfavourable in such homes. Furthermore, a whole range of adverse factors is often found together so that the resulting consequences on the child's development are in most cases both multiple and interrelated.

Some results from the Bureau's longitudinal study will illustrate this interlinked pattern of continuing and cumulative disadvantage. When both the father and mother stayed on at school beyond the minimum school-leaving age, they were likely to have a smaller family; also they were more likely to show a greater interest in their children's education (at the age of eleven years). In turn, both parental education and parental interest were, separately and measurably, associated with the children's actual level of scholastic attainment – the effect of each being the equivalent of, for instance, almost a year's reading age and a combined effect of nineteen months at the age of seven years.

At this early age, the overall effect of social disadvantage, and hence readiness to respond to educational expectations, is already clearly evident. After two years of schooling, the chance of a seven-year-old's being unable to read was fifteen times greater for a child from an unskilled working-class home (Social Class V) than from a professional (Social Class I); and the proportion of children from the former who would – in the opinion of their teachers – benefit from attending a special school was forty-five times larger than for those from a professional home.

Another example relates to housing. To begin with, there is a relationship between family size and over-crowding: the larger the former, the worse the incidence of the latter is likely to be. Thus whereas 57 per cent of children from families with five or more children were over-crowded, the incidence fell to only 4 per cent where there were not more than four children. Over-crowding remained a problem, so that by the age of eleven (i.e., in 1969), as many as one in eight of this nationally representative group lived in such conditions. Next, there was a very marked social class difference: children from unskilled working-class homes were ten times more likely to live in an over-crowded home than those from professional-class parents. Thirdly, the larger the number of children the less likely the family was to enjoy the sole use of such amenities as a bathroom, indoor lavatory and hot water supply.

Clearly stress and hardship are further magnified the larger the number of children. Cramped conditions which deny privacy, space for play and quiet for homework readily lead to irritability, restlessness and bad temper all round. Inevitably the brunt of the burdens carried by the mother who is rearing a family without the basic amenities which are taken for granted by the more fortunate majority.

These problems are further aggravated because outdoor play space is at a premium in practically all urban areas. The poverty of recreational provision is indicated by the fact that nearly three times as many mothers expressed dissatisfaction with available amenities as were dissatisfied with housing conditions (33 per cent compared with 12 per cent); a recent government study corroborated our findings (Department of the Environment, 1973). This situation is likely to be worse for children living in deprived city areas where houses and flats are commonly without a private garden or yard.

Again, over-crowding and a lack of amenities had considerable and measurable effects on educational attainment, social adjustment and health. For example, at the age of eleven years, over-crowding was associated with a retardation of about seventeen months in reading age and of twelve months where amenities were lacking – a combined effect of almost two and a half years. This is more marked than the effects had been at the age of seven years (nine months' retardation in relation to over-crowding and nine months also in relation to amenities).

Taken together these findings point to three conclusions. First, many children growing up in large families whose income is low, are beset by multiple, interrelated and interacting disadvantages which have a detrimental effect on the level of their educational attainment, social adjustment in school and probably also on their physical development, in particular height. Secondly, these effects usually work in combination and are cumulative. Thirdly, their adverse influence seems to increase over time so that the gap between the most advantaged and the most disadvantaged grows wider as the child grows older.

At least, this is the case in the Bureau's longitudinal study; for example, the combined effect of social disadvantage on reading attainment showed itself in a four-year gap at the age of seven (a good reader having attained the level of an average nine-year-old while five years is usually taken as the level of a non-reader). By the time the children were eleven years old, it had risen to a difference of eight years between the most advantaged and disadvantaged respectively (Davie, 1973; National Children's Bureau, 1972).

This finding of a widening gap in reading attainment during the junior school years confirms the results of an earlier study (Douglas,

1964). It also reinforces the view that equality of opportunity will not come about through changes in secondary or higher education. Rather it is during the pre-school and early school years that ways must be sought to overcome or compensate for the effects of environmental disadvantages on children's development. Limiting the initial gap is likely to be the most effective way of reducing the gap at later stages.

Effects on family relationships and on personal development

There is a tendency to paint a rather rosy picture of lower working-class life, according to which mutual self-help and support in child rearing, as well as in general family and financial matters, play a major part. It is doubtful whether this is in fact the dominant pattern in areas of high social need. In reality, more often than not, all members of the extended family in deprived urban neighbourhoods suffer from multiple disadvantages which stem from low income, poor housing and a limited ability to cope. Poor health and irregular employment not infrequently add to the difficulties.

For those at the lowest rung of the social and economic ladder, even collective resources have little to offer. Shared misery may temporarily lighten the weight of the burden but it is unlikely either to reduce its effect materially or to alleviate its causes. Grandparents may add another dimension to children's lives by providing a three-generation perspective; yet they also make heavy inroads on very limited family budgets. Other relations may contribute some cast-off clothes or a little cash in times of financial crisis, but usually they can do little to improve grossly inadequate housing or income (Leissner, 1972).

Another study concluded that

there was no doubt that individual and social handicaps marched together remarkably closely . . . It does not follow, of course, that because they are found together that personal maladjustment is caused by poverty; on the contrary, it could be argued that, under present day conditions, to be conspicuously poorer than one's neighbour is a consequence of personal inadequacy (West, 1969).

While favourable socio-economic conditions do not necessarily ensure that children's psychological needs are met, it is much more difficult to do so in circumstances of severe socio-economic strain.

Moreover, to be able to give and receive love it needs to have been experienced and many parents have themselves been unloved if not rejected in childhood.

The need for security may also remain unsatisfied because parental behaviour is unpredictable and contradictory. On the one hand, discipline tends to be autocratic; also physical punishment may at times be more of an outlet for parental anger and frustration, generated by the pressures of the daily struggle rather than a means of ensuring the child's conformity to desired standards of behaviour. Chastisement of this kind only succeeds in teaching its recipient to respect and to use force himself; even a verbal berating, coupled with threats of being 'put away', is more likely to make a child feel rejected than to enable him to understand what is expected of him and why.

On the other hand, living in a state of perpetual crisis and chronic frustration, the parents' capacity to deal with their own anxieties is often so limited that they feel helpless and overwhelmed by the problems of sheer existence. Hence they are unable to provide the necessary emotional support to their children at times of anxiety and conflict. Yet the children are in great need of such support just because family stability is inevitably so precarious.

The pressures of life in the most disadvantaged homes also prevent the parents from being adequate models for their children. The unskilled labourer, whose earnings are low and irregular and who leaves all family responsibilities to his wife; the mother who scorns or fears him, and who is herself weighed down by the burden of home-making and child-rearing – neither is able to present a picture of adult life and behaviour which is likely to evoke their children's respect or a desire to become like them. Worse still, as the children grow into adolescence they will become increasingly aware of how limited their chances are of escaping from the constricting net of their multiple disadvantages.

Thus many youngsters from severely disadvantaged families, being thrown back upon their own resources, come to look to their siblings and to their peers in the street for emotional support and for model figures. Is it justified to argue that turning to contemporaries and to gang life because parental support is so limited, shows early independence and self-sufficiency? At the same time, when faced with outside criticism, such youngsters show highly ambivalent attitudes, expressing strong feelings of family loyalty and affection. Probably this is because they have never known security or acceptance elsewhere. It is similar to the loyalty shown by children who have been neglected or even abused by their parents. 'The attachment of children to parents who by all ordinary standards are very bad is a never-ceasing source of wonder to those who seek to help them' (Bowlby, 1951).

Having had to adapt to precarious relationships as well as inconsistent or otherwise unsatisfactory parental models, and having lacked a predictable framework of discipline, the child will expect other authority figures, such as teachers, to behave in a similar fashion.

Because his needs for new experience, and for praise and recognition will probably have been inadequately met too, he comes to school ill-prepared to respond to what will be demanded of him. Even if aware of the value of play and of fostering language development, his parents will rarely have had the emotional or physical resources to provide either to a satisfactory degree. A limited range of experiences and limited language skills will make him an unrewarding, because unresponsive, pupil. From the outset, he confronts his teachers with both behaviour and educational difficulties so that they may soon come to expect low standards from him while he will be aware of their disappointment in him. And so all too often their mutual expectations will eventually become self-fulfilling prophecies.

He in turn will be bewildered by the, to him, alien achievement-orientated climate of the class-room; by the conflicting standards of behaviour expected at home and at school; by the displeasure and disappointment shown by his teacher towards his ineffective efforts; and by her disapproval and punishment of his lack of progress. Her assessment of him as 'hopeless' will make him feel 'hopeless' too. And so he may well come to view school life with the same attitude of resigned or resentful helplessness with which his parents view their own fate. Thus his educational experience only confirms the attitudes formed earlier by parental handling:

unable to identify with or to beat the system, he will expect nothing nor will he be equipped to do anything about it. Thus the child born into the lowest social bracket has everything stacked against him, including his parents' principles of child upbringing (Newson, 1972).

The fourth need, for responsibility, is often forced upon the child prematurely. He may have to fend for himself, both before going to school and when returning to an empty house afterwards. If there is a large family, he may have to assume pseudo-parental roles by taking care of younger siblings, to the detriment of his own development. When he fails to control them or when accidents occur he is likely to incur punishment. Yet he is given little chance to exercise responsibility appropriate to his age and ability level and with appropriate adult guidance.

Thus, on the one hand, being given responsibility is likely to be a source of anxiety and a burden, instead of an enjoyable opportunity which becomes increasingly challenging with age. On the other hand, in terms of his own personal life, his freedom of choice will be severely circumscribed by his lack of educational skills and social know-how. At best, a boring, poorly paid job with few prospects and fewer opportunities for exercising responsibilities lies ahead. At worst, there will be unemployment with its destructive effect on self-respect and self-confidence.

Social handicap and delinquency

Though the total and abject poverty of fifty years ago is now rare, today's greater general affluence may make a barren life and relative deprivation more difficult to bear: when the ownership of material possessions is widely advertised and equated with the good life; when having fun at parties, on yachts and at exotic beaches abroad, is featured prominently as the desirable way to spend one's leisure; then is it not likely that the dull, dead streets of inner cities and of redevelopment areas, as well as the windy deserts below high-rise tower blocks, feel even duller, deader and more frustrating by comparison? When everyone is poor or in danger, a shared fate makes for fellow feeling and solidarity. The more glaring the inequalities, the greater the divisiveness, resentment and hostility.

Yet, contrary to public fears, the majority of youngsters from severely disadvantaged homes are not angry and militant but apathetic and unassertive.

Far from challenging the world around them, they seem personally and socially incarcerated; their talents are consistently under-rated, their vision constricted, their most personal modes of expression stifled. Each self-image they have created for themselves has been repeatedly deflated, all futures prematurely and permanently foreclosed (Davies, 1969).

On the other hand,

For statistical purposes, basic social factors will undoubtedly prove the most effective predictors of delinquency, but cause and effect is another matter. This Study has also shown the remarkable concentration of parental pathology, in the shape of unsuitable discipline, unfortunate attitudes to children, personality deviations, etc., among the socially handicapped group. Personal inadequacies and external handicaps reinforce each other in these unfortunate families. Rather than trying to answer the conundrum 'Which comes first . . .?' it may be more useful to ask at what point to try to break the vicious circle (West, 1969).

HANDICAPPED CHILDREN

How well a handicapped child makes out in the long run depends far less on the nature, severity or onset of his condition than on the attitudes of his parents first and foremost, then on those of his peers and teachers, and eventually on society's. These determine how he feels about himself and his handicap. This has been confirmed by many recent studies (Tizard and Grad, 1961; Pringle and Fiddes, 1970; Dinnage, 1971 and 1972; Pilling, 1972 and 1973; Younghusband, Birchall, Davie and Pringle, 1970; Pringle, 1965 and 1970). It is illustrated too by the vivid biographies of those who have triumphed over severe disabilities (such as Carlson, 1952; Brown, 1954).

Difficulties in meeting basic psychological needs

In essence the needs of the handicapped are the same as those of normal children but the presence of a disability poses some special problems. These will first be considered in relation to the basic psychological needs outlined earlier (see Chapter 2).

Love and security To give a sense of security one needs to feel secure oneself. But this is just what many parents of a handicapped child do not feel: most are worried by their lack of special knowledge and afraid of being unable to meet his special needs; many feel guilty or ashamed: some may be completely at a loss, especially those parents of slow learning children who themselves are of limited ability and weighed down by all the demands of modern life. Inevitably there is less support from and sharing with relatives and friends since they also lack the experience of bringing up a handicapped child.

At school, too, special difficulties are likely to arise in meeting this need unless the child is among the lucky few for whom an early and correct diagnosis is made, a place is available in a suitable school (whether ordinary or special) and long-term educational guidance, in the fullest sense of the term, is provided throughout his school life.

If his disability is not recognised and he tries to hold his own with normal children, he will come to feel inferior and a failure, the more so the less obvious or easily understood the nature of his handicap. To the blind and to some kinds of physical handicap, sympathy is readily extended; mental handicap is more often met with ridicule or contempt. If his teacher lacks knowledge of and experience with handicapped children, she may feel unable to cope adequately; if in addition she is faced with a large class, it is not surprising that a handicapped pupil may seem to her, and thus feel himself to be, a severe burden.

That parents feel concerned, and often extremely anxious, about their handicapped child is entirely natural. This concern could be harnessed to provide the motivation for giving that extra care, time and thought to the handicapped child which can help him to overcome, as far as possible, the adverse effects of his disability. Instead, this concern often turns into over-anxiety or resentment: if left without any clear idea about the nature of the disability and its short- as well as long-term implications, parental uncertainty may show itself in insecure and inconsistent handling of the child. The more severe, complex or multiple the handicap, the more urgent it is to provide continuous supporting services for parents.

Adequate facilities for a comprehensive initial diagnosis and for periodic re-assessments would also greatly contribute to meeting the handicapped child's need for security. When parents and teachers understand his particular condition, they convey this to him by their confident and continuous encouragement and support. A happy, harmonious community – be it the family or a school staff – communicates warmth, confidence and hope to the child instead of anxiety, uncertainty or hopelessness.

The need for new experiences Here the handicapped child is inevitably at a disadvantage since a disability delays or even makes impossible the acquisition of some new experiences. As yet little is known about how different disabilities distort learning. For example, the physically handicapped may fail to acquire adequate experience of space and movement which will affect concepts of distance, of dimension and later of mathematics. The deaf all too often remain unstimulated by speech and language until much later than normal children, and even then benefit to a more limited extent; hence they may fail to acquire an adequate basis for abstract thought. Slow learning children are unable to benefit from new experiences at the time that normal children do; thus they may miss the opportunity for learning altogether if these experiences are not deliberately provided at a later stage than is usual; and the blind can never know the physical attributes of the world around them in the way the sighted majority do.

Not only is a distortion of learning difficult to prevent, it is also inevitably cumulative and progressive. The precise ways in which it affects the quality of learning have so far been little explored. Meanwhile the ingenuity of parents and teachers will be taxed to the full by trying to provide and adapt new experiences to the child's limitations without curtailing the range of these experiences more than is absolutely necessary.

Modifications may be required in the order and manner in which new experiences are presented; more careful grading and specially devised tools and apparatus may have to be used to ensure progress. Otherwise, new experiences may become a source of anxiety and defeat instead of an exciting challenge.

One effective way of learning, open to all handicapped children, except the deaf, is through speech. For some, such as the blind and physically severely disabled, it is a compensatory way of broadening their experience and understanding. Hence talking to and encouraging the child to speak from the earliest age are particularly important.

The need for recognition and achievement Here the handicapped face twin difficulties because of two tacit assumptions. First, praise habitually given for achievement rather than effort. This is at best unjust and positively harmful at worst. For example, writing a few lines of composition will cost a physically handicapped child a great deal more in terms of concentration and effort than it does the normal child to produce twice as much; yet the latter is more likely to be commended for his work. Secondly, the success of the handicapped tends to be judged by the extent to which their achievements approximate to those of the normal majority. In consequence, the more severe the handicap, the less likely is it that the child will be rewarded, genuinely and unreservedly, by recognition and a sense of achievement.

Thus to meet this need, we must grant the handicapped the fulfilment of another, specific to them, 'the need to be different and the need to be the same' (Mallinson, 1956). This means recognising that while they share the basic needs of all children, due allowance must be made for the differences imposed by the nature of a particular disability.

The need for responsibility The nature of a handicap may set a limit to the ultimate degree of responsibility a child will become capable of exercising. However, too low a limit may be set from a sense of pity or over-protection, or else through underestimating what he might become able to achieve, given the opportunity and necessary support. Also, one must guard against a whole household revolving around the handicapped child; rather he should be given the opportunity, both at home and in school, to shoulder some responsibilities, however limited in scope, so that he learns to give as well as to receive. In this way, self-respect and self-acceptance are fostered.

Social, emotional and educational adjustment

In recent years there has apparently been an increase in the number of children with multiple handicaps. To some extent this may stem, paradoxically enough, from the growth of medical knowledge: many babies are now surviving who would formerly have died (for example, those with spina bifida); and some conditions (such as retrolental fibroplasia or thalidomide limb deficiencies) were directly attributable to new treatment techniques. It may also be that an increasing understanding of, and attention to, potentially handicapping conditions as well as of their emotional and social concomitants is leading to their more effective recognition. In contrast, the development of appropriate treatment, educational and supportive facilities has lagged behind so that the complex needs of such children and their families are all too often inadequately met.

Since most disabilities burden the child with the additional handicap of distress or resentment about his condition, it is difficult to ascertain whether and to what extent any difficulties in behaviour, learning or adaptation are primarily 'organic' in origin. However, a few generalisations are justified on the basis of the literature reviews, covering the past fifteen years, which have been carried out by the Bureau (Pringle, 1967 and 1969; Dinnage, 1971 and 1972; Pilling, 1972 and 1973a, b, c and d).

What are the effects of different handicaps on adjustment and attainment? Blindness alone does not seem to be an insurmountable obstacle to the achievement of emotional or intellectual maturity. Blind children are able to reach the same standards as the sighted although they have to make prolonged and intense effort to develop abilities which come easily to the sighted. There is no research evidence that they are aided in this by any special compensatory faculties or attitudes. Parental support and understanding, as well as good intellectual ability in the child, appear to be the most crucial factors. Additional mental and physical handicaps – which are becoming more common in the blind child population – inevitably have detrimental consequences. Partially sighted children appear to be rather less well-adjusted than the blind and a higher proportion have educational difficulties.

Deafness, particularly if profound, almost always seriously impedes learning to communicate and to understand abstract thought; hence it restricts both intellectual and educational progress. More than any other handicap, except perhaps autism, it presents enormous barriers to the development of spontaneity and confidence in the parents towards the baby; and the child has to face similar barriers in building reciprocal relationships.

It is probable that the deep compassion aroused by blindness helps, just as the self-consciousness and irritation engendered by deafness hinder, good social, emotional and educational adjustments. Studies of those affected by orthopaedic handicaps and by thalidomide also highlight the central role of parental and society's attitudes. These determine how children cope with their difficulties far more than the severity of the actual deformity.

For example, of two seven-year-old thalidomide victims, one, a boy, was born without a left hand and the other, a girl, without arms and additionally unable to walk. Yet the girl was making good educational progress in an ordinary school where she had happy relationships with other children and with her teachers. The far less seriously handicapped boy showed signs of emotional disturbance and educational underfunctioning; however, his parents were over-protective while at the same time denying the existence of his deformity. The girl, on the other hand, was treated with loving care and compassionate but realistic common sense (Pringle and Fiddes, 1970).

This study also showed that though there has been much more emphasis on the limb deficiencies resulting from thalidomide, in fact many children suffered auditory impairment too; this had a much worse effect on intellectual ability, and on language and social development.

Among the cerebrally palsied the incidence of emotional, social and sensory difficulties is high. These are linked with intellectual and educational retardation as well as with a disturbed home background. After leaving school, only a minority, even of those whose physical disability is mild, lead normal social lives (Pilling, 1973a).

There are relatively few studies of the emotional, social and educational adjustment of children with spina bifida even though the number of those who survive has greatly increased since the introduction of the Spitz-Holter valve in 1958. Available results suggest that the incidence of difficulties may be higher among them than ordinary children (Pilling, 1973c).

In summary, most comparative studies show the handicapped child to be less mature and more disturbed than those without disabilities; nevertheless, there is no evidence that maladjustment or educational retardation are inevitable. Where the nature of the handicap imposes severe limitations, whether physical or social, then behaviour and learning are bound to be affected. However, available data do not show any definite association between a particular disability and a particular behaviour characteristic. So much then for negative conclusions.

On the positive side, there seems to be general agreement that parental attitudes towards the child and his handicap are of paramount importance. A conclusion reached by some early American workers has remained undisputed to this day: 'The child seems to adopt the same attitude to the disability that his parents do. If they worry about it, so does he. If they are ashamed of it, he will be sensitive too. If they regard it in an objective manner, he will accept it as a fact and will not allow it to interfere with his adjustment' (Allen and Pearson, 1928). This view has been endorsed by Carlson (1952), who himself succeeded in triumphing over severe physical disability; moreover, by becoming a doctor, he achieved a breakthrough in the attitudes to, and the treatment of, his own disability, cerebral palsy: 'Success or failure does not depend on what we lack but rather upon the use we make of what we have'.

CHILDREN IN ONE-PARENT FAMILIES

So far there has been relatively little research into the psychological and social effects on children of growing up in one-parent families. These will naturally vary, not only because of individual differences between children, but also because the age when one parent has to take over and the period during which only one cared for the child are bound to have a differential effect. Some of these questions will be examined in the Bureau's ongoing study of one-parent families; and they have already been explored in relation to illegitimately born children in the national cohort.

There is much evidence that a considerable proportion of one-parent families are likely to suffer financial hardship, if not actual poverty (Holman, 1970; Marsden, 1969; Pochin, 1969; Wynn, 1964 and 1970). Less is known about the emotional, social and educational effects. Results obtained from the Bureau's *National Child Development Study* made it possible to show that economic circumstances vary not only in relation to which parent is bringing up the family but also with regard to the reason why this is so. The rates of payment made by the Supplementary Benefits Commission were chosen as the general indicator of a subsistence standard of living.

As many as one in nine children (or 11 per cent) were no longer being cared for by both their natural parents by the time they were eleven years old, according to the results of the Study. Of these, some 5 per cent were being raised by one parent alone; the other 6 per cent were being brought up in more than thirty different types of 'anomalous' family circumstances. Here three particular groups will be considered: those being brought up single-handed by one natural parent; those born illegitimate; and children of divorce.

Single-parent families

The children in the study who – for whatever reason – were living in a one-parent family at the age of eleven years were more likely to have lost their father than their mother. In fact, the proportion of fatherless children was nearly five times as high as those who grew up without a mother. Although the rate of re-marriage was very similar for fathers and mothers respectively (about a third in each case), a further 25 per cent of the motherless children were being cared for by a mother substitute whereas father substitutes were provided for only 5 per cent of the fatherless children (Ferri, 1973).

Thus women are much more likely than men to be left caring single-handed for their families, following the loss of their marriage partner. This probably reflects differences in social attitudes: much greater sympathy is extended to the man who has been deserted by his wife and is trying to look after the children; also grandmothers, sisters or neighbours are more ready to offer help. However, there is perhaps less acceptance of a father staying at home and living on state support. The deserted wife calls out far less concern and assistance. There is a tacit assumption that it is easier and perhaps also more appropriate for a woman to combine the parental and wage-earning role than it is for a man on his own to do so.

The most common single cause resulting in one natural parent being left to bring up a family was marital breakdown; in fact, divorce, separation and desertion accounted for about half the cases. In the remaining families, where there was no mother, this was due to her having died; in households without a father, death was the reason in only a third of cases; the rest consisted mainly of illegitimately born children whose mothers were raising them.

In 1969, when the children were eleven years old, almost half (47 per cent) of the fatherless families had been dependent on state support at some time during the preceding twelve months; this compares with only 6 per cent among intact families. Motherless children were less badly off although their families were twice as likely to have received Supplementary Benefits than two-parent homes. Even single-handed mothers who did not have to rely on state support were probably worse off financially than their male counterparts since women workers are usually paid at a much lower rate. Mothers whose husbands had died were far less likely to have had to rely on benefits than when the marriage had broken down or the child was illegitimate.

Examining the quality of housing in terms of the availability of basic amenities, twice as many fatherless as two-parent families lacked the sole use of a bathroom, indoor lavatory and hot water supply; the situation of motherless children was also less favourable but not quite as bad as that of the fatherless (Ferri, 1973).

Children born illegitimate

A marked increase in the proportion of illegitimate births took place during recent years but this is now possibly being reversed due to easier abortion and the pill; also more unmarried mothers are choosing to keep their babies. Yet until recently little was known about how the mothers and their children were faring, in the short or medium term; or whether illegitimacy continues to present personal and social problems, even though attitudes towards extra-marital sexual relations have changed.

The *National Child Development Study* made it possible to seek some answers to these questions by comparing an unselected national group of illegitimate children, born in 1958, with their peers born in the same week (Crellin, Pringle and West, 1971). The findings clearly showed that to be born illegitimate is to be born 'at risk'.

As in other recent studies, there was no difference in social class background between mothers who have a legitimate and an illegitimate baby. However, the latter were at a potential disadvantage, right from the start, in respect of their mother's age and their own family position. There were five times as many very young mothers among the illegitimate and nearly twice as many were having their first child. Among both these groups, the perinatal mortality rate is higher as is the prevalence of low birth weight. The overall mortality rate and the proportion of low birth weight babies were in fact markedly higher among the illegitimately born.

Ante-natal care was also markedly poorer among mothers-to-be of the illegitimate. A higher proportion than among the legitimate did not seek such care or did so later than is advisable; and a higher proportion failed to make an advance booking for their delivery.

About a third of the illegitimately born babies were given up by their mothers for adoption; they were then being brought up in a much more favourable home environment than those who had remained with their own mothers. The development of these two groups, who had had a similar start in life, was compared when they were seven years old.

By that time, the majority of the illegitimately born was living in some kind of two-parent situation (including those who were adopted). However, a considerable number of homes lacked a stable father figure. Only one in four children lived with both their natural parents.

The most outstanding feature was the much more favourable situation of the adopted. Among the illegitimate not adopted many had to share household amenities or lacked them completely: in fact, this was twice as prevalent as among the whole legitimate group. The same was true of over-crowding, despite the fact that there was a high proportion of only children among the illegitimate.

A considerable number of children experienced supplementary or total substitute care. This was made necessary by the high proportion of mothers who worked outside the home before the child went to school, and by their difficult and unsettled family circumstances. Over three times as many illegitimate as legitimate children were placed in day care facilities; and this proportion is certain to be an underestimate. In the first place, nearly two-thirds of the mothers of illegitimate children worked before the latter went to school; yet only a quarter of the children were reported to have had day care. Even allowing for relatives helping out, a sizable discrepancy remains. Another reason is that information was lacking about child minders, whether officially registered or those with whom mothers had made some private arrangement.

The proportion of children who came into the care of a local authority or voluntary body was five times higher among the illegitimate than legitimate children.

It is evident, then, that the dice are still heavily loaded against the illegitimately born child. What were the effects on his development? In all aspects which were examined, consistent and marked differences were found between the illegitimate, the adopted and the legitimate group. Time and time again, the illegitimate were at the bottom of the league table, whether for general knowledge, oral ability, creativity, perceptual development, reading attainment or arithmetical skills.

Even in the relatively more favourable environment of middle-class homes, the illegitimate did less well than legitimate children in such homes. Over and above social class effects, there were important 'illegitimacy effects'. For example, they account for twelve months' difference in progress between the adopted and the illegitimate groups in reading. In contrast, the progress made by the adopted was similar to that made by legitimate children in the same social class.

Once they went to school the illegitimate also suffered disadvantages. They had more changes of school; their attendance was more irregular; and their parents showed less interest in their educational progress. Marked differences were also found between the three groups of children in behaviour and adjustment in school. The proportion of 'maladjusted' children was nearly twice as high among the illegitimate as the legitimate, while the adopted more closely resembled the latter.

Inevitably, many questions remain unanswered. For example, there was no information on the personality of the child's mother or other members of his family. Soon, however, it will be possible to say whether the problems encountered by the illegitimate differ from those who, for other reasons, live in one-parent families. Meanwhile, it is evident that illegitimacy still brings with it personal and social problems. The children were beset by a multiplicity of unfavourable circumstances; these gave them a relatively poorer start in life which continued to build up into a complex web of cumulative and interacting hardships and deprivations. To be born illegitimate is still to be born disadvantaged, at least for the present.

Can a favourable environment halt or reverse the effects of early disadvantage? To judge from the development of those children who were adopted, the answer is that it can. Of course, it remains to be seen what the later development will be of both those who were and those who were not adopted.

Children of divorce

Every year the family life of thousands of children is disrupted by divorce and the indications are that the number is still rising. 'In 1968, the total number of children affected was almost 73,000 of whom it is estimated some 60,000 were under the age of sixteen; by 1969 the total had increased to over 81,000' (Mortlock, 1972).

An even steeper increase occurred in 1971 when, largely due to the Divorce Reform Act of 1969, there was a 55 per cent increase in divorce petitions over 1970; the total number of children involved then rose to 116,726, three-quarters of whom were under sixteen years of age (Gibson, 1973). Indeed, the majority are likely to be quite young, since separation and divorce occur most frequently within five years or so after marriage.

There may well be a link between the rising divorce rate and the increasing trend towards early parenthood which allows young couples little time to adjust to the new relationships and responsibilities of marriage; then financial and housing problems are added with the arrival of a baby. If both spouses are under twenty when they marry the divorce rate (in England and Wales) is about three times the rate for all marriages. 'One of the most striking demographic features associated with divorce is the increased risk among wives who were pregnant at the time of marriage . . . marriages are now taking place at a younger age than previously and young brides are forming an increasing proportion of all pre-marital pregnancies so it is likely that a larger number of children than at present will be innocent witnesses of a broken home and family' (Gibson, 1973).

Remarkably little attention has been given to the effects which the break-up may have on children's development. What research there is has largely been confined to self-selected and probably atypical groups, namely those seen in psychiatric and child guidance clinics. 'We do not know whether it damages the child least to grow up in an unhappy home with both parents, or alone with one parent where there is no remarriage, or with one parent and a step-parent' (Mortlock, 1972). In relation to children's reactions to new marriages of either of their parents it has been suggested that 'overall, it seems it is better to have three or even four parents and six grandparents than no father or mother. This pattern of multiple marriages in fact produces a new type of extended family and consequently a variety of people with whom the child can identify and form relationships . . . Structurally, the family of the future will be polynuclear' (Benn, 1969).

Financially, there is often a drop in the standard of living since most children will stay with their mother who now depends on alimony which is not only a reduced but may also not be a reliable source of income. Even if she herself is earning a salary, it will be less than the previous joint income; moreover, she may have to incur additional expense in having the children looked after out of school hours and term time.

On the psychological side, it is difficult to help a child to understand the reasons for the marriage break-up, the more so the younger the child, and the more bitter the feelings between the parents. Not uncommonly they vie for the child's affections, blackening each other's character and motives in the process. At worst, the child may become a pawn in their game of mutual hurt and ascendancy which is played out during prolonged battles for custody; an extreme example being 'tug-of-love' children who are whisked from one home, and sometimes one country, to another in the fight for possession. (An even worse situation is a new phenomenon reported from the United States, namely that neither parent is willing to take on custody; such a degree of rejection is bound to have a most damaging effect on a child's sense of personal worth.) Even at best, when regular and frequent 'access' has been agreed so that the child spends some time with the parent who does not have custody, meetings at weekends and during holidays are not readily conducive to maintaining a close relationship.

What evidence there is suggests that a sizable proportion of children whose parents have been divorced show disturbed behaviour. Whether this is due as much, or more, to deteriorating relationships and possibly open quarrels prior to the final break-up of the marriage, or to the child's conflict of loyalties, or to the finality of the divorce itself, has not yet been established. What is agreed by many, including some lawyers, is that custody decisions, in the lower courts at any rate, tend to be arrived at too hastily and with too little attempt to take into account the child's own wishes or needs. If his long-term interests are to be regarded as of major importance, then some reform of divorce proceedings would seem essential.

CHILDREN LIVING APART FROM THEIR FAMILIES

The reasons why children have to live apart from their families range from parental inadequacy and intractable pathology to inability to cope with overwhelming circumstances; and from temporary crisis to permanent abandonment.

During the past twenty-five years, three major advances have been made in our understanding of the implications of substitute care for children. They are well supported by research, but none has yet been translated into action on the required scale. The first is that adequate physical care is not sufficient to ensure satisfactory emotional, social and intellectual growth; secondly, that prolonged institutional life in a children's home and especially in hospital can have very damaging effects on a child's all-round development; and thirdly that many, if not a majority, of children could remain in their own homes if effective and sufficient supportive services within the community were available.

To bring this about requires different social priorities and policies regarding housing, a minimum income and allowances for single parents as well as for handicapped children or adults. Though a detailed discussion of these changes is outside our brief, two official statistics clearly illustrate this fact: first, every year about half of all the children coming into care do so because of their mother's confinement or short-term illness. Secondly, chronic mental or physical illness, and desertion or death of one parent, account for a furthei 10 per cent of children. Research is now urgently needed to clarify how many children, in what type of situation, could be kept in their own home, and how successfully, both in the short- and the long-term.

A wide diversity of circumstances leads to the separation of children from their families. Are there, nevertheless, differences between them and other children of the same age and similar social background, who did not experience removal from homes; and what is the evidence that the former are more vulnerable? These questions will be examined in relation to three groups: those who have spent at least one period in residential care; or in foster care; or who have lived for long periods in hospital.

Children in residential care

The evidence quoted is based on four sources: first, a review of literature in the United States, Western Europe, Israel and Great Britain covering the period from 1948 to 1966, carried out by the Bureau (Dinnage and Pringle, 1967); secondly, a series of linked studies of seven-, eleven- and fifteen-year-olds (Pringle, 1971); thirdly, the Bureau's *National Child Development Study* (Mapstone, 1969 and 1973); and lastly, a study of children needing substitute parents (Rowe and Lambert, 1973).

130

Social, family and personal background Are there any features which distinguish those children who, by the age of seven, have spent at least one period in care, from all the others in the *National Child Development Study*? It proved possible, in fact, to draw quite a distinctive picture of them even though there will, of course, be much individual variation within the 'in care' group.

To begin with, nine out of every ten came from working-class homes. This is not really unexpected. Though separation experiences and unsatisfactory mothering are not confined to any one social group, nevertheless middle-class parents, who are unable or unwilling to look after their children, can usually make their own arrangements for substitute care. Their solutions – a nanny, *au pair* girl or boarding school – are quite unlikely options for the manual worker.

Next, the 'in care' group tended to live in homes which were more crowded and had fewer amenities than those of children in the comparable social class who had not been in care. Also, they had more brothers and sisters, and this was the case irrespective of social class. They had, too, experienced more home moves and changes of school.

Perhaps even more significant, their disadvantages dated back to the time of their birth. Already, as they lay in their cots, the group of children who later were received into care could be distinguished from the other children born during the same week. More of them were illegitimate, their mothers were likely to be younger and of smaller stature, they themselves tended to have had a shorter period of gestation and to be of lower birth weight. These characteristics are not, of course, independent of each other but, taken together, they indicate a group of children who were in these first few days of life already at a disadvantage compared with other children of the same age and social class.

Lastly, at seven years, proportionately more children who had been in care were short in height and light in weight for their age. In comparison with their classmates they appeared to their teachers to have poor control of their hands when writing, drawing or buttoning up their coats; they were fidgety; they tended to have poor physical coordination when running about, jumping, or throwing balls; they were clumsy; and hardly ever still. Their teachers also thought their appearance to be less attractive than that of the other children, one in five being said to look scruffy or very dirty, and one in ten underfed.

This group was not composed of long-stay, institutionalised children. Indeed about 25 per cent had had only one period in care, lasting four weeks or less; 66 per cent had been in care for no more than a year, even when there were several occasions. For most, the experience of being in care was of brief duration in relation to their total life span.

Thus the *National Child Development Study* results confirm that even children who come into short-term care, ostensibly because of their mother's confinement, tend to belong to socially disadvantaged families (Schaffer and Schaffer, 1968). Earlier findings have also shown that large families with low income, those where there is only one parent, or where there is physical or mental handicap, are at greater risk of disintegration, and that once a family is split up, reintegration may be difficult (Dinnage and Pringle, 1967). Hence, coming into care for the first time could be regarded as an early warning signal of a child's vulnerability.

Learning and behaviour difficulties Recovery from single, brief separation experiences has been shown to be fairly rapid. Therefore emphasis will here be given to the effects of long-term separations.

There is evidence of both language and intellectual retardation among infants and young children, which is the more serious the less adequate the psychological care (Dinnage and Pringle, 1967; Rutter, 1972). For example, a comparative study of four-year-olds showed both qualitative and quantitative differences: those in residential nurseries used smaller vocabularies, more immature sentence formations, expressed less fantasy and humour in their play or talk, and employed fewer active verbs. Also their knowledge of everyday domestic activities, such as cooking, was very limited and they were not even sure of the names of the various parts of their own bodies. The all-too-common absence of father figures, especially in homes for pre-school children, was reflected in their ignorance of male personal effects and apparel (Pringle, 1971).

Among children of school age, too, lower levels of language, intellectual and educational performance have been found in investigations carried out in the UK and elsewhere. Despite the fact that different research methods and different institutional settings have been used, there is considerable agreement that many children in long-term residential care function less well than their peers (Dinnage and Pringle, 1967).

This has also been demonstrated in a series of linked studies of seven-, eleven- and fifteen-year-olds (Pringle, 1971). At all three age levels, both intellectual and reading skills were found to be below average but the most serious backwardness was in language development. Admission into care at an early age (i.e., pre-school) and subsequent lack of contact with adults outside the residential home seemed to have a particularly detrimental effect on both achievement and adjustment. A higher proportion than among the ordinary child population showed behaviour difficulties, both at school and in the children's home, the commonest symptoms being anxiety, restlessness and aggression.

These findings, too, have been confirmed by the *National Child Development Study*. Once again, overall as well as within each social class grouping, the 'in care' group were doing less well in every aspect which was examined. In general knowledge, ability to express themselves in conversation, reading and arithmetic, the proportion performing poorly was twice or three times as high among them than among their peers. As one might predict, a proportionately large number were thought to need special educational help, either now or within the next two years.

Their behaviour at home (or if in care at the age of seven, in their substitute home) was characterised by frequent irritability, by a tendency to 'fly off the handle', by being miserable or tearful, by destructiveness with their own and other people's belongings, by aggressiveness towards other children and by an inability to settle to anything for more than a few moments.

In school they showed similar behaviour difficulties. The most marked difference between those who had been, or were still, in care and the other children was in the proportion showing hostility, both to other children and to adults, and 'inconsequential behaviour', i.e., lacking concentration and persistence; the teachers also described them as being untidy, slapdash and careless over appearance and with belongings, and impervious to correction. Thus, a picture emerges of children who, compared with their peers, are unhappy, insecure and immature.

Personal identity and relationships However adverse a home, the child lives in familiar surroundings and is looked after, however inadequately, by familiar people. Being taken from it means the collapse of the world he has accepted and trusted as the only one he knows. The younger the child, the greater the distress at being removed to an unfamiliar environment. The more limited his understanding of verbal explanations, the greater is his likely bewilderment and the more difficult the task of restoring his sense of security; also he may feel it was his naughtiness which led to his being sent away.

The most damaging effect, however, is probably on the growth of self-awareness and the development of a sense of identity. 'He has no single person who shares his own most basic and important memories, no one to confirm whether these memories are in fact correct or figments of his imagination, no one to polish up a fading memory before it is too late. Such a deprivation seems so damaging that I am not at all sure that we can ever fully make up for it artificially' (Newson, 1971). Not only does the child in long-term care have no reliable past; equally devastating, he has no predictable future except that he will come out of care at the age of eighteen.

In the ordinary home, both the store of personal memories and the framework of a personal future are built up through frequent everyday references and continuing discussions of family affairs. 'When you were little you had fair hair' and 'when you are older you can help dad in the shop' are phrases which crop up regularly, their predictability being a source of strength because of their very familiarity. The sense of a personal past as well as of a future lend perspective and continuity which are the essence of acquiring a sense of identity.

The youngster who has spent the major part of his life in care is often uncertain about why he came into care, why changes in placement were made, why other children moved on and why staff left; he may not know the names of the various people who have looked after him, let alone their current whereabouts; the same is true regarding the children who shared his life for certain periods; nor does he know what the future is likely to hold since long-term plans are rarely made. If he goes to boarding school, because of a physical or mental handicap, he may not even know until the end of each term in which children's home he will be spending his next holidays.

In consequence, children who have been deprived of a normal home experience difficulties, especially during adolescence and adulthood, in accounting for themselves. Ordinary personal questions such as 'where do your people live?' or 'what does your father do?' become loaded and embarrassing. In confused panic, inventions about imaginary relatives may be produced because the deprived youngster knows little or nothing about his own background. This adds to his feelings of insecurity in personal relations and may lead him either to shun them or to weave a web of lies when faced with the need to account for himself.

There is some evidence of the importance to the child of having at least one dependable and lasting relationship with an adult while in long-term institutional care (Pringle, 1971). Two groups of children were compared, one notably stable, the other severely maladjusted (according to four independently made assessments). All of them had been separated from their mothers before the age of five years and had spent the major part of their lives away from their own home; their ages ranged from five to fifteen years. The aim was to investigate possible reasons for the difference in their adjustment.

The most marked and consistent difference between them was in the amount of contact maintained with parents or parent substitutes: the stable children enjoyed a dependable, lasting relationship in contrast to the maladjusted group, where only one child had done so; also most of the latter had been separated from their mothers very early (within the first year of life), so that they had not had the opportunity of forming bonds prior to admission into care. Hence the maladjusted group had neither established nor maintained stable relationships and their outstanding characteristic was an inability to make relationships with adults or children. A second study confirmed these findings.

Three hypotheses could account for the findings. First, the maladjusted group might have been constitutionally inferior and hence more susceptible to emotional instability; however, there was little evidence to support this view. Secondly, their very early and virtually permanent separation might have done irreparable harm to their basic personality structure. This view of emotional development has been criticised as being too sweeping, narrow and deterministic (Clarke and Clarke, 1973; Rutter, 1972; and Wootton, 1959). At the same time, knowledge is lacking on whether there is in fact a point of no return if the child remains permanently deprived of a close personal relationship with an adult.

The third hypothesis holds that, although prolonged and early separation and residential life are disturbing and potentially damaging experiences, this is not inevitably so. The opportunity to maintain continuous, frequent and regular contact with an adult outside the institution appeared to enable many a child to cope with them. This was so even when his own family had been indifferent or rejecting, and when he had never lived permanently with the parental substitute (i.e., only for weekends and holidays). What seemed crucial was that someone cared sufficiently to maintain a stable, enduring relationship.

It looks then as if – at least in our type of society – a child needs to feel that he matters as an individual; that he is valued for his own sake and not only by someone who is paid for the job of caring for him fairly and impartially. If lasting and unconditional love and loyalty from an adult are never experienced, then the child may fail to develop these qualities; also the later he learns to establish such relationships, the more difficult and longer it will be before he learns to trust adults and eventually reciprocate affection. Thus a vicious circle is likely to develop; not having known a secure relationship, the child fails to learn in early infancy the responses appropriate and expected in such a relationship.

The effects of institutional life

Clearly children who come into care, even for a short period only, are not a random group. Prior to separation, the majority live in homes where verbal stimulation is minimal: over-worked and under-privileged mothers, often burdened with too many pregnancies or forced by economic necessity to go out to work, have little time and energy available to encourage the baby in his early experiments with sound and to elicit continued trial and effort by taking delight in his pre-speech vocalisations; similarly, once the child is beginning to speak, there is likely to be less verbal stimulation in the form of nursery rhymes, stories, songs and general conversation.

When the child enters an institution, the staff-child ratio as well as the training of the staff are of paramount importance: too low a staffing ratio and an over-emphasis on child training as against child development, are all likely to have a retarding effect on the growth of language. Furthermore, less than 4 per cent of all residential staff are fully trained for their work, and 62 per cent are totally untrained (Jones, 1973).

Being separated and having to live apart from their family for a time will then, at best, be another unsettling and, at worst, a deeply disturbing and damaging experience. Indeed, some may become the most disadvantaged group within each social class. It is difficult, if not impossible, to isolate and estimate separation effects from all the other unfavourable influences to which these children have been exposed. Also, the 'in care' experience itself will be different for each child, depending on his age, the length of time away from home, how often he was removed the quality of the substitute care provided, whether he remained in touch with members of his family or others close to him, as well as on his own resilience under stress.

On coming into care, establishing a bond of affection could help the child to regain self-confidence, but this requires time and continuity of daily handling. Many, if not most, residential nurseries and homes are unable to provide either. The rate of staff turnover also militates against their providing long-term relationships. The effects of this are well documented by now. Young children who remain in institutions tend to crave affection, to cling to visitors and later on to make indiscriminate friendships and to have difficulty in forming lasting relationships. Early and prolonged institutional care has also been shown to militate against successful fostering later on.

When in later life he is offered affection, he does not know how to reciprocate. His reactions will be immature, like those of a very young infant who naturally takes love for granted and demands unceasing devotion. In a normal family, the child learns as he grows older that he is expected to reciprocate: by delaying his demands for immediate or exclusive attention; by controlling his anger and selfishness; by considering the feelings of others; and by conforming to social expectations.

Not having learned all this at the usual time, the emotionally deprived child will later alienate and often lose any affection and goodwill offered because he seems selfish, greedy and ungrateful. This deprives him of the opportunity to learn the very skills needed in making close human relationships; instead he learns to mistrust affection when offered. Because of this mistrust, coupled with his emotional immaturity, he is likely to grow increasingly unable to respond when offered further opportunities for building up close, emotional ties. The more his ability to respond becomes stunted, the more his chances to build a reciprocal relationship recede. Eventually the vicious circle is closed: unloved and friendless, he is in turn unloving and hostile towards others.

Susceptibility to maladjustment and resilience in the face of rejection appear to depend on the quality of relationships available to the child while in care. By themselves, neither physical separation from the family nor living for long periods in institutions necessarily lead to emotional or learning difficulties.

Since most children coming into care are already disadvantaged socially, backward intellectually or educationally, and disturbed emotionally, it is insufficient for residential life to provide simply good physical care. If that is all, any positive gain is likely to be limited. Indeed, there is a danger that the 'cure', i.e., coming into care, will make the 'disease', i.e., being disadvantaged, even worse, because being in care itself has adverse effects. Only if children's institutions become 'therapeutic communities', aiming to remedy and rehabilitate the hurt, confused and damaged child, can they claim to provide a viable form of substitute care.

Children in limbo Are there children in the care of local authorities or voluntary agencies whose return to their families is uncertain or even unlikely? At a time when couples wanting to adopt greatly outnumber available children, one might have expected to find very few who need a permanent substitute family, living instead in long-term residential care. American work had shown that there are children who could have been placed in adoptive homes soon after they came into care; yet despite no real parental ties, they remained in institutions for so long that the likelihood of their being acceptable for adoption became remote. A recent pilot study in this country suggested that the same may be happening here (Laker and Tongue, 1972). Once again, the reason seems to be that greater weight is given to the (sometimes hypothetical) long-term interests of the parents rather than the child. Now the results of a more extensive study show that at least 17 per cent of children in long-term care need substitute parents (Rowe and Lambert, 1973).

The study covered thirty-three different voluntary or statutory agencies and examined nearly 3,000 children under the age of eleven years who had been in care for at least six months. In fact, over half of those aged between five and eleven years had already been in care for more than four years. Almost two thirds of the whole group were expected by their social worker to have to remain in care until they were eighteen years old; 80 per cent had been admitted under the age of five and 50 per cent before they were two years old. Half of all the children were illegitimate. Almost half had no contact at all with either parent, and for a further third it was infrequent (76 per cent altogether); less than one in four children saw one or both parents once a month or more often.

This then is the situation of children who are in need of substitute parents. Not unexpectedly, a very high proportion was reported to have behaviour problems and to be below average intelligence. One cannot help but wonder to what extent these difficulties are the consequence of long periods in care combined with minimal parental interest or contact.

The obstacle to placement most frequently mentioned by the social workers concerned was the presence of brothers or sisters; this would have meant finding a home willing to take more than one child. However, the study concludes that

in most agencies the main problem in homefinding was pressure of other work. In many areas only crisis work could be done because of inadequate staff and resources in the face of rising demand for social services of all kinds. Stereotyped reviews and inadequate recording were often noted...and decisions about placement had often been delayed for long periods while efforts were made to solve the family's problems or while new staff became familiar with the case...only about one child in three had been under the supervision of the same social worker during the two years preceding the study and one in five had had more than three social workers during this time.

Translated into national terms, the authors estimate that there are probably about 7,000 children waiting to be placed in a foster or adoptive home. Yet there are grounds for suspecting that the study underestimates the real size of the problem: the information was based on the judgement of social workers who by training and experience tend to be adult-centred; this tendency appears to have been further increased by a number of recent trends, including the Seebohm reorganisation of social services and the politically fashionable emphasis on 'parental rights'. In consequence, there is a reluctance to assume such rights even on behalf of children whose parents have not been in touch with them for years and whose whereabouts cannot be traced. Yet available evidence strongly indicates that if a child has been in continuous care for a period of six months, he is very likely to remain there until he leaves school.

May it perhaps bring about a much-needed change in attitude if the concept of 'parental duties' was substituted? A parent who disappeared without subsequently making any effort to find out about his child's well-being or even whereabouts for, say, twelve or eighteen months would then automatically be considered to have abrogated his parental responsibilities rather than having to be sought by social agencies for months or years as is current practice. This would free a considerable number of children for long-term foster care or, better still, adoption.

Foster care

Much of what has been said about children in residential care applies also to those who are fostered. Reviewing the literature, the most outstanding feature is the paucity of basic knowledge (Dinnage and Pringle, 1967). There is no nationally agreed policy or comparability of practice. There are very wide variations from one part of the country to another in the proportion of children being fostered (from 19 to 95 per cent); and so, not surprisingly, it is still as true as it was ten years ago that fostering is 'an important but nevertheless unpredictable part of the resources available for caring for children' (Parker, 1966). Worse still, recent evidence regarding private fostering indicates that there is an inverse relationship between the unsuitability of foster parents and the amount of supervision given by social workers (Holman, 1973).

Many of the disadvantages and difficulties encountered by children in long-term residential care will apply to those who have been fostered since they, too, have lacked family support and stability; indeed, many of them have been in residential care as well. But while 'institutionalisation' has been defined and described, this is not so far 'fosterisation'. There is no profile of the typical foster child and such studies as there are, have largely been concerned with failure rather than success. Similarly, little is known about the 'good', i.e., unbroken, long-term, successful foster placement or even whether the unbroken placement is generally or even necessarily 'good'.

Why should this be so? The chief reason may be the very complexity of the process, both administratively and psychologically. There is much more uncertainty and impermanence than in adoption; and the involvement is closer, more personal and intimate than in residential care. Some of the complexity arises from the rather ill-defined roles of, and relationships between, all concerned:

the child who is being placed; his parents; the foster parents; and the placing agency's caseworker. Furthermore the assumptions, expectations and needs of each are widely different. So it is perhaps not unexpected that conflicting perceptions of the foster care situation have continued to exist for close to a hundred years and to this day there is no consensus.

The following facts are supported by some evidence but all need substantiation: the first two years in foster care appear to be decisive in terms of both negative breakdown and positive rehabilitation; the younger the child when first fostered, the greater the likelihood that the placement will be a 'stable, successful' arrangement; the longer the child has been in institutional care during the first three years of life, the more likely fostering is to break down; this is the case, too, the older the child was when first separated from his mother; the breakdown rate is also related to the child's being emotionally disturbed, which in turn may well be due to his background and history, and in particular to rejection by parental figures.

As in so many other areas of development, sex differences are in the expected direction: boys have a higher incidence of behaviour difficulties and (possibly because of this) a higher rate of breakdown in their foster placements. Coloured children are liable to have additional difficulties, relating to identification with white foster parents.

An understanding of the meaning of foster care, and of the reasons which made it necessary, seems to have a positive influence on the foster child's adjustment. This one would expect both from developmental and clinical studies of emotionally damaged children which suggest that harmful consequences are likely when a child is kept in ignorance (or told half-truths) about his origin or about his own family. Coming to terms with illegitimacy or with a parent's being in prison, mentally ill or having disappeared altogether is inevitably distressing; yet this knowledge is less harmful than living in a depersonalised vacuum, created by passive silence or by active concealment.

Much more needs to be known about the actual feelings of the children and adults involved in fostering. Qualitative studies of successful placements are especially lacking; as are studies of how 'vulnerable' groups, such as bereaved children, adolescents and school leavers make out in foster homes. The criteria determining placements, the processes involved in decision-making, and community attitudes to fostering would also repay study. So would the proposal to make fostering a salaried and perhaps para-professional job. This practice is reported to operate successfully in Holland. The danger of exploitation and wrong motivation undeniably exists, but inadequate remuneration is no guarantee against either; nor are affection and money mutually exclusive. Indeed, 'love alone is not enough' in caring for someone else's disturbed, if not damaged, child.

Lastly, two kinds of longitudinal study are needed. First, a kind of 'natural history of foster parenthood': foster parents learn, and hence change, as they gain experience and greater understanding through their relationships with a variety of foster children, their parents and the case workers. The nature of these changes may well have implications for selection procedures and for the rate of successful placements.

Secondly, a longitudinal study, comparing foster children with those who have mainly been in residential care as well as with those who have lived with their own families would be valuable. One such project is under way as part of the *National Child Development Study* and some results have just become available. By the age of seven years, some 60 per cent of all the children who had been in care had experienced fostering. Of these, 53 per cent had been placed in two, and 8 per cent in three or more, different foster homes; 20 per cent had remained in the same foster home for one year or longer, and a further 25 per cent between two to eleven months; in the great majority of cases (86 per cent), the natural and foster parents did not meet nor did either of the natural parents visit the child while he was in foster care; over 40 per cent of mothers neither wrote to the child nor phoned the foster mother during the placement. These findings seem contrary to what is held to be good foster care practice.

The chronically handicapped child in hospital care

If it is difficult to satisfy a child's basic psychological needs while he lives in residential care, this is infinitely more difficult in long-stay hospitals. Their organisation, ethos, daily routine and staff training are in no way geared to do so. Acceptance of this fact has been very slow. Over twenty-five years ago it was advocated that long-stay hospitals should be reformed so that children lived in small groups under a housemother, and from there went to their lessons in a school, to their treatment in a sick-bay and to their entertainment in a central hall. There would be no disadvantage in the housemother having had a nursing training, but that in itself is not the qualification for the work she will do. Her duty is to live with her group of children and attempt to provide the things of which they have been deprived (Spence, 1947).

Some progress has, of course, been made. First, it has been recognised that thousands of children, who are chronically handicapped, mentally, physically or both, need not be in hospitals at all; this is necessary only because there are additional problems, connected with their home circumstances or with difficulties relating to special school placement. Several studies of mentally handicapped children have demonstrated this, but there are few comparable systematic accounts of physically handicapped children living in long-stay hospitals.

Secondly, some hospitals have over the years introduced more or less major reforms. Thirdly, a few experimental small units have been established, especially designed to replace hospital care altogether. Yet it is argued that 'what is needed is not wholesale closure of hospitals, but the recognition of their uniqueness and a reappraisal of their structure and function. Deprived and handicapped children need homes not wards. They need nursing in the widest sense, partly nursing, partly educational, and always parental' (Whalley, 1973).

A recent account of long-stay hospitals questions whether 'we have really advanced very much in the last hundred years when we tolerate the existence of forgotten, hidden children' (Oswin, 1971). The study highlights how inadequate an environment such hospitals are: the children are deprived of a mother-substitute, because care is fragmented and because staff changes are made deliberately (i.e., a three-monthly rota for nurses); they are deprived of play opportunities and of experiences outside the hospital walls; of a reasonable daily routine; of privacy and dignity when their physical needs are attended to; of pleasant meal-times which should be social occasions; and of achieving even a small degree of independence.

In short, the traditional way of treating the sick continues to be applied to the chronically handicapped.

Children cared for in a hospital ward regime tend to become depersonalised...the hierarchical medical and nursing approach is detrimental to their emotional, social and intellectual development...

those without a parent or guardian should be received into the care of the local authority while remaining in hospital, and all unvisited children should have a 'friend' appointed for them (Younghusband et al., 1970).

Weekend fostering for those whose parents cannot or will not have them home could provide at least some experience of ordinary family life.

There is then much evidence that even in good but large institutions the care provided differs both in quantity and quality from that in a family setting; and that the younger the child on admission and the longer he then remains institutionalised, the more likely that many aspects of his development will be adversely affected. Some experimental schemes have been introduced and monitored, showing that the ill-effects can be minimised or even avoided, provided major changes are made in institutional policy as well as in the daily regime (Tizard, 1972; Gibson, 1969). Also, the experience of the Kibbutz indicates that communal life in childhood does not inevitably lead to harmful consequences.

There is, however, no evidence for the view that 'better a bad family than a good institution'. Children's development is so gravely at risk in the worst families – which reject, ill-treat or batter the child – that even an institutional upbringing may be preferable. But this is anyhow a false antithesis since other alternatives are available for those requiring long-term or permanent substitute care.

BELONGING TO A MINORITY GROUP

In contrast to the various circumstances considered previously, belonging to a minority group is not in itself necessarily stressful. It will, however, become so when prejudice against a group is prevalent. A child belonging to it will become aware of the stigma or discrimination which may make his loyalty all the fiercer or may lower his self-esteem or possibly both. While little is known about the effects on emotional, social and intellectual development of feeling singled out in this way, it is likely to make a child more vulnerable, particularly if there are other stresses too.

Two very different conditions will be selected for discussion, namely being adopted and being coloured. Though adoption still arouses some prejudice, it is not necessarily 'discovered' by outsiders, since it is an 'invisible' handicap. In contrast, looking racially different is in our society a most visible means of recognition from birth onwards. The social attitudes towards, and assumptions about, these two minority groups are complex and highly charged emotionally; also both exert their influence from a very early age through parental reactions to the stress of facing prejudice.

Adopted children

To begin with, the inability to have children is for many couples a source both of sorrow and reproach. If a sense of personal inadequacy persists in either partner, this will affect their attitude to each other and also, directly or indirectly, to the child. Next, most adoptive parents have to come to terms with their own, and later their adopted child's attitude to illegitimacy. Though disapproval of it may be lessening and though it is not always explicit or even conscious, this in no way detracts from its potency. As long as it exists in the community, neither the adopted child nor the adoptive parents can entirely escape its influence, even if they themselves do not share the prejudice.

Another difficulty relates to the concept of the 'blood tie'. Because considerable importance continues to be ascribed to it, both in popular and even legal thinking, adoption is seen very much as a second best. This is likely to be conveyed to the child. Similarly, the myth about morals being inherited is still believed by many; because the majority of adopted children have been born illegitimate, adoptive parents as well as their relatives tend to be fearful, especially during adolescence and in relation to girls, of immorality and promiscuity. Such fears about the effects of poor heredity can then become self-fulfilling prophecies. In fact, practically all studies have shown that the most important conditions for a successful adoption are the kind of home and care which the adopters are providing for the child.

Right from before birth, children who will later be adopted, are likely to be subjected to stressful influences. The majority are conceived out of wedlock and are carried by mothers who are beset by problems, so that their pregnancy will be a stressful period. This can have adverse effects even while the baby is still in utero. Then, both the mother who relinquishes her child and the prospective adopters have, for different reasons, to cope with many more doubts and anxieties than are faced by ordinary families (Seglow, Pringle and Wedge, 1972, Chap. 17). Thus during the early months of life the baby will have been exposed to an anxiety-laden atmosphere. He has not only shared the vulnerability of all illegitimately born children but experienced additional stress compared with those who remain with their own mothers. Also, he may have had one or more changes in mothering while awaiting adoption.

One further set of potentially stressful circumstances relates to the way in which the meaning of adoption is conveyed to the child, and what and how he is told about his biological parents. It is difficult to explain the necessary facts, while also maintaining as satisfactory an image as possible of the natural parents, and without implying that they rejected him. Equally difficult is 'the double bind of "make the child your own but tell him he isn't" . . . "telling" is inevitably seen as setting in motion complex and emotion-laden wheels which must change the family dynamics and which may create problems for the growing child' (Rowe, 1970). Awareness of these dilemmas can lead to a reluctance to discuss his origin, so that it becomes a topic shrouded in uneasy embarrassment or, worse still, unmentionable mystery. Such a situation is calculated to lead to intense curiosity, or even obsession, during adolescence.

In view of these potential difficulties, the high proportion of successful adoptions is all the more remarkable. Available research evidence shows that 'adoption is one of the soundest, most lasting – and incidentally cheapest – ways of meeting the needs of certain children who are socially deprived and in need of a normal home life' (Jacka, 1973). In fact, it is the most satisfactory form of permanent care yet devised by Western society for children whose own parents cannot undertake it (Witmer et al., 1963; Pringle, 1966, Kadushin, 1970; Seglow et al., 1972). Its success also shows that loving care and a favourable environment can overcome, or even reverse, the effects of a whole range of early disadvantages and stresses.

Coloured immigrant children

Such children are probably the most vulnerable of all groups discussed just because a high proportion of them are affected by a whole range of adverse circumstances. Not infrequently the families of coloured immigrant children are large and have a low income;

their housing conditions tend to be unsatisfactory; family relationships may be more often impaired, either because one marriage partner came earlier or the children joined the family later on or because child-rearing patterns here differ markedly from those practised in their country of origin; language and hence educational handicaps are also bound to be more frequent; in certain groups at least, one-parent families are prevalent because unstable relationships and matrifocal households were sometimes enforced in their own country by conditions of slavery. Because of the multiplicity of these various pressures, a relatively high proportion of children come into care or attend special schools for the educationally subnormal.

Such a combination of unfavourable circumstances would by themselves be highly likely to have very detrimental effects on a child's whole development. But, worse still, coloured immigrant children must adapt – to a greater or lesser extent – to quite different cultural, social and climatic conditions, often with little prior preparation. Perhaps worst of all, however, they are living in a society where they are not always wholly accepted and in which they will become aware of racial prejudice.

For coloured school leavers, unemployment becomes a particularly serious problem. In Greater London, for example, 18 per cent of all unemployed young people were black (Hansard, 1973). A recent report by the Community Relations Commission (1973) stressed the seriousness of this situation. Inadequate educational opportunity was seen as one of the strongest links in the chain of deprivation and discrimination facing coloured people; unless broken now, it is likely to lead to unemployment or under-employment for the second and subsequent generations of coloured British children.

Current signs are that the cumulative and long-term consequences of the massive and multiple disadvantages affecting many immigrant children, have hardly yet begun to be identified, let alone constructively tackled.

7. Concluding Thoughts and Unanswered Questions

A willingness to devote adequate resources to the care of children is the hallmark of a civilised society as well as an investment in our future. Some argue that we do not know enough to provide positive care and creative education for all children; others object that child rearing is essentially a personal, private matter; while yet others retort that we cannot afford to spend more. So A. E. Housman's despairing appeal 'When will I be dead and rid of the wrong my father did?' continues to be a reproach to our affluent society.

Granted that more needs to be found out about how best to promote children's all-round development, surely enough is known already to take action. If even half of what we now know were accepted with feeling and applied with understanding by all who have the care of children, then the revolution brought about in children's physical health in the past forty years might well be matched by a similar change in their psychological well-being. By strengthening their emotional resilience and increasing their capacity for learning, they would be better prepared to adapt to a rapidly changing world.

In what follows, I shall summarise my views on the needs of children; indicate some changes which are required in the climate of opinion about children's rights and parental responsibilities; and, finally, raise some questions to which answers must be sought.

THE NEEDS OF CHILDREN

There are four basic emotional needs which have to be met from the very beginning of life to enable a child to grow from helpless infancy to mature adulthood. These are: the need for love and security; for new experiences; for praise and recognition; and for responsibility. Their relative importance changes, of course, during the different stages of growth as do the ways in which they are met.

148

The need for love and security

Probably this is the most important because it provides the basis for all later relationships, not only within the family, but with friends, colleagues and eventually one's own family. On it depend the healthy development of the personality, the ability to care and respond to affection and, in time, to becoming a loving, caring parent. This need is met by the child experiencing from birth onwards a continuous, reliable, loving relationship – first, with his mother, then father and then an ever-widening circle of adults and contemporaries. The security of a familiar place and a known routine make for continuity and predictability in a world in which the child has to come to terms with so much that is new and changing. Also a stable family life provides him with a sense of personal continuity, of having a past as well as a future, and of a coherent and enduring identity.

The need for new experiences

Only if this need is adequately met throughout childhood and adolescence will a child's intelligence develop satisfactorily. Just as the body requires food for physical development and just as an appropriate balanced diet is essential for normal growth, so new experiences are needed for the mind. The most vital ingredients of this diet in early childhood are play and language. Through them, the child explores the world and learns to cope with it. This is as true for the objective outside world of reality as it is for the subjective internal world of thoughts and feelings.

New experiences facilitate the learning of one of the most important lessons of early life: learning how to learn; and learning that mastery brings joy and a sense of achievement. Educability depends not only on inborn capacity, but as much – if not more – on environmental opportunity and encouragement. The emotional and cultural climate of the home, as well as parental involvement and aspirations, can foster, limit or impair mental growth.

Play meets the need for new experiences in two major ways: it enables the child to learn about the world; and it provides a means of coping with and resolving conflicting emotions by allowing fantasy to over-ride reality and logic.

Probably the single and in the long run most crucial factor which promotes intellectual growth is the quality of the child's language environment: not merely how much he is talked to, but how relevant, distinctive and rich the conversation is. Language helps in learning to reason and to think, and also in making relationships.

Going to school is itself a major new experience which opens up a larger and more impersonal world. The child's progress will come to be powerfully affected by his teacher's attitudes, values and beliefs. Wide interests, enthusiasm for things of the mind and receptiveness to new ideas – all these are infectious. Teachers are in a powerful position to preserve, to awaken or to rekindle the curiosity and joy in learning about new things, shown by almost all young children.

The need for praise and recognition

To grow from a helpless infant into a self-reliant, self-accepting adult requires an immense amount of emotional, social and intellectual learning. It is accomplished by the child's modelling himself on the adults who are caring for him. The most effective incentives to bring this about – which require a continuous effort, sustained throughout the years of growing up – are praise and recognition. Eventually, a job well done becomes its own reward but that is a very mature stage; and even the most mature adult responds, and indeed blossoms, when given occasionally some praise or other forms of recognition.

Because growing up is inevitably beset by difficulties, conflicts and setbacks, a strong incentive is needed. This is provided by the pleasure shown at success and the praise given to achievement by the adults who love the child and whom he in turn loves and wants to please. Encouragement and reasonable demands act as a spur to perseverance. The level of expectation is optimal when success is possible but not without effort. It cannot be the same for all children nor for all time. Rather, it must be geared to the individual child's capabilities at a given point in time and to the particular stage of his growth.

Teachers play a vital role too in meeting the need for praise and recognition; if for no other reason than because every child spends about half his waking life in school for at least eleven years. This provides an unrivalled opportunity to establish a favourable attitude to learning and also, where necessary, to improve or even rebuild the foundation for a child's self-esteem and hence his attitude to effort and achievement. To succeed in this task, a teacher must act on the assumption that every pupil has as yet unrealised potential for development which an appropriate 'diet' can call out, rather than accept past failures as indicating immutably limited learning ability.

The need for responsibility

This need is met by allowing the child to gain personal independence, at first through learning to look after himself in matters of his everyday care, such as feeding, dressing and washing himself. It is met too by his having possessions, however small and inexpensive, over which he is allowed to exercise absolute ownership. As he gets older, responsibility has to be extended to more important areas, ultimately allowing him freedom over his own actions. Eventually, in full maturity, he should be able to accept responsibility for others.

Granting increasing independence does not mean withholding one's views, tastes and choices, or the reasons for them; nor does it mean opting out from participating and guiding the lives of children; nor, indeed, condoning everything they do. On the contrary, children need a framework of guidance and of limits. They are helped by knowing what is expected or permitted, what the rules are, together with the reasons for them, and whether these are in their interests or in the interests of others.

How can responsibility be given to the immature and to the irresponsible? There is no way out of the dilemma that unless it is granted, the child cannot learn how to exercise it. Like every other skill, it needs to be practised under adult guidance which should gradually diminish. Training adolescents for responsibility is a particularly complex task. It requires a delicate balance between giving information and advice on the one hand and, on the other, leaving the making of decisions and coping with their consequences to the young person while yet being prepared to step in and help if things go badly wrong.

Schools have a vital contribution to make in this area. Those which emphasise cooperation rather than competition, which neither stream nor use corporal punishment have a lower incidence of bullying, violence and delinquency without any lowering of academic standards.

Failure to meet children's needs

If one of the basic needs remains unmet, or is inadequately met, then development may become stunted or distorted. The consequences can be disastrous (and costly) later on, both for the individual and for society. Symptoms of maladjustment are, like pain, danger signals, indicating intolerable tension between the personality and the environment. The range of possible symptoms is wide but basically they fall into two broad categories: fight or flight, attack or withdrawal. Aggressiveness calls forth much stronger adult reactions whereas the timid, over-conforming child tends to be overlooked; yet both types of behaviour are equally significant calls for help, indicating that emotional, social or intellectual needs are not being adequately met.

Prisons, mental hospitals, borstals and schools for the maladjusted, contain a high proportion of individuals who in childhood were unloved and rejected. Their number is high too among the chronically unemployable and among able misfits. Anger, hate, lack of concern for others and an inability to make mutually satisfactory relationships are common reactions to having been unloved and rejected.

A child growing up in a discordant home is also liable to become emotionally disturbed or anti-social. A quarrelling, inadequate or disturbed parent makes a poor adult model. Parental hostility has a particularly harmful effect on a child's later development, especially on his ability to give, as an adult, unselfish loving care to his own children. Thus parental hostility perpetuates itself from one generation to another in what is literally an extremely vicious circle.

If the need for new experiences is not adequately met throughout childhood and adolescence, then intellectual ability will remain stunted. Also, the more unstimulating, uneventful and dull life is, the more readily frustration, apathy, or restlessness set in. This is shown clearly by the contrast between the eagerness, alertness and vitality of normal toddlers whose life is filled with new experiences and challenges; and the aimlessness and boredom of adolescents with nothing to do and nowhere to go.

The urban environment is hostile to the young: there is little freedom or safety to explore or experiment, particularly without adult supervision. In seeking – legitimately – for the excitement of new experiences, where few are to be found or attainable, the forbidden, risky or dangerous are liable to acquire an aura of daring and excitement. What may start as a lark, giving vent to high spirits and the desire for adventure, can then all too easily turn into vandalism and mindless destruction.

Unfortunately, praise and recognition are almost invariably given for achievement rather than effort. In consequence, this need is most readily and often satisfied in the case of intelligent, healthy, adjusted and attractive children. In contrast, the intellectually slow, culturally disadvantaged, emotionally neglected or maladjusted get far less, if any, praise and recognition. Yet their need is immeasurably greater. Whatever small successes they achieve inevitably demand far more effort and perseverance; yet they receive less reward because they achieve less.

In school, praising for achievement instead of effort has very harmful effects on the slower learner as well as on the child with emotional or physical handicaps: he has no chance of shining and always finds himself near the bottom of his class. Such constant failure inevitably damages self-esteem and motivation. The teacher who believes that what matters most is the effort a child makes, and who praises whenever there is improvement however slow and limited, provides an appropriate incentive for all pupils, whatever their abilities. For better or for worse, the encouragement and expectations of parents and teachers have a most powerful influence on a child's progress.

There is controversy between those who demand equal educational opportunity for all; those who advocate that special attention ought to be devoted to the abler child; and those who argue that positive discrimination must be exercised in favour of the less able and under-privileged. The conflict between these viewpoints is, however, more apparent than real. It springs from the mistaken belief that all men are equal despite the enormous disparity in physical, intellectual and creative potential found in all walks of life. Equality of opportunity is the right of every child. To expect equal capacity to make use of this opportunity runs counter to common sense and experience.

Instead, we must act as if all children were equal and then respect, as well as accept and cater for, their differences. Within such a framework, it is legitimate both to provide a democracy of opportunity while at the same time to strive for excellence so as to ensure an aristocracy of achievement.

When the fourth basic emotional need, namely to exercise responsibility, is denied opportunities for fulfilment, then the child will fail to develop a sense of responsibility for himself, for others or for material objects. When such denial has gone hand in hand with a lack of training in self-control and in planning ahead, then such youngsters will tend to be impulsive, unwilling to wait and work for what they want, contemptuous of the rights of others – in short, irresponsible. A high proportion of the self-same young people will on leaving school find themselves in jobs which give them little, if any, responsibility. Work which fails to fulfil the need for involvement is likely to heighten the sense of alienation and rejection. Feeling that society has disowned them may well engender a feeling that they in turn owe nothing to society.

The cost of prevention

How costly would it be to ensure that children's needs are met, so as to promote and ensure their optimal emotional, social, intellectual and educational development? No one really knows because no serious consideration has been given to this question. How much would it cost to have supportive services available to the family, sufficient in quality and quantity, to prevent children who are 'vulnerable' or 'at risk' growing up emotionally disturbed, socially deviant, intellectually stunted and educationally backward? Again, no one can really say because the question has not been asked.

Nevertheless, some argue that as a society we simply cannot afford to pay either for wide-ranging preventive services or for comprehensive rehabilitation and treatment facilities. Is this not fallacious? Surely the question is: can we afford not to do so? Failure to provide the necessary programmes for children and their families merely postpones the day when the community has to pay the much higher price for not willing the means earlier. The cost in the long run is extremely high: not only in terms of human misery and wasted potentialities but also in terms of unemployability, mental ill health, crime and a renewed cycle of inadequate parenting. Even in the short run, it is by no means economic to do too little and to do it too late.

For example, in most cases, emotional, social or learning difficulties come to light when a child starts school. Inevitably, providing special classes, school psychological or psychiatric services is costly; but if the child's difficulties are so severe or his family background so unsatisfactory that residential facilities are required, then the cost is ten times as high (Pond and Arie, 1971). Moreover, because there are not enough trained personnel in any of the helping professions – whether remedial teachers, social workers, psychologists, psychiatrists or speech therapists – waiting lists are long and only those whose needs are the most urgent have any hope of receiving special help early. The later it is given, the more difficult and lengthy, and hence the more costly, the treatment and the less hopeful the prognosis. So in the event we may well be paying the most for the least effective intervention simply because prevention is not only better but cheaper than cure.

TODAY'S CHILDREN – TOMORROW'S PARENTS

Children inevitably depend on others for their well-being, care and education; they have no vote or voice in the running of the community, either at local or national level; and resources devoted to them are society's investment in tomorrow's parents. For all practical purposes of social policy, we must act on the assumption that the environment is of over-riding importance and that the early years of life are particularly vital. To develop the potential for becoming human, the baby must needs have a human environment; and the most efficient and economical system known to man for making human infants human is the family. Hence a long-term policy for children must be based on improving the quality of family care and of education from cradle through adulthood. To do so requires two wide-ranging changes: a different attitude to parenthood and child rearing; and a willingness to provide more adequate services for families and children, if only for the sake of the latter. The implication of the first change is discussed in this section.

Children's rights and parental responsibilities

The prevailing climate of opinion must be changed in a number of respects. First, children's rights and parental responsibilities need to be re-defined. Current attitudes on the paramountcy of 'biological' parenthood are ambivalent and contradictory. Both in law and in practice we often act as if the blood tie and 'natural' parenthood necessarily ensured satisfactory parenting. Yet we fail

155

to provide sufficient community support to enable a child to be looked after by his own family at times of difficulty (say mother's illness or pregnancy); in consequence, thousands of pre-school children come into public care every year.

Furthermore, we so over-value the child's ties with his natural parents that we are far too slow to consider severing them permanently when the parents are disturbed or rejecting, even to a pathological degree. Thus some babies who have been brutally assaulted are returned to their homes when both common sense and clinical evidence indicate that there is a high chance of it happening again with the risk of permanent injury or death. Similarly, this misplaced faith in the blood tie, and an unjustified optimism about the chances of successfully awakening or rekindling parental interest when a child has been to all intents and purposes abandoned, condemns thousands of them to remain in long-term public care without permanent substitute parents.

Secondly, the current over-romanticised picture of parenthood, and of motherhood in particular – projected by the media and the advertising industry – ought to be changed. A more realistic and perhaps even daunting awareness needs to be created of the arduous demands which child rearing makes on the emotions, energy, time and finances, as well as of the inevitable constraints on personal independence, freedom of movement and, indeed, one's whole way of life. Babies should be presented 'truthfully', warts and all – sometimes fretful and demanding, often wet, smelly, crying at night and 'unreasonable' – rather than with a permanent angelic, dimply smile and sunny temper. Deglamourising parenthood in this way will not deter those who truly want to care for children but it may act as a brake on those with unrealistic expectations.

Thirdly, several other notions, which have no foundation in fact, should also be dispelled: that having a child is the sole or most important or easiest way to feminine fulfilment; that a baby completes a home, rather like a T.V. set or fridge; that it will cement an unsatisfactory or failing marriage; that maternity has a therapeutic effect, particularly on girls who were themselves rejected in childhood; that a child belongs to his parents like their other possessions; and that he should be grateful to his parents even though he did not ask to be born.

Responsible parenthood

The myth of the blood tie should be replaced by the concept of responsible and informed parenthood. The ability and willingness to undertake its responsibilities are neither dependent nor necessarily consequent upon, biological parenthood. Rather it is the unconditional desire to provide a caring home, together with the emotional maturity to do so, which are the hallmarks of good parenting. Responsible parenthood also includes having only as many children as the couple can emotionally tolerate and financially afford.

Common sense suggests that very young parents, themselves not yet fully mature emotionally, are less able to provide the emotional support so vital to a child's optimal development. Being at the beginning of their working life, financial and housing problems are likely to be additional difficulties. But perhaps one of the main reasons why the rate of marriage failure is highest among those who marry young is the fact that neither partner has as yet reached his mature level of emotional, social and intellectual development. When the pace of this growth is markedly different for one spouse, then the couple will later on be no longer as well-matched as they had been. It would be in the long-term interest both of the future parents and of their children if parenthood were postponed until both partners are fully mature emotionally. For this to happen, a social climate will have to be created in which it is considered irresponsible to have children before, say, the age of twenty-two or twenty-three.

Preparation for parenthood, including family planning, could make an important contribution. Modern parenthood is too demanding and complex a task to be performed well merely because we all have once been children ourselves. Those who have been deprived of adequate parental care, thus not having had an opportunity to observe even those parental skills which were practised a generation ago, have little chance of becoming in turn responsible parents themselves.

An effective programme of preparation for parenthood would have to adopt a wide and comprehensive base. It should deal with the whole area of human relations and in particular with child development; first-hand experience of babies and young children should be an essential part of the programme; as should be an understanding of the ways in which the relations between a married couple are bound to change when they become parents.

Responsible parenthood must come to mean that the parental life style has been freely and deliberately chosen in the full realisation of its demands, constraints, satisfactions and challenges. Since the technological know-how is also now available it would be possible to translate into reality the slogan 'every child a wanted child'. Then there would be a much better chance than at present that the needs of children will be met. How to do so has been summarised in the following ten child care commandments. These are based on what has been said in Chapters 1, 2 and 3.

The art of child-rearing

These ten child care commandments are rather in the nature of guidelines. Inevitably only a few generalisations can ever be of universal application because of the uniqueness of each individual – father, mother and child; and for this reason the relationships between the parents themselves, and between them and each child, are also unique. A parent's best guide is his own quality of understanding, combined with his knowledge of developmental needs, both of which are then applied to the upbringing of each individual child. An understanding of a child's physical and mental abilities at any given stage, and hence his readiness at a given time to respond and adapt, is the most reliable gauge of whether parental expectations are appropriate.

It is an illusory, and sometimes even harmful, aim to treat each child alike. What is needed is a 'tailor-made' approach fashioned to suit each child but based on the general principles of child-rearing embodied in the ten child care commandments. Only by allowing for individual differences can we ensure an appropriate environment for each member of a family. In this way too we shall avoid trying to fashion a child in our own image and so avoid disappointment for ourselves and a sense of inadequacy in our children.

Ten Child Care Commandments

1 Give continuous, consistent, loving care – it's as essential for the mind's health as food is for the body.

2 Give generously of your time and understanding – playing with and reading to your child matters more than a tidy, smooth-running home.

3 Provide new experiences and bathe your child in language from birth onwards – they enrich his growing mind.

4 Encourage him to play in every way both by himself and with other children – exploring, imitating, constructing, pretending and creating.

5 Give more praise for effort than for achievement.

6 Give him ever-increasing responsibility – like all skills, it needs to be practised.

7 Remember that every child is unique – so suitable handling for one may not be right for another.

8 Make the way you show disapproval fit your child's temperament, age and understanding.

9 Never threaten that you will stop loving him or give him away; you may reject his behaviour but never suggest that you might reject him.

10 Don't expect gratitude; your child did not ask to be born – the choice was yours.

SOME UNANSWERED QUESTIONS

1 Why do we assume that the light of nature is sufficient for parents to know what the needs of children are and how these are best met? Is it because we have all once been children and have had the chance to learn from the child-rearing practices of our own parents? Yet most people would not accept the similar argument that because we have all been to school we could be adequate teachers without the need for any training; indeed professional teacher training has become increasingly longer to keep pace with the increasing knowledge in the relevant fields.

2 When and how would preparation for parenthood best be tackled? And who should undertake this task? None of these questions can be answered satisfactorily without experimenting with a great

variety of different methods, settings, ages and professionals, all the while monitoring and evaluating what is being done.

3 Should there be a new professional discipline undertaking preparation for parenthood? Personally I doubt it, but further training is likely to be essential except for a few people who are 'naturals' with the necessary flair and imagination.

4 Do we go too far in asserting that the way in which parents bring up their children is solely their own concern? Of course, the great majority give loving, concerned, responsible care. But just as the education and health care of children are shared with professionals on the grounds that most parents do not possess all the necessary skills, so it is evident that a minority are not able or willing to provide the care essential to a child's healthy personal development. Bringing up children is too important a task to be left entirely to those parents who are patently in need of support, guidance and, where necessary, sanctions on the part of the community.

5 What are the most effective ways of complementing and supplementing parental care at different ages and stages? To what extent is parental participation essential for optimal effectiveness? For example, some evidence suggests that pre-school enrichment programmes result in long-term changes only if there is active maternal involvement and that a child's progress in school is vitally influenced by parental interest.

6 What is the most effective balance between bringing supportive services for children and families right into the home and making them available in readily accessible community centres, child health clinics and schools? Need this balance be different at different ages?

7 What are the most effective ways of compensating for ineffective or harmful parental handling? And, where a substitute family is the only possible solution for the sake of the child's long-term development, what preparation and safe-guards are needed to ensure the success of this transplant operation?

8 Should there be comprehensive services which focus on the needs of the whole child and his family rather than on the specific nature of his particular type of deviancy or handicap? The former seems preferable since all children share the same basic emotional, social, intellectual and educational needs. Singling out a specific condition

may delay dealing with its consequences in a comprehensive way; this has happened, for example, in relation to services for handicapped children to their obvious detriment.

9 Should we ask ourselves the question: into what kind of people do we want today's children to grow? How it is answered materially affects child-rearing methods.

10 What are the qualities, circumstances or relationships which enable a child from a grossly impoverished, depriving or neglectful home to emerge nevertheless apparently unscathed? A great deal is known now about the harmful effects of impaired family relations, emotional deprivation and intellectual under-stimulation. Yet some children manage to triumph over appalling odds. Gaining some understanding of the mechanisms at work would aid prevention and possibly rehabilitation too.

To make man more perfect in body and mind has been an age-old dream. In the physical realm the prospect of positive good health is becoming a reality within reach of at least the developed countries. 'The developed, integrated human personality is without question the highest thing we know in the universe.' (Sir Julian Huxley.) Are we now reaching a cross-road? Given the will and willing the resources, science and technology may be able to provide the knowledge and to develop the techniques to bring the second part of man's dream of perfectibility at least within the realm of possibility. A compassionate society in which individual fulfilment and freedom are reconciled with the individual's obligations and commitment to the needs of his community – can there be a higher stake, a more worthwhile goal or a more exciting challenge than improving in this way the quality of life for all our children?

F

References

ALLAND, A. (1972). *The Human Imperative*, Columbia University Press, New York.

ALLEN, F. H. and PEARSON, G. H. J. (1928). The emotional problems of the physically handicapped child. *British Journal of Medical Psychology*, **8** (3), 212–35.

AMBROSE, J. A. (1963). The concept of a critical period for the development of social responsiveness in early human infancy. *Determinants of Infant Behaviour*, B. Foss (ed.), vol. 2. Methuen.

AMBROSE, J. A. (ed.) (1970). *Stimulation in Early Infancy*, Academic Press, New York.

ANDERSON, R. H. and SHANE, H. G. (1971). *As the Twig is Bent*, Houghton, Mifflin & Co., Boston.

ANDRY, R. G. (1960). *Delinquency and Parental Pathology*, Methuen.

ARGYLE, M. (1969). *Social Interaction*, Methuen.

ARIES, P. (1962). *Centuries of Childhood*, Jonathan Cape.

BANKS, O. and FINLAYSON, D. (1973). *Success and Failure in the Secondary School*, Methuen.

BARATZ, S. S. and BARATZ, J. C. (1970). Early childhood intervention: the social science base of institutional racism. *Harvard Educational Review*, **40** (1), 29–50.

BARTEN, S. S. and BLANK, M. (1971). Soviet research on speech and language: an American perspective. *Early Child Development*, **1** (1), 3–14.

BARNES, D., BRITTON, J. and ROSEN, H. (1971). *Language, the Learner and the School*, Penguin.

BAUER, R. A. (ed.) (1966). *Social Indicators*, The MIT Press, Cambridge, Mass.

BAYLEY, N. (1964). Consistency of maternal and child behaviors in the Berkeley Growth Study. *Vita Humana*, **7** (2), 73–95.

BELL, R. Q. (1968). A re-interpretation of the direction of effects in studies of socialisation, *Psychological Review*, **75** (1), 81–95.

BENN, C. (1969). Marriage breakdown and the individual. *Divorce, Society and the Law*, H. A. Finlay (ed.), Butterworth and Co., New South Wales, Australia.

BENTHALL, J. (ed.) (1973). *The Limits of Human Nature*, Allen Lane, The Penguin Press.

BERGER, M. and PASSINGHAM, R. E. (1972). Early experience and other environmental factors: an overview. *Handbook of Abnormal Psychology*, H. J. Eysenck (ed.), 2nd ed., Pitman.

BERLYNE, D. E. (1960). *Conflict, Arousal and Curiosity*, McGraw-Hill, New York.

BERNSTEIN, B. (1961). Social structure, language and learning. *Educational Research*, 3 (2), 163–76.

BERNSTEIN, B. (1961). Aspects of language and learning in the genesis of the social process. *Journal of Child Psychology and Psychiatry*, 1 (4), 313–24.

BERNSTEIN, B. (1971). Theoretical studies towards a sociology of language. *Class, Codes and Control*, vol. 1. Routledge and Kegan Paul.

BERNSTEIN, B. (ed.) (1973). Applied studies towards a sociology of language. *Class, Codes and Control*, vol. 2. Routledge and Kegan Paul.

BERRY, J. (1972). *Social Work with Children*, Routledge and Kegan Paul.

BIRCH, H. and GUSSOW, J. (1970). *Disadvantaged Children: Health, Nutrition and School Failure*, Harcourt, Brace and World, New York.

BIRLEY, J. L. T. (1973). The effect of the environment on the individual. *Proceedings of the Royal Society of Medicine*, 66 (1, part 2) 93–8.

BLANK, M. and SOLOMON, F. (1969). How shall the disadvantaged be taught? *Child Development*, 49 (1), 47–61.

BLOOM, B. S. (1964). *Stability and Change in Human Characteristics*, John Wiley, New York.

BLOOM, B. S. (1973). Affective consequences of school achievement. *Advances in Educational Psychology*, M. L. Kellmer Pringle and V. P. Varma (eds.), vol. 2. University of London Press.

BLOOM, B. S., DAVIES, A. and HESS, R. (1965). *Compensatory Education for Cultural Deprivation*. Holt, Rinehart and Winston, New York.

BLURTON JONES, N. G. (1971). Criteria for use in describing facial expressions of children. *Human Biology*, 43 (3), 365–413.

BOHMAN, M. (1971). A comparative study of adopted children, foster children and children in their biological environment born after undesired pregnancies. *Acta Paediatrica Scandinavica*, Suppl. 221.

BOWLBY, J. (1951). *Maternal Care and Mental Health*. World Health Organisation, Geneva.

BOWLBY, J. (1958). *Can I Leave My Baby?* National Association for Mental Health.

BOWLBY, J. (1969). Attachment. *Attachment and Loss*, 1. Hogarth Press.

BOWLBY, J. and PARKES, C. D. (1970). Separation and loss within the family. *The Child in his Family*, E. J. Anthony and C. M. Koupernik (eds.). John Wiley, New York.

BRONFENBRENNER, U. (1967). The psychological costs of quality and equality in education. *Child Development*, 38 (3), 909–25.

BRONFENBRENNER, U. (1968). Early deprivation in mammals and man: a cross-species analysis. *Early Experience and Behavior*, G. Newton and S. Levine (eds.), C. C. Thomas, Springfield, Ill.

BRONFENBRENNER, U. (1970). *Two Worlds of Childhood: U.S. and U.S.S.R.* Russell Sage Foundation, New York.

BRONFENBRENNER, U. (1973). Developmental research, public policy and the ecology of childhood. Paper read at the Annual Meeting of the Society for Research in Child Development. Philadelphia, 31 March.

BROWN, C. (1954). *My Left Foot*. Secker and Warburg.

BRUNER, J. S. (1965). The growth of mind. *Issues and Advances in Educational Psychology*, E. P. Terrance and W. F. White (eds.), Peacock, New York.

BRUNER, J. S. et al. (1966). *Studies in Cognitive Growth*. John Wiley, New York.

BURT, SIR C. (1937). *The Subnormal Mind*, 2nd ed., Oxford.

BURT, SIR C. (1946). *The Backward Child*. 2nd ed., University of London Press.

BURT, SIR C. (1962). The gifted child. *Year Book of Education*, 24–58, Evans.

BUTLER, N. R. and ALBERMAN, E. (eds.) (1969). *Perinatal Problems*. Livingstone.

BUTLER, N. R. and BONHAM, G. H. (1963). *Perinatal Mortality*. Livingstone.

BUTLER, N. R. and GOLDSTEIN, H. (1973). Smoking in pregnancy and subsequent child development. *British Medical Journal*, 8 Dec., 4, 573–5.

CALDWELL, B. M. (1970). The effects of psychosocial deprivation on human development in infancy. *Merrill-Palmer Quarterly*, 16 (3), 260–77.

CAMPBELL, D. (1972). Activity and attachment in early life. *Proceedings of the British Psychological Society*, London Conference.

CARLSON, E. R. (1952). *Born that Way*. Arthur James.

CARNEGIE UNITED KINGDOM TRUST. (1964). *Handicapped Children and their Families*. Dunfermline, Scotland.

CENTRAL STATISTICAL OFFICE. (1972). *Social Trends* (3). H.M.S.O.

CHAZAN, M. (1963). Maladjustment, attainment and sociometric status. *University College of Education Journal*, 4–7.

CHAZAN, M., LAING, A. and JACKSON, S. (1971). *Just before School.* Blackwell, Oxford.

CLARKE, A. D. B. and CLARKE, A. M. (1972). Consistency and variability in the growth of human characteristics. *Advances in Educational Psychology,* 1, W. D. Wall and V. P. Varma (eds.), University of London Press.

CLARKE, A. D. B. and CLARKE, A. M. (1973). *Mental Deficiency: the Changing Outlook.* Especially chapter on genetic-environmental interactions in cognitive development. 3rd ed., Methuen.

COHEN, LORD OF BIRKENHEAD. (1965). Foreword to *Investment in Children,* M. L. Kellmer Pringle (ed.), Longman.

COLEMAN, J. S. et al. (1966). *Equality of Educational Opportunity.* U.S. Government Printing Office, Washington D.C.

COOPER, J. (1969). Group treatment in residential care. *Caring for Children,* M. L. Kellmer Pringle (ed.), Longman in associaton with the National Children's Bureau.

COOKSEY, G. (1972). Teachers, parents and the social services. *The Challenge of Change,* M. Kogan and M. Pope (eds.), National Foundation for Educational Research, for National Children's Bureau, Slough.

COURT, J. (1969). Battering parents. *Social Work,* **26** (1), 20–4.

CREBER, J. W. P. (1972). *Lost for Words.* Penguin Books.

CRELLIN, E., PRINGLE, M. L. K. and WEST, P. (1971). *Born Illegitimate.* National Foundation for Educational Research, for National Children's Bureau, Slough.

DAVIE, R. (1972). The behaviour and adjustment in school of seven-year-olds; sex and social class differences. *Early Child Development and Care,* **2** (1), 39–47.

DAVIE, R. (1973). Eleven years of childhood. *Statistical News,* (22), 14–18.

DAVIE, R., BUTLER, N. and GOLDSTEIN, H. (1972). *From Birth to Seven.* Longman in association with the National Children's Bureau.

DAVIES, B. (1969). Non-swinging youth. *New Society,* 3 July, **14** (353), 8–10.

DAVIS, K. (1947). Final note on a case of extreme isolation. *American Journal of Sociology,* **52** (5), 432–7.

DE BONO, E. (1969). *The Mechanism of the Mind.* Cape.

DE BONO, E. (1972). *Children Solve Problems.* Allen Lane.

DENENBERG, V. H. (1969). Animal studies of early experience: some principles which have implications for human development. *Minnesota Symposium in Child Psychology,* **3**, J. P. Hill (ed.), University of Minnesota Press.

DEPARTMENT OF THE ENVIRONMENT. (1973). Children at play. *Design Bulletin* (27), H.M.S.O.

DEPARTMENT OF HEALTH AND SOCIAL SECURITY. (1971). *Two-parent Families.* H.M.S.O.

DEPARTMENT OF HEALTH AND· SOCIAL SECURITY. (1972). *The 'Battered Baby' Syndrome; an analysis of reports submitted by Medical Officers of Health and Children's Officers.* H.M.S.O.

DEVEREUX, E. C., BRONFENBRENNER, U. and RODGERS, R. R. (1969). Child rearing in England and the United States: a cross-national comparison. *Journal of Marriage and the Family,* **31** (2), 257–70.

DINNAGE, R. (1971). The Handicapped Child. *Research Review,* **1**: *Neurological Handicaps.* Longman in association with the National Children's Bureau.

DINNAGE, R. (1972). The Handicapped Child. *Research Review,* **2**: *Sensory and Physical Handicaps.* Longman in association with the National Children's Bureau.

DINNAGE, R. and PRINGLE, M. L. KELLMER. (1967). *Foster Care – Facts and Fallacies.* Longman in association with the National Children's Bureau.

DINNAGE, R. and PRINGLE, M. L. KELLMER. (1967). *Residential Care – Facts and Fallacies.* Longman in association with the National Children's Bureau.

DOBBING, J. and SMART, J. L. (1973). Early under nutrition, brain development and behaviour. *Ethology and Development,* S. A. Barnett (ed.), Spastics Society and Heinemann.

DODGE, J. A. (1972). Psychosomatic aspects of infantile pyloric stenosis. *Journal of Psychosomatic Research,* **16** (1), 1–5.

DONNISON, D. (ed.) (1972). *A Pattern of Disadvantage.* National Foundation for Educational Research for National Children's Bureau, Slough.

DOUGLAS, J. W. B. (1964). *The Home and the School.* MacGibbon and Kee.

DOUGLAS, J. W. B. (1970). Broken families and child behaviour. *Journa of Royal College of Physicians,* **4** (3), 203–10.

DOUGLAS, J. W. B., ROSS, J. M. and SIMPSON, H. R. (1968). *All Our Future.* Peter Davies.

EIBL-EIBESFELDT, I. (1967). Concepts of ethology and their significance in the study of human behavior. *Early Behavior : Comparative and Developmental Approaches.* H. Stevenson, E. Hess and H. Rheingold (eds.), John Wiley, New York.

EYSENCK, H. J. (1973). *The Inequality of Man.* Temple Smith.

FERRI, E. (1972). Children in one-parent families. *The Parental Role,* 20–1. National Children's Bureau.

FERRI, E. (1973). The single parent family: aspects of children's welfare. Royal Society of Health, 80th Congress, 1973 (published in the proceedings), 168–70.

FERRI, E. (1973). Characteristics of motherless families. *British Journal of Social Work*, **3** (1), 91–100.

FLAVELL, J. H. (1963). *Developmental Psychology of Jean Piaget*. Van Nostrand, Princeton, N.J.

FORSSMAN, H. and THUWE, I. (1965). One hundred and twenty children born after application for therapeutic abortion was refused. *Acta Psychiatrica Scandinavica*, **42** (4), 71–88.

GENERAL REGISTER OFFICE. (1960). *Classification of Occupations*. H.M.S.O.

GEORGE, V. (1970). *Foster Care: Theory and Practice*. Routledge and Kegan Paul.

GEORGE, V. and WILDING, P. (1972). *Motherless Families*. Routledge and Kegan Paul.

GEWIRTZ, H. B. and GEWIRTZ, J. L. (1969). Caretaking settings, background events and behaviour differences in four Israeli child rearing environments: some preliminary trends. *Determinants of Behaviour*, **4**, B. M. Foss (ed.), Methuen.

GIBSON, J. (1969). The mentally retarded child in hospital. Suggestions for improving care and stimulation. *Clinical Pediatrics*, **8** (5), 256–7.

GIBSON, C. (1973). Social trends in divorce. *New Society*, 5th July, **25** (651), 6–8.

GIL, D. (1971). *Violence against Children*. Harvard University Press, Cambridge, Mass.

GLUECK, S. and GLUECK, E. T. (1962). *Family Environment and Delinquency*. Kegan Paul.

GOLDFARB, W. (1943). The effects of early institutional care on adolescent personality. *Journal of Experimental Education*, **12** (2), 108–29.

GOLDSTEIN, J., FREUD, A. and SOLNIT, A. J. (1973). *Beyond the Best Interests of the Child*. The Free Press.

GOOCH, S. and PRINGLE, M. L. KELLMER. (1966). *Four Years On*. Longman in association with the National Children's Bureau.

GRAY, P. H. (1958). Theory and evidence of imprinting in human infants. *Journal of Psychology*, **46** (2), 155–66.

GROSSER, G. M., WECHSLER, H. and GREENBLATT, M. (eds.) (1964). *The Threat of Impending Disaster*. The MIT Press, Cambridge, Mass.

HADINGHAM, E. (ed.) (1970). *Youth Now*. Kingston Grammar School, Surrey.

HALSEY, A. H. (1973). E.P.A. Problems and Policies. *Educational priority*, **1**, H.M.S.O.

HAMPSON, J. L. and HAMPSON, J. G. (1961). The entogenesis of sexual behavior in man. *Sex and Internal Secretions*, chap. 23, 1401–32. W. C. Young (ed.), Baillière, Tindall and Cox.

HANSARD. (1973). Unemployment among young black people. *House of Lords*. 25th July, column 1926–7, H.M.S.O.

HARLOW, H. F. and GRIFFIN, G. (1965). Induced mental and social deficits in rhesus monkeys. *The Biosocial Basis of Mental Retardation*, S. F. Osler and R. E. Cooke (eds.), John Hopkins Press.

HARLOW, H. F. and HARLOW, M. K. (1969). Effects of various mother-infant relationships on rhesus monkey behaviour. *Determinants of Infant Behaviour*, 4, 15–36, B. M. Foss (ed.), Methuen.

HARLOW, H. F. and HARLOW, M. K. (1970). Developmental aspects of emotional behavior. *Physiological Correlates of Emotion*, P. Black (ed.), Academic Press.

HEBB, D. O. (1949). *The Organisation of Behaviour*. John Wiley, New York.

HELFER, R. E. and KEMPE, C. H. (eds.) (1968). *The Battered Child*. University of Chicago Press.

HELFER, R. E. and KEMPE, C. H. (eds.) (1971). *Helping the Battered Child and his Family*. University of Chicago Press.

HEMMING, J. (1974). Emotional and moral aspects of adolescence. *Advances in Educational Psychology*, 2 chap. 15, M. L. Kellmer Pringle and V. P. Varma (eds.), University of London Press.

HESS, R. D. and BEAR, R. (eds.) (1960). *Early Education : Current Theory, Research and Action*. Aldine, Chicago.

HESS, R. D. and SHIPMAN, V. C. (1965). Early experience and the socialization of cognitive modes in children. *Child Development*, 36 (4), 869–86.

HEWETT, S., NEWSON, J. and NEWSON, E. (1970). *The Family and the Handicapped Child*. Allen and Unwin.

HITCHFIELD, E. (1973). *In Search of Promise*. Longman in association with the National Children's Bureau.

HOLLOWAY, B. (1973). Too many right men for the jobs. *The Times*, 20 July.

HOLMAN, R. (ed.) (1970). *Socially Deprived Families in Britain*. Bedford Square Press.

HOLMAN, R. (1972). *Unsupported Mothers*, 2nd ed. Mothers in Action.

HOLMAN, R. (1973). *Trading in Children*. Routledge and Kegan Paul.

HOME OFFICE. (1972). *Girl Offenders aged 17 to 20 Years*. J. Davies and N. Goodman, H.M.S.O.

HOTYAT, F. (1974). How children learn new skills. *Advances in Educational Psychology*, 2. M. L. Kellmer Pringle and V. P. Varma (eds.), University of London Press.

HOUSE OF COMMONS PAPER 384. (1973). *Community Relations 1972–1973*. H.M.S.O.

HUDSON, L. (1968). *Frames of Mind*. Methuen.

HUDSON, L. (ed.) (1970). *The Ecology of Human Intelligence*. Penguin.

HUDSON, L. (1972). *The Cult of the Fact*. Jonathan Cape.

HUGHES, A. (1967). The battered baby syndrome. *Case Conference*, **14** (8), 304–8.

HUSÉN, T. (1974). The purpose of futurologic studies in education. *Advances in Educational Psychology*, **2**. M. L. Kellmer Pringle and V. P. Varma (eds.), University of London Press.

JACKA, A. (1973). *Adoption in Brief. Research and other Literature in the United States, Canada and Great Britain, 1966 – 72 ; an annotated bibliography*. National Foundation for Educational Research, Slough. (A National Children's Bureau Report.)

JAFFEE, B. and FANSHEL, D. (1970). *How they Fared in Adoption; a Follow-up Study*. Columbia University Press, New York.

JARUS, A., MARCUS, J., OREN, J. and RAPAPORT, C. (1970). *Children and Families in Israel*. Gordon and Breech, New York.

JENCKS, C. et al. (1973). *Inequality : A Re-assessment of the Effect of Family and Schooling in America*. Allen Lane.

JENSEN, A. R. (1969). How much can we boost I.Q. and scholastic achievement? *Harvard Educational Review*, **39** (1), 1–123.

JOBLING, M. (1973). Non-accidental injuries in children. *Highlight* No. 7., National Children's Bureau.

JONES, K. (1973). Notes: social work. *New Society*, 1 March, **23** (543), 478.

JOSEPH, A. and PARFIT, J. (1972). *Playgroups in an Area of Social Need*. National Foundation for Educational Research, Slough. (A National Children's Bureau Report.)

KADUSHIN, A. (1970). *Adopting Older Children*. Columbia University Press, New York.

KAGAN, J. (1970). On class differences and early development. *Education of the Infant and Young Child*. V. H. Denenberg (ed.), Academic Press.

KAGAN, J. (1971). *Change and Continuity in Infancy*. John Wiley, New York.

KAGAN, J. (1973). The importance of simply growing older. *New Society*, 14 June **24** (558), 610–12.

KAGAN, J. and MOSS, H. (1962). *Birth to Maturity*. John Wiley, New York.

KAHN, A. J. (1969). *Studies in Social Policy and Planning*. Russell Sage Foundation, New York.

KAHN, A. J. (1969). *Theory and Practice of Social Planning*. Russell Sage Foundation, New York.

KAHN, A. J., KAMERMAN, S. B. and MCGOWAN, B. G. (1972). *Child Advocacy*. Columbia University School of Social Work. New York.

KEMPE, C. H. et al. (1962). The battered child syndrome. *Journal of the American Medical Association*, **181** (1), 17–24.

KITZINGER, S. (1969). Communicating with immigrant mothers. *Caring for Children*, M. L. Kellmer Pringle (ed.), Longman in association with the National Children's Bureau.

KITZINGER, S. (1972). West Indian immigrant children with problems. *Therapeutic Education*, Spring issue, 5–18.

KITZINGER, S. (1973). Personal communication.

KNIVETON, B. H. (1973). The very young and television violence. Paper read at the 17th Annual Conference of the Society for Psychosomatic Research, on 18 October, London.

KOGAN, M. and POPE, M. (ed.) (1973). *The Challenge of Change*. National Foundation for Educational Research, Slough. (A National Children's Bureau Report.)

KOHLBERG, I. (1968). Early education: a cognitive-developmental view. *Child Development*, **39** (4), 1044–55.

KOLUCHOVA, J. (1972). Severe deprivation in twins: a case study. *Journal of Child Psychology and Psychiatry*, **13** (2), 107–14.

KUSHLICK, A. (1967). Comprehensive services for the mentally subnormal. *New Aspects of the Mental Health Service*, H. Freeman and J. Farndale (eds.), Pergamon Press, Oxford.

LABOV, W. (1971). Variations in language. *The Learning of Language*, C. Reed (ed.), Appleton-Century-Crofts, New York.

LAING, W. A. (1972). *The Costs and Benefits of Family Planning*. P.E.P.

LAKER, C. and TONGUE, I. (1972). New rights for foster parents. *Concern*, (Journal of the National Children's Bureau) (8), 19–25.

LASLETT, P. (1972). *Household and Family in Past Time*. Cambridge University Press.

LEISSNER, A. (1967). *Family Advice Services*. Longman in association with the National Children's Bureau.

LEISSNER, A. (1969). *Street Club Work in Tel-Aviv and New York*. Longman in association with the National Children's Bureau.

LEISSNER, A. (1972). Parents and Children in high-need areas. *The Parental Role*, 22–7. National Children's Bureau.

LEISSNER, A., HERDMAN, A. and DAVIES, E. (1971). *Advice, Guidance and Assistance*. Longman in association with the National Children's Bureau.

LENNEBERG, E. H. (1968). The capacity for language acquisition. *Man in Adaptation, the Biosocial Background*, 2 vols. Y. A. Cohen (ed.), Aldine, Chicago.

LEVY, D. (1943). *Maternal Overprotection*. Columbia University Press, New York.

LIPSITT, L. P. (1967). Learning in the human infant. *Early Behavior –*

Comparative and Developmental Approaches. H. W. Stevenson, E. H. Hess and H. L. Rheingold. John Wiley, New York.

LIPSITT, L. P. (1972). Reciprocating relationships in infant behaviour: congenital and experimental determinants. *Proceedings of the British Psychological Society,* London Conference.

LUNN, J. BARKER. (1970). *Streaming in the Primary School.* National Foundation for Educational Research, Slough.

LYNN, R. (1966). *Attention, Arousal and the Orientation Reaction.* Pergamon Press, Oxford.

MacALLISTER, J. and MASON, A. (1972). A comparison of juvenile delinquents and children in care: an analysis of socio-economic factors. *British Journal of Criminology,* **12** (3), 280–6.

MCCLELLAND, D. (1973). Testing for competence rather than for 'intelligence'. *American Psychologist,* **28** (1), 1–14.

MALLESON, A. (1973). *Need your Doctor be so Useless?* Allen and Unwin.

MALLINSON, V. (1956). *None can be Called Deformed; Problems of the Crippled Adolescent.* Heinemann.

MAPSTONE, E. (1969). Children in care. *Concern* (Journal of the National Children's Bureau) (3), 23–8.

MAPSTONE, E. (1973). *A comparative study of children in care, based on the National Child Development Study.* Unpublished.

MARSDEN, D. (1969). *Mothers Alone.* Penguin.

MASON, M. K. (1942). Learning to speak after six and one-half years of silence. *Journal of Speech and Hearing Disorders,* **7** (4), 295–304.

MAYS, J. B. (1973). Delinquent and maladjusted children. *Stresses in Children,* V. D. Varma (ed.), University of London Press.

MAYS, J. B. (1974). Social aspects of adolescence. *Advances in Educational Psychology,* **2**, chap. 16, M. L. Kellmer Pringle and V. D. Varma (eds.), University of London Press.

MEYERS, E. O. (1973). 'Doing your own think': transmission of cognitive skills from parent and/or paraprofessional to children in the inner city. *American Journal of Orthopsychiatry,* **43** (3), 242–3.

MIDWINTER, E. (1972). *Projections: an Educational Priority Area at Work.* Ward Lock Educational.

MILLAR, S. (1968). *The Psychology of Play.* Penguin.

MILLER, J. G. (1964). Adjusting to overloads of information. *Disorders of Communication,* D. M. Rioch and E. A. Weinstein (eds.), Williams, Wilkins and Co., Baltimore, Maryland.

MINUCHIN, S. et al. (1967). *Families of the Slum: an Exploration of their Structure and Treatment.* Basic Books, New York.

MONEY, J. (1963). Cytogenetics and cytosexual incongruities. *American Journal of Psychiatry,* **119**, March 1963, 820–7.

MOORE, T. (1972). The later outcome of early care by the mother and substitute daily regimes. *Determinants of Behavioural Development,*

F. J. Monks, W. W. Hartup and J. De Wit (eds.), Academic Press.

MOORE, T. V. (1948). *The Driving Forces of Human Nature and their Adjustment; an Introduction to the Psychology and Psychopathology of Emotional Behaviour and Volitional Control.* Grune and Stratton, New York.

MORRIS, P. (1969). *Put Away.* Routledge and Kegan Paul.

MORTLOCK, B. (1972). *The Inside of Divorce.* Constable.

MUSGROVE, F. (1966). *The Family, Education and Society.* Routledge and Kegan Paul.

NASH, R. (1973). *Classrooms Observed.* Routledge and Kegan Paul.

NATIONAL CHILDREN'S BUREAU. (1972). *The Second Follow-up at the Age of 11 Years of the National Child Development Study (1958 Cohort).* Unpublished.

NEWMAN, O. (1973). *Defensible Space.* Architectural Press.

NEWSON, E. (1971). Who am I – where do I come from? *Concern* (Journal of the National Children's Bureau) (8), 26–7.

NEWSON, E. (1972). Towards an understanding of the parental role. *The Parental Role*, 28–35. National Children's Bureau.

NEWSON, J. and NEWSON, E. (1963). *Infant Care in an Urban Community.* Allen and Unwin.

NEWSON, J. and NEWSON, E. (1968). *Four Year Olds in an Urban Community.* Allen and Unwin.

NEWSON, J. and NEWSON, E. (1972). Cultural aspects of child rearing in the English-speaking world. *The Integration of a Child into a Social World*, M. P. Richards (ed.), Cambridge University Press.

OAKLEY, A. (1972). *Sex, Gender and Society.* Maurice Temple Smith Ltd.

OFFICE OF POPULATION CENSUSES AND SURVEYS. (1973). *Family Planning Services in England and Wales.* H.M.S.O.

OLIVER, J. E. and COX J. (1973). A family kindred with ill-used children: the burden on the community. *British Journal of Psychiatry*, **123** (572), 81–90.

OSWIN, M. (1971). *The Empty Hours.* Allen Lane, Penguin Press.

PARFIT, J. (1971). Spotlight on physical and mental assessment. *Spotlight* (1), National Children's Bureau.

PARFIT, J. (1971). Spotlight on group work with parents in special circumstances. *Spotlight* (2), National Children's Bureau.

PARFIT, J. (1972). Spotlight on services for the young handicapped child. *Spotlight* (3), National Children's Bureau.

PARFIT, J. (1973). Spotlight on sources of information on children. *Spotlight* (4), National Children's Bureau.

PARKER, R. A. (1966). *Decision in Child Care. A Study of Prediction in Fostering.* Allen and Unwin.

PARRINDER, D. (1972). Housing for children: a second look. *Housing Review*, **21** (3), 85–6.

PFUHL, F. H. (1970). Mass media and reported delinquent behavior: a negative case. *The Sociology of Crime and Delinquency*. M. E. Wolfgang, L. Gavity and N. Johnston (eds.), John Wiley, New York.

PIAGET, J. (1950). *The Psychology of Intelligence*. Routledge.

PIAGET, J. and INHELDER, B. (1958). *The Growth of Logical Thinking from Childhood to Adolescence*. Basic Books, New York.

PIDGEON, D. A. (1970). *Expectation and Pupil Performance*. National Foundation for Educational Research, Slough.

PILLING, D. (1973). The Handicapped Child. *Research Review* **3**: *Mental and Intellectual Handicap*. Longman in association with the National Children's Bureau.

PILLING, D. (1973a). *The Child with a Chronic Medical Problem – Cardiac Disorders, Diabetes, Haemophilia. Social, Emotional and Educational Adjustment: An Annotated Bibliography*. National Foundation for Educational Research, Slough. (A National Children's Bureau Report.)

PILLING, D. (1973b). *The Child with Spina Bifida. Social, Emotional and Educational Adjustment: An Annotated Bibliography*. National Foundation for Educational Research, Slough. (A National Children's Bureau Report.)

PILLING, D. (1973c). *The Child with Cerebral Palsy. Social, Emotional and Educational Adjustment: An Annotated Bibliography*. National Foundation for Educational Research, Slough. (A National Children's Bureau Report.)

PILLING, D. (1973d). *The Orthopaedically Handicapped Child. Social, Emotional and Educational Adjustment: An Annotated Bibliography*. National Foundation for Educational Research, Slough. (A National Children's Bureau Report.)

POCHIN, J. (1969). *Without a Wedding Ring*. Constable.

POND, D. A. and ARIE, T. (1971). Services for children in trouble. *Child Care*, **25** (1), 16–20.

PRINGLE, M. L. KELLMER. (1963). 'The happiest day of my life' as judged by junior school children; a longitudinal study. *Current Problems of Developmental psychology; Festschrift for Charlotte Buhler*, L. Schenk-Danzinger and H. Thomae (eds.), C. J. Hogrefe, Göttingen, Germany.

PRINGLE, M. L. KELLMER. (1964). *The Emotional and Social Adjustment of Blind Children*. National Foundation for Educational Research, Slough.

PRINGLE, M. L. KELLMER. (1964). *The Emotional and Social Adjustment of Physically Handicapped Children*. National Foundation for Educational Research, Slough.

PRINGLE, M. L. KELLMER (ed.) (1965). *Investment in Children.* Longman.

PRINGLE, M. L. KELLMER. (1966). *Social Learning and its Measurement.* Longman.

PRINGLE, M. L. KELLMER. (1967). *Adoption – Facts and Fallacies.* Longman in association with the National Children's Bureau.

PRINGLE, M. L. KELLMER (ed.) (1968). *Caring for Children.* Longman in association with the National Children's Bureau.

PRINGLE, M. L. KELLMER. (1969). Policy implications of child development studies. *Concern* (Journal of the National Children's Bureau), (3), 40–8.

PRINGLE, M. L. KELLMER. (1970). *Able Misfits.* Longman in association with the National Children's Bureau.

PRINGLE, M. L. KELLMER. (1971). *Deprivation and Education.* 2nd ed., Longman in association with the National Children's Bureau.

PRINGLE, M. L. KELLMER. (1973). The pre-school comprehensives. *Where* (81), 165–7.

PRINGLE, M. L. KELLMER, BUTLER, N. and DAVIE, R. (1966). *11,000 Seven-year-olds.* Longman in association with the National Children's Bureau.

PRINGLE, M. L. KELLMER and FIDDES, D. O. (1970). *The Challenge of Thalidomide.* Longman in association with the National Children's Bureau.

PRINGLE, M. L. KELLMER and NAIDOO, S. (1974). *Early Child Care in Britain.* Gordon and Breach.

PRINGLE, M. L. KELLMER and VARMA, V. P. (eds.) (1974). *Advances in Educational Psychology*, 2. University of London Press.

PROSSER, H. (1973). Family size and children's development. *Health and Social Services Journal.* (4325 (suppl.)), 11–12.

RABINOWITZ, A. I. (1969). Co-operation in a multi-purpose school for children aged 2–11 with various handicaps. *Caring for Children*, M. L. Kellmer Pringle (ed.), Longman in association with the National Children's Bureau.

RIST, R. C. (1970). Student social class and teacher expectations. *Harvard Educational Review*, 40 (3), 411–51.

ROBINS, LEE N. (1966). *Deviant Children Grown Up.* Williams and Wilkins, Baltimore, Maryland.

ROSENSHINE, B. (1971). *Teaching Behaviours and Student Achievement.* National Foundation for Educational Research, Slough.

ROSENTHAL, R. (1969). Empirical vs decreed validation of clocks and tests. *American Educational Research Journal*, 4 (6), 689–91.

ROSENTHAL, R. and JACOBSON, L. (1968). *Pygmalion in the Classroom.* Holt, Rinehart and Winston, New York.

ROWE, J. (1970). The realism of adoptive parenthood. *Child Adoption* (59), 23–9.

175

ROWE, J. and LAMBERT, L. (1973). *Children Who Wait – a Study of Children Needing Substitute Parents*. Association of British Adoption Agencies.

RUTTER, M. (1966). *Children of Sick Parents: an Environmental and Psychiatric Study*. Oxford University Press.

RUTTER, M. (1972). *Maternal Deprivation Reassessed*. Penguin.

RUTTER, M. and MITTLER, P. (1972). Environmental influences on language development. *Young Children with Delayed Speech*, M. Rutter and J. A. M. Martin (eds.), Heinemann.

RUTTER, M., TIZARD, J. and WHITMORE, K. (eds.) (1970). *Education, Health and Behaviour*. Longman.

SANDAY, P. R. (1972). On the causes of I.Q. differences between groups and implications for social policy. *Human Organisation*, **31** (5), 411–24.

SARGEANT, W. (1963). *Battle for the Mind*. Pan.

SCHAFFER, H. R. (1965). Changes in developmental quotient under two conditions of maternal separation. *British Journal of Social and Clinical Psychology*, **4** (1), 39–46.

SCHAFFER, H. R. and SCHAFFER, E. B. (1968). Occasional Paper on Social Administration (25). *Child Care and the Family*, G. Bell.

SCHON, D. (1970). Reith Lectures. Change and Industrial society. *The Listener*, 19 Nov–24 Dec, **84** (2173–8), 685–8, 724–8, 772–6, 810–12, 835–8, 874–7.

SCHORR, A. L. (1966). *Poor Kids: a Report on Children in Poverty*. Basic Books, New York.

SCHRAMM, W., LYLE, J. and PARKER, E. B. (1961). *Television in the Lives of our Children*. Stanford University Press, California.

SCRIMSHAW, N. S. (ed.) (1968). *Malnutrition, Learning and Behavior*. MIT Press, Cambridge, Mass.

SEARS, R., MACCOBY, E. and LEVIN, H. (1957). *Patterns of Child Rearing*. Row, Peterson, Evanston, Ill.

SEGLOW, J., PRINGLE, M. L. KELLMER and WEDGE, P. (1972). *Growing Up Adopted*. National Foundation for Educational Research, Slough. (A National Children's Bureau Report.)

SELYE, H. (1956). *The Stress of Life*. McGraw-Hill, New York.

SHELDON, E. and MOORE, W. (1968). *Indicators of Social Change*. Russell Sage Foundation, New York.

SHERIDAN, M. D. (1973). *Children's Developmental Progress*. National Foundation for Educational Research, Slough.

SILBERMAN, C. E. (1970). *Crisis in the Classroom; the remaking of American Education*. Random House, New York.

SILVER, H. K. and FINKELSTEIN, M. (1967). Deprivation dwarfism. *Journal of Pediatrics*, **70** (4), 317–24.

SKEELS, H. M. (1966). Adult Status of Children with contrasting Early

Life Experience. *Monographs of the Society for Research in Child Development*, **31** (3).

SKINNER, A. E. and CASTLE, R. L. (1969). *78 Battered Children: A Retrospective Study*. National Association for the Prevention of Cruelty to Children.

SKODAK, M. and SKEELS, H. M. (1949). A final follow-up study of one hundred adopted children. *Journal of Genetic Psychology*, **75** (2), 85–125.

SMILANSKY, S. (1968). *The Effects of Socio-dramatic Play on Disadvantaged Children*. John Wiley, New York.

SMITH, S. M., HANSON, R. and NOBLE, S. (1974). Parents of battered babies: a controlled study. *British Medical Journal*, **4** (5889), 388–91.

SMITH, S. M., HONIGSBERGER, L. and SMITH, C. A. (1973). E.E.G. and personality factors in baby battering. *British Medical Journal*, **3** (5470), 20–2.

SPENCE, J. C. (1947). The care of children in hospital. *British Medical Journal*, **1** (4490), 125–30.

STINCHCOMBE, A. L. (1969). Environment: the cumulation of effects is yet to be understood. *Harvard Educational Review*, **39** (4), 511–22.

TALBOT, N. B., KAGAN, J. and EISENBERG, L. (1971). *Behavioral Science in Pediatric Medicine*. W. B. Saunders.

TALBOT, N. B., SOBEL, E. H., BURKE, B. S., LINDEMANN, E. and KAUFMAN, S. B. (1947). Dwarfism in healthy children: its possible relation to emotional, nutritional and endocrine disturbances. *New England Journal of Medicine*, **236** (21), 783–93.

TANNER, J. M. (1974). Physical aspects of adolescence. *Advances in Educational Psychology*, **2**, chap. 17. M. L. Kellmer Pringle and V. P. Varma (eds.), University of London Press.

THORNDIKE, R. L. (1968). Review of R. Rosenthal and L. Jacobsen (*Pygmalion in the classroom*). *American Educational Research Journal*, **4** (5), 708–11.

TIZARD, J. (1972). Research into services for the mentally handicapped: science and policy issues. *British Journal of Mental Subnormality*, **18** (34), 1–12.

TIZARD, J. and GRAD, J. C. (1961). *The Mentally Handicapped and their Families*. Oxford University Press.

TIZARD, J. and TIZARD, B. (1971). The social development of two-year-old children in residential nurseries. *The Origins of Human Social Relations*. H. R. Schaffer (ed.), Academic Press.

TIZARD, J. and TIZARD, B. (1972). The institution as an environment for development. *The Integration of the Child into a Social World*, M. P. Richards (ed.), Cambridge University Press.

TOFFLER, A. (1973). *Future Shock*. Pan.

TOLSTOY, L. (1949 edn.). *Anna Karenina*. (Translated by L. and A. Maude), Oxford University Press, World Classics.

TRASLER, G. D. (1960). *In Place of Parents*. Routledge and Kegan Paul.

TRASLER, G. D. (1962). *The Explanation of Criminality.* Routledge and Kegan Paul.

TUCKEY, L., PARFIT, J. and TUCKEY, B. (1973). *Handicapped School-Leavers: Their Future Education, Training and Employment*. National Foundation for Educational Research, Slough. (A National Children's Bureau Report.)

VARMA, V. P. (ed.), (1973). *Stress in Children*. University of London Press.

VERNON, P. E. (1969). *Intelligence and Cultural Environment*. Methuen.

WALL, W. D. (1955). *Education and Mental Health*. UNESCO, Paris: Harrap, London.

WALL, W. D. (1959). *Child of our Times*. National Children's Homes.

WALL, W. D. (1965). The role of education. *Investment in Children*, M. L. Kellmer Pringle (ed.), Longman.

WALL, W. D. (1968). *Adolescents in School and Society*. National Foundation for Educational Research, Slough.

WALL, W. D. (1973). The 'problem' child in schools. *London Educational Review*, 2 (2), 3–21.

WALL, W. D. (1973). *Constructive Education, 1*. Harrap.

WALL, W. D. and VARMA, V. P. (eds.) (1972). *Advances in Educational Psychology, 1*. University of London Press.

WARD, C. (ed.) (1973). *Vandalism*. Architectural Press.

WEDGE, P. J., ALBERMAN, E. and GOLDSTEIN, H. (1970). Health and height in children. *New Society*, 10 December, 16 (428), 1044–5.

WEDGE, P. and PROSSER, H. (1973). *Born to Fail?* Arrow Books in association with the National Children's Bureau.

WEST, D. J. (1969). *Present Conduct and Future Delinquency*. Heinemann.

WEST, D. J. and FARINGTON, D. P. (1974). *Who becomes Delinquent?* Heinemann.

WHALLEY, T. (1973). The needs of the hospitalised child. *Special Education in the new Community Services*. J. W. Palmer (ed.), Ron Jones Publications.

WHITE, B. L. and HELD, R. (1966). Plasticity of sensorimotor development in the human infant. *The Causes of Behaviour*. J. Rosenblith and W. Allensmith (eds.), Allyn and Bacon, Boston.

WHITE, J. and WHITE, P. (1971). Slogan for crypto-elitists. *Times Educational Supplement*, 5 January, (3006), p. 2.

WHITE HOUSE CONFERENCE ON CHILDREN. (1970). *Report to the President*. US Government, Printing Office, Washington D.C.

WILLIAMS, J. M. (1961). Children who break down in foster homes: a psychological study of patterns of personality growth in grossly deprived children. *Journal of Child Psychology and Psychiatry*, **2** (1), 5–20.

WINNICOTT, D. W. (1964). *The Child, the Family and the Outside World*. Penguin.

WISEMAN, S. (1966). Environmental and innate factors and educational attainment. *Genetic and Environmental Factors in Human Ability*. J. E. Meade and A. S. Parkes. Oliver and Boyd, Edinburgh.

WISEMAN, S. (1972). Environmental handicap and the teacher. *Advances in Educational Psychology*, **1**. W. D. Wall and V. P. Varma (eds.), University of London Press.

WITMER, H. L., HERZOG, E., WEINSTEIN, E. A. and SULLIVAN, M. E. (1963). *Independent Adoptions – a Follow-up Study*. Russell Sage Foundation, New York

WOLFF, S. (1970). *Children under Stress*. Penguin.

WOLFGANG, M. E., FIGLIO, R. M. and SELLIN, T. (1972). *Delinquency in a Birth Cohort*. University of Chicago Press.

WOODMANSEY, A. C. (1969). The common factor in problems of adolescence. *British Journal of Medical Psychology*, **42** (4), 353–70.

WOOTTON, B. (1959). *Social Science and Social Pathology*. Allen and Unwin.

WYNN, M. (1964). *Fatherless Families*. Michael Joseph.

WYNN, M. (1972). *Family Policy*. 2nd edn. Pelican.

WYNN, M. and WYNN, A. (1973). Using maternity benefits for preventive measures. *Concern* (Journal of the National Children's Bureau), (11), 13–16.

YOUNGHUSBAND, E., BIRCHALL, D., DAVIE, R. and PRINGLE, M. L. KELLMER (eds.) (1970). *Living with Handicap*. National Children's Bureau.

Index

Index